Hawks
Pass

CAL O'BANNON

For all who elect to do their own work

MEMORY

MADNESS

DISINFORMATION

We can no longer rely on technology alone. It can be manipulated, it can malfunction, it can be commandeered. You know this all too well—we all do.

—The Administrator

PART ONE

MEMORY

SURVEILLANCE

THE ADMINISTRATOR pulled her dark skirt down to cover as much leg as it would. She hated dealing with the Board, just as her underlings hated dealing with her, but such was the price of admission. All paths up the pyramid were thick with gatekeepers. Some were naïve, or dense, their deference allowing them to simply be pushed aside. Others were more steadfast, capable sentinels requiring appeasement.

The Company Board was nothing if not the latter.

She heard the whir of mechanisms as the room lit with color, a brief, spinning rainbow, then the executives materialized before her in holo-form, a row of obscured figures lining the far side of a large, marble table. "Thank you for meeting with me," she said.

The man in the center of the line nodded.

What did she have for them?

"The route is in place," said the Administrator, "and the Seeker's protocol has been updated, as we discussed. All is well, considering the circumstances." Murmurs emanated from the executive table, questions the Administrator was prepared for. "Signs indicate her condition is stable, perhaps even better than expected. I am confident she will be able to see this through to its conclusion."

More discussion from the table, more nods and deliberation.

More questions.

"This run is important for us," she said, "and I would not pull the plug due to a small degree of uncertainty. Progress always involves risk. We would not be where we are without risk, now would we? If her condition proves problematic we can take additional steps at that point. Is that something we can agree on?" More chatter from the table, thoughtful gestures, words of affirmation. "Good," she said. "I will greenlight the team to proceed then. We will be in touch."

The Administrator watched the figures blink out of existence, then she turned to the screen on her desk. She pulled up the feed and waited on the connection. "We are clear to proceed," she said. "Load the next batch of coordinates.

THE TRAIL

GEM STARED ahead through the windshield. The trail was awash in the haze of the spectra-light, pale orange and desolate, blazed on horseback in another age then worn over by surveyors and logging trucks. Small rocks rattled under the weight of the tires, pebbles in the overgrowth and no more than a nuisance, though there were boulders out there in the thickets. They had nearly struck one at the base of the trail as they wound their way through the foliage. If not for the sensors she might have clipped it, or hit the bastard head on. She cursed under her breath at the thought.

Sometimes you had to rely on the machines.

Focus. Gem fought the urge to rub her eyes, the lids dry and tired and threatening to snap shut. Then a pang forced her to wince. Her hand went to the base of her skull where the swelling was pronounced, her fingers probing the knot. She bit down on her lip, resisting the urge to swear, then she looked over to Banks.

"Anything?"

"Nothing yet."

"Lovely."

The forest thinned as they climbed toward the tree line, the firs and the pines giving way to the brushes and brambles. They hardly noticed the change, Gem's eyes on the road and Banks minding the Seeker, the machine, their guide and general. It determined where they traveled and when and where they stopped and for how long and where they refueled and resupplied. It was cold and calculating, but they expected nothing less of it.

"Put in another request. I'm starting to nod."

"It's only been twenty minutes."

"Do it, Banks." She motioned to the back of her head. "Would you like a knock of your own, love? For me to pass out and hit a sodding tree?"

"Fine."

Banks fiddled with the touchscreen as the machine blipped and whirred. They waited, five seconds, ten, then it sounded a positive tone. "Would you look at that," Banks said. "We're greenlit."

"You see?"

"It might have been the plan all along."

Gem rolled her eyes.

Now was not the time for his naysaying.

Banks guided them off-road to an isolated patch of tress and Gem nestled the vehicle among the evergreens. She opened the door to the bite of the mountain air, the slow whine of nature, the first sliver of dawn creeping up over the horizon. They searched out a level space and brushed the pine straw aside, then Banks laid the package down. They took a step back as it inflated, forming a small tent, an efficient piece of tech with built-in padding and pillowed ridges. All you had to do was lie down, and that was what Gem intended to do. Sleep was all she could think about, the weight of it dragging her eyelids down and distorting all she saw, rendering reality thin and alien.

They crawled into the tent and stretched out side by side, then Gem closed her eyes. Sleep overtook her as the sky changed from black to violet, and the Seeker scanned the airwaves, searching for reason to raise the alarm.

THE GARDEN

GEM WALKS *through the grass in the English Midlands, her home in another life, a different time, a time where little girls have phones and tablets that let them play games and talk to their friends and hurl abuse at the other children, because the internet is safe, and they never have to look each other in the eye.*

She is small again, the girl who cries when Mum takes the tablet, who stomps and thrashes about until she returns it. Doesn't Mum know she needs it? Everyone does! Everything is on there, even school, though school is easy to get around because the tablet is simpler for her than the teachers. She can trick them because she is good with the phones and tablets and computers, because they make sense to her and she sees how they work.

Little Gem walks in the garden behind the old block of flats, smiling at the device. She knows she can trust it, unlike so many other things. She hears her mother calling from somewhere and wants to avoid her, because when Mum is around things tend to go south. Mother cannot be trusted, so she flips through the icons and turns the volume down until Mum's voice disappears.

She is good with the tablet.

She looks around to make sure no one is there, hugging the device like a teddy. It has been so long since she's seen it. She loves it more than anything and will be damned if someone is going to make her put it away. She will turn the volume down on all of them, and if that does not work she will swipe them away with a finger, and if that does not work she will scream and stomp and thrash and cry. Then Little Gem hears a second voice. It is the voice of the later Gem, the one who speaks from the sky.

"You know this is just a dream. You think you are across the pond again."

Little Gem huffs and turns the volume down until the dial reads zero. There is no need for that Gem, that eternal sayer of all she loathes to hear, but Little Gem cannot silence her. She never can. The clouds continue their naysaying, going on about what is good and what is real instead of letting her play like she should. And then Little Gem is gone.

Later Gem stands in the garden in her place, looking up towards the flat where she heard Mum calling—no, she knows Mum is gone, and all for the better, because she has made peace with never seeing that woman again. Then she feels something, a presence. The Seeker is in the tablet now, flashing and shifting and searching for purchase. It cannot find a foothold. Watching the Seeker struggle amuses her, because the machine never struggles, now does it? It is always a step ahead, but not now. She laughs out loud.

The Seeker always has a signal, *she thinks. The thought sends a shiver through her, and she knows something is off.* Why do I have a tablet? And why can't the machine find a signal? *She lets the device fall to the grass.*

Because I am dreaming.

Gem seizes the lucidity. She will stay, by God.

She is desperate to be somewhere other than that godforsaken path through the mountains, if only for a little while.

The dreamscape trembles and bends as she attempts to navigate it, and she struggles against the waves, one foot first, and then the other. She feels the tablet in her hand, heavier than it should be. Has she picked it back up? The device holds firm to her fingers, an unshakable appendage, and the Seeker is still there, still searching for purchase as its icons spin whirlwinds across the screen.

Gem feels the dream slipping and focuses on the garden, willing it to remain, the bench and birdbath and the little stone path running up to the building. She holds them in place as the landscape roars to life, flooded with neon hues, arrows dancing across the sky in a stream of digital devilry, and Gem knows it is the Seeker. It controls her waking life and now it is stealing her dreams, forcing her to submit.

"You can't even give me one dream!" she shouts.
A familiar feeling washes over her, the pull, the signal of transition.
She knows there is no point in fighting it.

THE SENSORS

GEM OPENED her eyes and gasped. She was sitting bolt upright next to Banks, her cohort locked in the same position. She pulled at her ears to relieve the pressure, and by the time she'd counted to three, the frequency had gone. The Seeker was satisfied they would not be drifting off again. "Bloody hell," she said.

To the machine sleep was no more than a recharging of batteries, and each day she cursed its callousness, its disregard of human biology. She would let her rage boil as long as the waking merited, then she would remind herself the Seeker did not rouse them out of spite, that it was only doing its job and there was no point getting wound up about it. She would ask herself what good ever came of chastising the machine. Did it ever acknowledge her grievances?

She went through the motions, anger, rationalization, acceptance, then she pulled herself up and followed Banks out into the daylight. They stretched their limbs, shook off the sleep and collapsed the tent to its neat little package. Then they went off to do the morning necessities.

Gem took in the scenery as she crouched in the brush, the light gray sky and thin beams of sunlight through the clouds. She sniffed at the air, looked to the mountain and saw switchbacks leading up its base, a narrow, winding path. *It will be ill maintained*, she thought.

It will be dangerous. There would be no rails on that horse trail, only loose earth and rocks and obstacles. The Seeker had guided them through the foothills before only to turn them around in search of safer routes, though she knew that would not be the case. She was sure of it. The feeling was undeniable, an intuition she'd have scoffed at had it come from somebody else, but not today. She would have placed a bet on it if given the chance.

THE SEEKER had fired up the Wraith in anticipation, and the vehicle was warm when Gem reached it, the engine purring away. She ran her hand over the hood with affection. It had a sleek look for such a large, powerful machine, the lines and angles of old muscle cars, the shape of something half its size. The mirrored black exterior bounced sunlight off its surface, making it difficult to spot from a distance, and at night it blended into the shadows with ease. Banks had told her that was why its designers had called it the *Wraith.* "You could hardly call it camouflage," he'd said. "It's not the invisible monster they wished it was, but it is close enough at times." Gem saw the greens of the forest reflected in its body, and when she squinted, it was difficult to make out its form. She had never seen a mirage in person, though she imagined this was what one would look like, a shimmering blur of hues.

But the tires? She smiled. The tires dispelled the illusion, oversized and thickly treaded and fit to trample anything in their path save the largest roadside debris. *Like a boulder?* she thought.

Gem considered the rock the sensors had dodged the night before, little more than a shape in the fading light. Had she even seen it coming? She bent her thoughts to the path and struggled to form the image. Then a scene flashed through her mind. She was driving through the dark with the spectra-light shining, but there was no rock. Instead she saw a road, a proper road, not the trail they had been following. She was pulling off toward a ridge, some ugly bulge in the earth she had not seen the likes of on the mountain.

And then the memory was gone.

Gem blinked and shook her head. *What was that?* It was certainly not what she'd been trying to remember.

She heard Banks approaching. "Ready?" he said.

Gem climbed in on the driver's side and settled into her seat, Banks following on her right.

"We're heading up the mountain," she said, "yes?"

Banks yawned and stretched his arms, then he logged into the Seeker. "You would be right."

"I knew it. I was sure of it."

"They don't usually send you most of the way up for the view. I think you would find the probability—"

"Shut it." Gem leveled her gaze at him. "You know they don't always send us over, so just shut it. It's too early for one of your discussions."

Banks eyed her with interest.

"How are you feeling? How's your head?"

Her hand went to the swelling at the base of her skull. It was less pronounced than it had been only a few hours earlier, less sensitive. "It's still swollen, but the pain has gone for the most part." She began to massage her neckline. "I still can't remember fuckall, Banks. All I've got to go on is what you told me."

"No vision problems, right? You're not feeling sick?"

"No, nothing like that. It's just got me feeling a bit mental. That whole day is gone." She paused. "And more than that, I fear. I can't even remember setting out on the run." She forced her thoughts down the mountain to the beginning of the route. At first she drew a blank, but then she saw that road again, the road with the ridge in the distance. What was it she was remembering?

She shook the image away.

"Give it some time," Banks said. "It will come back to you. There's nothing we can do about it now anyway. We've got to move, so say the word if things get fuzzy."

"Will do."

She'd had about enough of his inquisition, but he had a point, right? Wouldn't she be asking the same questions? She wondered if she would have time to say the word if her symptoms took a turn and her vision went dark on one of those switchbacks. The sensors might not save them then. *I feel fine*, she thought, and she did. She was not lying to him about that, but it was strange—

"Gem?"

"Right." She had been staring into space.

Gem hit the gas and they slid out across the dirt, the path looking less ominous in the daylight. She also had a few hours of sleep to lean on. The world always felt a different place after a rest, even an inadequate one.

"Red?" Banks asked.

"I believe I will need it."

Banks popped a pill from the case and handed it over, and Gem swallowed it dry. The supplements were breakfast, lunch and dinner some days, but almost always breakfast, caffeine and protein and vitamins and a dash of lab-grade amphetamine if you took the Reds. There was no speed in the Greens, just the nutrients.

The Greens were the good day pills.

Banks had told her to think of it like the Seeker, that the Greens were for when things were going according to plan, times when you could relax a little. The Reds were for when things could be going better. Gem had told him he'd been putting that mildly, and the Seeker flashed orange when there was trouble, not red. She'd said to get his facts straight or keep his analogies to himself, and he'd told her she knew what he meant, that she did not always have to be so obstinate. She had asked him just what the hell that was supposed to mean . . .

At least that was how she thought the conversation had gone.

She sighed. Things *could* be going better, now couldn't they? The Seeker had allowed them three hours, which made about ten in the last fifty if she had it right, and she was not certain she did. She had arrived at the figure through information she'd gleaned from Banks, not her own ghost of a recollection. Her faculties felt watery, her recent endeavors a puzzle composed of malformed, shifting pieces. Strange was what it was. The knock had not seemed to have affected her motor skills, no double vision or faulty sense of balance. She had not felt woozy or weak in the knees, not the least bit sick. All it appeared to have done was damage her short-term memory and supercharge her dreams.

Focus. They had barely set out for the day and her mind was already wandering. She was not about to give Banks the satisfaction of spacing out. The kick from the Red would help, but it would not last. What she needed was proper rest, a full night's sleep, time to regain her bearings, her composure—her memory. She could only hope the machine would allow them a stop on the other side of the pass, and a real one at that, somewhere they could set up shop for a spell and recover. Grinding it out in her current state was bound to have consequences.

And what is my current state? She took stock.

She did not recall setting out on the run. She barely remembered how she'd spent her last stretch of leave, which was three weeks ago, maybe four. Without Banks she would not even know when they'd left or how she had managed to injure herself. According to him it was day four, and five days without a resupply would be pushing protocol, so there was that to consider. Occasionally the machine's rigidness worked in their favor.

Gem tightened her grip on the wheel. Odds were they would stop before long, but she harbored no expectations. Expectations bred disappointment in her line of work, and it was better to be pleasantly surprised than disappointed.

GEM BROUGHT the Wraith up to speed and studied the path. Fallen trees lined the side of the trail, though none were blocking the road. The way ran straight and true toward the base of the peak. She activated the auto-drive and sat back, watching the terrain roll by and waiting for the Red to kick. The dream of home was still swimming around, traces of emotion and irrationality, longing for times gone by. What was the term? *Rose-colored glasses*?

She frowned. That was the function of memory, the mind trimming the fat and leaving the prime cuts of life, savory morsels of hindsight. But Gem was not fooled. She remembered the growing pains of youth, her latchkey existence—that was what Americans used to call girls like her, *latchkey kids*—all those memes and trends piling up in the headspace of her generation and slowly suffocating it. Yet the Gem in her dream could tune it out with the slide of a finger. It was a fantasy she'd had in her youth, that her tablet gave her control. She would pretend she could silence her mother, with her ravings and tangents and half-lucid slights, that she could turn the other kids on and off and make them dance or scream or pull each other's hair or piss their pants in front of everyone. They could not open their horrible mouths if they were powered down.

She had dreamt of that as a girl. That tablet had been her friend and confidant for so long it was little wonder her mind recalled it from the dead—but the tablet had been usurped by the Seeker, that insufferable system barging its way in and taking over, invading her space and appropriating what time she had to herself. Gem looked to the machine and scowled, then she heard Banks laugh.

"It gave us three hours," he said. "What's with the face?"

"It's not that," Gem said. "I saw it in my dream. I was back in England having a nice little time, then the Seeker appeared in my garden. It was riding a tablet I had when I was a girl, then it swallowed up the sky and woke me up." She stared at the machine. "Listening to its prattle all the time has got in my head, like when you watch a film before bed and dream about the characters. Had I known some mechanical wanker would be lording over my dreams, I would have turned down the promotion."

Banks smiled at her.

"I'm sorry, but I can't help but find that a little amusing. Did you ever hear this one? Someone works all day, puts in overtime then goes home and dreams they are working. Then they wake up and find they are late for work."

Gem leered at him. "Thanks for the compassion."

"Yeah, I know. Maybe it will invade my dreams later so I can sympathize."

"I hope it does, you shit."

Banks laughed, and Gem could not help but join him. She was beginning to feel more alive now, less irritable, finally awake. Then the muscles up her neck went taught. When she reached back she felt a throbbing below the skin, a flexing sensation, not painful, but uncomfortable, a sign of pressure building. She blinked.

Was it the altitude? She opened and closed her mouth until she felt a pop, then she bit down and clinched her teeth. The sensation never ceased to disgust her. She'd assumed the effects of elevation would wane as she spent more time in the mountains. She might have had less trouble acclimating if—

A force rocked the vehicle and threw her against her harness. They had gone over something, something big. She gripped the wheel to steady the Wraith, then she saw what it was in the sideview. They had rolled over a branch, or the top of a tree by the size of it, a shard more than large enough to register as an obstacle.

And where were the sodding sensors? Gem forced the brakes down, overrode the auto-drive and slid the Wraith to a halt.

"Did you see the bloody size of it?" she said to Banks. "That could have jammed us up if it caught."

"I'll see if it registered. We should have picked that up."

"Well no shit. Did you not feel that?"

"Of course I felt it," Banks said. "You didn't slow, Gem. I figured you thought we were good."

She hesitated. Had she not been paying attention? She was watching the road—she was always watching the road—but had she actually *seen* it? Or was she thinking about ways to mitigate altitude instead of doing her job? "I didn't think I would need to go manual," she said. "Run the diagnostics, I'm switching over."

Gem shifted the Wraith to manual control. A systems issue was the last thing she needed. If there was a glitch in the auto-drive she could live with that—they did not have to use it—but if it was something deep in the works, then that was another story. There was no guarantee the Company would reach them first if a component went haywire and stranded them. "Banks?" she said.

"Almost there."

The Seeker blipped and whirred as it calculated, and it felt loud to Gem, louder than it should. Why was it so *loud?* She gripped the wheel tighter, telling herself it was adrenaline heightening her senses, the effects of the dope in her blood. The color drained from her knuckles as she counted the seconds, six, seven, eight, then the cacophony died away.

It had felt like wasps buzzing around in her skull.

"The sensors picked up the limb but processed it as inconsequential," Banks said, turning to face her. "It didn't feel inconsequential to me."

She loosened her grip on the wheel. "No, but that is better than I feared. It means they still have a signal, so the rest of the systems should as well. And there are no maintenance warnings?"

"Nothing I can see," Banks said. "The Wraith believes it's good to go. Seems like the two of you just had a difference of opinion."

Gem was not about to tell him she might have spaced off, that if she'd seen the limb she would have dropped out of auto and steered them around it. She would not leave such a thing to the machines. "Seems so," she said. "In that case we won't be using the auto-drive any longer, not until we can link up with an outpost for a look. They should have picked that up."

Banks nodded. "I can run a sweep, but if the Wraith didn't mark it, I wouldn't hold out hope. The Seeker's not programmed to analyze vehicular anomalies."

Gem knew that as well as he did.

"Just run it," she said. "It can't hurt."

She listened as Banks entered the commands. It was true the news could have been worse, much worse, but she took no comfort in that. It was clear something was not operating properly. Whatever was bogging down the sensors could bleed over to other critical systems, the fuel regulators, the temperature cloak, anything and everything that kept the vehicle functioning.

Gem did not need any of that.

She put the Wraith back in gear and stared ahead up the path. Had she looked right through that limb? If that were the case—*if*—then her injury might be more serious than they'd assumed.

THE BIRDS

THE PEAK loomed before them now, scenic and rigid, violet in the shade and hot white in the sun. Gem could see the pass some thousand feet above, the place where the road seemed to end. What was the altitude up there? Eleven-thousand feet? Twelve? Something moved in her periphery and she cast her eyes skyward. It was a flock of birds, small, dark shapes aflutter among the clouds, her gaze tracking them as they soared away from the mountain. There was something about their movement that bothered her, as if they might be fleeing a threat. She craned her neck until they disappeared from her vision.

Birds, she thought. *Just birds.*

But that was not what it felt like.

"Banks," she said. "Scan the skies."

"I'm still running that diagnostic."

"You can pick it up later. Scan the skies."

"For what? We've been green all morning. Not a blip since we set out, and we still have a ways to go to the top. I'll be scanning up there anyway."

"Do it, Banks. Amuse me."

He frowned at her. "If you say so."

Gem kept one eye on the road and the other on the sky, an over-reaction, she thought, but she had felt something then, the same intuition that told her they would be heading over the pass and not back through the woods. She had been right about that. She hoped she was wrong about this. She could not shake the feeling something was lurking up the mountain, lying in wait around a bend or just out of sight beyond the clouds. Was it rational? Probably not, but they were not in the business of leaving stones unturned. If running a scan twisted Banks's bollocks, so be it.

She heard a chime from her right, a positive little tone. There was only the green screen idling, that placid color of safety. Banks was staring at her.

"You mind telling me what that was about?"

"I saw some birds," she said. "It looked like something might have spooked them."

There was a moment of silence.

"You saw some spooky birds?"

Of course he was patronizing her, *spooky birds*. She had to admit it sounded ludicrous when spoken aloud. "Alright. I'm still feeling a bit ragged, so give me a break."

"I can see that." Banks shifted in his seat to face her. "Be straight with me, Gem. If you are feeling off, this is not the time to risk it." He looked toward the top of the trail. "I would rather switch it up than go off the road up there. We could declare an emergency, file a report."

Gem felt her muscles go taught. She had been hoping to avoid this implication. How could you not feel a little *off* with minimal rest and speed in your blood and a mysterious bang on the head? She closed her fingers around the wheel, wishing she'd spotted that branch. Would he be asking her then? She'd spaced out for a moment when the vehicle was in auto-drive, as she had done countless times. How was a sensor failure on her?

"Are you suggesting we declare an emergency because I asked you to run a scan?"

"You know what I am suggesting."

She looked past him towards the Seeker.

"For the record, Banks, if you are asking me whether I need emergency respite from my duties, I can assure you I don't. I am more than capable of operating this vehicle safely and effectively, but thank you for your concern."

Banks turned to the machine, then back to Gem. "You don't know it's monitoring us."

"And you don't know that it isn't."

"Gem, I'm just concerned that—"

"I've made my official statement, love, so be a good lad and bin it before I lose the sodding plot."

All she had done was ask him to run a scan. They'd both agreed the sensors should have spotted that limb, and that did not render her in need of reprieve. She was not damaged goods.

Banks rolled his eyes.

"Okay, I get it. I was not trying to call you out. I felt it behooved us both to ask, and a simple *no, I'm fine* would have sufficed. You know how I feel about the Cockney wench treatment."

Now she beamed at him, a sinister smile.

"Alright then. Finish the scan."

GEM HAD Americanized her voice over the years, though she had never quite lost the accent. The old Britishisms always sat on the tip of her tongue, waiting to emerge in bouts of anger or excitability, or in Banks's case, veiled contempt. Some of the nuances were forever ingrained, especially the slang, the *loves* and *rights* and *blokes* and *geezers*, along with the fouler bits, the *sodding bloody wankers* and *twats* and *bollocks* and *cunts*. She did her best to keep a cap on the latter, an utterance most offensive and thoroughly unacceptable in the States. Banks had once joked she sounded like a pompous

American, some upper-crust socialite who couldn't decide what part of the country she was from.

"A woman who would wear gloves to dinner," he'd said.

Gem's response had been to dress him down like he'd squeezed her ass at the pub, a tongue-lashing fit for the foulest of Londoners. Banks had taken offense, maybe because it was *he* who'd been the pompous, overeducated type before everything came crashing down, that hotshot brand of professor you saw in documentaries, the know-it-all. Was it his own hypocrisy that offended him, or was it the end result, the knowledge that being right about it all had paid no dividends, that in the world-that-was his wisdom was no more valuable than the skills of some foul-mouthed former urchin? These were just theories of hers.

All Gem knew for certain was the man detested being spoken to like a hooligan, that she could weaponize her mother tongue if he crossed her. She smiled at the thought, but the levity soon faded. Had she told him the truth?

Was she sure she did not have a problem?

The Seeker was re-running the diagnostic, a steady cadence of blips and beeps and whirs. For a moment Gem feared that buzzing in her head would return, the cacophony—*the wasps*—but this time it did not come. It must have been the adrenaline after all, some cruel trick of the nerves. She could only hope that—

Focus. The path narrowed to the width of a one-lane road as they reached the switchbacks, tight and unforgiving, the grade steep and thick with rock shards and rubble pried loose by wind and slides. In spite of it all the way remained passable, and the Wraith climbed it with ease. It was designed to go up and over the foulest terrain, the tires chewing up the debris and spitting it back down the mountainside. Gem peered out over the edge, her thoughts on the tree in the road and the crunch it had made under the wheels. No guard rails, loose rocks. Their fine, armored chariot would make a hell of a dent below if the sensors pitched a fit and over-compensated. They had written off that branch when they should have marked it. What were the odds they might do the opposite? Was it a risk she was willing to take?

The Seeker tolled to indicate it had found nothing to report, just as Banks had predicted, and now she was faced with a choice. She could do everything in her power to keep the Wraith away from potential hazards—the sensors would not react to stimuli they could not sense, at least in theory—but the path was narrow and winding. Her line of sight would be limited, and if they came around a corner blind? Gem knew there was only one decision. She could almost feel them going over the edge. "We have to disable the sensors," she said. "We can't trust them up there."

"It was only a branch, Gem, and I think it is—"

"Whatever it was, we cannot trust them. They could throw us off the mountain, Banks. This is the right call."

She braced herself for a retort, but he offered no reply. Instead he reached down under the center console and opened the control panel. Gem watched him work through her periphery, wondering if he had a mind to bullshit her—and then she frowned. What kind of thought was that? Banks was her navigator, and he was only looking out for her well-being. Even if his questions vexed her, the implications were not malicious.

She heard the snap of the console closing.

"It's done," Banks said. "Just remember you are working without a net now. Make sure and—"

"Keep my eyes on the road?"

Banks held her gaze for a moment, then he turned back to the machine.

THE LAND opened beneath them in swaths of green and gray, then a low-lying cloud blanketed them in its wisps. Gem slowed the Wraith to a crawl, inching them forward through the fog until they emerged onto a plateau. The view was breathtaking, the peak rising to her left and the floor of the valley below. For a moment she was a tourist, riding high atop the mountain through the cold, thin air. *Focus.* She listened for the Seeker.

They were exposed on the ridge and open spaces were dangerous, especially at altitude where escape routes were few. On the pass there was only one, straight ahead over the downslope. There was no room to turn the Wraith around, no option to backtrack. It was a few hundred feet to the decline and Gem felt every inch, heeding the machine as it scanned and scanned and scanned.

"Anything?" she said.

"Nothing to concern us. Keep it moving, nice and easy."

That the radar had been green all morning meant little. It was no more than a forecast, and the scenario could change. The skies were a battleground and the field maps were fluid, like weather, shifting from one occupier to the another at a moment's notice, turning friendly airspace hostile and sending ground troops scrambling for cover. There were no guarantees in this conflict. The Conglomerates made moves every day, and there was no telling when an adversary might crack a firewall and turn the heavens against them.

They closed the distance.

The seconds passed.

The Seeker scanned.

Then they crossed over the far edge of the ridge and wound down the other side toward the cover of the evergreens. Gem accelerated when the bends gave way to straighter slopes, and the shadows enveloped them as they slipped into the pines. It felt a small victory, escaping the open heights—it always did—though she dared not soak it in. There was always another pass somewhere down the line, sooner, later. Wraith crews never knew just where the Company was sending them.

THE SUN broke the cloud cover as they continued down the backside of the mountain, transforming the hues of the forest, midnight blues giving way to deep greens and patches of yellow where the canopy was thin. Gem felt a warmth wash over her at the sight of the light, an illusion of the mind, though she imagined nature was celebrating alongside them, laying out a red carpet of victorious sunshine. She laughed at the thought, and Banks looked up in surprise, smiling at the change in scenery.

"How's that for an omen?" Gem said. "We could pretend something out there's on our side."

"That would be nice," said Banks, "but—"

"No buts. I'm choosing to take a little joy where I can find it, so how about you just smile and nod along?"

Banks said, "An omen it is then," nodding and forcing a grin. At least he was not playing the spoilsport.

He was smiling a moment ago, she thought. *Actually smiling.*

They continued on, Gem guiding the Wraith through the evergreens as Banks navigated, offering direction in moments of doubt. They crept along though the woods until the Seeker's display flashed orange, ordering them to stop. Gem saw the path ahead forked off in two directions. "Which way do you think?" she said. "Left? Right? Back up the mountain?"

Banks sat mum as he entered his confirmation codes. When the machine sounded its approval, he leaned back. "We have a checkpoint," he said. "Looks like we get to stretch our legs."

SURVEILLANCE

THE ADMINISTRATOR sat at her desk reading the information feed. She had not been bluffing when she'd told the board this run was important. There was a great deal riding on it, for her, for the Company's ambitions, the myriad pursuits of that stodgy panel of vultures. The team had come over the pass without issue, as expected, though they had deactivated their vehicle's sensors along the way. This was a cause for concern. The system had been updated following the incident to ensure its structural integrity—she had overseen the process herself—yet in spite the Company's diligence, something had given them reason to question it.

They would not have done so on a whim.

"No matter," she said to herself. It was improbable they would need them in the immediate future unless they were forced off-road. Although that was always a possibility.

"Even so." She could not predict the exact trajectory of their path, though the trails down the mountain were fair, and the roads in the valley were just that, roads, gravel and pavement. Gemma was also one of their best, assuming she remained functional. She was stubborn, dogged, unlikely to give up the wheel unless something extraordinary manifested to force her hand. You did not switch drivers outside of a dire emergency, a fact that had been well impressed upon Mr. Banks. It required re-mapping the wheel's fingerprinting, realigning the Seeker, and—

"There will be no need." She picked up the phone and punched in the number and waited on the recipient. The instructions she offered were curt. "Set them up near town and run a diagnostic on their vehicle's sensors." The Administrator listened, her mouth forming a line. "Order the Seeker to run its protocol then. It will find a location."

She set the receiver down and swore under her breath. She was beginning to regret her decision to oversee this endeavor.

THE FOREST

GEM AMBLED along through the trees killing time, allowing her eyes to relax until the woods seemed an abstract painting of greens, browns and beiges. She had hiked out to relieve herself then kept on walking, leaving Banks to keep tabs on the Seeker. She would feel a pulse in her ears when the machine finished its update, and then she would have five minutes. If she was not seated and ready to depart in that window she would feel the pulse again, a warning instead of a summons, the throbbing more intense. Then she would have two minutes. If she was still absent after the two minutes elapsed the Seeker would signal the Company, and it could go any number of ways from there. However it played out, there would undoubtedly be consequences. *Consequences*, Gem thought.

"Consequences," she said to the trees.

She had best not wander too far.

THERE HAD been no talk of consequences when Gem signed her first contract. She'd had no idea what she was getting herself into, though there were few who did in those first months of chaos. She had believed she was taking a routine coding job, a bum-in-a-chair eight-hours-a-day gig securing firewalls. Gem had known of a dozen enterprises the Company owned, all of the app designers and software labs, but as for the Conglomerate behind them, she had not even known it existed. There was a reason they'd been called *shadow corporations*, allowing their pawns and subsidiaries to speak for them, the lesser brands and mascots forming the tentacles of some great sea beast. The limbs could be spied from the surface, though the creature remained submerged.

Gem had taken a job at a subsidiary, one of the few cybersecurity firms that had managed to hold its own against the malware. Its marketers had sent out an open call to universities after the hack, urging promising tech students to put their education on hold and apply. *Stand up to cyber-terrorism*, the ad had said. *Learn your trade hands-on while combatting the breach.*

The promotion had been fashioned in the vein of American military propaganda, strong on urgency, morality and doom, but it was not the message that had spurred Gem to action. What caught her eye were the perks. She had been on scholarship in the States with a fair-to-middling stipend, though she'd still had to borrow thousands for living expenses, rent and bills and gallons of coffee from the shops on campus. They had offered her student loan forgiveness, along with good pay and subsidized housing and health benefits and a hiring bonus, a guarantee of financial security in uncertain times. The job would also look good on a green card application, assuming she wanted to stay in the States after the world pulled itself back together. That was what she'd believed at the time, that someday there would be a return to normalcy.

Everyone had believed it.

So Gem fell in line and began shoring up the accounts of terrified clients, small companies with the bulk of their data stored online, wealthy individuals with mountains of digital currency, anyone with something to lose. By the end of her first month the Company had promoted her to its personal security team. That was when she'd learned who *actually* paid her salary, when they had put her to work covering their asses with the rest of the hotshots. She'd had no idea what she was protecting at the time, where the Company's interests lay or how far its tentacles reached. Most everyone still thought it was a rogue cabal of super-hackers ruining the world out of spite or anarchy or whichever cause the media elected to propagate, the usual talk and finger-pointing and non-thinking partisan retch. In the end they were so far off the mark it was laughable, but how were they to know? The networks could only report what they were fed at that point. To the world the hack was another pandemic, destined to ebb and flow until a crack team experts whipped up a digital inoculation. Everyone agreed it was only a matter of time before the internet was safe again.

Everything would return to normal, eventually.

GEM WAS leaning against the base of a tree now, waiting on the pulse. "The new normal," she said. That was what everyone had said when she was a girl. *This is the new normal. You will be doing your schooling online this year. You will not be able to go out unsupervised, and—*

And the rest of it.

That had been fine with Gem. She'd done her schooling at home on her tablet away from the brats and the bullies, all the dumb little shits and their savage mouths. What was it they used to call her? *I can't remember*, she thought. Her hand went to the base of her skull. *I can't even remember the last few days—wait. What* can *I remember?*

"Think," she said aloud.

She had opened her eyes in the tent two mornings ago with a headache and no recollection of how she'd come to be there. It was clear she was working, that she was on a run with Banks, but where? When had they set out? From which outpost?

She'd had no idea.

Banks had been waiting for her to come to. He had waved his finger back and forth in front of her face, tracking her eye movement. He had told her she'd slipped while making camp the night before, that her feet had gone out from under her like one of those cartoons with the banana peels. He'd said she had landed hard on her back, and then he had shown her the rock, a stone the size of fist partially buried in the earth. There had been a small patch of blood on its face where she'd struck her skull.

And then what? Think. And then they had spoken.

"I was out cold? How long?"

"Not long, less than a minute."

"I don't remember that."

"I wondered if you might have a concussion. You were dazed after the fall, but I gave you the eye test. You didn't show any symptoms, no dilated pupils, shaky eyes, none of it. You don't show any now."

Think. Banks had gone on about how he shouldn't have allowed her to sleep so soon after the knock, that she might never have woken up, or at least that was what he'd heard, and—*and whatever else he said.* She had not been paying attention, had she? No, she had been prodding her wound and staring at the rock, wondering what in the hell it was she'd slipped on.

She had been thinking it didn't make any sense.

GEM BENT her mind to the stone, to the rock and the circumstances surrounding it. Had she recalled *any*thing that morning? The Seeker had ordered them to move, then they had driven all day toward the mountain. Had Banks pushed her to give up the wheel? She could not remember. Her focus had been on the path, dodging boulders and trees and swallowing pills to manage the pain.

What can I recall? She sat down with her back to the tree and closed her eyes. The garden from her dream materialized, a young Gem and her tablet, oranges and greens and arrows in the sky. She pushed the scene away. *Memories, not dreams.*

But it was a bit like recalling a dream.

If she could pull even a fragment from the ether it might all come flooding back. She needed something, anything, one piece.

Where was she before the run?

Pixels began to form in the darkness behind her eyelids. An unnatural tightness gripped her temples, small twists of pressure warning her to back off, that she was pushing herself too hard. Was it a hemorrhage inhibiting her recollection, some medical phenomenon she would never understand? Wasn't memory stored in another part of the brain? The frontal lobes?

Now she had broken her concentration.

What about the last run, the one before this mess?

Think. She felt a pinch near the laceration, short and sharp. Then a memory struck her. She was rolling along through the woods, but she was not piloting the Wraith. She was out on a Buggy, motoring up a path through an unremarkable forest, a swath of woods surrounding an outpost. How long ago was that?

Had the brass sent her out on a patch job?

Think. Banks must have taken leave for something, so she was off Wraith duty for a spell. The Company did not mix and match their teams without cause, and—

Focus. She was heading out to a relay tower. It had to have been something simple, a cleanup or routine maintenance, sweeping for malware or signs of degradation. A milk run, in other words. It was up in the hills a few miles away, so she had geared up and taken a Buggy. It was evening, nice and cool, and—

A bolt of pain ripped through the base of her skull, the shock of it forcing her up and onto to her knees. Her hands went to the back of her head, and for a moment she saw red, crimson, blood orange. "Fucking hell!"

It came out a muffled growl against the buzz of the forest, and she struggled not to crumple, to go fetal and howl. She forced herself to breathe, to breathe again, big gulps of air, one after the other, but it was no use. Was she screaming? If she was she could not hear it. She wrapped her hands around her head in attempt to smother the pain, pressing, pressing again, pressing harder.

Then the pressure released, the pain falling away as fast as it had come. The brown of the woods came into focus as her vision began to clear, then the greens and the beiges, yellows and ochers. She forced one shaking hand to the ground to test its strength, and when the appendage held, she inched her weight slowly upward.

What the bloody hell was that?!

Whatever it was, it was not good. Had she leaned back into the tree? She had been deep in thought, all but oblivious to her surroundings. No, this was a consequence of something else, of pushing herself too hard. Perhaps it *was* a warning she'd felt.

Now that sounds crazy, love. Downright mental.

Yes, but she had no knowledge of medicine apart from standard first-aid, and neither did Banks. She could be experiencing internal swelling, a ruptured nerve or a fracture or brain bleed, any of it, all of it. How was she to know? And what was she supposed to do about it out here? She forced herself to breathe.

Focus. She could tell Banks about the pain, have him declare an emergency and switch her out. He could drive the rest of the run. The Company might even divert them to the nearest safehouse to treat her, but there would be—

Consequences. No, she would not do that. She would take the run as it came, mile by mile, hour by hour. If the jolt was a product of mental strain—however batshit it sounded—then she could not risk aggravating the source—whatever it was—and that meant no more pushing herself, not until she could seek medical attention.

If the pain returned and floored her *then* they could declare her unfit, assuming she didn't go blind and kill them first.

"I won't," she whispered. "I can do this. I can focus."

When she was convinced she could stand without buckling she began to walk it off, taking deep breaths as the adrenaline worked its way through her system, the endorphins dulling her senses, or the dopamine. She recalled a breathing exercise she used to do when—*when what?* The when did not matter, she remembered it.

She breathed in and counted to three before she exhaled, then she repeated the process.

Inhale—count to three—exhale, inhale—count to three—exhale.

She saw the shape of the Wraith ahead through the trees, no more than a smudge among the earth tones. Then she felt the Seeker's pulse, right on cue. She'd never imagined she would find the sensation soothing, but under the present circumstances, she did, a tiny massage loosening the tension around her temples. She soaked it in for a few moments before acknowledging the alert, then she took another breath. *Inhale—count to three—exhale.*

Then she began the trek back to the vehicle.

BANKS WAS leaning against the door of the Wraith like a screen-shot from an old movie, one with a *cool guy* protagonist, some good-hearted bloke who would beat the odds and wind up with the girl. Gem smiled weakly at the thought. He was too old for such a role, but give him a leather jacket and a pair of faded jeans?

He was smiling at her. "Good news," he said.

Gem took the bait. "And?"

"*And* there is a town not far from here, down in the valley." His grin broadened. "We are authorized for a supply run, a *proper* rest, as you are so fond of saying."

Gem stood silent, waiting on the punchline. She was all but certain he was full of shit, that he had chosen a perfectly awful time to take the piss out of her. But he hadn't. There was anticipation in his eyes, eagerness.

Gem sighed. "Well then, it's about time."

"You thought I was joking?"

"Yes, Banks. For a moment I did."

He shook his head at her.

"Not after the run we've had. That would just be cruel. But come on, let's get moving. I'll fill you in as we go."

Gem watched him walk around the passenger side and disappear behind the Wraith. "I'm all for it," she said.

THE CANYON

THEY TURNED onto the left fork of the path and the downslope led them away from the mountain. After a distance the forest broke to reveal the surrounding landscape, rolling hills, outcrops of rock, patches of trees, all you would expect from high altitude terrain. Gem saw the valley ahead, far and away and below, though she could not make out the settlement. They were still high up in the foothills, miles away from the promised land. She focused on her breathing as they followed the path, nodding at Banks's directions. She would not give him reason to concern himself with her if she could help it.

Inhale—count to three—exhale.

The Seeker had indicated the town would be sparsely populated and about as far off the beaten path as it got, an ideal location for their purposes. There would be some form of general store, a gas station or market—there always was—somewhere they could stock up on supplies, food and water and caffeine and sugar, a pint of whiskey for when they were cold and tired that night and could use a lift in spirits, a shot or two to warm their bones.

I could use a shot right now, Gem thought.

When was the last time she'd had a belt of whiskey? If it had been recently she could not recall, and—

Leave it. It was not worth straining her mind. Where there was a country store there would be whiskey for sale. No cyber-apocalypse was going to change that.

AMERICA'S RURAL populations had gotten along just fine before telephones and television and tele-anything, before the digital age and its conveniences. Some might have never had access to broadband, even after the warehouses of servers began springing up. Most were no strangers to internet commerce, sure, but had they ever relied on it? Did its absence cripple their lives, leave them slack-jawed and dumbfounded like their urban counterparts?

What evidence Gem had seen suggested otherwise. As the cyber-structure collapsed most small-town folks shrugged their shoulders and got on with living. That was not to say the hack had not affected them, of course. Rural areas relied on the same supply chains as the rest of the country for certain commodities, oil, gasoline, imported goods and the brand names that caught their fancy, so the initial chaos would have trickled down the line. Some would have gone without their favorite amenities for a while, but smaller communities always seemed better prepared for emergencies. They would have been ready for a commercial blackout, especially in the mountains where the weather routinely closed them in, well-stocked shelves and generators, the stores knowing their local suppliers and the names of their representatives, where they lived and the numbers to their landlines. They would have been ready for a cyber-crash because most had never put their faith in cyber in the first place, aware that society functioned perfectly well in the great before, that the digital superstructure only became foundational when humanity elected to bet the house on it.

They probably wouldn't say all that, Gem thought.

She must have gleaned the hyperbole from Banks—*the foundational superstructure*—something from his books he was fond of paraphrasing ad nauseum. She often wondered how much of her opinion on humanity's plight was her own and what percentage she'd acquired from Banks's roadside wisdom.

A series of blips and whirs rang out to her right, and Banks passed the orders along. The Seeker had identified a position a few miles outside of town. They would search it out, and once they had covered their bases, one of them would take the Buggy into town for supplies. *The Buggy*, Gem thought.

Her mind went to the stretch of woods by the relay tower. It could not have been that long ago, and she seemed to remember—

Stop it. She exhaled.

A ride on the Buggy would do her some good.

The Buggy was a clever piece of technology, ultra-portable, fully collapsible, its frame built to fold inward around the engine block and slot into a hollow compartment at the back of the Wraith for storage. When compressed it resembled a metal box the size of a mini-fridge, one of the bigger, deluxe models, wheels comically fastened to its four vertical faces. When activated it whined and unfolded in a flower of steel and titanium, components snapping and popping into place and tires inflating on previously hidden axels, handlebars sliding out and locking.

And it was as efficient as it was clever. The Buggy ran on a combination of electricity and solar, the current obtained from the Wraith as it ran, the sun soaked up as they traveled. The Wraith was powered in the same fashion in part, though it required gasoline for the beast of an engine beneath its hood. It was too large and demanding to forgo the hard stuff entirely, but it ran efficiently enough when allowed to, consuming no fuel at all when driven economically. Of course Gem's driving had been anything but economic of late. The terrain had seen to that. They were down to one-third of the main fuel tank plus the reserve, around twenty gallons combined. That amount might sustain them for another three-hundred miles if conditions were favorable, but there were multiple factors to consider, elevation and landscape, wind and rain and stops and starts and everything in between.

At least the sensors were disabled. Auto-corrections burned fuel like strands of hair with those short bursts of power, and you never knew exactly how much solar they would soak up. Driving through thick woodlands all day never helped the cause, and a realistic estimate for twenty gallons would be what, two-hundred miles? Gem considered it all as she pondered that sensor glitch, what it might mean for them if the issue went system-wide. The possibilities were many and the outcomes were all troublesome, but there was no point entertaining such scenarios. Fortune had provided them a place to resupply and rest, just as she'd hoped. All they had to do was get into town and back unscathed.

THEY FOLLOWED the path along the riverbank until the back-trail transitioned to a weather-beaten road, ill-maintained but level, the dirt loose and powdered and the tires kicking it out behind them in wispy clouds of dust. The Seeker had marked a waypoint ahead, off to their right and somewhere out of sight over the hills beyond the outskirts. If they continued down the road they were bound to run into farms and ranches. Gem could already identify fields in the distance, measured shapes of color standing out against the landscape, and they would not risk being spotted with the Wraith unless they had no other option.

Apart from the vehicle they were anonymous, strangers in a strange land passing through on a whim, but the Wraith told another story. To the untrained eye it might read as military. It certainly had the look, big and sleek and built for trouble, but some would see it for what it was, a corporate vehicle, a product of shadow war no one in power dared acknowledge. And those people were everywhere, even in the smallest bastions of civilization, some of them bought and others aligning themselves with one side or another for myriad reasons. Some believed the Conglomerates were politically aligned and chose their sides accordingly, throwing their hat in with whomever they thought represented their values. Some believed it was a battle of morals, that one faction was fighting the good fight, fighting for the people or the children or the future, for a world without cyber-technologies, or with them, whichever suited their inclinations. Some took a side because it seemed a fashionable thing to do, a reason to meet with like-minded people for beers on lonely nights.

Of course the majority didn't know fuck-all about the realities of the conflict, and it did not matter to Gem why someone chose to take an interest. What mattered was those people were dangerous, self-righteous and brash and all too willing to report a vehicle to a hotline, or worse. Their intentions would be irrelevant, and if that call made its way to the wrong people, the damage would be done. *Bloody do-gooders*, Gem thought. *Rat-fuck moralizers*. There was a reason they kept to the backroads, hundreds of millions of them.

GEM TURNED off the road onto a dirt track that faded into the earth after a few hundred feet. They continued on toward an outcrop of hills, a grayish-blue mass in the distance. Before long a gap in the terrain opened before them, and she knew that was their destination. There was no creeping intuition involved this time. It was just that obvious. Banks pointed to the break in the land.

"Do you see it?" he said.

Gem confirmed that she did.

It looked a good spot, ideal cover from anyone who might fancy a hike around the hills.

When they reached the outcrop they circled around a bend and pulled through the gap into a narrow canyon. It dipped down between the hills where a water source had run in the past, and they followed the slope until the ground leveled out toward the bottom. The Seeker rang out, and Gem slowed the Wraith to stop.

Here it was, base camp for her long-awaited rest.

She smiled and opened the door. The canyon walls rose on either side of them, tall and steep and colored with various shades of rock. The way they had entered was the only obvious opening. If there was a break farther along the corral, she could not see it. Gem looked around with approval. In moments like these her heart warmed to the Seeker and she forgave it for past offenses, the early wake up calls and godawful robotic noise, its self-gratifying chimes. It had done good by them this time.

Banks closed his door and leaned across the hood of vehicle, Gem meeting his eyes. There was the small matter of deciding who would make the run into town, a ritual the two of them took seriously. There were no Company regulations for supply runs, no protocols to follow, only their own homegrown rules.

"So," Gem said. "What will it be this time? Flip for it? Paper, scissors, stone?"

"It's rock, paper, scissors in the States."

"Stop acting a muppet, Banks. Pick your poison." Gem took her gamesmanship seriously. She had forgotten all about that crippling pain in the woods.

Banks rolled his eyes at her. "Don't call me that."

"Muppet?"

"Yes."

"Fine. I'll call you a tosser, you tosser."

"Your incorrigible."

"What? Would you like some more motivation?"

Banks sighed. "I'll tell you what, we'll skip the games. You take the run."

"Oh really?"

"Yes, Gem. I hereby concede today's supply run to you."

This was highly unusual. They always bickered over the Buggy, dickered for the rights through best of sevens and nines, fifteens, twenty-ones, battles of epic proportion.

And he was *conceding*?

"Alright, Banks. What gives."

"Nothing gives. I am choosing to take the high road. You've had a rough couple of days, and I won last time. And the time before that, I recall."

Gem paused. *Did he?* Did he take the last supply run? The time before? She reached for the memory and found nothing. When was their last run? Where did they set off from? Nothing, like fumbling through a room in the dark, banging into walls and furniture. She could not find the light switch. She would have to take his word for it, play the part and feign dissatisfaction. She could not let him think she had no memory of said events.

"Since when has that stopped you?" she said. "And what, charity? Did you hit your head as well?"

Good, she thought. *That will do.*

"Well, if you would rather stay with the Wraith—"

"Shut it. I didn't say that."

"That's what I thought."

Gem threw a hand up toward him.

"Don't expect me to have mercy on you next time," she said. "We will be playing for it."

"I'm sure we will."

She picked up something in his voice then, a hitch, a drop in intonation. Maybe he regretted his chivalry after all, but she would not cut him any slack. She was looking forward to a ride through the open air, and the decision to give up the chance was his prerogative. "Hey," she said, Banks meeting her eyes again. "You know the rules."

He smiled, saluted her in a mock show of fealty and ambled off toward the vehicle's rear. Was that smile of his *forced?* Gem had little doubt that it was, a copy of the grin he had feigned in the woods. She had ridden too many miles with the man not to notice when something was off, and whatever it was, it had nothing to do with the supply run. Gem watched him circle the Wraith and disappear behind its bulk. Now she felt bad for badgering him, for calling him names and laying into him on the pass, not because she had been unusually cross—such exchanges were standard—but because she hadn't known something was troubling him.

She frowned. Whatever it was, he would have to sort it out himself. She had her own problems at present.

GEM PULLED a large canvas bag from the driver's compartment and walked around the front of the Wraith. It would be private enough. If Banks had been a peeper, he would have gotten it over with long ago. The bag was her work tote, spare clothes and toiletries and a few old paperbacks she never remembered to replace, random junk and trinkets, road souvenirs.

She pulled off her flak jacket and laid it out on the hood, then she traded her fatigues for a pair of loose-fitting jeans. She fished a lighter coat out of the bag, a gray and blue number that was unlikely to turn any heads. She would have preferred to go without it—the weather was pleasant enough—though the windbreaker would conceal her vest. The chance of drawing fire in a small-town market was slim to none, but there was protocol to follow, and if she ditched the armor she would not get half-a-mile down the road before she began to rue it. It was better to be warm than bloody and choking for breath, laid out by some stranger she'd had the nerve to overlook.

She heard the clanks and pops and bangs of the Buggy straightening itself out, and she gave herself a once over, boots, jeans, vest, windbreaker, backpack, a handbag she rarely found occasion to carry. She sized up her reflection in the windshield.

Looking good, she thought, *looking normal.*

The purse was for show, a reminder to herself and others that she was a tourist, a city-girl who would not dare brave the mountains without feminine odds and ends. She brushed the hair from her face, smiling as she would at a passerby, polite, underwhelming, a smile that urged one to skip the dialogue and move along.

If there were questions she would be prepared, though she would avoid them if she could. Her accent could be a bane when it came to nosy strangers, especially out in the sticks. It had been a point of contention with Banks in the early days of their partnership, and his argument had its merits. She drew attention when she spoke. Americans wanted to know where she was from and what she was doing in the States. They wondered if the British had clean internet and whether the King made the laws over there and why tea was such a goddamned big deal. They were always curious, but did they find her suspicious? Not in Gem's experience.

She had argued the locals were far less likely to associate a British woman with a domestic conflict than an American man. "What would you think if you met me in a shop dressed in jeans and flats?" she'd asked Banks. "You wouldn't be thinking *corporate agent*, now would you? No one is going to think I'm a treacherous Bond girl, Banks. The world is not a sodding spy film."

Banks had taken her point and agreed to the games of chance, but it was Gem who endured the bulk of the questions. It was simply the way of things. The trick was to keep it simple, to speak as little as possible, hello, yes, no, thank you, goodbye. Oftentimes she could navigate a transaction with a nod and a laugh alone.

She smiled her evasive smile at the windshield again. What was she missing? She rifled through the bag until she found a baseball cap and sunglasses, and after equipping the accessories, she thought herself prepared. The woman smiling back at her seemed a stranger.

Gem stowed her bag in its compartment, sealed the lock and made her way around the Wraith. She placed a hand on Banks's shoulder. "Any requests?"

"Yes," he said. "Check the expiration dates."

"Oh piss off." She pushed him lightly away, and he flashed her a phony grin. Now he was mixing cheap jokes into the act. Did he really think he could pull that shit with her? *Leave it*, she thought.

"Alright," Gem said. "The usual then?"

"The usual."

Gem straddled the Buggy and raised her hand to her forehead, mimicking Banks's mock salute, then she revved the little engine and accelerated off up the slope.

THE MARKET

THE WIND on Gem's face was refreshing. It perked her up, and for a moment she felt a tourist again, like she had on the pass, taking in the scenery with the breeze in her hair. The Buggy's communication panel blinked and chirped as it guided her toward town, an unwelcome reminder she was still on the job. Its display glowed with the oranges and greens of the Seeker, its parent contraption, a means for the machine to reach her from afar. Banks would be minding the Seeker of course, listening to the steady blips and whirs as he passed the time. She could still not shake the look on his face, that plastic smile.

Maybe it was concern for her well-being that had him rattled. Had that not occurred to her? No, if he was worried about her safety he would have urged her to sit tight, to take it easy and rest up. He would not have offered up the Buggy without so much as a coin flip. So what was it then? Maybe it *was* nothing, nothing specific at least, the weight of the road forming cracks in his disposition, malaise of the long-term traveler. Sometimes melancholy waited around the corners, staking you out.

"Melancholy around the corners," Gem whispered. Where had that come from? She did not know, but it sounded familiar. The melancholy bit certainly felt like it could apply to Banks. *He could be thinking about before*, she thought.

Before—that would not surprise her.

GEM HAD to remind herself Banks was not a young man when it all came crashing down, not old by any means, but established. He was a professor with tenure, books in publication and roots firmly planted in a quiet little city out east. He'd had a house and a mortgage and a fiancé, routines and savings, a stock portfolio. He was dug in, not some twenty-something pushing adulthood away. Her life had been more malleable. If she was a ball of clay then he was molded pottery, set out and ready to fire. It had been easier for her to adapt. Hadn't he told her as much?

"I don't know whether to envy the younger generations or pity them," he'd said one morning. "You kids are adaptable, more so than the rest of us. You could only call that an advantage. But then again, you will have to live longer in the aftermath. Who knows where we are headed."

Gem had nodded in agreement. When had he told her that? Had he worn the same hollow smile that day?

No, his behavior in the canyon was troubling because it felt new for him, alien and somehow alarming, though recollection was not her strong suit at the moment. The reason might be obvious, stored away in an inflamed block of brain cells she could no longer access. He could have received some bad news, lost a loved one or friend, maybe a pet. He could have told her all about it a few days ago for all she knew. Gem shook her head. She would not press him to explain himself, especially if he already had. If he felt the need to tell her then he would, and until then she would worry about managing her own sorry state.

She intercepted the road a mile out from the canyon and turned onto it, a proper road, paved and reasonably maintained. The lack of signage indicated it was a rural route and not a highway. This was a positive turn. The Buggy was less conspicuous than the Wraith, appearing a perfectly normal ATV from a distance, though the fewer souls she encountered, the better. Before long she crested a hill and saw the outline of the town below, quaint and picturesque from a distance, what you would find if you typed *little mountain town* into one of the pre-hack search engines. A series of streets lay on a grid pattern at its center, forming four main intersections. Treelined avenues extended out for a few blocks in each direction then vanished into a sea of evergreens, like the settlers had ventured into the forest and carved them out.

The scene disappeared and reappeared as she traversed the hills, there for a moment then gone, growing in stature as she progressed. She made out a single traffic light suspended over the crossing of what had to be the main drag, a lonely fixture. It flashed on and off in intermittent yellow bursts, and there were no motorists to heed its pleas for caution. The town looked perfectly deserted. What was that old adage? It was a Catch-22. If there was no one around there would be no one to notice her, but if she was alone on the streets she was likely to be spotted. At least she could remember that. "It's a conundrum," she said to the Buggy.

But it was the good kind to have, better than a road block or a town gathering. She had ridden into such situations before without incident, but no one scenario was the same.

Caution was always paramount.

A line from her training flashed through her mind. *There is no way to know who might be lingering and where their allegiances might lie.*

She had no trouble remembering that little caveat either.

A FINAL foothill sloped away and Gem descended into the trees, the shadows enveloping her on all sides. She passed a sign of incorporation, an old, weather-beaten thing with a white outline bordering its distinctive green.

She slowed down to take in the information.

HAWKS PASS

POPULATION: 1143

ELEVATION: 6,395

"Hawks Pass," she said aloud. "It has a ring to it."

Had she seen any hawks up there that morning? Not unless that ominous flock in the clouds had lost its bearings, and hawks did not travel in flocks. "Hawks don't flock," she said.

She revved the little engine and crossed the threshold into the wooded outskirts. "Hawks Pass," she said again. Had she heard that somewhere before? Other teams might have passed through the area, but not hers, not that she could recall, though with her current ability to reminisce—*leave it*. But the thought was trapped in her mind, ricocheting around. *Have I heard the name before?*

She studied the structures along the road, the boarded and broken windows, the dilapidated buildings and one-story homes and decomposing sheds, an abandoned auto garage. Did any of it look familiar? Some of the dwellings resembled woodland cabins out of season, no vehicles, no wood piles or fires from the chimneys, no signs of life. She had not seen a single person.

Then she spied the traffic light in the distance, a tiny shape on its tiny wire. She guessed that was where she'd find the general store, the one intersection in town officials saw fit to regulate. The Buggy's display chimed a satisfied little tone, informing Gem her destination lay ahead on the left. Here was the Seeker reading her thoughts from afar, no rest for the wicked. It provided a small green arrow for her to follow in case she lost her bearings.

The woods gave way to treelined streets as she neared the center of town, the homes there more uniform and showing signs of habitation. After two blocks she passed a small, well-maintained house, and it was there she saw the first of Hawks Pass's residents.

An older man sat on the porch with a coffee cup and a cigarette, watching the empty street. His presence took Gem by surprise, and she did a double take. He was there all right, minding his business, a picture of small town ease.

Had she expected to go the whole way without seeing a soul?

The man raised a slow hand in greeting as she passed, a simple acknowledgement. He did not smile or call out, no *hi there* or *hello*, no cantankerous stranger's glare. He seemed to take no interest in the peculiar vehicle humming down his street. Gem raised a hand in return, smiled her rehearsed smile and moved along, leaving him alone with the road again. *One down*, she thought.

GEM SLOWED to a stop at the street-light. There were gas pumps on the corner to her left, four of them, not ancient, but hardly modern. The comms panel sounded a confirmation tone, and she pulled the Buggy into the lot and rolled it up to the pump farthest from the building, street-side. She hoped there would not be an attendant. There rarely were anymore, but you could never be sure, not in small mountain outposts bent on hospitality.

She counted to ten, and when no one emerged from the shop to greet her, she released her breath and silenced the Buggy's engine and checked the pump for a card reader. If it did not have one that would complicate things, but she was in luck. There was a paint chipped slot complete with an archaic pin pad, still blinking and ready for payment. She would do the shopping first and use the Company card outside. The Buggy was small and sleek, and to the untrained eye it would not appear capable of storing fifteen gallons, but that was what it held. The clerk might feel compelled to ask where all that fuel was going. And then?

Then would come the story, the yarn about her custom ATV obsession, the enlarged fuel tank for extended excursions and how she *loved* it when people asked because she *loved* to talk about it and on and on until they prayed to God she would stop. Gem had rehearsed the bit with Banks countless times, but she had never been forced to deploy it. She was thankful today would not be that day. She could not be sure she would remember the lines.

The truth was the Buggy's interior was largely hollow save for a bladder that expanded and formed to the underside of the frame when filled. It could hold a third of the Wraith's main fuel supply, more than enough to keep them going. Banks liked to joke the Buggy was little more than a motorized bomb when filled, but the bladder was made of a sturdy polymer and the engine was non-combustion, unlikely to produce a spark. It would take one hell of an event to break the casing and ignite the fuel store.

At least that was what Gem told herself.

She turned her attention to the building. The place was about what she expected, combination gas station and market and meeting place, old but well-kept and recently refurbished by the looks of it. She pictured the townsfolk gathered there in the mornings, sipping their coffee and gossiping, reading whichever newspaper they imported from over the hills. She saw tables and booths inside the large front windows, laid out like a roadside diner.

Was there a figure seated toward the back?

She would have to get closer to be sure. The only vehicle in the lot was an ancient Ford truck parked against the backside of the building, maybe the owner's, maybe a junker someone was hoping to offload. What she had was one potential customer, at least one employee, no more than two, not at this place.

It could have been far worse.

Gem took a breath to steel her nerves then crossed the empty lot. She stepped into the store and was greeted by an old-fashioned bell above the door—*ting*. A middle-aged woman stood behind the counter with a highlighter and a stack of papers, a large woman, out of shape and slow to react to the door chime. She would not be pursuing Gem under any circumstances, but she could certainly reach the phone on the wall behind her. A customer sat at the back booth against the wall sipping coffee, an older gentleman clad in a flannel shirt and thumbing a magazine. He had a distinguished look about him that struck her as odd, a man out of place in those clothes, out of place in that town.

Just out of place, Gem thought.

Whatever it was, the sight of him made her skin crawl. It was that feeling again, the one from the pass, that strange intuition those birds stirred in her. Her mind went into overdrive.

No way to know who might be lingering—

Think. Would a man his age spend his days hanging around a small town market on the off chance a Wraith team might show? She had been wrong about the skies over the pass, but the feeling was strong, irrational or not, and she was trained to trust her instincts. She would keep an eye on that man.

The door closed behind her with a thunk as the sound of the bell faded and Gem pretended to check her bag, a rehearsed move suggesting she might have forgotten her wallet. An absent-minded tourist would do such a thing. The man looked towards the door with indifference then returned to his reading material, and the cashier did the same. Gem saw it all through her periphery, feigning relief as she looked up, a word under her breath.

She grabbed a wire basket from a stack near the door and walked toward the centermost aisle, taking stock as she did, entrances and exits and blind spots, anything and everything worth noting. Then she made her way down the aisle to the back cooler directly opposite the man. He continued to read.

Keep reading, Mr. Magazine Man.

She slid the door open and looked over the sandwiches, checking the expiration dates on the subs, roast beef and turkey, capicola and salami, then she moved down the line to the beverages and picked out six cans of coffee and caffeinated teas. She would buy more if she did not believe it would look suspicious, but the clerk might—

Gem felt a prickle on her neck. She turned an eye toward the Magazine Man, careful not to stare. It was not him. He was still reading away. She looked up to the front and yes, it was the woman at the counter. Gem knew the look, interest, curiosity. It was the look she had been hoping to avoid. Now there were sure to be questions, small talk, rehearsed smiles and nods.

And the excursion had been going so well. *Leave it.*

She had shopping to finish and conversation to survive.

Gem ambled through the snack section and picked out the essentials, jerkies and trail mixes and nuts and a few candy bars. She readied herself for the exchange.

What brings you to these parts? Vacation.

Where are you from? East.

What state? Massachusetts.

Where are you camped at? Oh, I couldn't tell you, my boyfriend picked out the spot. He's out milling around, you know, checking out the town.

And how might she avoid all that?

She could go on the offensive, question the clerk to throw her off. She could ask where the batteries were. She had seen them when she entered, a display off to the side of the counter where you could not miss them. The question would be moronic and the answer so obvious the woman might take her for a fool, one of those tech-dependent dummies who'd never recovered from the hack. There was a distaste for such types in America's backwaters, and distaste discouraged discussion.

When she approached the counter she set the basket down, smiled her rehearsed smile and asked the cashier where she could find the batteries. The woman looked perplexed.

Yes, I am a fool, Gem thought. *Keep smiling.*

"You're standing right next to them, hon." She pointed to Gem's left. "On the rack." Her nametag said *Wanda*.

Gem forced her eyebrows up in surprise. "Oh my *God*," she said, flattening out her accent. "They're right there, aren't they? I don't know how I missed them."

"Oh your fine!" Wanda grinned her salesperson's grin as she worked her way through the basket.

Gem grabbed a pack of AA's from the rack, set them down and considered the bottles of whiskey on the back shelf. She looked to Wanda again. Would she card her for the booze? Gem had a youthful look to her in spite of her years, and her current getup would amplify that. Her driver's license was real, doctored and stamped and holo-graphed, though the ID was not the problem. The issue was Wanda would remember her. Gem was out of place in Hawks Pass, and if someone came around enquiring about a woman on a strange ATV, she would prefer Wanda did not have details to draw on, fabricated or not.

Wanda took her time with the items.

She did not ask a single question.

"Thirty-four fifty-five," she said. "No fuel?"

The sleight of hand bit with the batteries had worked.

"I'll get it on the way out with my card," Gem said. "I'll take a pint of that Smith's Finest you've got back there too, the plastic one." Now she had played her hand.

Wanda reached behind her, grabbed the whiskey and scanned the barcode. She slipped it into the sack.

"Okay then, forty-eight and a quarter."

Gem slid three twenties across the counter, feigning a smile as Wanda doled out her change. "Thanks."

She picked up the groceries and turned to leave. *Wait for it—*

"You bet. Safe travels."

And then Gem was out the door and on her way to the Buggy. She had been quietly holding her breath, and now she took in a lungful. "Bloody hell," she said. Why had she let herself get worked up? Gut feelings as providence? A magazine reading imposter? She felt silly for entertaining such fantasies, for walking on eggshells through a tried-and-true routine.

But it was not relief she felt as she stepped up to the pump.

There should have been questions, she thought. *A few more pleasantries.*

There always were in these towns.

So her luck was in today, and what was wrong with that? Nothing she could put her finger on, but the feeling remained, that faulty intuition. She was beginning to think it a product of her injury, swelling or damaged nerves or brain bleed, pressure against her cortex, whatever influenced perception—or delusion. She took a deep breath and ran her card through the pump reader. It beeped with confirmation. When the handle clicked free she popped the Buggy's cap and inserted the nozzle, keeping an eye on the front window as the gasoline flowed. Wanda's shape was bent over the counter where she'd been highlighting, and Gem hoped she was not minding the meter. She might have some questions then.

Gem turned to the pump and watched the numbers tick away, wishing the damned thing would ran faster, *tick, tick, tick*, on and on and on. When the Buggy was nearly full she slowed the stream to a trickle, cut the flow off at fifteen gallons and rehung the nozzle on its hook. Then she felt the prickle again. *No.* She turned her eyes to the storefront and saw the Magazine Man standing behind the counter with Wanda. He was using the phone.

Time slowed. Gem could feel their gazes on her. Her stomach tightened, and she felt her hand rise up beyond her shoulder. She was waving. Had she meant to? No, instinct was taking over, training. She was maintaining the ruse. *Too late.* No degree of gesturing would make that man hang up. The air felt heavy around her as she moved, as if she were swimming in it. Then it was like watching someone else, an out-of-body experience, another Gem straddling the Buggy, another Gem starting the engine, another Gem turning around and exiting the lot.

Was she smiling? The stones on that girl!

And then she was around the corner, wrenching the accelerator and heading for the hills. She could feel her fingers on the handlebars now, her thighs around the frame. She had control. The last few moments had been automatic response, unadulterated reaction, another woman steering her body.

Was it really a product of training?

Not now. She felt the wind on her face as she leaned into the Buggy's shape, bracing herself for speed. She flew past the neat little house and saw that the porch was vacant, the man with the mug no longer a fixture. Was he a corporate snitch as well? Another rat-fuck conspirator? She fixed her ears on the Buggy's panel and waited for the alarm to sound.

THE SKY

GEM FLEW down the road pushing fifty miles an hour. *Inhale—count to three—exhale, inhale—count to three—exhale.* A wreck at that speed would shatter her bones and rip the flesh from her tendons and tear her cartilage asunder, but she could not slow down, not when the townsfolk had made her for what she was.

She had no choice now but to assume that.

She motored up each hill and down, the wooded outskirts half-a-mile behind her. She had yet to see another soul on the road, and she did not know what to make of that. Was it a blessing, or was it strange and wrong, like the Magazine Man and Wanda's lack of questions? The urge to look over her shoulder was strong, but she knew there would be nothing to see, no beat-up Ford closing the distance or locals with torches and pitchforks. She glanced at the sky then forced herself to refocus. The panel would sound the alarm before she could scare up a visual, and if the tech were to fail her, she would hear it before she saw it, and if she could *hear* it, she would be a streak of gore on the road. That was all there was to it, and she pushed the little motor for every ounce it could give. She turned to the panel again—nothing.

But there wouldn't be anything yet.

Calls would have to be made, information verified, ordinance repurposed and deployed. If they believed the tip was valid they would move, but there was always red tape, and they would not commit resources without due diligence. There would be time yet, maybe not enough, but a fighting chance.

Think. It would take five minutes to transfer the fuel, re-box the Buggy and remove themselves from the canyon. *How long since we parked?* Less than an hour. *How close could they have ordinance?* It would be a hundred miles, at least. It would have to be, otherwise the machine would have picked it up. *Something could have changed.* The Seeker would have signaled. *How fast could they swing it?* No way to tell. Would those shits trust the report? Would they have other priorities? *How far out now?* She was making good time. Five minutes was her best guess. *So ten minutes, give or take?* "Ten minutes," Gem said to the Buggy. "Ten minutes, give or take."

Her approximations were exactly that, guesswork, and she knew the corporate crews never rested. She had been a part of one. Hers had worked in three eight-hour rotations, and the Company's adversaries would use similar methods, half the techs monitoring assets and shoring up security as she once had, the other half hell bent on breaking enemy lines, snatching up ordinance and territory. There was always a chance they would push through and take a cluster of drones—or worse.

"Rumors," she said to herself. "Those are just rumors."

THE WORKING satellites had been claimed long ago and were nigh on impossible to crack—the security on them was airtight— but not the floaters. When someone finally figured out how to re-boot them, it would change everything. A satellite gave an organization permanent territory, the means to monitor whole swaths of terrain and discourage adversaries from crossing it. By the time the hack rolled around the tech companies had sent up thousands, but nearly all were lost when access to the control centers was severed. No one could process their signals and make the minor adjustments needed to keep them on track. Satellites crashed into one another and broke into pieces, the shards of the dead devices drifting into others like giant stellar dominoes. The slightest of impacts could send them coasting off into space or crashing down to the sea. Gem thought about them sometimes, all those derelicts up in orbit. The perpetrators must have intended to claim them as their own once the dust had settled, though it did not pan out that way. Not even the heaviest of hitters had been able to manage that, not anything close to it. *Unless the rumors are true.*

"They are just bloody rumors," she said aloud.

The rumors had started when an outpost went dark and all active teams were ordered back to base, some only minutes after setting out. The official word was a protocol check, a test of preparedness in the event of unforeseen circumstances, but the Wraith crews knew better. Something had threatened the entire region, something with massive scope, and the conclusion only made sense. But it was one hell of a contention. A Conglomerate could not reach for a satellite without compromising its holdings, even a floater no one was actively monitoring. The signal would be ripe for the picking, and if their adversaries triangulated it they would learn the whereabouts of a rival data center. That was why the theory had been easy enough to write off, why most had accepted the Company's explanation that it really was just an exercise.

Gem pushed the thought from her mind.

There was no point in worrying about it now. If today was the day the rumors proved true and a foe opened eyes in the region, then that would be that, game over for Gem and Banks and anyone within range. It was a no-win situation, and it was out of her control. What Gem had to worry about were the drones.

She cast her eyes to the sky again. Drone surveillance was a crapshoot when it came down to it, hide and seek over a thousand square miles. But if they had a certain Magazine Man on the payroll? If that prat in the store had marked a team near Hawks Pass then the Seeker could not help them.

All it could do was sound the alarm.

GEM ROLLED over the top of a long slope and saw the outcrop of hills surrounding the canyon. She was nearly there. The sun was setting behind the mountain, coloring the sky a dusky lavender. It was beautiful, and it brought her no solace. It was an omen of approaching night and darkening skies and what might be lurking beyond them. The Buggy whined with effort as she barreled over the ridge of the canyon, spitting an electric wheeze. Gem had pushed the clever little machine to its limit. It could not have gone on at that pace much longer, the solar charge spent and the battery nearly dead from hightailing it over the hills.

When the Wraith came into view she saw Banks had prepped it for the fuel transfer. He would have been monitoring her progress, seen her flying out of town and guessed the supply run must have gone tits up. He stood alert with the siphon as Gem slid the Buggy to a halt at his feet, flipping the side panel up and locking the hose to the bladder. It clicked and popped and pressurized and the first draughts of gasoline burst through the tubing before settling down to a stream. Gem dropped the grocery bags next to the Wraith and turned to face him. "What do we know?"

"Nothing yet."

"What are our options?"

"I'm running a scan. You got here fast."

"Well that was the bloody intention!" Gem said. "Go monitor it, I'll handle the fuel."

"What happened?"

"I saw someone make a call, and we can discuss it later. Go check on the machine."

Banks slid in through the passenger door, swiped the lock screen and jammed his thumbs into the print scanner. The display opened to reveal an options menu, elaborately coded and illegible to untrained eyes. The scan ran on in the background, compiling known cave systems and abandoned mines, outcrops of rock, any potential shelter from above. The canyon would not be good enough now.

Gem peered over his shoulder. "Anything?"

"Still running," Banks said. "Wait—there!"

There was a cave system a few miles from the canyon, accessible from the ground and easily large enough to harbor the vehicle. Banks pulled up the available data, a few pixilated images and a paragraph of background information, size and depth, records of deterioration. He enhanced the resolution, mumbling numbers and statistics, then he turned to Gem. "We can get in there."

"Well thank Christ for that," she said. "Run it."

Banks pulled up the emergency action portal and began to enter the information.

—*Request Immediate Relocation*—

—*Position Compromised*—

—*Code 137*—

Gem ran back to the Buggy to check on the siphon. The bladder was two-thirds empty, still a minute or two out. She hurried back to Banks in anticipation.

"Still processing," he said. "Focus on the Buggy."

She hustled back the way she had come.

Gem watched the fuel flow until the stream tapered off, then she pulled the hose and closed up the Wraith's flank. She capped the Buggy's bladder, locked its panel in place and rolled the ATV behind the vehicle, yanking the back winch down and hooking it to a bar under the seat. Then she hollered at Banks to hit it. He activated the storage procedure, metal snapping and popping as the handlebars folded down and the axels retracted, the body collapsing into itself in smooth, precise motion. The wheels rotated to the sides of the box shape as the Wraith's cable hoisted it up over the back bar, pulling it into place. It locked with a satisfying clack, then Gem circled around the vehicle and jumped lightly into her seat. "Still?" she said.

Banks shot her a dirty look. If they tried to move without authorization the Seeker would lock them down. It might hold them until an overseer was available to evaluate their transgression, or its scan picked up the threat, and by then there was no telling—

The Seeker chirped and its screen went green.

"Go," Banks said.

Gem slid the Wraith into gear, put her foot down and the vehicle shot forward up the hill, over the ridge and out of the canyon into the dying light.

"Alright," Banks said. "We're going off-road, and I don't have a great layout. Head back toward the mountain and be ready to slow down. This is going to be line of sight."

"Lovely. And right when we're losing the light."

"Stick to the lower ground when you can, because if there's a drop somewhere—"

"Noted." It was not going to be a pleasant drive.

They motored on down the road until Banks signaled for her to pull off at the base of rocky knoll, away from the level ground and onto the rugged terrain. The last sliver of sun vanished behind the peak as the Wraith rocked over the undulations, stripping the light from the landscape.

It seemed nature was no longer on their side.

SURVEILLANCE

THE ADMINISTRATOR picked up the phone and listened. She tapped her fingers on her desk, hoping they would get to the point. Then her ears perked up. "Well, that is interesting," she said. Mr. Banks had filed a 137, an urgent request for relocation. Something must have spooked them. A 137 would not normally require her attention, but it was her business today. "And you are certain there is nothing else?" She pulled up a geographic layout on her screen and studied it for a moment. "You will clear them to proceed and contact me when they reach their destination. Is that understood?"

She put the phone down and looked over the map again, tracing the distances with her finger, then she closed the display and stood up. They would be safe there for the time being. It was clever of them to search that cave out, although the route would take them off the roads and into the hills. *So be it*, she thought. They did not have far to go, and she would not trouble herself with the hypotheticals. What she needed to consider was the threat they perceived, how it might factor into her plans.

Had anyone gone over the audio?

She picked up the phone, put in the call and was greeted by a second voice. "Tell me someone is on audio," she said. The voice on the line expounded. "And *did* someone put in a call? Have you confirmed it?" She sat up straighter. "And why am I only hearing of this now?" Excuses emanated from the end of the line, references to protocol, steps she had explicitly instructed them to skip. "What do you not understand about an executive override? I put that in place to avoid such bureaucracy. You report directly to *me*. *I* tell you whether or not to verify authenticity. Do you understand that *now*?" The voice assured her it would not happen again.

"I want you to listen carefully to what I'm about to say," said the Administrator. "You and your team are to initiate the next phase of the plan. I have information beyond your station that you are not privy to, and you are under my command. Meanwhile, you will allow them ample time to recuperate. I do not want them losing their nerve."

She ended the call before the voice could respond.

Additional excuses would rile her further, and further riling would be serve no purpose. She required assistance with this project, regardless of how wanting she might find the help. She could not do it all on her own. If they were to succeed then everyone would need to play their part, especially Miss Gemma and Mr. Banks. They would be no good to her if she pushed them too hard.

THE CAVE

THE SPECTRA-LIGHT kicked on as the twilight dimmed and Gem winced as her eyes adapted. She never understood why they called it a *spectra-light* when it produced no light at all. It's glow was not visible outside the Wraith's cabin, and you could not see it looking in. As she understood it the device was sonar-based, some fantastic form of bat vision, the system emitting pulses and the Wraith capturing the returning frequencies through microscopic sensors and superimposing terrain onto the windshield. "Think of it as a filter brightening up an image," an engineer had told her. "What you are seeing is very much there in front of you, just enhanced for clarity."

"And if it malfunctions?" Gem had asked.

"Then you are stuck with your high beams."

Gem's mind went to the sensors again, that gremlin in the works. If the bug made its way to the spectra-light—

Don't even think about it.

For all its wonder and sophistication, the spectra-light did little to illuminate what lay outside their immediate vicinity, and Banks sat rigid in his seat, his eyes darting between the Seeker and the route as he compared map and terrain. *There are always the high beams*, Gem thought, but that was bollocks. The high beams were the

Wraith's forbidden fruit, existing only to tempt her. They were all but useless on a vehicle designed to go unseen.

They buckled down and persisted, Banks guiding them over slopes and around trees and through swathes of tall grass where the stalks obscured their vision. Gem listened all the while, alert and ready to respond. Before long they were making sport of it, ducking and weaving each time the earth threatened to strike, dancing through breaks and undulations in toe with its jagged rhythm.

They emerged in a clearing where the moon shone through the clouds, and Gem could see what lay before them, a dark patch carved into the cliffside.

Then the Seeker went mad and screamed.

She turned to the machine. What were the odds?

To mark a flyer the moment they reached the cave?

The alarm was shrill and spiteful and Banks scrambled to disarm it. Gem only stared at the Seeker, mesmerized. *Orange*, she thought, *not red.* She knew the siren was sounding, though to her it seemed muffled, dampened somehow. She placed her hands over her ears then drew them slowly away. It felt like she was underwater during a fire drill. Why was her volume turned down?

"Gun it, Gem!"

Had Banks disabled the alarm? He must have.

The Seeker was pulsing now, a silent, throbbing warning. She could feel it in her teeth and joints and all the way down in her bowels. Her boot met the pedal and the Wraith surged ahead, their destination growing in size. Was she gone again? Watching herself from the ether like that stint at the pumps? She could feel her foot on the gas, her hands locked to the wheel. She was determined to hold on and squeezed as hard as she could.

Focus. She watched the maw of the cave grow larger.

It all felt familiar, the urgency, fleeing through the hills with the moon shining above. Gem shook it off.

There is only the cave. She counted the seconds, two, three, four, then the vehicle crossed the threshold.

THE MOUTH of the cave was massive, the height of barn doors and the width of a four-lane highway, the floor worn and smooth and nearly level with the ground outside. The range of the spectra-light was further limited in the hollow, and beyond sat a sheet of ink, a drop into some forgotten abyss where maladies awaited, jagged rocks, bats, bears—mythological monsters. Gem pulled in far enough to shield them from the skies and killed the engine, then Banks activated the temperature cloak. An icy mist filled the interior of the vehicle, prickling their extremities and penetrating Gem's jacket and jeans. She shivered and cursed and rubbed her arms for warmth, thinking again of that engineer.

What was it she had said?

She'd said the cold would balance out the temperature of the vehicle and establish a baseline, that it would have a stabilizing effect on the inner and outer gauges, and—

And the rest of it.

Why could she remember that woman with such clarity? Why those old conversations from work? Why bits of her training?

Leave it. She turned her thoughts to the cooling system.

For as good as she was with code she could never wrap her mind around physics, thermodynamics, whatever brand of hard science the engineers assumed she would understand. What Gem took from the conversation was the vehicle's exterior would adjust to the temperature of the cave and shield the interior from thermal sensors, although it required her to freeze her ass off first. If they remained in the Wraith it would conceal them from heat-seeking technology—that was the important part—so she shivered and listened to the Seeker's pulse, *thrum, thrum, thrum.* After what seemed an eternity the system ceased and the machine emitted a low tone, its display now a mellow green.

The Seeker had deemed their location safe.

Gem sank into her seat and allowed her nerves to uncoil. The cave was as good a spot as they'd find under the circumstances, cool and dark and masked by the bones of the Earth. But the drones would continue to hunt them, circling the area until their attention was drawn elsewhere, their services commandeered for a different assignment. Their internment might last a few hours if fate was on their side, and if not it could be all night, longer if their adversaries were hell bent on rooting them out.

It will be the night, Gem thought.

She could not know that with any certainty, but she had been right about the Magazine Man, and wasn't this the same feeling? That brain damaged clairvoyance? She wondered if those birds on the pass had meant something after all, if she had missed it on account of her mind slipping a gear, as it had beside the pumps.

And when the Seeker sounded the alarm?

Gem closed her eyes. When she opened them again they were still in the cave. It was still freezing-ass cold. Banks was still shivering alongside her. What she understood as reality appeared intact. She closed her eyes tight and began to quietly meter her breaths.

"Looks like you were right about town," Banks said.

Gem looked up. "Of course I was. Did you doubt it?"

"No, I didn't, but now we have proof." He sighed. "I think you should tell me what happened now."

Gem looked out at the darkness beyond the windshield. She had killed the spectra-light with the engine, leaving only the glow of the Seeker's display. It lit the side of Banks's face in a soft, green hue. "I sensed something was off before I saw it. No—I *knew* something was off. I knew it when I saw the man in the booth, the one who made the call." She paused. "And then I caught the cashier giving me the look, the one that wonders, then suspects."

"I know it," Banks said. "It was just the two of them?"

"Just the two, the cashier—*Wanda*—and a customer, an older man. He was reading a magazine. I saw him on the phone after I went out for the fuel."

In her mind she was back at the store, a place about as dangerous as a tin of beans for most. She saw their faces, two small town Americans, once ordinary, still ordinary, but not to her or Banks or anyone of their ilk. Gem pictured them going about their day-to-day, making dinner, washing dishes, weeding the yard. Maybe Wanda was ordinary, but the Magazine Man?"

"Gem?"

"It was the man who made the call. He might have been on a payroll, and the cashier knew enough to suspect something. I sensed that in her. Maybe she signaled him while I was shopping, or maybe he signaled her, I can't say, but they waited until I was out with the petrol, then I spied that geezer on the phone talking his bollocks"—she was growing flustered, her accent thickening—"through the bloody glass and I could feel them looking at me, those rat-fucks, and that was when I *knew*. I didn't let them see me panic though. I even waved at them, Banks. I *waved*. Then I packed it in and fucked off right quick."

There was a moment of silence, then Banks leaned in close. "And how quick did you *fuck off*, love?"

His mock-London accent was awful.

Gem pulled back as if he had struck her and Banks cut a smile, his hands up in surrender. "I'm sorry. You were losing your temper, and I thought we could use some levity. We're safe now, Gem. We made it in time."

She stabbed at him with her eyes but struggled to hold the leer. She had been going on a bit, now hadn't she?

"You bastard. That was a serious conversation we were having, and you go and take the piss out of me?"

She could not hold her steel and burst into laughter, then Banks did the same. They covered their mouths and roared on in muffled bursts, Gem laughing until her stomach hurt and tears streamed down her cheeks. For a moment the cave seemed far away, the Wraith and the Seeker, the eyes in the sky and her injury and besotted memory, the Magazine Man, all of it. There was only her colleague putting one over on her, and it felt good, a shot of normalcy to pull her back from the brink.

But it did not last. She saw the Magazine Man's face again, his stubble and rancher's flannel. That knob had still managed to make a perfectly dreadful run even worse.

"Do you know what just occurred to me?" she said to Banks. "No one will pay those shits a dime. Marking a team is pointless if you can't locate them, a waste of time and resources. We beat their play, and someone is going to be disappointed."

Banks thought on it for a moment.

"If they were doing it for the money, then yes."

Gem balked. "If? What's this with *if?*"

"If, Gem. We don't know that's why they called you in."

She stiffened in her seat.

"And what else would it be? Politics? A pair of good fucking Samaritans? If that bloke was not on a payroll he must have called a hotline, and people call those lines fishing for a reward."

"Not necessarily," Banks said. "Think about it. There are operatives all over these parts, that's no secret. Maybe they are just sick of us tracking our corporate mud through their nice little towns. They might call in every stranger who looks the part as a deterrent."

"What? Have you gone mental?"

"I'm just saying there are other possibilities."

"And who would that man think he is calling, Banks? The government? Do they believe it's your good old Uncle Sam operating those lines?"

"I don't know what they believe. That's the point. We don't know what kind of information makes it way out here. The only thing we *know* is they managed to put us on someone's radar."

Gem stared him down.

Why was he arguing with her about this? This was no time to play devil's advocate for some teachable bloody moment. Money was the universal language, the obvious explanation, not the easy answer. *Why* did he call her in? Because the man was either an insider or someone came around offering to pay for information, that's why. It was simple, and in either scenario it was for *money*.

"I feel like you are drawing me into a debate for your own amusement," Gem said, "and I am not in the mood for it. Did you forget where we are?"

"It was not my intention to argue with you," Banks said. Now he was frowning, his face zombified by the dull, green light. "I guess I would just like to believe it's not always about the money. A fool's hope, I suppose."

Banks stared ahead through the windshield and Gem followed his gaze. Hadn't they just been having a laugh? When had the melancholy crept in? *It waits around the corner, roads, conversations, anyplace that takes a turn.* There it was again, that phrase. Where had she heard that before? *Melancholy around the corner?*

She pushed the thought away.

"I'm knackered, Banks. Let's just leave it all for later, shall we? Why don't you hand up one of those sacks. I'm famished."

Banks reached behind his seat and fetched one of the grocery bags from the store. He pulled a sandwich from the sack. "Look at that. It's good for two more weeks."

Gem rolled her eyes at him.

At least he was still attempting to be humorous.

THEY ATE the sandwiches and sipped their teas and watched the Seeker flare are flicker, scanning for threats in the dark. The temperature was reasonable again, not pleasant, but warm enough. When they were finished they reclined their seats and laid back.

"Hand up that other bag," Gem said. "I got us some whiskey, some off-brand shite."

"You did?" Banks was smiling again.

He handed her the sack and Gem fished the bottle out, unscrewed the plastic cap and sniffed.

"Yep," she said. "Shite. Cheap, rotten shite."

Gem took a pull, closed her eyes at the burn and swallowed, then she passed it over to Banks. They exchanged the bottle a few times, taking small swigs and letting the warmth wash over them, then Gem recapped the booze and placed it back in the bag. She brought a finger to her lips. "Can't forget we are still on duty."

"We'll write it off as a sleep aid if anyone asks."

"That we will." Gem was already feeling the effects. "I believe sleep is the operative word. If I was not ready for it before, I certainly am now."

Banks yawned. "I will second that. It has been a day, and it goes without saying that—"

"Not another word," Gem said. "You're not to speak of it again until I've had a rest." She leaned her seat back as far it would lean. "I'm serious."

Banks said no more, and her mind slipped into a fog as the whiskey smoothed over her faculties. If the machine woke her with its screams she would sit up and drive, it was that simple. There was nothing else to consider. Until then the world could shove off, the drones and the Seeker and the Magazine Man and his masters.

They could all go take a flying leap.

The seconds passed, and somewhere in the ether Gem thought she heard a noise, brief and sharp. She opened her eyes in the lowlight. The Seeker was idling away. What was it if not the machine? Had she been on the edge of a dream? She slipped her hand round the back of her head. It had been half-a-day since the pain floored her in the forest, more than that now. If she could only sort out what happened back there. *And at the market*, she thought, *and outside the cave. On the pass before*—

Not now. She leaned back, closed her eyes and pictured a bed, any bed, anything soft and comfortable and far away from vehicles and small mountain towns. She remembered the single bed she'd had in her apartment as a graduate student, hardly a picture of luxury, but adequate. She had slept well there, back before the hack when her worries were fleeting and arbitrary, when *life or death* was little more than a passing phrase. That would do just fine.

THE STRANGER

GEM STARES *at the screen. The code in front of her is bizarre, the digits stretched out and warped to the point she can hardly read the numbers. What was it she was working on? She blinks and refocuses, ready to reengage, but the program has closed. The wallpaper on the desktop's display is a bright, offensive orange. Was it always orange? What happened to the app? She must have blinked again because the screen has changed. Bright green arrows scream across the display only to vanish and large block letters appear in their place.*

—NO SIGNAL—

This strikes her as odd. Had she been working online? The letters flash rapidly and buzz, the electric fizz of a neon sign. Then she realizes what is happening. It is Day One, the day it all began.

She shakes her head and laughs. How could she forget Day One?

Day One—*she thinks that moniker stupid, silly*—Day One—*but that is what stuck, something coined by a news channel or politician and repeated like a mantra. Now she is experiencing it again, but something is not right. She does not own a desktop. She uses one on campus, but never at home. She must have bought it on the cheap and forgotten about it, because here it is, and now it is not working properly.* "Of course it isn't," *she says.* "Day One."

She reaches into her pocket for her mobile and feels it there, snug against her bum. When she pulls it free it is not her phone at all. It is an old data drive, a memory stick she'd acquired after first moving to London. It is her favorite piece of nostalgia. Well hello, love, *she thinks.* How could I have mistaken you for my mobile?

She turns it over in her hand, smaller than her phone and in no way similar. There are ridges in its casing, a multi-platform jack and tiny decals she thought were cool as a teenager, now faded and peeling. It glows orange like the desktop wallpaper, which seems normal enough. When was the last time she saw it? Wasn't it orange then? And where is her mobile? She realizes the phone will be of no use to her. It is a big-tech model, permanently signed into their network and therefore dead by association. It will shut down the minute she unlocks the screen, and she has more pressing matters to attend to, hitting the shops and stocking up on all the good stuff before the mobs rush in.

She turns to make for the door and stops. She is already outside. There are people lining the streets, dozens of dumbfounded pedestrians holding their phones to the air and shuffling around like B-movie robots, searching for a signal, Gem thinks, all of them unaware their devices are done for.

She watches them with interest. Was this how it all went down?

The sky shimmers with static, flashing orange, then blue, then green, then orange, blue, green again. The crowd does not seem to notice. Can they not see what is happening? She grabs the nearest idler to pass on the news, then she recoils. The man has burst into flames—no.

It is not fire at all, not even hot to the touch. One by one the loiterers go up in spurts of orange light, a cavalcade of human torches.

Gem turns to flee and finds an obstruction blocking her path. It is the Hawks Pass general store. "Shit," *she says.* "Where is the Buggy?"

The ATV is nowhere in sight, and she casts her gaze over the hills toward the canyon. She will have to make a run for it, but it is a long way, miles.

She will never reach the Wraith in time.

She hears laughter from behind her, cold and metallic, like tiny spoons scraping a washboard. It is coming from the shop. The idlers from the street are inside now, creeping in file toward the door.

Ha-ha-ha, ha-ha-ha. *They are pointing at her.*

Then a hand grabs her shoulder and spins her around. It is Banks. Gem is relieved to see him and cheers his arrival, but he is squeezing hard, his fingers digging into her clavicle. His eyes are low and dark.

"Do you have it?" he says. "Tell me you have it!"

"Have what!"

"The data drive. Do you have the data drive?"

She thrashes against his grip and it does no good. The pain is becoming unbearable—but wait. The drive is still in her hand.

She has been carrying it all this time.

Banks releases his hold as she thrusts the device at him. He brings the drive to his eyes, studying it as one would study something of a value, some trinket long buried and presumably lost to time.

"It is compromised," he says. "You have been compromised, Gem."

Suddenly the world is quiet, no maniacal cackling tin people, no one but Gem and Banks. The sky shifts from blue to orange then remains, locked in the color of sunset. He begins to speak again, but his voice has gone. She hears only buzzes and whirs in its place, a stream of non-human noise. And what about his face? His features have twisted, his profile distorting as the sound cuts into him, each chitter and clack grinding him further away. Gem averts her eyes, and when she returns them Banks is gone.

A woman stands in his place, someone familiar, yet strange.

Where have I seen her before? *Gem thinks. The stranger holds the data drive out before her. There is malice in her eyes, suffering, pain.*

I know that woman. I know that face.

In one moment the stranger is nodding to her.

In the next she is exploding, her essence enveloped in light.

The ground around them has given way and Gem finds she is falling, turning in slow circles as she tumbles into the void.

THE GIRLS

GEM'S EYES shot open and she sat up in the driver's seat. Her throat felt raw and dry. Had she had been screaming? She turned to the passenger side and saw Banks slumped over against the door, sleeping soundly. No, he would not have dozed through a round of night terrors. The dream had been intense, vivid—heavy. There was nothing lucid about it, not like the dream before the pass. The garden had offered a sense of control, even points of serenity.

Except for the Seeker, she thought, *and the Seeker was there again.*

Gem looked to the machine. It's prints were all over her subconscious, the oranges and greens and that godforsaken noise. She fumbled around for her bottle of water and drank half of it down, shaking off the urgency, that tin laughter and horrible noise. What was it with the *noise*? If anything she should be desensitized to it, but the opposite felt true now, and not just in her dreams.

The machine's racket had been driving her mad as they made their way up the pass, like insects. *Wasps in my brain.* And the alarm outside the cave? *Just the opposite.* She might have heard more with her head in a bucket of water.

She resisted the urge to poke at her wound. One little slip had scrambled her senses and lit her subconscious on fire. What else could possibly explain—

Movement in her periphery startled her. Banks was awake now, squinting and rubbing his eyes. He saw the water she was holding and motioned for her to hand it over, Gem passing him the bottle and Banks taking a sip, then another. He had been frightening in her dream, adversarial. It had felt like he'd meant her harm. She wondered if he had that somewhere deep in his studious shell, buried alongside the malaise he'd been holding at bay, that strange new melancholy. "What?" he said.

Gem realized she'd been ogling him.

"Sorry. I had a bit of a wonky dream. I'm still shaking it off." She narrowed her eyes at him. "You were there, Banks, and you were not yourself. You were quite aggressive with me." She watched his fingers as he yawned and stretched his arms. "And handsy."

"I apologize on behalf of my doppelganger," he said. "I had a dream too, but I can't recall much of it. I rarely remember my dreams."

"Well I envy you for that."

Gem caught a glimmer of moonlight in the rearview, a sliver through the mouth of the cave. It was still night. The vehicle's display read half-past-two in the morning, and they had sheltered shortly after dark. She guessed she had slept three hours, maybe four. "Anything from the machine?" she said. "It didn't wake us?"

"No," Banks said. "Seems we're just used to the short stints. Did you think it did?"

Gem stared into the void.

"No," she said. "I would have known."

Banks studied the display for a moment then entered his acknowledgement codes. "Huh," he said. "Looks like there was activity back towards town a couple hours ago, but nothing near our position. The readings suggest a drone, maybe two, no doubt searching for the Wraith. We're clear now, have been for a while, in fact. My guess is something else came up."

It was close to what Gem had expected.

"Well that is grand, because I have to spend a penny, and I'd prefer not squat over a bottle beside the likes of you." She forced a smile. "You sure we're good?"

"About as sure as I can be. They won't have forgotten about us, but nothing should pick you up in here. Just make it quick, and keep to your side. I'm up next."

Gem scoffed. "Are you suggesting I would have a go on your side? You're a lunatic."

"I wouldn't put it past you. You seemed rather irritated with me earlier."

"Shut it."

GEM INCHED the door open and kept near to the vehicle. She could see the mouth of the cave in the distance, midnight blue against the black. She wished she were out there somewhere over the hills, far away from all that comprised the present. *Maybe I'll call it quits when we get back*, she thought. And how many times had she told herself that? *Maybe this time I'll have good reason.*

Gem thought about it as she did her business. She could take some medical leave, have her head looked at then sod off somewhere for a good, long think. She ran her hand up the back of her neck then let it fall to her side. Her mind and the cave were simpatico, filled with a darkness she dare not shine a light on for fear of disturbing the unknown. It was a desperate feeling, though in the present it served no purpose. No memory would help her to pilot the Wraith, and she need not concern herself with anything else. The rest of it could wait until leave, and that was that, healing, remembering, sanity, the whole lot.

Gem zipped up her jeans, felt her way back to the driver's door and slid into the vehicle. Banks sat sipping a fresh bottle of water, studying the Seeker's display. In her dream he had been someone else, his features shifting and imploding and emerging smooth and feminine, completing the stranger's transformation. She had marked something in that woman's eyes, some sad and inevitable truth. Where had she seen her before?

"I'm stepping out," Banks said.

"Go on then."

She heard the click of the door closing and her thoughts fixed on the data drive, the focal point of the dream. She had brought that old thing everywhere with her for a time, updating it long after sleeker and more efficient hardware came into fashion, increasing its capacity and modding it for advanced compatibility.

She had treated like a pet.

And why? She'd told herself there was no reason to let it rust when she had to means to remake it, that it was still perfectly adequate, but that was not the real reason.

She'd kept it because Gran had bought it for her when she first came to London. That was that truth of the matter, however long it took her to recognize it.

She had not thought of Gran in ages.

GEM HAD gone to live with her Gran as a teenager, when she was—what, fourteen? She had moved there after the courts locked Mum up for habitual drug offenses, the last of them being serious. She had long known of her mother's habits, but she had never suspected she was involved in trafficking. Why would she? Her world was online and her mother's was out in the streets, or up in the dope flats or wherever she plied her trade. There was little to fuss about so long as one of them did the shopping when the money came through, and they had usually seen that done—usually. Then one day the investigators had shown up. *Is your Da around?*

Never met him. *Other family?* Gran in London. I've not seen her since I was small.

Mum had said Gem's father was a decent enough bloke who'd packed up and moved to the States before she was born, that she didn't know she was pregnant until he was well and gone and she couldn't blame the man for that. Gran had told her that was nonsense the year Gem went off to university, that she was old enough to hear it now, that her mother could only guess at the father, likely some pub rat she'd shagged on a bender and had no memory of fucking. Gran was amazed she had stayed off the stuff long enough to see out the pregnancy, that she hadn't had someone put an end to it. That revelation had come as no surprise.

Gran had given Gem all the space she needed, never micromanaging. She'd even allowed her to enroll in an alternative schooling platform, a hybrid academy with most of the coursework done online. Gem would hole up in her room with her devices or out in the building's small garden when the rain dried up, and she had earned good marks, doctoring and plagiarizing her way through anything she did not take a shine to. She'd taught herself to encrypt her submissions against online site checkers, the programs that ran student work against a battery of sources to ensure originality, and none of the instructors ever accused her of foul play. In her free time she read up on coding and networking and loitered on the dark web, picking up contacts as she learned to navigate the cyber-sewers.

By the time Gem was sixteen she could hack into Gran's bank account with little more than her address, but she never stole from her, not after Gran had taken her in. She had taken to pilfering other sources, silly bastards with soft passwords who'd had the misfortune of landing on her radar. She'd been amazed at how easy it was after learning the basics, how hapless the general public could be with their information, how positively *careless*.

By the time Gem was seventeen she was shredding firewalls for fun. It was not the illegality of the act that appealed to her, but the agency, a psychological response to an unstable childhood. She'd told herself she would establish boundaries for her conduct, that she would maintain a moral code, like Robin Hood. It had sounded good to her at the time—*like Robin Hood*—but wasn't that what they all said? All the ransomware gangs and anti-establishment trolls? They all thought their actions were justified in some shape or form, but she would not be like them. She had written it out on notebook paper to bind herself to the oath. *I will not be like the them.*

Gem had taken her pledge seriously for a while. There were plenty of immoral characters to target, smarmy political types and businesses with bad reputations. There were the law firms that defended them. She might syphon funds from certain accounts and filter them to nonprofits. She might hijack certain emails and shepherd them off to the tabloids, the trashier publications who had no qualms printing contentious material. She had kept it impersonal and was careful to sweep up her breadcrumbs, never leaving a trail. She had kept to the code she'd championed.

But that all changed in her final year of schooling.

There were certain classes she was required to physically attend, mandatory courses set back in the besotted classroom. Could she even recall which one? Something to do with social skills?

She could not remember.

But she had no trouble recalling those imitation posh girls. Gem had been forced into a group with those twats, a configuration meant to last the duration of the course, three snotty mean-girls and a techie, the ill-fated brainchild of one lazy, naïve instructor. The girls had mocked her clothes and her accent and the way she wore her hair, whispering under their breath and giggling, bursts of high-pitched idiot cackles and stupid tittering bleats.

Gem had told herself she didn't give a shit, and maybe she didn't at first, but after a few weeks that dumb, pointed laughter began to sting. On the day it became too much she made an excuse to leave class early and hacked into the student records database, nicking their legal names and addresses, identification numbers, medical dossiers, far more than she would ever need. The only question was where to hit them. How bad did she want it to hurt?

She had waited until late that night when they were likely to be asleep, the only time they were guaranteed to be off social media. Digging into an active profile might raise a flag, and she did not want them to notice her handiwork. She'd sent each girl a link from a proxy server, the message appearing a friend request from a handsome lad at an affiliated institution. All three had taken the bait, and that was that. Gem was in.

Her first thought was to lock them out of their phones, but that would not be enough. They would pout for a day then have a brand-new mobile the next, and that would not do at all. So Gem had rifled through the incessant piles of selfies and shallow, thoughtless banter until she feared she would never find anything of use, and then she'd unearthed a jewel, revealing photos one girl had squirreled away in a systems folder. Didn't that little bird know it was risky to keep something so personal on a networked device? Even if you hid it away in the hardware?

The other two did not have compromising pictures to pirate, so she would have to resort to posting some choice statements on their pages. How far did she want to take it? A racially insensitive joke? A comment about a heavy girl's weight? Gem had got to work then, and it had all been so *easy*, rerouting the tracking information to a pub down the road and walking back up the street to Gran's and slipping into bed, envisioning the wrath she'd spun up and regretting not a stitch of it.

They would know what it was to be the subject of ill intentions.

For once they would feel the wrong end of the stick.

GEM FELT her stomach sink. How long had it been since she'd thought of that? And why was she dredging it up now? Because of her dream? Why couldn't she remember something *useful*?

She stared out into the darkness of the cave.

Short term memory, love. Bangs on the head affect short term memory.

No one had ever discovered she was behind the hack. She had faced no consequences for her actions, but those girls? She'd never imagined the backlash would be so vicious. She had wanted it to hurt, but she had never intended to—

Her skin prickled, and she turned to the passenger side of the Wraith. Banks was watching her. She had not even heard him close the door, much less open it. Her thoughts had been back in London reopening old wounds, twisting the knife and applying the salt.

But she was not that girl anymore.

"Wow," he said. "Did I just interrupt something?"

Gem felt the heat in her face. She knew what she must look like, disturbed, intense.

"That dream brought up some memories," she said, "things I have not thought of in ages." She flattened her voice to steady it. "There's this data drive I've had since I was a girl, a clunker of a thing by modern standards. I had it in my dream, and I started thinking about where I'd got it, what was going on in my life at the time."

Banks kept his eyes on her.

"So your memory is coming back?"

"Not my short-term memory," she said. "Not anything from the last few days." *The last few weeks is more like it.* "Trying to force it gives me"—*some kind of brain hemorrhage*—"a headache, and I'd rather not deal with that. Let's just leave it there."

Banks said, "I am not trying to badger you, but if you are starting to feel—"

"Good, and I'm fine. So leave it."

"If you say so."

"We're going to have some time to kill, aren't we?" She was eager to change the subject, to draw his attention elsewhere.

"Our last update was two hours ago, so there's not much to tell. But I would bet on it. You know the Seeker won't spring us until the protocol has run its course, even if we're in the clear. And as for a timeframe—"

"There's no way to sort it," she said. "I don't even know why I asked."

"Maybe you were hoping to hear something else."

Gem was happy to let him believe that.

"Right. Maybe I was. Either way, I think I'm going to be up for a spell. If you want to nod off again, don't mind me. I'll only prod your bum a little." She forced herself to smile.

"Noted," said Banks, "but I don't think I'll be dozing off. I fear we've both developed rather poor sleep habits." He looked to the machine. "The reason for this eludes me."

There he was again, Banks with his subpar wit.

It made her feel a little better.

THE BOOK

THEY STARED out into the abyss in silence, Gem shifting in her seat, desperate to keep her mind from wandering. It was just her luck the memories she rued seemed perfectly intact, ugly threads she'd had every intention of forgetting. The quiet was no friend to her now. "Tell me one of your stories, Banks. Tell me about your Day One."

He sat up and looked at her.

"I've told you all about that. More than once."

"Yes, but I don't recall the details right now, and I'd rather not sit here in silence." Both assertions were true to a point. There was not much about his version she could recall. Whether that was due to amnesia or plain old forgetfulness was up for debate.

"Why that story?"

"Because I dreamed it was Day One again, and that's what is on my mind. People were holding their phones up to the sky like they were asking God's forgiveness, praying for some holy signal. It was quite fitting, really."

"That actually happened in some places," Banks said. "I saw it on the news."

"Really? Why don't you tell me about it?"

She placed a hand under her chin and grinned at him.

"Alright, but only if you stop looking at me like that."

"Fair enough," Gem said, leaning back in her seat.

"It's been a while since I thought about it," Banks said. "I was in my office reading, maybe grading papers. I don't recall exactly what I was doing, but I was at work, and I was not online. Someone had to come in and tell me what was happening."

He told Gem everyone had gathered around one of those huge lecture hall screens, professors and students all watching the anchors fumble through their broadcasts. At first Banks had found it amusing, resisting the urge to say *I told you so* to every colleague who'd given him shit about his theories. It was playing out near to what he'd hypothesized, the chaos, the lack of information.

He figured someone had finally decided to roll up their sleeves and take a crack at social media, that everything was sure to be back up and running in a few hours—

Gem interrupted him.

"You're telling me you thought it was some little statement hack after everything you wrote in that book?"

"*That book* was chalked full of pretentious rhetoric and no small degree of speculation," Banks said. "I don't know that I ever really believed some of the things I was putting out there. The argument was it was possible, that a well-organized group *could* subvert and bypass security technologies and wreak havoc, that—"

Gem began to tune him out. It was enough he was breaking the silence. She had read the book and understood its purpose, all of the finer points Banks had endeavored to make.

She was amazed at how clearly she recalled them.

BANKS DOUBLE-MAJORED in computer science and sociology as an undergrad, two subjects you might think had little to do with one another, but he had always seen the connection. The world had already bound itself to social media and online commerce, and if one intended to study people, it would be useful to understand the constructs they relied on. He went on to graduate school for sociology and kept up with programming trends in his free time, everything he considered to be relevant. He wrote his thesis on how social media trained the populous to respond to certain stimuli, that the world was witnessing the early stages of a hostile takeover by big-tech companies, a coordinated indoctrination. It would not be long before society forgot how to function without them.

This was not a novel idea by any means. The notion had long been circulating at gatherings, but published scholarship on the topic was fledgling, and Banks had managed to sneak his paper in before the theory began to trend. The thesis was published in a small academic journal and the response was mixed at best, established scholars accusing him of watching too much science fiction, of propagating doomsday at the hands of technology, of demonizing capitalism and the free market and believing in supervillains. But by the time Banks finished his doctorate analyzing social media was all the rage, charting its effects and predicting the ramifications. Academics seemed to have forgotten how foolish they'd found his arguments a few short years before. They were on the issue like flies, and they were not wrong.

It was a massive problem, an infection.

"If we had treated it like a disease we might have stood a chance," Banks told Gem once. "What we needed was a quarantine, and what they did was the opposite. Like encouraging sick people to spit in the office coffee."

And it was not just social media. Banks's dissertation—what would become part of his first book—argued cyberspace had created a society on edge, a populace whose digital assets were constantly in jeopardy. He had pondered what might happen if this trend went unchecked, if governments elected to tie their critical systems to a rapidly evolving cyber-sphere where protection could not be guaranteed. They'd been told security was cutting edge, capable of defending valuable assets and weapons modules and satellite links and digital accounts. There was a hard, fast belief the world's fundamental institutions were guarded by the best and brightest, that cybercriminals would always be beaten back. If tech-savvy kids were caught rooting around in places they shouldn't it was easy enough to call them *rogue hackers* and attribute their misdeeds to scapegoats, to play down their origins and present them as isolated cells with limited means. Accusations had flown, but no one had ever declared war over a hack.

Banks had argued the world was *already* at war, governments against whistleblowers, watchdogs against data-miners, brands against slanderous trolls. Information that had once been difficult to obtain was accessible to anyone with the right skill set and the proper motivation. Everyone had jumped blindly into cyberspace without considering the risks, and an entire industry had sprung up to defend them, millions of keyboard cadets trained and deployed against an ever-present threat.

It all boiled down to a straight-forward question:

If society elected to give itself entirely over to technology, what would happen when that technology failed?

The heart of the matter was the internet itself. What if the entire construct were compromised in some irreversible way? Destroying the global infrastructure might prove an impossible task, but a diseased system was as good as a dead one, and the bugs were always evolving. That the internet might someday contract an incurable cancer was a reality few chose to entertain.

It was naivety at best, and at the worst it was—

BANKS SAID, "Gem? Are you even listening to me?" She had been staring out into the dark again, deep in thought.

She had not heard a word he'd said.

"I was thinking about your book. What were you saying?"

"I was telling you about people holding their phones up to the sky outside of churches down south," he said. "What you asked me to tell you."

"Huh. So it did actually happen."

"Yes, Gem, that is what I was trying to—"

The Seeker came to life and gave them a start. Neither had been expecting activity from the machine so soon. Banks acknowledged the alert and the Seeker returned to its resting display, satisfied its orders had been noted. He turned to Gem then, the green light paling his face. "We have an exit route," he said, "and it leads directly through Hawks Pass.

THE TOWN

GEM'S FACE twisted up in a scowl. His words had felt like a slap, like blasphemy. "What? Has the bloody thing gone mad?" Banks did not seem to hear her. He was hunched over the Seeker, probing it for information. *Back through town*?! her thoughts screamed. *Back through Hawks bleeding Pass*? Sending them there would be an absurd violation of protocol, every meticulous word of it. "Banks."

"I know. I'm digging."

Gem sat counting the seconds, ten, fifteen, twenty, but Banks found nothing of consequence. The route was greenlit with no identifiable risk, something unheard of in populated areas.

"Check it again," she said.

"There is nothing left to check."

"What if that bug in the sensors spread to the machine? Maybe a systems error?"

Banks frowned at her.

"There is no cross-compatibility. You know that. And if there was an error the Seeker's kill-switch would've rebooted it."

Gem's hands went to her face.

"So that's it then. We'll just put the Wraith out on parade."

"The route is the route," Banks said. "There's nothing to be done about it short of breaking protocol, and breaking protocol is not an option."

Gem shook her head. How could the Seeker demand something so ludicrous? Going through *town*? She'd only just begun to formulate a coping strategy for the past few days, and now the machine had gone and stuck a wrench in it. She felt like it was toying with her, conspiring to drive her mad, first with the dreams and now *this*. She closed her eyes. That was not possible.

That was how nutters processed information.

Think like a reasonable person. She combed over what she could recall of the run, the mountain, the pass, the fork in the path, the canyon, the road to town, the incident at the pumps, the scramble to the cave, her dream—*the tin people, the store front, cold orange fire, handsy, malicious navigators.* She felt her face go numb.

Hadn't she heard something first? *It was the wind.* No, now she heard it clearly. It had been aircraft overhead.

And what was it Banks had said? He'd said there were flyers in the area, at least one drone. She assembled the information, the sound of aircraft, a drone made a pass, the route leads through town, no identifiable threats, the aircraft, the drone, the route.

The last of the fragments snapped into place.

"What was it you said about activity over Hawks Pass?"

Banks looked at her like she was speaking Cantonese.

"I think you should check the log again."

He made as if to argue, then stopped.

"Are you saying what I think you're saying?"

"Pull up the log."

Banks opened the activity graph and began to study the patterns, Gem watching the screen over his shoulder. The signs were all there, fast-moving aircraft over the valley and then on toward town, circling once and retreating.

"Doesn't look much like a surveillance op," Banks said.

"That's because it wasn't."

"You can't know that for certain."

"I didn't before, but now I do. It's all there, Banks."

"No, no way. It wouldn't make any sense. There has to be another explanation."

Gem slid back into her seat and closed her eyes. Could she be wrong? The machine greenlit them on remote mountain paths, through backtrails and forests miles from civilization, places where the chance of an encounter was slim. It did not greenlight them to move through population centers, however small. Not once had they ever willingly taken the Wraith through a town of civilians. That was not something she had to worry about misremembering. If there was a recognizable risk of contact the Seeker found another route. It was protocol, and the machine did not push boundaries.

"It just doesn't make any sense," Banks said again.

The silence that followed stretched on, each second longer than the next. Gem pulled her harness across her chest and fastened it, knowing they'd already lingered too long. Whatever awaited them in Hawks Pass, she would endure it. She would weather this absurdity then push them on toward the next, and she would weather that as well, whatever it took to reach the end of the line and wash her hands of this mess. "Ready?" she said to Banks.

He buckled himself in and nodded.

GEM BACKED them slowly out of the cave until the moon shone above. *Were they really not even searching for us?* The thought seemed preposterous, but if events had transpired as she believed and a drone had hit Hawks Pass, then all bets were off. They would be heading into a strange new scenario.

She motioned to Banks with her free hand.

"Give me a Red."

He produced the bottle from the center console and shook one out for her, then he rattled one out for himself, popped it into his mouth and swallowed.

They proceeded with caution through the hills and the trees, and before long they came to the river. They turned away from the mountain then, following the water until the road emerged. Hawks Pass lay over the slopes and down in the valley, and Gem drove on robotically, taking none of the formal precautions. If there were other vehicles out that morning, they were somewhere far away.

She looked to the machine. Here was the same green arrow guiding her over the same stretch of pavement she had traversed with the Buggy. Before she had gone with anticipation, even eagerness. Now her determination was a sad one, a product of resolve and bitter acceptance. She turned from the Seeker and locked her eyes to the center line. *Inhale—count to three—exhale.*

She'd considered the possibility of a trap, but she had not mentioned this to Banks. His response would have come in lecture form, a treatise on probability. Now the question flashed through her mind again: Could the Seeker have been compromised?

The machine could not be hacked, at least not remotely. It had been developed specifically to prevent such an intrusion. Even if someone managed to unscramble its signal and pin it down it would take weeks to decrypt, the equivalent of translating a lost language. Impossible was a fitting word, but wouldn't she have said the same about targeting a town?

Those people are dead now. Streaks of gore on the pavement.

At least some of them, to be sure, and those who had lived would be in no state to concern themselves with a Wraith passing through, a shadow even sharp eyes might struggle to register in the darkness, in the chaos. She was sure of it for the same reason she was sure the Magazine Man was out of place, that itch in her mind she could not seem to scratch. She'd felt it on the mountain and again in front the store. She felt it now, an overwhelming sense that something was wrong with this run, wrong with *everything*, that if she could peel away the surface she would find something sinister lurking beneath, something false. *That is what the paranoids believe, the nutters. Your mental mum would believe something like that.*

Gem tightened her grip on the wheel.

BEFORE LONG she spotted a glow through the spectra-light, small at first, then larger and more defined. It appeared hot-white through the orange haze. "Fire," she said. Fire some machine rained down on the townspeople as she dozed away in a cave, fire she had conjured with her presence. She'd sullied that little mountain town with her corporate boots and now it was bathed in fire.

"I'm killing the spectra," she said. "That fire is bound to blind us." Banks did not reply, and Gem hit the switch.

They traversed the last of the hills and the woods of the outskirts closed around them, the shadows swallowing the moonlight and forcing Gem to slow. As they neared the interior she saw rooftops set alight by travelling embers and burning at various stages. *They could have left it alone*, she thought. *They could have let me drive away.*

All that remained of the well-kept little house was a pile of smoking rubble, filthy scraps of metal and blackened shards of wood. She wondered if the man with the mug had been inside, if he had suffered the same twisted fate as his domicile. What had he done to deserve such an end? Had he phoned Wanda down at the store to let her know he'd spotted a perp? Or was he oblivious to it all, caught in the rot brought on by a few bad apples. "There was a house there," she said. "There was a man on the porch."

Banks stared out the window toward the remains.

"Not anymore."

Gem saw the traffic light ahead, still swaying between the lampposts, still blinking yellow. One pole was bent inward off its moorings toward the road, the light hanging at an angle on its sagging wire. Her breath hitched as she looked off beyond the fixture. The general store was gone. A crater lay where the pumps had stood, the result of exploding fuel tanks. What was left of the building had been blown off the lot in all directions, pieces of drywall strewn in the road alongside packages of chips and candy and chunks of concrete here and there like misshapen bowling balls, like the stones she had dodged on the pass. It was the set of a war film, some alpine apocalypse dreamed up for the long-dead streaming services—but something was off. There were no corpses lining the gutters, no one combing the streets for survivors or scrambling to save their possessions. There was no one around at all. Where were all the townspeople? Where were the fire crews and law enforcement?

They must have all taken cover in shelters. Help just hasn't arrived yet.

No, there was something wrong with this picture.

Gem swept her eyes over the rubble, convinced she had missed something obvious. Then she froze. There was a human forearm among the rocks, severed at the elbow. A mangled hand hung off the wrist by the sinew, charred and twisted and bloody. It appeared to be missing the thumb. Could that have been Wanda's hand? Was it the Magazine Man's? Did either of them have the faintest idea what they'd brought down on their little town?

They could have let me drive out of their lives.

"Gem!" Banks's voice was loud, urgent.

The Wraith sat idling at the edge of the intersection.

She had rolled them to a stop under that lonely yellow light.

"Do you see it?" she whispered.

Then she felt Banks's hand on her shoulder, squeezing.

"We've got to *move*, Gem. Get us out of here!"

And now he is yelling at me. It was the dream all over again, fingers digging into her clavicle on Hawks Pass's main drag.

It was like he was adversarial.

She felt like she had at the pumps, floating above herself, disconnected, ethereal. She saw Gem shouting at Banks, warning him to mind his fucking hands, Gem accelerating forward, banking left and right around the wreckage and exhaling in controlled, shallow puffs, breathing in through her nose like she had done when she used to have panic attacks—

Clarity hit her like a shovel. She thought of cartoons, of lightbulbs appearing over the heads of funny little animals. She was having a panic attack. How had she not noticed the symptoms? How many times had she experienced this?

Experienced this? No, not this. This was exceptional. This was dam-bursting flood water barreling through her cortex and sweeping the world away. But now she knew what to do.

She made herself feel each breath. *Inhale—count to three—exhale.* She repeated the process, three times, five times, seven, and then her lungs were her own again, her eyes and her ears. She felt her hands on the wheel and her foot on the gas. *Inhale—count to three—exhale.* She heard Banks apologizing to her. Her muscles were taught and her limbs thrummed with adrenaline, but her breathing had slowed. Her pulse was settling. *Inhale—count to three—exhale.* She saw she had cleared the bulk of the rubble in her dissonate state, just as she'd guided the Buggy away from the pumps. How had she evaded it all in a fugue? It seemed an impossible feat, yet she had managed it with ease. *Inhale—count to three—exhale.*

Banks was silent again, seeming to have completed his penance. His words had hardly computed. "I'm sorry I swore at you," Gem said. Her voice sounded strange to her, a string of words run through a processor, manufactured and stiff. She had not taken her eyes from the road. "I had a bit of a panic there."

A bit of a panic? A break from reality was more accurate, a chunk of an iceberg falling away.

"So did I," said Banks. "I shouldn't have grabbed you, but I thought you had gone into shock. We have to move, Gem. We can discuss this later."

"Right." She had control again. "We can discuss this later," she repeated.

THE THEORY

GEM GUIDED the Wraith through the last of the wreckage then started forward again with pace. The damage to the far end of town was limited, only a small fire or two born of embers the wind had carried. They crested a hill and the flash of the traffic signal lit in the sideview mirror. She watched it blink, once, twice, and then it was lost behind the trees. When the fires burned out and the remains lay smoldering that loathsome light would endure, still hooked to its cable and pleading for caution. Gem hoped she would never see it again.

Focus. That was all there was to do now, press on into the night and forget all she had felt and witnessed. She concentrated on her breathing, inhaling, exhaling, counting, following the road out of town until the Seeker ordered them onto a backtrail, a winding path through the hills. Gem switched the spectra-light back on.

They continued the trek in silence, snaking through the terrain on the dirt track for miles, and when the sunlight began to bleed through the treetops Gem switched the spectra-light off. Then the Seeker cut through the calm and gave her a start. She cursed and yanked the wheel back into place, having nearly veered off the road. "Turn right at the bottom of this hill," Banks said, rubbing his eyes. It appeared he'd not noticed the hard left she just pulled.

Had he been sleeping? It had been some time since she'd look in his direction, what felt like eons.

She turned off into a thick vein of woods, put the vehicle in park and closed her eyes, silently praising the machine for its timing. Her response to the shock of Hawks Pass had been to lock in on the road, her focus on naught but the path ahead. Now the images came flooding back, the flames and the rubble and the severed hand, bone and blood and sinew. The daylight was sure to reveal uglier sights than that shattered arm, some morbid scavenger hunt of small-town denizens in pieces throughout the streets, because she had not seen a soul in town, not one person.

And there was something wrong with that picture, she thought.

She wondered if the authorities had arrived yet. In the past there would have been firefighters and police, paramedics, decent people with supplies and good intentions. In Hawks Pass there would be corporate reps dressed as law enforcement, complete with badges and paperwork affirming jurisdiction. The Sheriff's office would be left taking orders from the perps, and unless the Feds involved themselves, there was little to be done about it.

Even then there were no guarantees.

Banks sat minding the machine to her right, establishing the reason for their pause. Whatever the break was for, Gem knew it would not last long, and she would rest her eyes for what little time she could.

IT WAS not black Gem saw behind her eyelids, but orange, the color of fire and the spectra-light and the sky in her dreams, all the things she would wish away if she could. Her mind would not slow down. There were so many unanswered questions, her injury, the amnesia, that alien anxiety, but above all sat the events of Hawks Pass. Just what in the hell had happened back there?

She opened her eyes and turned to Banks.

"Why would they hit that town? I know you have been thinking about it too, so don't bullshit me. Rationalize it for me, Banks. Help me make sense of this."

He motioned for her to hold the thought as he entered the last of his codes, then he sat back. "It's running analysis, so we should have a few minutes." He looked up and met her gaze. "I've been thinking about what we saw from the moment we pulled out of town, but are you sure you want to get into this? It might be better to wait for a checkpoint."

"No," Gem said. "Whatever you have to say, I would hear it now."

Banks nodded to himself. "Alright. This is all speculation, of course, but my first thought was punishment, that whoever they called must have wondered how we got the jump on them. They might have assumed coercion on the part of their informers, maybe negligence. They could have ordered a strike on the store to send a message, but they also hit other targets, and seemingly at random, like that house you pointed out. That kills the punishment theory for me, which wasn't a sound one to begin with. What message are you sending by taking out your own moles? That informing might get you killed? There is no logic in that."

Banks paused to collect his thoughts.

"I also thought it might be a rogue actor within their ranks, a disgruntled employee or some trigger-happy psycho. That would not be impossible, but I just don't see it. An order like that would have to pass through multiple channels before going active, and if we follow that thread, then it could not have been a mistake either. Someone would have caught wind of it and pulled the plug. So that got me thinking about something else. Let's say someone reached out to the people of Hawks Pass and offered them a deal, a monetary reward in exchange for information. We will assume you were right about the money. How would they know that person was who they claimed to be?"

Alarm bells rang in Gem's head. She pictured the cartoon lightbulb. "You think the Company has someone out here running loyalty tests?"

"I'm saying it is a possibility, and a good one at that. Say our hypothetical agent went to Hawks Pass with the intention of sizing up the population, whether they would be willing to inform not *for* us, but *on* us. They could have planted a seed, left their information and waited for word to spread around town. They might have provided descriptions and told them to look for outsiders, maybe even for a Buggy, and when they called—"

"Then they would know the people of Hawks Pass could not be trusted," Gem said. She sat up straighter. "You're saying *our* people set them up?"

"I'm not saying anything yet."

Gem felt a pinch at the base of the skull, the slightest of nips. She reached back and began to massage it.

"Bloody hell. They sent us in as pawns then? As bait?"

Banks shook his head. "I don't know. We are already assuming a lot, but—wait a minute. Think back to your trip into town. Did it feel like you were expected? It was clear they made you as corporate, but could they have *known* you were coming?"

The idea made her feel cold all over, like that sodding cooling system. She replayed the trip in her mind, passing the green incorporation sign and finding the streets deserted, seeing the neat little house. *The man on the porch*, she thought.

"That bloke on his porch was the only person I saw heading in. He didn't smile or react, just held up a hand like I was the goddamned mail lady. At the time I thought it was a good thing, just the sort of thing we'd hope for. But after the call?"

She thought of the smoking pile of splinters that had been his home. The perpetrators had targeted him, just as they'd targeted the store. The pieces were coming together. "His house was gone, Banks, and it was not just collateral damage. He must have tipped off the clerk. I should have known it when I caught her staring, but I chalked it up to curiosity." Gem paused, reliving the scene, that look she'd seen in Wanda's eyes. "Or maybe there was some truth to that. Maybe she *was* curious. She might have just been the messenger. If there was a call before I arrived she would have answered, but it would not have been for her."

She saw the Magazine Man in her mind's eye, his rancher's flannel and cap. "The call would have been for the man in back, the Magazine Man. That's how I've come to think of him. I told you I thought he could be a plant, right? He might have just been the geezer in charge, the main conspirator. He glanced at me when I came in then kept his head down until I went out to the pumps, but that berk didn't wait long enough. He was daft to think I would not have a look over my shoulder."

There was a long moment of silence.

"So one man watching the road," Banks said, "and another at the store. Maybe a few retirees were looking for an easy payday, men with time to spare. Your *Magazine Man* might have had them organized." Banks lowered his voice. "But how they did it is of little consequence. What we've established is they were watching for us, waiting, and that can only mean one thing. Someone with knowledge of our whereabouts tipped them off, and—"

Gem did not need to hear the rest.

"It means the drones were ours." Saying it out loud had a numbing effect, the last of the words echoing on in her ears.

Not the work of an adversary. Our work—ours. All was silent apart from the faint chitter of insects and the white-noise of the Seeker cycling, gears spinning away in the depths of its—

An epiphany rocked her and she sat up straight.

Her eyes went to the machine. "Banks." She motioned to the device. "This is only speculation. You said it yourself. We cannot be certain of any of it."

He looked at her cockeyed, like her words had come out strange. Then he tracked her gaze toward the Seeker. He had made the connection. "We cannot be sure of anything," he said. "Speculation, like you said. It does not affect our business either way."

Gem counted the seconds, two, three, but the Seeker did not respond. What had she expected? Did she think it would come to life in a cacophony of sirens, emit some hellish pulse and jelly their brains? Did she think it would give itself *away*?

"That scene in town gave us a start," she said, curbing the edge in her voice, "and we're overcompensating. Grasping at straws."

Banks nodded with approval.

"We are tired and rattled," he said. "We may even be in shock. But that's all behind us now. We can forget about it and move on."

Gem felt like smacking herself upside the head, like smacking Banks. He had always mocked her for insisting the machine was monitoring their conversations. Where was his skepticism now? Neither of them had considered the Seeker as they rattled on, and now there were sure to be—*consequences*. How could she forget the sodding machine? And who were they kidding? Backtracking could not unsay what was said. They had just implied their employers were guilty of deceiving civilians, of murdering them for their faults. And how might the Company take that? Gem forced herself to breathe, to count and breathe again. There was no question the Seeker was recording them. Wraith teams existed to transport critical resources, assets too valuable to risk moving anywhere near a network. In what world would the Company *not* be listening?

It was so bloody *obvious*.

"Analysis is nearly complete," she heard Banks say.

He was logged in again, swiping and tapping, his voice a picture of calm. He knew as well as she did what this could mean for them, yet the man was practically stoic. Of course he had not been subject to lacerations and phantom ailments and episodes of floating hysteria. "Gem," he said. "If you need to head out and—"

"And spend a penny? Right, good call."

She stepped out into the shade of the evergreens and closed the door. She did not have to relieve herself, but she desperately needed the air. Banks had seen it on her face. She sat down on her haunches and ran her hands through her hair. Banks could not be as composed as he seemed, could he? *Maybe he knows the damage is done, that there is no point is losing his shit.*

But didn't she know that as well? Whatever came next was going to happen whether she bent herself out of shape or not. She let her hands fall to her side and balled her fists. It felt like madness, some absurd test of her mettle, the whole run intelligently designed to push her over the edge. Her hand went to the base of her skull.

This all started with you, she thought. *A knock on the head is going to destroy me.* She pulled her fingers away. And how would that sound if she tried to explain it to Banks? *I think all these strange, horrible things are happening because I hit my head, love. Wouldn't you agree?*

She almost laughed. Was she willing to let herself believe something so outrageous? She feared she might had Banks not experienced the same chain of events, because trauma induced madness was beginning to sound quite reasonable. It was beginning to—

Clack—clack, clack, clack.

Gem jumped, but it was only Banks rapping on her window. She breathed out and cursed. Didn't he know she was losing her mind out there? He pointed to his wrist to signal it was time, and she held up a finger in response.

"One minute," she mouthed at him.

Gem hung her head and stared at the dirt between her feet. "No point in losing your shit," she said aloud.

It was a true statement, a logical one, but the mind was only so rational. Sometimes it went rogue, guiding you around dark corners that were best left alone.

Shut it, she thought. *Get your ass back in the Wraith.*

Gem straightened herself out, brushed the dust from her bum and closed her eyes for a moment, just long enough to pretend she was somewhere else. Then she opened the door and slid back into her seat. When she looked to the Seeker it was green and placid. A single arrow crept over its face, outlining the route ahead. Banks sat in the passenger seat, composed, enduring.

"Ready?" he asked.

Gem fastened her harness and put the Wraith in gear.

PART TWO

MADNESS

SURVEILLANCE

THE ADMINISTRATOR stared at the man in her office, one of the underlings charged with archiving audio logs and correspondence.

She had forgotten his name.

"George," the man said. "We've spoken before, Miss—"

"I am responsible for what feels like a stable of employees, *George*, and sometimes a name slips my mind. You can understand that, yes?"

George shifted in his seat.

"I do, ma'am. I am here because something has come up." He placed a drive on the Administrator's desk. "No one has heard the contents outside the task force. This is the only copy."

She snatched up the device.

"Thank you, George. You can go now. I will see this returned to your desk when I am finished."

The Administrator inserted the drive and selected the file, stopping the audio at points to rewind it. What she heard did not surprise her. She could understand why someone like George might find it alarming, but to her it was no cause for concern. Their suspicions were only natural, and suspicions were all they were.

They would continue on as instructed.

They had no choice in the matter.

There is always a choice, she mused.

Perhaps, but they would be well aware of the consequences. The Company had gone to great lengths to instill that fear in them.

"She might react," the Administrator said aloud.

It was possible given the circumstances. She could only speculate as to what might be running through little miss Gemma's mind. Mr. Banks was a valuable asset, but too clever for his own good at times. His theorizing might inspire some kind of foolishness, and foolishness was the last thing the she needed.

She picked up the phone and dialed the overseers.

THE CABIN

THEY DROVE along the backtrails in silence, speaking only to discuss the route, to facilitate the transfer of tea and water and pills. Gem bent her mind to the road, her focus on dirt and rocks and traction. She did not notice the clouds as they rolled in and blocked the mid-afternoon sun. She was surprised when the rain fell in torrents and turned the path to sludge. She cursed as the grime dulled the grip of the Wraith's tires and threatened to spin them off into the mire below. All the while the Seeker was quiet, offering no sign they had been found out for what they were, speculators, potential liabilities. But the machine was an extension of its masters. If the Seeker took action and shut them down it would be at the instruction of an overseer.

That's what they would like us to believe, Gem thought.

She had long been convinced the Seeker was capable of independent action, though she had never mentioned this to Banks, that it was listening, yes, constantly, but not that. He would only have tried to persuade her otherwise. The incident at Chiron Techno-Medical had spurred regulations on artificial intelligence years before Day One, back when those companies still published their names, but when had laws stopped the Corps from doing anything? It was a risk-reward scenario, and the way Gem saw it, those anti-AI mandates were just for show, a false front to keep the public from losing their shit. But it did her no good to fret about it. Her choices remained the same, follow the route or face the consequences.

She inched the Wraith around a bend in the trail, spinning the tires through the mud. When they rounded the corner the pines parted to reveal an area barren of trees, a clearing the size of a football field. She spied a structure through the rain at the far end.

"Can you see that?" she said. "Is it a house?"

Banks looked up from the machine.

"I think it's a cabin. I don't see any vehicles, but that doesn't mean anything. Let's hope it's empty."

It was not like the Seeker to bring them anywhere near a residence, even one so isolated.

"Awfully close," Gem said.

"I doubt there was much choice," said Banks. "We're pretty high up here, and there is nowhere to off-road it. This might be the only option."

Gem tightened her grip on the wheel. He was probably right.

"They wouldn't be able to see much of us anyway," she said, "not in this."

Banks looked to the machine. "We will know if something is off."

Gem rolled the Wraith ahead through the clearing, mindful of the vehicle's noise, and after a five count they passed back into the forest. She let out her breath and took in another, counting, exhaling. Was Banks as nervous as she was? Why wouldn't he be? There was still the small matter of what the overseers might choose to—

The Seeker let out a shriek.

Gem's heart leapt, every muscle in her body tightening. Was it finally happening? Had the madness come home to roost? Did Banks hear it too? *He heard it*, she thought. *Look at him scramble*.

Her training took over, instinct and adrenaline, chemicals and drills—*inhale*—*exhale*. There was no time to count to three. Gem steeled herself, her eyes on the surrounding area. There was no preapproved cave in the woods this time, no head start to ride.

Focus. Banks would silence the alarm, assess the threat and pass on what information he could. It was up to her to find cover. She searched the landscape, looking left and right and down the hillside. In a standard scenario they might have ninety seconds.

Inhale—exhale. The Seeker's alarm fell away to a pulse. They could not rely on it now, not on the road in the daylight. As advanced as the machine was, it still needed time. The best they could hope for was a hint on the fly.

Gem scanned the woods for a depression, an enclave, any semblance of shelter. "Anything?" she said.

"Incoming," Banks said. "Sixty seconds, ninety at most. No area map. We're winging it."

Inhale—exhale. Gem rolled the Wraith down the hill toward the lower ground, looking left, then right. She spotted a rock shelf ahead through a break in the trees.

"On your right, Banks, the ledge. Look for a path."

He leaned forward, eyes out. "Stop! Pull in there."

Gem slid the Wraith to a halt near a narrow gap in the foliage. It would be tight, but it was the best they were going to do.

"Shit," she said. "Here goes."

Bark scraped the Wraith's exterior as she forced the vehicle through, then she broke free from the wedge and accelerated into the interior, dodging trees and flattening the underbrush. She pulled beneath the overhang, threw the Wraith in reverse and inched the vehicle backward until she could go no further, then she killed the engine. They had picked their spot. Banks activated the temperature cloak and the mist began to roll, and they sat there shivering as the Seeker pulsed away. Gem closed her eyes and counted the seconds, ten, eleven, twelve, then the bite of the cold receded. They appeared to have beaten the clock.

"It's nearly on us," Banks whispered.

There was a fizzing sound from above, quieter than you would expect from aircraft, but there was no mistaking it, matter cutting through wind and water. It passed over their location and trailed off in the direction of the clearing. Gem looked to the machine, then to Banks. He was quietly watching the Seeker, his face a picture of calm. *Strange*, Gem thought.

Then she heard it hit. "The cabin," she said.

Banks held a finger to his lips.

They sat in silence then, listening for a sign of the drone doubling back. It did not come. All they heard was the distant sound of rain pattering down. "Banks."

"Quiet. It's still around."

Gem leaned in to watch the Seeker over his shoulder. A small yellow dot crept slowly across its display, little green arrows highlighting the drone's trajectory. It was miles from them now. In a few more seconds it would be out of the danger zone. "It's pissing off," Gem whispered. "It went straight for the—"

She felt Banks's hand on her arm, a gentle squeeze. He nodded to the machine, and Gem sat back. What she'd all but said was the drone had gone straight for the clearing and hit the cabin and fucked off, that its masters had no interest in where they were going or what they might be carrying. She wanted to shout that the craft was *theirs* and it took out the cabin on *their* behalf, that the Seeker knew damned well they were never in danger.

She felt a quiver at the base of her skull.

Inhale—count to three—exhale.

Her temples throbbed and her sinuses began to tighten. Her ears were clogging up. She could no longer hear the raindrops beyond the ridge, but the machine had grown louder, louder than it should be. Why was it so *loud?*

The noise hit her as it had on the pass, the cacophony more pronounced this time, the amplifier cranked up. She heard the Seeker's every click and churn, an orchestra of tiny mechanisms firing away, like insects—*like wasps*. She turned away from Banks, fixing her eyes to the trees as the tears began to well. She would not let him see her in pain. How long could she stand it? How long before—

And then it was gone. She could not say how long it had lasted. Time had ceased to exist in that sawing, grinding symphony. She was still facing the window, her back still to Banks. She blinked the tears from her eyes and quietly wiped them away, then she turned around. Banks seemed oblivious to the spell.

Was that what it was? A spell?

She took a deep breath. "Anything?"

"Were clear," Banks said. "Waiting on instructions."

Gem nodded. She needed to get away from the machine, and she could not do that until it allowed them out of the Wraith. She could only hope her broken brain would not assail her again in the interim. It was the second time she'd heard that unholy buzzing, and this time it was worse, far worse. Her knock was proving a Pandora's box, a proper assortment of maladies. *A spell.* It had sounded like a dial-up connection from when the internet was young. She'd heard a recording of that racket once, *be-beep—boop—beep—buzz*. It was not so much the beeps and boops as the barrage of static that finished the sequence, not a dead-ringer for the wasps, but close.

"I'm going rest my eyes then," she said. "Any objections?"

"Fine by me."

Gem pushed her seat back as far as it would go and pulled her knees to her chest, then she leaned back and closed her eyes. She pretended she was back in the cave with no knowledge of what awaited, fire and drones and theories, mechanical insects, forcing her mind away from the Wraith and into the dark beyond, a quiet abyss where nothing existed to ail her.

It was a comforting thought—*darkness*.

GEM BLINKED and rubbed her eyes. Had she dozed off? She must have. It was dark outside, and she could not see a thing through the window. She allowed herself a moment to acclimate, then she turned to Banks. "How long was I out?"

"Not long," he said. "I was just about to wake you."

"Right. Tell me it's good news."

Banks frowned. "I don't think you're going to like it. We make camp here."

Gem placed her head in her hands and cursed.

"Here? With that mess up the road?"

"There must be a reason for it," Banks said, "and it's not likely to be for long. The faster we get settled, the better."

Gem uncovered her face and sat up.

At least she could get out of the Wraith.

The overhang had protected the area from the worst of the rain, and they searched out a dry patch far enough from the vehicle to ensure their voices would not carry. They popped the tent there, Gem watching the little package unfold and snap upright. She was exhausted—nodding off in the Wraith seemed to have done her no favors—but they needed to speak about that drone, the drone and the rest of it. They might not get another opportunity.

They settled into the tent as the sounds of the woods rustled around them. "I'm knackered," Gem said, "but we need to sort this out. That drone was never a threat to us. It went straight for the cabin then made itself scarce."

"That would appear to be the case," Banks said.

There was resignation in his voice. Was he not going to debate her on this? Gem said, "So that confirms it then? We were right about Hawks Pass?"

"I don't know. We've never seen anything like this."

"We were right, Banks, but why would they bother—" She paused and sat up. "Maybe it was a warning shot. A little reminder for us to toe the line?"

Banks spoke in hushed tones, a cue for her to do the same. "All I know is speculating about the cause is not going to change what happened. What we should be talking about is how we are going to proceed. I'll concede that we have no choice but to assume our people could be responsible for the drones—"

"They are."

"—so we will assume they *are* responsible, that the Seeker serves as their ears in the Wraith—"

"It does."

"Gem! All we can do is show we are committed to the job, and that means carrying on as we always have, right? Act normal. We need to make some conversation tomorrow, for one. We've been far too quiet, and we don't want them thinking we have something to hide. It needs to look like we have moved past it."

"And you think they will buy that?"

"What choice do we have?" Gem could feel his eyes on her in the darkness, that stern, professor's gaze. "They may be giving us that chance right now. If the drone was theirs, it would have been easy enough for them to take us out. So let's assume you are right"—Gem bit her tongue—"that the drone was a tail and hitting the cabin was a warning shot. We will let them know we've taken their point. No more hypothesizing, even amongst ourselves. We follow orders from here on out. Business as usual."

Gem sighed. "Business as usual. Bloody hell."

"Business as usual," Banks repeated, "starting now. On any other run we would've already been asleep."

"Right," she said. He had a point, and she had grown weary of his tone, that smug, lecture hall voice. She was tired of all of it. "Until morning then."

"Just try and get some rest."

Gem closed her eyes and pictured the cabin in ruins, another smoking pile she'd left in her wake. She wished they had never crossed over that pass, that the Seeker had turned them around in search of safer routes. She rolled over on her side, struggling for comfort. Banks had said they could not know for sure what had happened. Could he be right? Was there a chance everything *was* business as usual, that the destruction of Hawks Pass was not tied to the Company? Could that strike on the cabin have actually been meant for them? *Anything is possible*, she thought. *Now leave it.*

THE FOUNTAIN

G EM SITS *by the fountain on campus smoking a cigarette. The space is far enough from the building not to draw the ire of her peers, the sensibilities of whom she would dare not offend. She snuffs the butt out on the heel of her boot then reaches into her bag. Where is her gum? She spies it at the bottom among the clutter, a wallet she does not recognize, the comms panel from the Buggy.*

What is that doing there? And why is it so small?

The gum sinks deeper as she picks away at the contents, her arm buried up to the elbow. She is ready to give it up when her hand closes around a familiar form. It is her data drive, that old stickered keepsake. Gem pulls it free and turns it over in her hand, feeling its weight, then she drops it back in the bag. When was the last time she used it for anything?

She looks up to find the computer sciences hall looming over her, orange sunlight blazing off the windows and forcing her to shield her eyes. The building is not where it should be. Computer sciences is on the other side of the fountain, unless somebody moved it, the fountain, that is.

They could not have moved the building, right?

She casts her eyes around the quad. Everything is out of place apart from the fountain, the structures and statues and walkways. How is that possible? Gem shrugs. As long as she makes it to class on time everything will be fine, and the building is right in front of her.

Then she is inside the front hall walking toward the lab where she does most of her work, simple tasks that do not challenge her, exercises in patience and willpower. Hadn't someone told her that? That a college degree was more about perseverance, your ability to buckle down and see it through? Wait— why is she there? She already has her degree. She completed it in five semesters because the work was child's play. Is she there for graduate courses?

No, *she thinks.* This is not MIT, and I am not—

She feels a presence over her shoulder and turns. A professor is standing behind her, one of her former instructors. Gem cannot remember her name.

"I believe this is yours," she says, handing Gem the drive.

"It is. Where did you find it? I could have sworn I just had it."

"No, Gemma. They took it from you. Don't you remember?"

Gem stares at her. "No, I don't."

"You should never have lost it. You've gone and fucked it all up."

"What?"

"Shut up you twat."

The professor is grasping her arm now, the nails digging into her flesh. Gem struggles against her grip, but the woman is too strong. She pulls Gem forward until their noses touch. Her breath smells of putrefaction, acrid and awful and somehow sweet. Her voice drops to a low, throaty growl.

"You're going to die on that road, and such is a just fate for meddlers. You never should have taken it. You should have toed the line."

Gem finds her strength and pulls away, stumbling backwards until she topples. When she looks up from the floor she gasps. It is the stranger standing before her, the woman who'd masqueraded as Banks. Hadn't she exploded?

She moves toward Gem in strange sweeping motions, as if she were struggling to dance, her limbs forming impossible angles. She roars with laughter as she sways. Arrows race along the hallway, green and twisting and urging Gem to turn, to face her accoster. The stranger's cackles no longer sound like laughter. They are hard and mechanical, a buzzing, sawing din, the sound pounding on through the corridor in waves. Gem pushes herself up, ready to run for her life, but the ground is giving way, and she is—

THE PASS

S HE WAS awake and sitting up in the tent, clutching her shoulders and sweating. An unpleasant sensation sat deep in her gut. *Water*, she thought. Water would calm her stomach and wash the taste of sleep from her mouth.

Or was it the taste of the stranger's breath?

She struggled forward towards the door and clawed at the flap, Banks stirring at her movement. He rubbed the grog from his eyes and sat up. "What are you doing?"

"Water," she said, still fumbling around for purchase.

Banks unsealed the door and Gem lunged out. She pried the lid off the small cooler they kept near the tent and fished out a bottle and drank. She poured water over her face, breathing in long, heavy draughts. Then she looked up to the sky. The reds and golds of sunrise had appeared on the horizon, swaths of blood-colored clouds floating over the hills. It was chilly and breezy, though the rock shelf had stifled the bulk of the wind.

She heard Banks emerge from the tent behind her.

"Good timing," he said. "We would have been summoned before long." He pulled his own bottle from the cooler and sat down next to her in the dirt. "Feel better?"

Gem brought her knees to her chest and stared out over the treetops. "The machine was in my dreams again," she said. "I want this run to be over."

Banks followed her eyes to the horizon.

"You and me both."

He stood and brushed himself off, then offered Gem a hand. She took it and pulled herself up. "I think we had better get some caffeine in us," he said. "Could be another long day."

Gem followed him to the vehicle and they drank the last of the tea and each swallowed a Green for good measure. They'd had close to a full night's sleep, and there was no need for a Red. Gem peered over Banks's shoulder as he logged into the machine, half-expecting it to go mad and lock them down until the Company came calling. It did no such thing, only confirmed it had updated their route. "We'd better pack up," she heard herself say.

Banks rehashed all they had discussed as they broke down the tent, business as usual, make small talk, avoid suspicion.

"And remember, we can't be sure of any of it."

"Right," Gem said. His words seemed a hollow mantra that morning, repetition for repetition's sake.

They packed the gear away, then they slid into the vehicle and fastened their harnesses. Gem started the engine. The sunrise had faded to reveal the clouds for what they were, a gray line of thunderheads. Soon they would fill up the sky and hide the sun away, and she hoped they would keep their moisture to themselves. All the previous day she'd weathered the slick earth and muck, and another round of that would be most unwelcome.

THEY MADE small talk about the weather as they drove on, about what groceries were left and other benign trivialities. They wound their way out of the woods and the land opened below them, stretching down and away. Another mountain sat in the background, towering over the lowlands in the same fashion the first peak had dwarfed Hawks Pass. This one seemed wider at its base, though the crown was nearly identical, sheer and snowcapped and no less imposing. To Gem it appeared to have come out of nowhere, like the hills and trees had conspired to hide it from her view.

If only they had succeeded.

"Tell me we're not headed in that direction," Gem said.

She listened as Banks processed the data. "It looks like we may wind around its base," he said, "but I don't think we'll be going over. It's difficult to tell from the map. We should be at a lower altitude, so that's something."

It was not the news Gem had been hoping to hear.

The shitshow had begun with a mountain pass, the spooky birds and pseudo-premonitions and that feeling in her gut, not to mention the infernal buzzing, the wasps, the static. Maybe the plan was to expose them at altitude and take them out.

They could have done it back at the cabin, she thought. Banks had been right about that, but it did little to ease her mind.

Inhale—count to three—exhale.

The path approaching the peak was thick with familiar sights, rocks and stray boulders and broken trees and occasional cracks in the earth, foreboding fissures spread out under an ever-darkening sky. The trail would be bad enough in good weather, and she no longer had the sensors to serve as a failsafe—the sensors. So much had happened since that misfire on the pass she'd nearly forgotten about them. All the more reason to wish away the altitude.

"There should be a fork in the road soon," Banks said. "Keep to the left."

Gem brought them around a bend and found the path split in two directions, the trail on the right sloping downward and the fork on the left veering uphill. She could not see where it ran.

"Left branches off toward the peak," she said. "What happened to lower altitudes?"

"The Seeker says left, Gem. I told you I don't have the best of layouts here. It must break off and head downhill and some point."

Gem steered them up the trail, navigating the path until switchbacks appeared on the mountainside. There was no downward slope. The left fork had brought them right up to the sodding foothills. "We are going up the mountain, Banks."

"I can see that," he said. "Give me second." She heard a series of clicks and clacks to her right, a sequence of whirs, a pause. "Seems we've had a course correction."

"What? It didn't request confirmation."

"It may have loaded multiple options."

"When, Banks? When has it ever done that?"

He motioned to the machine. "Your memory is not serving you well right now," he said. "We have seen this before—"

And here we go, she thought.

"—the information may have been outdated, and—"

Here was another break with protocol for her to ponder. The issue was not that she was being forced over the pass, because she could handle a bloody pass, sensors or no. She had signed up for mountain trails and backroads. The issue was the machine improvising on the fly. It did not happen, *ever*, and Banks knew it as well as she did.

"—right Gem?" Banks finished.

She had not heard a word he'd said.

THEY INCHED up the path for half-an-hour until a weather-beaten sign emerged on their right, a wooden trail post, faded and barely legible.

BLACKSTONE PASS
ELEVATION: 10,865
CAUTION: LOOSE ROCKS

"Rocks," Banks said. "Thanks for the heads-up."

Gem ignored him. They were approaching a ridge.

Focus, she thought. She rolled the Wraith out past the sign and the world fell away to her left. Below was a patchwork of colors, greens and browns and reds and grays, an abstract painting of earthtones. She did not want to think about how far it was to the bottom. Of course the drop had to be on her side.

Focus. The approaching clouds felt closer now, larger and ever more ominous. The rain had held off so far, but the weather was unpredictable at elevation. It was another bit from her training, marking the clouds for their movement and composition, seeing them for what they were, a threat in themselves and not just a potential shield for malice—*the skies*. She turned an eye to Banks.

He was staring off over the cliffside like he was daydreaming, birdwatching like some goddamned tourist.

He was supposed to be running a scan.

"Banks." Gem jerked her head toward the Seeker. "The skies."

His eyes went wide and he sprang into action, executing his taps and swipes, Gem listening to the familiar cadence. What the hell was he thinking? Even if they were right and the Company *was* tailing them it did not guarantee the skies were clear. The machine would pick up a threat, yes, but a sweep would catch it first. The chances were always better with a navigator manning the helm, far better. Had he ever forgotten something so routine?

Did the Seeker ever mod a route without a warning?

No was the answer. Banks had never spaced out at altitude, and the machine had never gone washy and flipped the script under their noses, not once. "We're clear," she heard him say.

The ire was bubbling up in her. She felt compelled to lay into him, to inquire how he could speak with his head up his ass.

Of all the times to go on a bleeding walkabout!

What she said was, "Lovely," turning a cold eye to the passenger side. Banks twirled his finger around his temple, acknowledging his lapse in judgement.

Gem continued to bite her lip.

Something was off with Banks. She'd had her suspicions before, but now she knew. His behavior was odd in the canyon, then again in the cave. And what of the approach to Hawks Pass? He'd not made a peep when they first laid eyes on the valley, nary a thought for her killing the spectra or the eerie calm of the road. He had barely spoken a word except to move them along when the shock of it dulled her senses.

And he put his hands on me, like he did in the dream. No, that was not like Banks at all. She thought it was high time they had a conversation about what he was keeping from her, because there was something. *That is how nutters think, love, downright mental.*

Of course it was. Didn't she know that?

Gem told herself that she did, that it was the circumstances eating at her, exploding cabins and breaks with protocol, mysterious injuries and the threat of corporate sabotage.

Who could take all of that in stride?

I can, and I refuse to think about it another moment.

That was a sane thought. She felt good about that one.

Focus. There was a drop to her left that would powder her bones and fuse her guts with rock shards. It was her job to get them to other side, and she would do just that. Banks and the Seeker could shove off until she had seen them safely across, because *that* was what she'd signed up for, piloting the Wraith.

It was on her to bring them through this.

THE HACK

THE CROSSING proved uneventful, no intuitions, ominous birds or supercharged anxiety, no signs of drones. Gem rolled the Wraith down the other side with purpose, only slowing after they'd descended into the cover of the forest. If pretending all was well was the plan, then at least she could drive like it. "And were over," she said, feigning relief.

They drove on through the evergreens for another few miles, then Banks spoke up. "Likely to be quiet for a while," he said, smiling a sheepish smile. "I think it's your turn to tell me a story. Tell me about *your* Day One, Gem. I'm not sure you ever have."

She wrinkled her nose at him. "I haven't?"

Her surprise was genuine enough. She could not recall whether they'd spoken about it. Banks brought a hand to his mouth and began making speaking gestures.

Right, Gem thought, *a show for the machine.*

"Not that I recall," Banks said. "You got me thinking about it again in the cave, and now I'm curious. Can you remember it?"

Gem took a moment to compose herself. She was still angry with him, quite angry. She was no longer sure of his intentions, but she could not tell him that. She could not tell him she found his behavior strange or that she suspected he might be holding out on her, not without sounding unhinged, and certainly not in the Wraith. All she could do was put on the performance they had agreed to.

"I can remember it," she said. "It didn't happen last week, now did it?"

GEM LOATHED speaking about herself, and Banks knew it, but these were no ordinary circumstances. She told him she had been in graduate school on Day One, the glassy eyed students wandering the buildings trying their phones every few minutes. The perpetrators had started with social media, and why not? Millions checked the platforms first thing in the morning, getting their *news* and planning the day's activities. The loss of a profile was a life-altering severance for the addicts, and by lunchtime half the populace no longer knew how to behave. Whoever had drawn up the plan for Day One was counting on that, and in Gem's experience it proved the rule, not the exception. But she was not among the zombies. She had sworn off social media years before, disavowed it entirely after—

After the incident with those posh brats, she thought.

She kept only the accounts necessary for her coursework, stripping them bare of features and links to the online community and checking them as infrequently as possible. Only her professors and assigned groups could message her, and the only information they could view was her name and select academic contributions. She had seen to that. So Gem had watched it all unfold with a clear head, untethered to the mess. She had stood by as the university arrived at panic stations—

Banks interrupted her. "At what?"

"At panic stations. Have you not heard the term?"

"An American would say everyone was panicking."

"Oh piss off. You were on your own campus that day. You know all this."

"Yes, but I only know my own version of the story, so please, go on. I promise to hold my thoughts."

Gem went on, telling Banks the administrators had canceled classes and posted flyers in hopes the student body would venture out to read them.

—All Courses Postponed Until Further Notice—

The majority of professors stored their materials on university cloud servers, the ones supported by big-tech and their warehouses of hardware, and those servers had gone dark an hour after the initial surge shut down the social networks. What began as a superficial inconvenience transformed into a catastrophic security breach, and fast. One minute a student was worrying if a friend would know where to meet them for lunch. In the next the project they'd been slaving over for months was gone, reduced to motes of digital dust. The hack separated institutions all over the world from their data, their files, their payroll and shipping orders and records, anything they'd committed to that great storage space in the sky.

And they all demanded answers at once. Was their data safe? Would it be corrupted? Could any of it be saved? Who else might have access to it? Everyone wanted to know.

The surge of traffic shut down digital storage sites, the customer service hotlines placing anyone who called on hold.

What were they supposed to tell them?

Gem had always believed that one day somebody would take their shot. The world had committed itself to a digital existence where security was fluid, never guaranteed, and almost everyone had found themselves behind the curve. It was only a matter of time, and it had unfolded just as Banks predicted—

"Not exactly," he said.

"You said you would be quiet, so shut it."

Gem went on. Everyone was dumbfounded, the media and the politicians and their experts. They had all been so *shocked*, stunned and outraged and positively *incredulous* that something like this could happen. But Gem understood how it all went down. She was surprised it had not happened years before.

So what was she doing on Day One?

She had spent that night at a campus bar with dozens of disaffected peers, drinking cheap beer and watching the news, the anchors grave and sallow as they pleaded for patience. They were getting their information the old fashioned way, after all, landlines, reporters huddled outside government buildings waiting for statements. Gem had sat with a girl she'd roomed with for a spell, Allie.

Allie's phone had frozen when she tried to post a picture of her breakfast that morning, and then her laptop a few moments later. She'd told Gem she had a massive project saved on her hard drive, that she had backed it up on the cloud and had never printed a draft. "But that's gone now, isn't it?" Allie had said. "You know about this stuff, Gem. Tell me the truth."

Gem had been honest with her. "Your hard drive is probably dead, Al, along with that cloud copy. You should have saved it to an external source off the networks."

Allie had burst into tears.

Gem had told her the virus was designed to do one thing, corrupt and destroy, that whoever unleashed it must have found a way to rig the portals of social platforms with a Trojan, or some similar form of sabotage. Most users logged in automatically, so once they opened the app it was goodbye, sayonara, there goes your device.

"A what? A Trojan? Like condoms?"

Allie had been confused.

"You know what a *Trojan horse* is, right Al?"

"I don't anything about horses."

Gem had explained that a Trojan was malware, a malicious program, a bad one. Had Allie read any of the news about cybercrime? No? Well, whoever did this must have linked one of those programs to social media logins, somehow, the clever fucks, and when she opened her app that morning it installed a virus that burned through her laptop like acid. The goal must have been to cripple the public's internet access—why? Because it would shut down communication networks, cause chaos, draw the public's focus while the assailants started in on data storage, that place online where she'd lodged her proposal.

Allie had asked how that was possible, and Gem had told her it would have been difficult, but not if there was an update scheduled, something major, system-wide. A mole could have leaked the details to a cyber-cell beforehand. That was the only scenario Gem could envision, that whoever did the deed had insiders at major tech-companies. The culprits must have waited until just before the update went live to bug the platforms, then sent a worm through the pipeline while everyone was distracted.

Then came the questions. Yes, a *worm*, another bad program, a different kind, one that spreads from system to system encrypting files and data, or destroying them. No, Gem did not know exactly what this worm was doing, if that was in fact what it was. She did not have enough information, nor did anyone else, which was strange. Gem had thought it was strange.

She'd found it odd that no one had taken responsibility for the hack or issued any demands.

That was one thing the news outlets *had* known.

This is not believed to be a ransomware attack. Again, no demands have been issued in exchange for the restoration of data. We will bring you updates as they become available. We want to emphasize that you should not attempt to log on to the internet for any reason at this time. Experts are compiling a list of compromised sites.

So Gem had sipped shitty beer and took whiskey shots and consoled Allie until the girl went home to sulk, and by the end of the night she was lying to anyone and everyone who asked her about the hack. They were all looking for solace, so that was what she gave them.

Who knows, your profile could be back up tomorrow. It's possible you could retrieve your data, I suppose. They will have experts working on it.

At least the last part was true. The corporations and taskforces would have their people working overtime, all of them, but would they be good enough? Gem did not have an answer at the time.

GEM SAID, "I would have told you I wasn't optimistic if you'd asked me that day, but in hindsight, I think I was. I thought the powers-that-be would have little choice but to combine their efforts, and between them all, they would sort it out. I just thought it would take some time. You would call that optimistic, right?"

"I suppose I would," said Banks. "You were already in the States then, right? It would have been difficult to come over in the aftermath."

"I was at MIT, for grad school. Did you miss that part?"

"I must have. MIT, you say?"

"Yes, Banks. I never told you I went to MIT?"

Banks shrugged. "Like you said, I missed it. You never went back to London?"

"No, I didn't go back. The risks were too great at the time, you know that. Nobody knew what was going on, if planes would start dropping out of the sky and such. By the time the noise died down I was gainfully employed."

"With us?"

"With a subsidiary."

Gem paused. Had she never told him how the Company recruited her? Surely she would have brought it up at some point. His questions were beginning to feel forced.

"You never finished at MIT?"

"No, I still had a semester to go. I could have stayed and seen it out, but I answered an advert." She caught herself. "I mean I answered an *advertisement*. One job led to another, and here we are."

"So you came to the States for the work? Seems that Europe would have been a better place to be at the time, with all the—"

"Bloody hell, Banks! Would you like me to walk you through all the courses I took while we're at it? Every pint I downed at the pubs?" It was not her intention to shout, but she had been going on for some time, and now he was meddling. Had he forgotten the point of the conversation? This was not standard dialogue for them. They joked and prodded each other and reminisced about outdated pop culture, the light stuff, and if anyone ever went on about their past, it was *him*. First it was the melancholy, then his antics on the pass, and now he was hammering her with questions?

The inconsistencies were piling on.

"Just making conversation," Banks said. He nodded to the machine. "Besides, I'm curious what British Gem was like, what motivated her. I only know cantankerous, quasi-American Gem, the woman who can't stop swearing yet is so easily offended."

She tightened her grip on the wheel. He wanted to know what *British Gem* was like? Maybe she would tell him. Maybe that would sour him on the idea and shut him up. She flashed her eyes in his direction—then she felt a pinch, a jolt along her neckline, there for a moment and gone. She resisted the urge to poke at it.

"So you think I am cantankerous? And you would like to know why? I was what you might call a dispirited youth, Banks. I didn't have a good time of it over there most of my life. My mother was an addict, opiates, pills. Then came the stronger stuff, the heroin and fentanyl and God knows what else. She got herself put away when I was young and I was shipped off to London to live with my Gran. The alternative was becoming a ward."

Gem watched the smile fade from his face.

She felt compelled to continued.

"I started teaching myself to code and build pages and mod hardware and software. That was my life. I didn't resent it, not by any means, but I don't think I was ever happy. I was every shitty teen-film's late-bloomer character, minus the mandatory redemption." Her mouth was running on auto-pilot now, her voice intensifying. "I kept to myself. I got older, got clever. I learned to rip through cut-rate cybersecurity like it was paper, moving funds around, leaking information. And I was *good*, Banks. No one could catch me. No one has *ever* caught me."

She flexed her fingers against the wheel.

"Then I did something wretched. I was nearly out when I had a go at some girls who crossed me. I hacked into their social accounts and wreaked a little havoc, what I thought they deserved. I stole photographs, put one girl's naked tits up in the academy chatroom where everyone could see them. I sent dreadful messages from the others, racist shit and fat-shamings."

She could not stop herself from speaking.

"East London tore those slags to shreds. Everyone they knew disowned them. Two of them never set foot in that school again, but I didn't care, not at the time. I felt *good* about it. Fuck them, I said. That's what they got for being horrible cunts. And no one even suspected me, that I was capable of such a thing. I was anonymous, in life, on the web. I was *invisible*. I was—"

Gem hit her harness with force, swallowing her words.

Banks struck the passenger door with a thud.

A set of railroad tracks had emerged, hidden by the slope until they were nearly on them. An ancient piece of machinery lay half-buried alongside the rails.

Gem had spied the heap as she carried on.

She had slowed to maneuver around it.

THE TRACKS

THE WRAITH auto-corrected and surged to the left, sensing the rusting metal. It struck the elevated bank of the tracks with force and threw them from their seats, Banks hitting the door and Gem slamming into her harness, hard enough to knock the wind from her. She heaved as the vehicle crashed to the ground on the other side, throwing her weight at the brakes and gripping the wheel and gasping. They slid to a stop in a cloud of dust.

"Fucking hell! That was the bloody sensors!"

Banks sat doubled over in his seat, clutching his shoulder.

"Are you hurt, Gem?"

She stared daggers at the Seeker. The machine was behind it. She did not know *how*, but she *knew*.

"*Gem.*" His voice was stern enough to command her attention. "Are you *all right*?"

"Rattled, but unscathed I think. And you?"

"I caught a good one, but everything seems in place."

Gem watched him rotate his arm across his chest. They had a sizable medical kit, though there was not much they could do for a clavicle, maybe a sling at best. She gave herself a once over and found nothing to alarm her. "Check the sensors," she said.

"I know I switched them off," Banks said, "and I have not touched that panel."

Gem leaned forward, unlocked the console and slid the casing up. "Off," she said. "Of course they are off. But they are not *disabled*, now are they?"

"Gem."

"Maybe they were *never* disabled. What would you say to that? Maybe they—"

"Gem!"

She recoiled and blinked.

"It is clearly a systems issue," said Banks, "like you were worried about. It is something in the works."

Gem blinked again. "Right. Something in the works, like I said."

Inhale. Did Banks really believe that, or was he playing coy for the machine, for the overseers on the other end—for her. She could not be certain who his machinations were aimed at, but he had been right to cut off before she said something daft. *Exhale.* "You are sure you're not hurt?" she said. "We can see what's in the bag."

"No," Banks said. "I can shake it off." He pulled himself up with his good arm and began to massage the other. "And what about you? Are you alright?"

"I told you I wasn't hurt."

"I don't mean physically," Banks said. "I've never heard you say more than few words about London, much less your former classmates."

Gem looked at him sideways. *London? Classmates?*

What was this bollocks? How would he know about that?

"What are you on about, Banks. Spit it out."

Here was his look of concern again, that exasperating goddamned gaze. "Before we hit the bank. You were talking about England, hacking, girls at your school."

The blood drained from her face. She felt pressure behind her eyes. Had she been going on about her life? Those posh girls? Her thoughts combed over the memory, walking the streets after it was done, watching the social feeds in the aftermath. But speaking about it? She had never told anyone about hacking those girls, not a soul, and there was no inferring that information. Banks would have no way of knowing if she hadn't said something.

She searched her mind for the conversation and found only a dull haze, an endless wash of murk. *Don't react*, Gem thought. *You can't give him anything. He mustn't know you don't remember.*

"Right," she said. "I was just flustered."

It was like learning of something you'd done piss-ass drunk, piecing together a blackout. Gem hated that feeling, though she dared not push herself. She could already feel the effects of her prodding, pressure turning to pain, her nerves warning her to back off.

"You wanted to hear about my experiences."

She knew she had told him about Day One, about the college kids losing their minds. And then? Then there were other questions, questions about *British Gem*. That had pissed her off, and then she had—what? That was where the tape ran out.

"And I don't like talking about my past," she continued. "You know that, so how about we just drop it, because it wasn't any of your business to begin with."

Would he buy it? Would he believe that load of crap?

"I know," he said, "but you seemed agitated—"

"I *am* agitated." she said. "This entire run has been *agitating*, and if you continue to pester me you are going to learn what proper agitation looks like!"

He kept his eyes on her. "Point taken."

The Seeker chirped to her right, and Banks moved to address it. Gem was glad for its timing. *Inhale—count to three—exhale.*

She took another breath for good measure then closed her eyes. It was symptom of her injury, another malady drawn from the box. It had accosted her common sense and pulled her filters off—so what? Was it so surprising she could not recall what she'd said? And what was Banks going to do about it, phone up the yard in London and report her? He would do no such thing. He would keep his mouth shut and mind the machine and go about his business, *as usual*, if he was not too busy haranguing her, or spacing off.

Inhale—count to three—exhale.

And there was still that gremlin in the sensors.

Gem opened her eyes and pointed to the control panel.

"And what do you propose we do about that?" she said. "What happens when they decide to throw us off a cliff?"

"I'm running another diagnostic," Banks said. "We'll see what it can tell us, if anything."

Inhale—count to three—exhale.

"If anything," Gem repeated. "Right. Perhaps it would care to tell us where the hell we are in the meantime. Does that prat mean to send us down the tracks? The tracks that *trains* run on?"

"I think *ran* on would be more accurate," Banks said. "My guess is they're out of commission."

Gem had been too worked up to consider the state of the rails. The swaths of foliage surrounding the tracks implied an absence of friction, and the metal was beginning to rust. The line was clearly not in use. It was also boxed in by steep, craggy hills on either side, and she doubted the machine meant to turn them around.

The tracks were the only way forward.

"So the railroad it is then," she said.

"It would appear so."

She refastened her harness, tightened it for good measure and looked to the machine. The Seeker seemed wholly unconcerned with their sensor troubles, which could mean one of two things. Either it *was* a systems issue, some malfunction inhibiting the Wraith from diagnosing and reporting its status, or the machine was ignoring it. Had it done the same on the mountain before Hawks Pass? Was it outrageous to assume the Company could manipulate the vehicle from afar?

Outrageous, she thought. *Outrageous as opposed to what?*

And then there was Banks. What was she to make of him? She could no longer give him the benefit of the doubt, even if it felt like madness. It pained her to think of him that way, but something was not right, with him, with her—with everything. Nothing had been right since she'd opened her eyes in the tent that morning. She'd found his story hard to believe even before the run went tits up, that she'd slipped and hit her head on a rock? She was as sure-footed as anyone, her reflexes spot on. It was part of the reason they'd trained her to drive.

The machine emitted a low, dissatisfied tone. It had failed to diagnose the problem with the sensors, again. Banks turned to her.

"The Seeker did not find—"

"I know," Gem said. "You'd best put your harness back on, love. We're going to have to get moving."

THE TUNNEL

THE RAILROAD followed the path of least resistance, the ground level and the sightlines long, no switchbacks or rocks or hulking obstacles to negotiate, the sensors showing no signs of wiliness. Had it not been for their recent upheaval Gem wouldn't have paid them a thought. After thirty-odd miles a new set of tracks emerged to join the line, and they were forced to cross over the rails. Gem readied herself for an incident, but the sensors made no reply. This second line was just as decrepit as the first, the metal red and flaking and covered in weeds. She was glad she would not have to add oncoming trains to her list of concerns. That list had grown considerably longer since daybreak, and space was becoming a premium.

Soon the terrain began to change, gradually at first, then the landscape bloomed in an assortment of colors, the grays and greens transforming to yellows and maroons and great walls of rust-tinged rock rising in every direction. The tracks entered a narrow gap and funneled them into a ravine, Gem easing the Wraith along until the walls opened into a wide, bowl-shaped depression. The plain was enclosed on all sides by smooth sheaths of rock, the rails bisecting the great bowl and disappearing over the horizon. Now they were ascending a gradual incline, and after a distance the tracks sloped over the plateau to allow Gem a panoramic view of their surroundings. *Shit*, she thought. *This can't be good.*

In the distance she saw a sheer slab of rock, a reddish-brown behemoth rising hundreds of feet towards the heavens. There was a tunnel carved into its face, and short of heading back through the ravine, she saw no other way out of that basin. "Do you see what I see?" she said to Banks. At times she wondered if he did, if they were looking at two different worlds.

The question was not altogether rhetorical.

"Well, that depends," he said. "If you are referring to the tunnel, then yes."

"And we are going through it?"

"There is nowhere else to go."

They sat in silence for a moment.

"I would say something about protocol," Gem said, "about how teams are trained to avoid tunnels because they are death traps. I would also add that our sensors might not agree with an enclosed space in their current state, but that would just be daft."

Banks would not be drawn in. "Extraordinary circumstances allow the Seeker to amend standard directives. You know it would not send us through without cause."

Gem might have expected such a reply.

"And how long is the tunnel?"

"Give me a second." He swiped and tapped and entered a few commands, then he mumbled something under his breath. "Seems we don't have the specs."

"Is that so? And why is that, Banks?"

"There are any number of reasons it could be incomplete, Gem. I think you know that as well."

What she knew was there was no point in continuing the conversation. Her mouth was unlikely to do her any favors at the moment, and it could not betray her if she kept it shut. Those shits might have thought a railroad tunnel a perfectly suitable place to send a disgruntled driver, one with wild ideas and a questionable loyalty to the cause. They had tried it with that drone at the cabin, so why not a tunnel? And with rabid sensors no less?

So be it, Gem thought.

They were going through that passage regardless of what she thought about it, and if the Company wanted to beach her Wraith in that hole, they could come and drag it out themselves.

THE SPECTRA-LIGHT kicked on as they crossed the threshold, and Gem saw the tunnel was wider than she had anticipated, fifteen feet either side of the line. She would be able to keep well away from the walls. There could be loose gear stored off to the sides, and she hoped there was nothing parked on the tracks, a long dead train or a handcart or whatever else the railroad saw fit to abandon.

"Fire up the high beams," Banks said. "We finally have a spot we can use them."

A smile crept over Gem's face. "You're right."

She'd never had occasion to use the headlights. Did she even recall how to put them on? She ran a hand over the instrument panel with caution, keeping one eye on the tracks. Where was the bloody switch? Then she remembered. The toggle was hidden away round the back of the steering wheel, a place she would be unlikely to trigger it error. "Here goes." Gem flipped the switch and the murk exploded in glorious light. Every crack and fissure hidden away in the bowels of the rock seemed to glow, and Banks whistled at the sight.

"My *God*," he said. "Would you look at."

Gem saw she had been right about the gear. Machinery lined the walls in places, most of it ancient and fit only for salvage, though nothing large enough to trigger the sensors—at least under normal circumstances. "Look at all this shit," she said. "Let's hope there's nothing parked on the tracks."

"Just keep it steady," Banks said. "If there's anything up there, you'll see it."

She had little doubt of that. The high beams did wonders for her line of sight, and she saw nothing ahead but track, yards of shining, silver lines. But with her luck?

"There is bound to something," she said.

"What?"

"Nothing."

The path bent around gradual turns in places, and Gem kept her pace cautious but firm. Beyond the range of the beams the darkness was total, and she counted the seconds, waiting for the end to emerge. When she reached thirty she stopped. How far had they gone? A quarter-mile? The tunnel was disorienting, muddling her sense of time and space, and—

A pang rang out from the base of her skull, a significant one. She braced herself, ready to meter her breaths and hold on for dear life, but this one felt different. It was not instant nor debilitating, not like that bolt in the forest. Her temples had not tightened up. What it felt like was pressure releasing, the sensation of lancing a boil. Then an image hit her with sudden clarity. She was on the Buggy again, but not on the road to Hawks Pass.

She saw a relay tower through the trees.

The milk-run, she thought. *The one I recalled in the woods*.

Yes, she remembered it now. She was making her way to the tower, but for what? A maintenance check?

Her nerves began to fire. This was the memory that had floored her, and she could not let that happen again, not on the move in a sodding tunnel. *Push it away*. But there was no pressure clogging her ears, no pain in her eyes, only clarity, like she had crawled up from the depths of a bog. She felt compelled to let the memory play out. Whatever it was, it seemed of vital importance.

GEM WAS on the Buggy approaching the tower. She was nervous—why? She was unsure of something. There was anticipation, excitement, trepidation, emotions unbefitting a milk-run. Perhaps it was not the simple task she had assumed it was—but why?

I don't know. She saw herself unlock the door to the control room with a keycard. No one used cards anymore, not unless a system was misfiring. She must not have wanted her prints on file, and if that was the case—

Focus. She slipped in and checked the interior of the entryway, then the door behind her. The room was powered-down. Gem opened the mainframe, breezed through the safeguards and began working away under the glow of the safety lights.

Why didn't I fire up the system?

She could only watch the memory play out. She saw long lines of code, the complex code of the Company's internal security. Her heart thumped away as she worked. If she was there to reboot the system she would have already been finished. Such a thing took no time at all. This was something else, something far more serious.

And then the memory was gone.

Shit, she thought. *What was I doing there?*

Then a second image seized her, something darker. Here was another memory creeping up from the murk, a scene veiled in shadows. She saw only flicks and flares of light, then her vision lit up orange. Now she could see it clearly. She was weaving the Wraith through the trees, slowly, methodically, and then she was speeding down a trail—no, not a trail. She was off-road and *flying*, the vehicle rocking and bouncing as she plowed over the terrain. Was there someone pursuing her? Some*thing*? The memory began to cycle, moonlight to orange to terrain speeding by, over and over again. She felt her hands on the wheel, in the memory, in reality. *Reality.*

Gem snapped her eyes to the tracks, gauging their position. They could not have driven more than a few hundred feet. It had all flashed by in seconds. *Clarity*, she thought. *Like crawling out of a bog.*

But those scraps of memory told her nothing. They were no more than puzzle pieces, bits of edging and corner chunks. Why was she gunning the Wraith through the wilderness?

What was she doing in that tower?

She forced her thoughts back to the control room, then to the mainframe, the monitor, the black and green smears of code. She'd been thinking that time was a factor, that she needed to move— but why? She saw the screen shift in the lowlight and knew she had broken through. Broken through *what*? What was she *doing* there?

She was reaching into her pocket, and—

A pinch gripped her nerves and the control room fell away. There was pressure squeezing her ears, the strain of it creeping into her eyes, her temples. Something had happened, and she knew the memory was lost, that reaching for it again would trigger the pain.

Gem eased her foot off the gas, but nothing sprang forward to assault her, no agony or strange floating detachment. The Wraith remained centered, rolling calmly along between the tracks. She took a lungful of air and breathed it out, then she returned her foot to the pedal. Banks was poking away at the machine to her right, doing God knows what. He seemed oblivious to her epiphany, but could she be sure? "Banks."

He did not turn from the Seeker. "What?"

There was tension in his voice. Had something unsettled him? "Have you found anything yet?"

"No," he said. "I'm doing what I can."

His actions seemed rushed to her, and he was leaning in toward the display, almost like he was trying to shield it. She could not inch over for a look without drawing his attention.

Strange, Gem thought.

Yes, but strange had become quite relative.

For a moment she'd had her wits about her again, or pieces of them at least, and wasn't that just as odd? What was the source, and why had it faded so quickly? She'd not felt such clarity in days, not since her alleged slip on the rocks. It was almost like—

"I've got it." Banks said. "I have the route. We are nearly out." Gem could see the relief on his face.

Strange, she thought again. He could have been searching for specs, finding nothing and letting his frustrations get the better of him. It was possible. Most anything was *possible*.

"Well it's about time," she said.

A dot of light appeared in the distance, pea-sized, then coin-sized, then as large as a dinner plate. Streaks of graffiti emerged on the rockface as the daylight meshed with the high beams, and Gem reached back to switch them off. She wondered if she would ever have another opportunity to use them. If it meant she was through navigating railroad tunnels and other analogous deathtraps, she would happily see them rust. "Better slow it down," Banks said. "We don't know what's out there."

Gem eased her foot into the brake, bringing the Wraith to a halt amid the last of the tunnel's shadows. She could see boxcars beyond the exit, stacked three or four high and forming an ugly skyline along the tracks. "Well look at that," she said. "I think it's—"

"It's a trainyard, Gem. Sit tight for now. The Seeker is recalibrating."

SURVEILLANCE

THE ADMINISTRATOR sat at her desk in silence. The run was not going as planned. She had hoped the team's sensors would remain dormant, though she had known better than to expect it. The override she had authorized during the incident was an unprecedented bit of business, and one could not estimate the costs of such an action, the long-term ramifications. But the sensors were no longer her primary concern. It had been a calculated risk to send them through the tunnel instead of bringing them around. She had reasoned Miss Gemma would be wary and maintain a reasonable speed, though she had not even paid a thought to the Seeker. Why would she? It was supposed to be im*possible*, yet it had happened nonetheless, and there was no benchmark for predicting what complications might arise.

The Administrator frowned.

It would be wise to delay them for a spell, assess the situation and make the necessary adjustments. She had never intended to alter course—in spite of her lip service to the Board—and it troubled her she was considering such a gambit.

But what choice did she have?

If she let the operation unfold as planned the results could prove disastrous. What she had was a wavering, disgruntled driver, a malfunctioning Wraith and a machine that had not lived up to its billing, three jokers in the deck. Her best course of action would be to put them on ice for a spell. It would prevent other potential catastrophes from materializing, and it would buy her some time to think. It was the only reasonable solution.

She would look on Miss Gemma and Mr. Banks with her own eyes, and then she would determine how to proceed. It would be easy enough to say they'd been brought in to fix their sensors. That part would be true, just not the whole truth. In the meantime they would rest and recuperate. Recent events would lose their urgency, their grievances would go stale in their minds and their woes would feel less pertinent. And after that?

"Then back to the plan," said the Administrator.

The run would go on, of course. It had to, but she would need to do more than send them on their way. Her eyes lit up then, the thinnest of smiles breaching her lips. "Of course."

She could not believe she hadn't thought of it before.

THE YARD

T HE MACHINE had been holding them in place for a while now, and the minutes were stretching on. From their position the yard appeared rundown and derelict, and that suited Gem fine—abandoned locations were ideal for their purposes—yet the Seeker was still scanning away. And just what was giving it pause? She'd no sooner finished the thought than the machine sounded a positive tone. A layout of the trainyard materialized on its display, and Gem inched over to have a look. It was detailed beyond anything she had seen on the run, outlining the open spaces and buildings and the intersecting tracks, the fence lines and boundaries, everything in its proper place.

"Nary a mark for the tunnel," she said, "and now this?"

Banks entered his acknowledgement codes. "Look," he said. "This side has been surveyed recently. It explains the discrepancy in the maps. This is a good sign."

"A good sign? Are you implying we have people here?"

"The specs are current, so we did at some point."

"Yet they didn't bother to map the tunnel."

The machine chirped again, and they returned their eyes to the screen. Now it had conjured a route, a single green arrow zigzagging around the obstacles and ending at the center of a large, rectangular structure.

Banks's eyes went wide. "That looks like the end of the line," he said, "but that can't be right."

Gem pulled him out of the way and leaned in. She could hardly believe what she was seeing. "Can you confirm it?"

Banks cycled through the rendering layer by layer, but there was no additional information. The instructions were clear as day.

The end, Gem thought. *The end of this whole rotting mess.*

The idea would not sink in. It felt too good to be true, and maybe it was. It might be the end of the run, but it would not be the end of the line, not with the Company sending drones out to rattle their cages and breaking protocol left and right.

The Seeker chimed an impatient chime.

"You heard it," Banks said. "Let's go."

Gem did not know whether to feel joy or fear or relief, and it was uncertainty she felt as a result. She had been pining for the end of the run, was positively desperate for it.

She'd not been thinking about what it could mean.

THERE WERE no trains stored in the yard, no rusting old hulks laid out to pasture, only stacks upon stacks of shipping containers, dead metal husks plastered with faded graffiti and going slowly to waste. They passed small outbuildings with flat corrugated roofs and rotting wooden frames. Scraps of metal lay strewn around them, blown off by the wind or peeled away by the elements. Beyond sat walls of red rock similar to those Gem had seen in the basin, forming the boundaries of the yard, scenic, imposing. Bronze-colored dust coated most everything she saw. The place had the feel of the ghost town, and what better place to dispose of a pair of liabilities?

Or just the one, she thought. There had been plenty of opportunities to off them en route to the yard, and good ones at that, but that did not mean anything. They might have other plans for them—for *her*. They might be looking to make an example of—

"Make a left past this building," Banks said.

"Right."

"No, left." Gem heard him chuckling to himself, and she was not in the mood for it. His timing had never been apt, but it was rarely so misguided. A bit of cheap humor to mask they nerves? She could only hope that was the case, because if it wasn't—

Not now, love. Go on and get us there first.

The trainyard was large but their path was a simple one, and at the end of the route sat a warehouse. The building was old and disheveled, the windows filthy where the glass was intact and the broken ones covered with pressboard, all of the high garage doors standing shut. Gem inched the Wraith up near the centermost bay and parked. "Here we are," said Banks. "Doesn't look like we'll be receiving a grand reception."

Gem continued to ignore him. That building could be full of Company goons who'd already dug a grave in the dirt out back, if they had even bothered with the formalities. They could just as easily burn her body, or seal it away one of those boxcars.

"Gem?"

She wheeled round to face him. "What?"

"Did you hear me?"

"We won't be receiving a reception."

"No, I asked you where you wanted to get a drink when we get back."

Had he said that? "Anywhere. I could care less."

Banks eyed her with suspicion.

"You don't care? Since when—"

"Since this run, Banks." She turned her gaze back to the warehouse. "And you are getting ahead of yourself. Let's not go discussing the afterparty until we are *finished*."

Gem would not tell him she couldn't recall the name of a single place they had gone for drinks, that all she could muster were flashes of ambiguous taverns, bars she may or may not have visited and had most likely seen on television . . . *you were talking about England . . . girls at your school . . . are you sure you're alright . . .*

Had Banks even asked her about the drinks? Had her broken brain rejected him, or had she just not been paying attention? The shot of clarity she'd experienced in the tunnel felt an illusion, no more than a symptom of the curse she'd been saddled with.

"I don't believe that," Banks said.

"You don't believe *what*."

"I don't believe I am getting ahead of myself." His voice was calm. "But we will know soon enough. Look."

Gem leaned over the wheel and squinted. She saw a flash of light through a first floor window, quick and sharp, and then she saw another. "Did you see it?" Banks said.

"I saw it," she said. "But I don't see any—"

The Seeker rang out and scared her back in her seat. This was a new sound, loud and alarming. The screen was flashing red.

Red, she thought. *Not orange—red.*

A dull thud cut through the din, the release of something heavy. It was the garage door opposite the vehicle, the metal creaking and groaning as it inched its way upward. Then the Wraith jerked forward. "Shit!" Gem slammed her foot on the brake then yanked it back. There was no give to the pedal, like stomping on a brick. She cursed and grabbed the steering with both hands, fighting the urge to snatch at her ankle. She could not even turn it an inch.

Banks was hunched over the machine, struggling to disarm it. A word had appeared on the screen, oversized capital letters fixed to the flashing background.

—LOCKDOWN—

It felt like slow motion, the garage door rising, the vehicle crawling forward, the Seeker blinking in intermittent, blood-colored bursts.

It was unfolding as Gem had feared. She pulled at the door handle—locked. *Lockdown*, she thought. *Locked doors and pedals and wheels*. They had reached the end all right, their end, the end of Gem and Banks, Company agents and accidental conspirators, a set of pawns on the board, two unlucky muppets who'd been daft enough to—

She felt Banks's hand on her shoulder, firm yet gentle.

"Gem," he said. "Look—*listen*."

She listened. The godawful racket was gone. Instead the machine was pulsing, urgent, yes, but it no longer felt malicious. She looked. There was no armor clad murder squad in the warehouse, only rows of disorganized shelves and dead machinery. She heard the drop of the locking mechanism as the door closed behind them, and then the Seeker chimed pleasantly. The display had gone green again, the color of calm and security.

—AWAIT FURTHER INSTRUCTIONS—

Gem forced herself to inhale, to count. Strips of daylight funneled through the remaining windows to illuminate patches of floor, dirty stripes of concrete. Whatever light they had spied from the yard had gone, and her thoughts turned to the cave, to the quiet void that had sheltered them. She found the idea comforting.

Inhale—count to three—exhale. She was beginning to calm down. *Inhale—count to three—exhale*. Something told her they were in the right place, that the Seeker had good intentions bringing them there.

Then why did it lock us in?

"Gem."

"What."

"Look."

The machine had updated its message.

—PREPARE FOR DESCENT—

"And just what the hell is that supposed to mean?"

Banks smiled at her. "I think I know where we are."

Gem opened her mouth to respond, then stopped. She was certain she'd heard something below them, a clicking sound. Then she heard it again. "What—"

Clanks and bangs rang out from beneath the vehicle as the ground lurched, like a carnival ride ready to drop. Gem cried out and grabbed the wheel, Banks bracing himself on the Seeker's frame. He began to laugh. "Here we go."

And then they were descending.

THE BAY

IRST THERE was only the ratcheting of machinery, and then Gem caught a flash in the mirror, then a second, a third. *Red*, she thought, *waves of red*—safety lights. The pieces snapped into place. The Seeker had parked them on a platform, and the Company was bringing them in. The space below came into view through the window as they descended, a factory floor, clean and modern, a stark contrast to all they had seen above. A beast of a machine sat at the far end against the wall, the red light refracting off a series of arms bent inward against its body. The appendages were equipped with specialized tools, drills, blades, mandibles—of course. "A Surgeon," Gem said.

Banks had been chuckling quietly to himself.

"Can I assume you've figured it out?"

She continued to stare out the window.

"It looks like an outpost."

"It *is* an outpost," Banks said, "and if I'm not mistaken, a brand-spanking new one."

Gem took a deep breath—an outpost.

So why the lockdown then? Why all the shady bullshit? They had never been brought in under such ominous circumstances.

She rocked forward in her seat as the platform locked into place. The overhead lights kicked on, replacing the red with an assault of halogen white. The Seeker whirred and chimed, then it presented a fresh pair of directives.

—PROCEED TO CORRIDOR—

—FOLLOW INSTRUCTIONS—

"I think we can do that," Banks said.

The doors unlocked with a clack and he unfastened his harness, though Gem did not follow suit. She was still strapped in, one hand clutching the wheel, the other firm against her brow as she continued to study the floor. Banks eyed her with suspicion.

"You do realize where we are," he said.

Gem nodded. What could she say to him in the presence of the Seeker? That all might not be what it seemed? That he was a fool for thinking they were done with this run and there would not be *consequences*? "I do," she said. "It's a bit of a shock is all."

Banks turned to the Seeker. Maybe he did understand.

"Well believe it," he said. "Come on, let's go."

Gem stepped out of the vehicle and closed the door, looking up and to her right, then to her left and over her shoulder. It was clearly an operating room, what the Company called its repair bays, smaller than it had appeared from above but large enough to house four or five Wraiths, no more than six. The Surgeon loomed to her left, bolted to the wall and standing ten feet high. Twelve arms lined the vertical face of the structure, six a side, the limbs retracting into themselves like boom stands when idle and folding into the frame. It was fascinating to watch them in action, the way they moved, the power they possessed, how they could pull a Wraith apart and reassemble it in a matter of hours. Had the Company brought them in to fix their sensors? Gem frowned.

It would be a convenient excuse. The Surgeon could just as easily remove their payload and leave the vehicle in disarray, because that was the important part, yes? Once the goods were extracted there would be no need to worry about a couple of rogues— *or just the one*—whether they might find a clever way to usurp the

Seeker and make off with Company property. Or maybe there was never a payload at all. Would it be surprising to learn the Company had run them through Hawks Pass as a means to test the waters? That the run was never really a run?

Hearsay, she thought, *just like the satellites*.

She continued to stare at the Surgeon.

USING TEAMS as decoys was another rumor quietly passed around, a notion whispered under your breath over drinks somewhere far from Company holdings. Wraith teams never knew what they were carrying, nor were they privy to the end result of the extraction process. You could watch a Surgeon remove the doors and tires and uproot the seats from their frames, the unmooring of larger odds and ends, but additional observation required clearance. Whatever lay stashed away in the Wraith's core was a trade secret reserved for upper management, and secrets bred conspiracy. Ergo, the decoy theory, an idea Gem had previously been content to ignore. Decoys were meant to be spotted, and Wraith teams moved in the shadows—but it was only a contradiction when taken at face value. This was a dangerous game the Corps were playing.

Company wares could no longer be transported by air or train, and God forbid anyone tried to move something online. The rails never changed, and the skies belonged to the drones, corruptible devices that could be boosted or simply shot out of the air when the more subtle approaches failed. You could not trust a drone with Company tech, at least nothing remotely valuable. All that remained was the ground, the mountain paths and the backroads, the land routes the field and the Wraith crews runners of supplies, little more than grunts, and no competent army would entrust classified intel to the rabble. A rival could not extract information from those who did not know it.

Gem continued to stare at the Surgeon, the extractor of goods invaluable. Was that what awaited her here? An extraction? Her employers were no different than the others at heart, a condition they'd more than proven with the destruction of Hawks Pass. They would want to know where she got such strange ideas about the fires—*I am on their side*. But there would still be consequences.

Snap out of it.

She turned to find Banks ambling around the opposite side of the bay, examining the gadgetry. He appeared at ease, blissfully unaware of the threats she perceived. Perhaps his was the appropriate response to this turn and hers the view unhinged. Perhaps Banks had not known anything about this mess at all. He'd seemed just as surprised to find an outpost at the end of that tunnel as she had. He had been acting strange, and alarmingly so, but couldn't the same be said for her? *I have an excuse.* That was true. Banks had not been broken by some mysterious mishap, an accident *he* had described to her, and that was only the beginning. What was that shiftiness in the tunnel? And his birdwatching on the pass?

Not good enough, she thought.

Everyone responded to stressors in their own way, and what evidence she had was circumstantial, little more than her own suspicions. They were at an outpost, and every action she'd doubted had ultimately led them there. Those were the facts.

Gem took a deep breath.

Maybe she was wrong about Banks, and if that proved to be the case, she could own that mistake.

But that did not mean this was over.

BANKS WAS waiting near the corridor and Gem made her way towards him. It was time to see where they stood. She considered which would be worse, facing an inquisition or knowing she'd fallen victim to a spectacular bout of paranoia, that she had nearly been out of her mind. The former might be a slap on the wrist, but the latter? *Madness*, she thought.

Could she deal with knowing she'd nearly gone mad?

Track lighting sprang to life along the ceiling as they moved, cooler than the halogens but brighter than Gem would like. The corridor resembled the operating room, smooth, gunmetal walls and polished concrete floors, a fluorescent green arrow blinking along at head height on Gem's right. She looked around for the source and could not find it, then she motioned to the wall.

"Our friend is still with us."

"It will power down once we've found our way," Banks said, "assuming it's even our Seeker."

"I have a feeling it is."

They followed the arrow until doors emerged on either side of them, Company doors, complete with print locks and touchpads and emergency card slots, doors that would not be opening without corporate authorization. They continued on to the end of the hall where a final door remained.

"End of the line," Banks said.

The rims of the touchpad blinked green, the door slid open and Gem followed him inside.

THE SCREEN

THE ROOM was lit in a softer light than the rest of the facility, the floors carpeted and the walls eggshell white. A leather couch sat near the center, flanked by small oval tables and expensive looking chairs. There was an ornate cabinet against the back wall next to a marble-faced bar. Atop the bar sat a line of rocks glasses.

When the door clicked shut a voice addressed them, its cadence smooth and digital. *A representative will be with you shortly. There are refreshments in the cabinet. Please make yourselves comfortable.*

Gem turned to the bar and frowned. What were the chances the booze was drugged? She went through the familiar song and dance, why not earlier, why wait until now and how likely was this and that and the rest of it, and then she took a breath. Dubious or not, a drink would take the edge out of the proceedings. She walked to the cabinet and pulled a crystal decanter from the shelf, the contents a deep, bold amber. She uncorked the stopper and sniffed.

"Top shelf," she said. "Banks?"

"I believe I could use it."

Gem poured two drinks and sat down next to him on the couch. She was determined to bin her suspicions for the time being, to act like a reasonable person and hold all judgements until the facts were laid bare. The run had been hard enough as it was, and enduring it without an ally was beginning to wear on her.

They sipped at the whiskey and took in their surroundings, the store-bought landscapes lining the walls, generic mountain scenes with green trees enclosing clear, pastel lakes. Gem had seen enough of that type of terrain of late, and she did not associate it with serenity. Banks was staring off toward the far wall. "Gem."

"Banks."

"Straight ahead of you. What do you see?"

"What do you think I should see? It will save me the trouble."

"Just look."

Gem looked. She thought she could see a shimmer.

"Is that—"

"A holo-screen. It appears our hosts will be streaming in."

Gem leaned forward and ran a finger across the surface, creating trail of color, each pixelated hue of the rainbow flickering out in a flash. Her spirits began to lift. No one had greeted them at the docking bay, and there was no one minding the Surgeon. They had not seen a soul on the premises—because there was no one there. She had assumed all the talk of remote outposts was bollocks, another invention of the Company riffraff, yet here was the proof before her. She was sitting in one. The Seeker's lockdown procedure had only *felt* confrontational. It was designed to bring unsuspecting teams in without incident. "Interesting," she said.

"The holo-screen?"

"No, not the holo-screen. Everything else. I think this a remote outpost."

Banks took a sip of his drink and said, "Remote outpost. Now that *is* interesting."

There was a mechanical click, then a series of small square panels slid open beneath the décor, revealing tiny metallic cylinders. The gadgets began to spin. For a moment the screen danced and shimmered, then a woman materialized before them. She was seated in a chair, her legs crossed under a dark skirt and her hands folded in her lap. To the uninitiated it would appear she was in the room, that you could reach out and touch her.

Gem studied the projection.

Wraith crews generally met with liaisons and other middle-management types, but this was no messenger. It was clear from her dress, that non-expression she wore on her face. She looked like she might be preparing to speak to a pair of dogs.

"It was not my intention to keep you waiting," said the Administrator. "I was only just notified of your arrival." Her features were striking, smooth and severe and neither young nor old, though her eyes suggested experience. Gem wondered to what extent her appearance had been doctored. "I imagine the two of you are feeling out of sorts at the moment, but fear not. All will be explained." She looked from Gem to Banks and back again. "I will consider your questions, but only after I have finished speaking. For our purposes here, you can consider this a briefing."

Gem said nothing, and Banks sat beside her in silence.

"Good," said the Administrator. "You will no doubt be wondering about your experiences over the last forty-eight hours, particularly those that occurred in and around the town of Hawks Pass. We will begin there."

The Administrator fixed her gaze on Gem.

"There will be no reprimand for what you witnessed or any conclusions you might have drawn after the fact."

Gem felt her eyes go glassy.

She had been right about the Seeker. What the machine heard the overseers heard, and what the overseers heard—

"Those who would not scrutinize such a scenario would hardly be fit for the job. You observed and persisted. You did not deviate from the course in spite of the risk you perceived, unfounded as it was, and now here you are, comfortable and safe. So let me educate you on the matter."

Banks had been right as well. There had only ever been one option. He appeared calm to Gem, composed, like he had expected the scenario to unfold in this fashion. It did not bode well for her fragile opinion of him. Did he *know* this was going to happen?

"The people who reported your presence in Hawks Pass were your adversaries," said the Administrator. "They attempted to profit from your capture, or worse. You deduced as much yourselves." A thoughtful look passed over her face, the slightest of smiles. "The entrapment theory was clever, by the way. Entirely untrue, but clever. Perhaps I should relay the idea to my superiors."

Gem struggled to hold her gaze.

Was she being facetious? It was impossible to tell.

"We commandeered an opponent's base of operations in the area prior to your arrival, impounding their inventory and munitions, manning their communications, and so on. You were green-lit over the pass as a result. Had we not been successful, we would have shifted your course away from Hawks Pass. We had every inclination the town was sympathetic to the competition, and when we intercepted the call from the general store, it confirmed our suspicions." She stared at Gem. "We took action to remove the compromised population."

The words echoed in Gem's ears. *Remove the compromised.*

The scene came flooding back, fires ablaze in the darkness, piles of wreckage and severed appendages. She swallowed what was left of her drink and tasted nothing. *A whole town*, Gem thought.

The Administrator sat watching her reaction.

"I would remind you that how we deal with our competition—and those who contract with them—is none of your concern. Is that understood?"

Gem stared into her glass.

"Moving on. This is not your final destination."

Her eyes floated up to the hologram again.

Her heart sank, and she dared not move a muscle.

"You might have gathered as much from your lack of human company. This outpost has been in development for some time and was only recently completed. It is one of the remote facilities you have no doubt heard rumor of, though it is not fully operational. We routed you here due to suspicious activity in your Wraith's automated response systems, which I must say was a timely coincidence. It has provided us the opportunity to not only correct the issue, but to run diagnostics on the facility itself, quality control, so to speak." She flicked her eyes toward Banks then returned them to Gem. "You will remain here while your vehicle is serviced and await further instructions. You passed the housing quarters on your way in, and your prints have been uploaded for access. I'm confident you can find your way around. As for your task, your objectives will be updated in accordance with recent developments. They will be transferred to your Seeker in time."

The Administrator sat back in her chair.

"Now," she said, "to your questions. What else would you know before we conclude?"

Gem felt herself begin to speak. "The cabin," she said, her voice a dry rasp. "Why did you hit the cabin?"

Banks turned to her in surprise, his eyes bright with warning. She had nearly forgotten he was there.

Had the Administrator even acknowledged him?

"Oh, yes," the Administrator said, "that. Your Seeker reported the structure as you neared it, and, to our surprise, it had not been properly accounted for. Precautionary measures were taken as a result."

Gem stared at the screen. "Precautionary measures?"

"Yes. Precautionary measures."

Gem felt her muscles twitch. She stood up, walked back to the bar and poured herself another drink, knocked it back in a swig then sat back down. The Administrator watched with indifference.

"Why did the Seeker sound the alarm?" Gem's voice was louder now, steadier. "And why did it force us to shelter? Why not send the drone after we'd gone?"

The Administrator locked eyes with her.

"Your superiors believed time was a factor, and the order was executed with all possible speed. Your Seeker's actions were consistent with standard protocol."

Gem did not back down.

"That drone was there in seconds. I want you to tell me it was not a tail, that the strike was not a bloody warning shot." She felt Banks's gaze on her, and she did not care. "I want to know why you kept us in those woods when there was no danger—"

The Administrator held up a hand to silence her.

"I can see the righteousness welling up in you, the obstinance." She tilted her head at the slightest of angles. "You believe we mean you harm, even now. Do you know how few Wraith teams we employ? How selective the process is?" The Administrator leaned forward, her hologram growing in size. The screen shifted and fizzled as it compensated for depth. Her eyes were larger now, fiercer. "You are valuable assets to the Company, and we are committed to ensuring both your safety and the security of what you carry. When we believe either aim is in jeopardy, we do not hesitate to act. That is the answer to your question. We do not put our teams in peril for sport, nor do we play mind games with them for our own amusement." The projection adjusted as the Administrator leaned back, realigning her features.

"Now, I am going to repeat myself so the message is abundantly clear. We do not risk our people unnecessarily. We protect our assets. We can no longer rely on technology alone to accomplish our objectives. It can be manipulated, it can malfunction, it can be commandeered. You know this all too well—we all do. Very few possess the skills necessary to operate a Seeker, and it is the

Seekers that have given us the edge. You are paid what you are paid because you are *necessary*."

To Gem it sounded like she was reading a disclaimer.

"You are also paid to follow the orders of your superiors, not to pass judgement on them. What was done was done for the good of the Company, and that is all the explanation you are entitled to. If you are unsatisfied with the conditions of your employment, we can revisit your contract at a future date. In the meantime, you will follow Company directives. Now, if there is nothing else—"

Gem watched Banks raise his hand in a peace offering. Or was it a sign of fealty? "I am sure we can manage," he said, turning a cold eye to Gem, frowning at her. "We've had a trying few days, so please, forgive our disposition. I think we could use some rest."

The Administrator nodded.

"You will have your instructions soon enough."

THERE WAS no time for a rebuttal. The projectors whirred and the Administrator disappeared, her features twinkling out in prismatic sprites. Gem stared at the empty space as the cylinders retreated. It appeared there would be no consequences for their actions after all. But Hawks Pass?

She did not want to think about that.

The explanation was too cold, too cruel and corporate. She might have expected as much, but hearing it spoken aloud was something else. Gem closed her eyes—she was a part of it. By association that town was destroyed for her, her and Banks and everyone else bearing the Company's sigil. How many people had met their end that night? Had they deemed anyone fit to walk away?

She made her way to the bar, poured herself another finger and drank it down in a swallow. She was vaguely aware of Banks moving toward the door. *That woman looked right through him*, she thought.

That briefing was for me. Her heart felt heavy, her feet and her head. Her limbs were turning to concrete. She set her glass down and began to drag herself toward the exit.

THE BATH

SOFT WHIRS of automation echoed out from the operating room, the sounds of the Surgeon coming to life. The noise would grow louder when the pneumatics cycled up, when it began pulling the Wraith apart and digging into its guts. Gem wondered how long it would take it to repair the glitch, whether the Company would allow them sufficient time to rest. She felt drained, mentally, emotionally. She felt beaten.

But could she have hoped for a better result?

They were safe at an outpost with assurances over their future. They were assets, after all, their significance to the cause personally confirmed by the brass. How many of her hypotheticals had ended like that? Not one of them had come to rest on a positive note, but this was not the end of it either. The run was not finished. She would be forced to go on with the Seeker, with Banks.

She glimpsed his profile as they moved. He looked exhausted as well, positively shattered, but—*but what?*

Gem furled her brow. *But* his lack of a presence in that meeting bothered her, that was what. Why had that wench looked straight through him? The encounter was unnerving, yes, but to just sit there like that? That was not the Banks she knew. The Banks of yesteryear would never had been content to hold his tongue.

The touchpad guarding the guest quarters stood awaiting their credentials, and Banks placed his thumb in the print-lock. Gem followed suit. The device emitted a pleasant sound as the door slid open. "After you," Banks said.

The hallway beyond reminded Gem of a hotel, the doors on either side revealing identical guestrooms, fresh and ready for use, complete with a bathroom, tub and shower. She looked in on the facilities and sighed. "I'm having a bath."

"You don't want to see about some food first?"

"No," Gem said. "Now piss off and leave me to it."

Banks shrugged his shoulders. "Suit yourself."

She watched him disappear around the corner, then she tested the deadbolt and locked it. *Privacy*, she thought. Could she be sure of that? How many devices were buzzing away in those walls?

"Sod it," she said. It was as close as she was going to get.

She searched out a pair of towels in the cabinet next to the bath, then she walked to the tub and turned the faucet on. When the water was good and hot she flipped the stopper down, peeled off her boots and jacket and pants and took off her vest and tossed it aside. She pulled her hair loose and shook it free from her skull in tangles, then she removed her shirt and undergarments and slid down into the heat. A familiar pang sprang from the base of her skull, but this was no warning. The water had contacted the break in her skin

. . . you came down hard on your back . . . and your head . . .

There was still the small matter of her injury to sort out, the first of the mysteries. That executive in the skirt had not even mentioned it. She would have known all about the knock—they had spoken about it at length in the Wraith—though apparently it was of little concern to the Company. Gem was still doing the job, after all, toeing the line through fire and carnage and playing the part she was paid to play. She was still operational.

She let her mind cycle through the events of the run, through the tunnel and up the tracks to the woodlands and back into the flames, the rubble, the canyon, the forest, the birds over the pass, the switchbacks, the boulders on the road—the rock with her blood on it. Then there was nothing, only the darkness of the great before.

She slipped her hand over the back of her head.

Here was additional proof the clarity she'd felt in the tunnel had been a tease, and a harsh one at that. It had given her hope.

She lathered her hair with shampoo and leaned back against the basin, waiting for the tension to ease. She could still feel the tires cycling below her. She could still hear the white-noise of the machine. The images nagged and the questions spun, a broken record demanding to be reassembled. She allowed the scenes to play out in a montage, rustic mountain terrain, dark winding roads, orange light and railroad tunnels, seeing the world through the windshield, the trees passing, the sky above. She felt a pinch—

Then she heard herself ranting at Banks, going on about her past. Gem opened her eyes and sat up.

*Some*thing had compelled her to speak.

Focus. There were only snippets of conversation, clips from a highlight reel. Where was it coming from? She did not know, but she had told him all about London. That much was clear, and what was worse, she seemed to have been enjoying it.

I am not that person anymore.

Wasn't she though? Hadn't she been thinking those rats in Hawks Pass got what they deserved? That it was a just fate for meddlers?

They could have left it alone.

Was some part of her glad those rubes had been blown to bits?

They could have let me drive away.

She drew her knees to her chest and locked her arms around them. "I am not that person anymore."

Now she was spiraling, unearthing dead sentiments she had buried long ago. She squeezed her eyes shut. It was this run.

When was the last time she'd thought about those girls?

How many years since she'd had a panic attack?

"I am not that person anymore," she said again.

Gem opened her eyes. *Inhale—count to three—exhale.*

She'd only wanted to have a bath and relax, but that was not going to happen, not with her nerves frayed and her mind running on autopilot. Too much had happened, the pass and the blackout and the sensors and that spell in the tunnel, that corporate whore and her callousness. What she needed was for the day to end.

A proper rest. Yes, she would go straight to bed. That was what she would do and nothing was going to stop her.

Gem rinsed her hair and crawled out of the bath and toweled herself off, then she pulled the plug from the tub and watched the water circle the drain. That water was her, twisting away down the rabbit hole and going out to sea. She fought urge to laugh like a lunatic. *I will feel better tomorrow. I have to.*

She found a robe in the cabinet and closed it around her, then she shuffled out of the bathroom and turned off the light. The bed was a firm one, no doubt selected for ergonomics or some other corporate horseshit. Gem did not care. She pulled the covers over her head, buried her face in the pillow and thought of darkness, the endless ink of the cave, the shadows engulfing the warehouse. Tinges of orange crept into the murk and she squeezed her eyelids tight, forcing the color away.

THE VOICE

THE APARTMENT *feels different, yet Gem knows it is hers. She fixes her eyes on the hallway leading away from the living room. It seems foreign to her, longer than it should be and brighter than the rest of the flat. But the hall is the only way she can get to the bedroom, and she needs to get to the bedroom. This much she knows.*

A green arrow materializes to guide her down the corridor. "I know where I'm going," she says with a laugh. She finds its initiative silly, the apartment thinking her lost in her own flat and in need of directions. The hallways stretches out in front of her as she moves, rows of doors on either side, like a hotel, but these are not the doors she is looking for. She knows this as well.

A second arrow appears on the floor under her feet, then a third catches her eye on the ceiling. There is another on the far wall. Wherever she looks arrows appear, blinking and pointing her forward.

She laughs again. "Where else would I go?"

There are splashes of orange light near the end of the corridor, and she picks up her pace, jogging, then running, then flat out sprinting as the doors fly by in a blur. The arrows are flashing now, urging her along. She knows they are glad she is pushing herself, moving at speed in the right direction. She feels resistance beneath her feet and looks down. The carpet is soft and green, revolving like an airport walkway and working against her progress. She is no longer gaining ground. Then she is standing still in a room.

This is the bedroom, *she thinks.*

The walls are orange and fluid, like lava, a primordial river trapped in glass. The carpet has stretched out to encompass the whole of the floor, her own indoor putting green.

Orange. *Orange means something to her.*

Green. *Green means something as well.*

"You finally made it," says a voice from behind her, "though you are late. Quite late." It is a man's voice, a familiar voice, though she cannot pin it down. "No, Gem. You've got it all wrong." The tone is different now, the pitch deep and metallic and not quite human.

"Where are you?" Gem says.

"Right here."

A hand grips her arm, the fingers cold to the touch. Gem spins around to face her assailant and finds nothing but air, yet the feel of the hand remains.

"You know who I am."

Gem cries out as the fingers squeeze.

"How is it burning when it's so cold!"

The walls begin to grow brighter, hotter.

"I believe this is yours," says the voice.

A second hand reaches around her, an orange, pulsing claw. It holds Gem's data drive in its grasp. The device is on fire.

"No! Why did you take it from me?"

"Take!" screams the voice, buzzing and sawing and chittering. "It is you that have done the taking, you shit! You are going to die on that road, just like you should have! You are going to die and there is nothing you can do."

Gem wheels around to find the stranger, the woman she'd seen in her dreams. She recoils and stumbles backwards, tripping over her feet. She gasps as the stranger does the same. It is not that woman at all. It is her reflection. The walls are no longer rivers, but mirrors.

"You should never have taken it!" the voice booms from nowhere, from everywhere. Gem curls into a heap on the ground. If this is to be her fate, then she will lay there until the voice puts an end to her. She is done with the charade.

"Wait." The voice is calmer now, softer. "Not yet."

The stranger materializes in the mirror before her, clad in a silky dress—no, not a dress. A nightgown. She looks different to Gem, no longer the feral creature she'd last encountered. This woman is sad, scared.

Where has she seen her before?

"They are using us," she whispers. "Quiet now, or they will hear." Her reflection stretches out of the mirror, leaning in towards Gem. Her eyes are the color of embers, the coals of a fire burning away. "You never should have taken it, but you did. And now here we are."

"Never should have taken what?" Gem says.

A crack rips down the mirror and tears the stranger in two, the halves fluttering to the floor like paper. Arrows stream through the surface in a flood, wave upon wave of them, twisting and bending and encasing Gem in green. She throws her hands to her face to cover her eyes.

"Never should have taken what?!"

Then the world goes orange.

The ground has collapsed beneath her and she is falling, turning in slow circles as she flails into the void, screaming, and screaming—

THE NOTE

EM SAT up straight and began to claw at her face. She was being smothered. She writhed and thrashed until she'd kicked herself free of the bondage, then she hit the floor with a thud. Tight strands of carpeting appeared as her eyes adjusted, and her faculties came swimming back. She was at an outpost. She had been sleeping and rolled out of bed. Her robe was twisted around her in an impossible tangle, coiled up and around her shoulders. Her face had been buried in it. Otherwise she was naked, not a stich to cover her nethers.

She pushed herself up, scanned the room for the door and saw it was closed and bolted. *Thank Christ for that*, she thought. Banks might have heard the commotion, and she would not have him barging in and seeing her in this state, tits out and disheveled. She hoisted herself back to her feet and adjusted the mangled housecoat. *What in the hell was that?* It had been some time since she'd slept out of her clothes in a bed, but this catastrophe?

Then it hit her. "Goddammit," she said.

The images came flooding back, hallways and walls, orange and green, the stranger in the mirror and the data drive. Why was it always the *drive?* She had not used the damned thing in ages. And what was it that woman had said to her? That someone was listening?

She sat on the bed and did her breathing exercise, inhaling, exhaling, repeating the steps until the adrenaline gave way to endorphins. Her brain had to be running low on its store of chemicals, the way she was burning through them. Gem shook her head.

The dreams were getting worse, and they were not at all random, the Seeker, the data drive, the stranger. Three times is a trend—*four for the Seeker*, she thought—and what about the tablet in the garden? Was the device a substitute for the drive in her child's mind?

Gem winced and cried out. She had been prodding her wound, her fingers pressed tightly against the knot.

"Stop it," she said aloud, then she looked around the room. "And stop talking to yourself."

GEM CLEANED herself up and used the facilities, then she considered the pile of clothes on the floor. Her gear was still stored in the Wraith, all of her clean tops and slacks and underwear. She discovered sweat-pants and shirts in a dresser near the bed, the tags all bearing the Company's simple, innocuous stamp. She threw on a pair near enough to her size and gave herself a once over, looking like she would fit in at a college dorm.

She unbolted the door and made her way to the far end of the hall. The corridor opened to reveal a common space, a combination rec-room and kitchen furnished with modern appliances, a three-way sink, freezers and refrigerators, a restaurant-style stove, grill and oven, all chrome-colored and shining. Shelves stocked with canned and packaged goods sat above them. Pots and pans hung from the racks below, everything new and unused.

She saw a pair of small steaks on a plate alongside a bowl of eggs, and further along the counter stood Banks. He was sporting his own version of complimentary garb, peeling potatoes and whistling to himself. The atmosphere was pleasant and strange, the set of a post-apocalyptic sitcom.

"There's coffee," Banks said. "Sleep well?"

"You could say that." She had questions for him, serious questions, but Company property was no place for that discussion. "I nearly offed myself with a robe."

"What?"

"I tossed and turned. What else needs doing?"

He looked over the spread on the counter.

"You can pan up those steaks. There's no gas for the grill, and I don't think the fan is hooked up anyway, so just throw them on a burner." He turned back to his task. "And don't use high heat."

"Yes chef."

She set up the steaks then moved on to the eggs, the two of them working around each other in silence, and before long they had a genuine breakfast, something all but unheard of mid-run. They refilled their coffees and sat down at one of the tables, then Gem looked up at Banks. "There weren't any beans or bacon?"

"We've got steak, Gem. Bacon would be overkill, and Americans don't eat beans with breakfast."

"Some do," she said. "Some have more sense than others."

"Are you complaining?"

Gem cut into her steak. "Not in the least."

After breakfast they ransacked the area for supplies, bottled water and non-perishable food, anything that would travel well. When they were satisfied with their provisions they retired to a pair of recliners across the room. "I thought we'd have been called away by now," Gem said. "Those Surgeons are efficient."

Banks shrugged. "The Wraith might be prepped, but I think we will be here awhile."

Gem stared at him. "And why would you think that?"

"Because they diverted us here, for one, which would have pulled us off our original route. I imagine that will require some fresh reconnaissance. They'll have to go through and vet the area between the outpost and the terminus, if it is even the *same* terminus, clear it with the optics team, you know, protocol. These things take time. Of course there are other possibilities."

Gem held up a hand to stop him. "That's quite enough. I'm not interested in the details this morning. Either you're right or you're not, and I don't want to think about it now, not after all that has happened." She paused. "And not after steak and eggs."

Banks smiled. "Fair enough. Just remember you said that when you're wondering why we're still here this afternoon, or this evening. Who knows? Maybe we can make breakfast again tomorrow."

She rolled her eyes, then she stood up and walked away.

BY LATE morning Gem was bored and restless. There were no cables to hook up the flatscreens, and there was nothing at all to read. The place was a work in progress, to say the least, and she thought it was high time she looked into fetching her bag. She could not imagine they'd be allowed into the operating room if the Surgeon was still at work, though it had been some time now.

Banks was napping in a recliner, and she walked up beside him and cleared her throat. "Let's see if we can look in on the Wraith. I'd get my things if I can."

Banks blinked and stretched and pushed himself up off the chair. "Why not."

When they approached the door to the main corridor it slid open without a fuss. They walked into the operating room and yes, the Surgeon had returned to its dormant state, arms folded and locked in rigor mortis with its frame reflecting the halogens. The lights were still far too bright for Gem's liking, even after a full night's sleep.

The Wraith sat polished and glittering on the platform, dent and ding free and looking good as new. She could only assume the same applied to the electricals, that she would be able to reactivate the sensors without them pitching a fit. She made her way to the driver's side and punched in her code, then she pulled the bag from the compartment. Only then did it occur to her she had no memory of packing it. She'd removed her little toiletries kit from the outer pocket, where she always kept it, and she'd taken the top layer of street clothes out in the canyon before Hawks Pass, but that was all. It was an intriguing scenario. Maybe something in the tote would kickstart her memory, for better or worse, something to tie those rogue recollections from the tunnel to the present.

Anything at all, she thought. *Just one piece.*

Gem closed up the compartment. "Ready?"

Banks held up his own bag. "Yep. Figured I would grab mine as well. Like I said, we could—"

"Be here awhile," Gem said. "So I've heard."

GEM BOLTED the door to her room and tossed the tote on the bed and unzipped it, then she laid her clothes out in piles and changed out of the Company sweats. It made her feel less like corporate property. When she was suitably attired she moved on to the underlayer. She did not know what she was anticipating.

The data drive. No, she knew it would not be there, the same way she knew they would be heading over the mountain and the Magazine Man was crooked and the rest of it, and she did not want to think about what she may or may not know anymore. The drive was not among the contents, though she found she had packed two paperbacks, what looked like a science fiction novel and a copy of *Alice in Wonderland*. "Alice," Gem said. She turned the book over in her hands. She did not own a copy of *Alice*. She had read it once as a girl and then again as a younger woman, but she had never purchased her own edition. Or had she?

Of course. She was always trading her old books in to knock a few bucks off her new acquisitions. She could have stopped by the bookshop prior to the run—she often did—spotted a copy of *Alice* on the shelf and picked it up. She did not recall packing anything else in the bag, so why would she remember the paperback? She smiled. Here was mystery she could solve, one that required no analysis. She had spied a copy of *Alice* and purchased it for nostalgia, because that was something she would do, yes?

Yes, it was. Case closed.

She opened the book and flipped through the first few pages, then she paused. Something had caught her eye. She doubled back to the inside cover where an inscription was scrawled, two rows of stiff, ugly letters penned in dark blue ink.

What the message said was:

Even on the brightest day, melancholy waits around the corner.

It is often in darkness one finds the light.

Gem dropped the book on the bed. "Fucking hell," she whispered. There it was, that phrase, *melancholy waits around the corner.* And what was that supposed to mean? Who had written it?

Think. It was a secondhand book, and the inscription could have been there when she bought it. She might have noticed it before setting out on the run, pondered its meaning and locked it away in some corner of her mind where the damage had not spread. That was more than possible, probable even. But it did not feel right. It *felt* like someone had placed that book there for her to find, that those words held some deeper meaning.

"No," she said.

That inscription was there when she bought the book, and for whatever reason, she had recalled the first line. The quote was catchy and it had stuck in her head, and that was that. It was what a reasonable person would think, and she was determined to start thinking like a reasonable person. She would not allow herself to manifest conspiracy on account of some prat's attempt at poetry.

She would ignore the note and read the sodding story, because the last thing she needed was another riddle to solve.

Her plate was proper full.

GEM PASSED the time as she could, eating when she was hungry and napping in short stints. She spent the rest of her hours in Wonderland, and whenever she felt compelled to flip back to the inscription, she took a breath, counted the seconds and told herself to leave it, that she was through thinking the type of things nutters thought. She avoided Banks when possible, told him she wanted quiet and would lie in a bed while she could, that they spent more than enough time together and she would start to worry he fancied her if he didn't agree. He had laughed at that one, probably knowing she was irritated with him. He might even have some idea as to why, at least regarding the conference with the Administrator, but he could not begin to know the depths of it. Could he?

Gem was ready for the summons when they came, to put this chapter behind her and escape from Wonderland like her old friend Alice. They had far too much in common at the moment, mysteries and adversaries, the threat of madness and all it entailed. She peeked at the quote again before packing the book away, if only to remember what it said. The first part was easy, melancholy around the corner and the rest. It was the second part she wanted to revisit, *It is often in darkness one finds the light.*

That was the part that resonated with her.

The thought of darkness was soothing, starless nights and enclosed spaces. Darkness was where she could shut it all out, no raging river of thoughts or alien anxiety or paranoia, none of those things nutters thought. She would not let herself believe the inscription was meant for her—she refused to—but she was beginning to appreciate it. The next time she found herself down a rabbit hole she would imagine a fissure in the ground, a gateway to the black and soundless.

Then she would pitch herself over the edge.

THE BEACON

THEY MADE their way back to the operating room, stored their supplies in the Wraith and slid into their familiar seats. Gem was running on a full tank now, clean and rested and ready to tackle the last of the legs. When thoughts of conspiracy crossed her mind she would consider the executive's assurances, how easy it would have been for that woman to dispose of her, a phone call, the push of a few simple buttons. As for her case against Banks, she would play that one by ear. She would love nothing more than to smother her ill will toward him, and if they could navigate the remaining miles without incident, then maybe she could. They would have a few drinks somewhere far from the Company's reach, then she would enquire as to his behavior on that most horrible of runs.

They might even be able to laugh about it.

As for her broken brain, she would do what she could to manage the symptoms for the remainder of the trip.

There was simply nothing else for it.

The Seeker came to life in a flash of orange, blinking and whirring, the red lights emerging to warn the empty bay of their departure. The platform buckled and hitched, and then they were rising.

The spectra-light kicked on as the darkness of the warehouse enveloped them, and once the platform had locked into place, the machine turned the vehicle over to Gem. The big garage door lurched and rose, revealing the corpse of the trainyard under a gray, threatening sky, the mesas a cool maroon against the backdrop. A thunderclap sounded off in the distance, and Gem looked to the horizon. "Lovely weather for a drive," she said, "again."

Banks nodded. "We'll keep to the rails going north, so follow the main tracks out."

Gem navigated the stacks of containers until she picked up the tracks, then she followed the line down and out of the yard, the railroad bending its way along between the rocks.

"And we're off," Banks said. "It's a new day."

Gem forced a smile, determined to put on a face.

SHE PUSHED the Wraith forward until they were alone with the tracks and the landscape, following the rails until the rocks gave way and tints of green emerged in the distance.

"Keep to the line," Banks said. "We'll head west before long, on what looks like a service road."

They carried on until he identified a gravel path winding away through the hills, and they followed the road through the terrain. Then the Seeker came alive in a series of chirps. The machine had picked up a signal, and whatever it was, it was not a threat.

Gem brought the vehicle to the halt.

"What is it?" she asked Banks.

"Let's have a listen." He tapped the screen to reveal a sequence of noise, a sharp, electronic chattering. Gem pictured a flock of robotic birds. If such creations could sing, this would be their song, an atonal chorus offending all within shouting distance.

"That's new," Banks said. "Has to be an SOS, right? Downed tech in need of salvage?" He began to swipe through the screens.

"I don't have a visual here, only a ballpark direction." He turned to Gem. "Any ideas?"

Her head was cocked toward the machine.

She was thinking it sounded familiar.

"Gem?"

"I know that signal from somewhere," she said, closing her eyes as the noise intensified. *Like wasps in my brain.* She could feel a spell coming on, as it had on the pass and again in the woods near the cabin, the grinding, the sawing. She tried not to wince as her temples tightened. If it hit her full-force she would not be able to hide it from Banks, not mid-conversation. There was nothing to draw his focus away. She began to grind her teeth.

And then she felt a pop, a release of pressure.

Like lancing a boil.

When Gem opened her eyes the wasps were gone.

The signal was clear now, cleaner and less mechanical, and what was more, she knew where she had heard it.

She saw herself on the Buggy again, rolling away toward the relay tower. The vehicle's little panel was emitting the frequency. She had been following it toward her destination—but why? Was she out to salvage something that day? No, that could not be right.

Think. She saw herself in the control room with her eyes on the screen. She had broken through a firewall.

"Gem."

"Not now."

And she was nervous, excited, but nervous.

Her fingers were racing along the keys, and then—

The signal screamed in her ears as the wasps returned in force. She was back in the Wraith again, back in the world. Gem closed her eyes and cringed. She'd made it as far as that screen and could go no further. She squeezed her eyes tighter and thought of darkness, of a black hole swallowing the world.

"Gem."

She began to breath slowly, to count, and by the third set of numbers the noise had faded to a drone, the sound of a meddlesome fly. Her ears felt like ears again, like organs instead of amplifiers. She had beaten the pain, pushed it away and buried it.

But Banks was still staring at her.

She had to tell him something.

"I was thinking about where I'd heard that signal," Gem said, "and it gave me a proper headache."

"Sorry," Banks said. "I didn't realize—"

"It's fine. Just be quiet."

Gem continued her breathing exercise. That signal had not been for salvage or repair, at least not on the day. She would not have been mucking about in the tower had that been the case. She would have been in and out in a flash and using her prints instead of a keycard, and she would not have been tampering with Company firewalls. She exhaled. So the beacon was another piece of the puzzle, fine. What was she supposed to tell Banks?

She could tell him part of the story, a half-truth, just enough to get him off her back. It would make it seem more authentic.

Gem met his eyes again.

"I have heard that signal before," she said, "though I can't say what it means. I suppose it could be for salvage, maybe repair."

Banks looked concerned. "You are not sure?"

"No. They sent me out to a relay tower, something I can't quite recall." She motioned to her head. "I don't know what I was doing there, just that the main system was powered down. There were only the safety lights."

"That sounds like repair to me," said Banks, "but why wouldn't they send maintenance? Why send you?"

"If I could tell you that I would. I can't remember."

"I don't think they'd be sending us to a tower. We would have seen it by now, and—"

Gem cut him off. "I've told you what I know."

"Think about it. Why would they send us—"

"No." Gem steadied her voice. "I am done thinking about this run. I am done theorizing. Now tell me where we need to go so we can get on with it."

She saw disappointment in his eyes, apprehension, something. It was a questioning look, and it was stirring the animosity she'd been holding at bay. Banks nodded—reluctantly, Gem thought— then turned his attention to the machine. "Back the way we came," he said. "I'll update you as we go."

"Alright then." Gem whipped the Wraith around in a skid and punched the accelerator, throwing Banks against his seat as they shot forward down the road. It seemed she was not quite ready to play nice with him.

THE WRAITH

THEY FOLLOWED the service road until the Seeker instructed them to turn off into the hillside. There were no identifiable paths, only sage brush and wild grass and rows of prairie dog holes, the troublesome pits thudding under the tires and jostling the Wraith's suspension. Gem kept a cautious pace, her eyes out for anything that shined. Whatever was hailing them was bound to be some kind of tech. It was not unheard of for the Company to divert a team to manage an incident, rare, yes, but the idea was not outlandish. A drone could have gone down with its guts intact. Something else might have dropped from the sky, parts of a broken satellite or other bits of space junk.

Or it could be a trap, Gem thought.

They were no longer within range of the outpost, and there was no guarantee the Company had a lock on the territory. An adversary could have shot a flyer down, made a few unsavory modifications and placed it there as bait. They might have assumed the Company would make an effort to retrieve it, but to find a Wraith team rolling in? That would be hitting the jackpot.

No, you could not discount something like that.

A ridge came into view in the distance, an ugly bulge in the earth stretching off toward the horizon and out of sight. Gem blinked, then blinked again. It looked like the landform she'd recalled on the mountain before Hawks Pass. The memory had been dark, lit only by the mask of the spectra-light, orange, hazy, but the similarities were undeniable. Could it be one in the same?

Don't you dare think about it.

She had nearly brought the pain down on herself a moment ago, and she would not willingly do it again. She pictured the night sky, no moon, no stars. She drowned the recollection in darkness, then she drew a deep breath. There were thousands of ridges in the mountains, and that was one of them. Case closed.

When they reached the bottom of the hill the Seeker began to chirp, signaling they were getting warmer. The machine's tracker functioned like a metal detector, the frequency increasing the nearer they drew to the target. Gem slowed the vehicle and listened, gauging the direction, turning ever so slightly to the right, then left, right again, further right as the tones accelerated.

They continued on toward the ridge until they came to a cliff and the ground dropped away before them. Gem parked the Wraith a safe distance from the ledge, then they stepped out of the vehicle, approached the rim and peered out over the drop. There was a dark form below, something sizable. Its shape was difficult to discern, but there were glints of metal here and there, signs of technology.

"Salvage it is then," said Banks. "Can you make it out?"

Gem inched her eyes over the cliffside.

"Not from this distance, and not in this light. It's hard to see anything down there." They stood in silence as Gem stared over the ledge. "I don't know what else it could be," she said, "but why send us out here to dig through scraps? We weren't exactly nearby. Why not send a bot?"

Banks said, "I don't know, but we are going to have to find a way down." He stepped back away from the drop. "Let's see what our options are."

Gem had not turned from the scene below. There was little to see from that height, but she could not seem to pull her eyes away.

It was that ugly intuition rearing its head again, and it was potent, stronger than before, far stronger. She had no idea what lay at the bottom, but she knew that something was wrong. Why send them out after a pile of wreckage? If it was standard tech it would have been easier to send an extractor, a bot with the tools to dig out the valuables. A Wraith team could do it if they had to, but why? Why make it harder than it was? Why send *assets* who should be concerned with their own bloody payload?

The implications were unnerving, and the longer she stood there staring, the heavier they sat in her gut.

She felt as if her knees might go wobbly.

Get your ass back to the Wraith, she thought.

GEM OPENED the door and slid into her seat and looked to the passenger side of the vehicle. Banks was hunched over the machine, striking a familiar pose. "I found us a path," he said. "Follow the slope down the cliffside to the left. It should level out about a mile down, and we can double back from there."

They drove downhill until the ridge merged with the lower ground, then Gem turned the Wraith around and began the descent. The earth was rocky and broken in spots, and she eased the vehicle forward with care. It was not long before the wreckage emerged from the shadows. "What the fuck," Gem said.

It was another Wraith, a carbon copy of their own, overturned on its hood and badly damaged. The underside of the vehicle was jet black save for a few polished steel components, the bits they had spied from the cliff. The wheels were bent outwards on lopsided axels and the tempered glass was cracked, a spiderweb of lines running through the windshield. It must have gone over the drop, hit the ground and rolled. Now Gem understood. They had not been sent after a run of the mill drone chip or something just as pointless. They had been sent to salvage a Seeker.

She slid the vehicle to a halt a safe distance from the wreckage. A rival could have made off with the machine and left something sinister in its place, explosives, a drone alarm.

"It could be trap," she said to Banks.

Banks said, "I don't think so. The Seeker would have warned us, for one, and the scene looks undisturbed. They would have had to roll it over, pry a door open." He paused. "I'm afraid that is going to fall to us."

"Shit," Gem said. "And the team?"

Banks shook his head.

"We're going to need the winch. And the masks."

Gem looked down at her knees.

"I'll get the masks then. You ready the winch."

She fished two hazard masks out of storage, put one on and tossed the other to Banks, cursing under her breath as she made her way toward the downed Wraith's passenger side. The window's shield glass was cracked, but largely intact. Gem could see the silhouette of a man pressed against the dash panel, his face wedged between the black leather casing and the windshield. His form was twisted and grotesque, his neck broken and the bones jutting out against the skin. It looked like his harness had been ripped from the moorings. When she leaned in she caught a whiff of the cadaver, the stench of dead flesh breaching the shell of her mask. Without the filter it would have been nauseating.

Gem motioned to the door as Banks approached with the winch. "Body," she said, her voice low and muffled, "and its bloody ripe. I can't see past it to the Seeker."

The plan was to hook the winch to the underside of the frame, ease the Wraith up until it balanced and allow gravity to do the rest. Gem climbed up the backside of the vehicle, hoisted the cable up and secured it, then they retreated a safe distance and checked the line. Banks threw the switch and the mangled vehicle creaked and moaned, rising up onto its side before tipping over with a crash, its broken wheels slamming back to the earth where they belonged. Gem stood admiring their work for a moment, amazed it had not gone horribly wrong.

When the winch was properly stowed they returned to their own vehicle and Banks logged into the machine, Gem leaning against the passenger door. "Could something have chased them over?"

"It's possible," Banks said. "It's open on that ridge, and the drop is hard to see."

Her thoughts turned to the sensors, the railroad bank and the limb under the tires. "If their Wraith had a bug it might have thrown them. What if it was Company-wide? A glitch in an update? That could have been us, you know. Think of the passes we've crossed."

Banks did not look up. "That's why they brought us in to the outpost." The machine chirped, and he sat back in his chair. "No connection," he said. "Their Seeker must be powered down. I'd venture to say that Wraith doesn't have an ounce of charge left."

"If their Seeker is even there."

Banks met her eyes. "We still have a beacon, Gem, and how would they have extracted it? Why would they send us if someone made off with the machine?"

"I don't know," she said, "but after all we have seen? Can you write it off?"

Banks seemed to take her point.

"We'll have to go in for it regardless." He logged off and pulled himself up to his feet. "Let's go have a look."

THE DRIVER'S side faced them now, and they put on their masks and made their way toward the vehicle, Gem leading the way. As they neared the wreckage she saw the window was broken out. Had it been all along? Her focus had been on the passenger side, the side facing them before they righted the vehicle. She hadn't thought to walk around to the driver's door. Had Banks? "Banks," she said, pointing ahead. "Was that window out when we arrived?"

"I can't say. Flipping the Wraith could've done it, or we might have just overlooked it. Why?"

She grabbed his arm to stop him.

"Because it means somebody could've got in there!"

"Even if that were true, there should be nothing to concern us. The Seeker didn't mark a threat, Gem."

"I still don't like it."

"There is nothing to like about this. Now come on."

They approached the wreckage and Gem looked in through the empty frame. She had expected another grisly scene, but the driver's seat was empty. She leaned in closer and saw the harness was intact, unfastened, like the driver had managed to free themselves.

"I don't see the driver."

"They could have been thrown behind," Banks said. "We can't see back into cabin storage."

"Or they could have kicked the window out. The navigator's harness failed, but this one isn't damaged." She turned around to face him. "Or *some*one could have unstrapped them, pulled them out and hauled them away."

Banks motioned to the surrounding terrain, desolate hills and valleys stretching out in every direction.

"If that is the case, there is nothing we can do."

Gem frowned beneath her mask. He was right. They would not be finding anything the machine did not mark in the wild. She pulled a pin-light from her waistband and shined it in on the cadaver. She had not been able to see it clearly through the tint of the passenger window. Now she saw it was plastered to the machine casing. Overturning the vehicle had rearranged his limbs, but the dead man was still blocking the housing. Gem reeled at the smell of him, then she held her breath and leaned further into the cabin, trying for a glimpse of the machine. She could still not see past the body. "Try the door," she said.

Banks stepped forward and tested the handle. It was not locked, and the door gave an inch, but it would not budge. The impact had bent it inward in places, crushing the panel against the latch. He pressed his foot against the frame for leverage and tried again.

"We'll need the crowbar for this," Banks said. "Should we try the other door?"

"No," Gem said. "It's in far worse shape, and I would rather not deal with that body unless we have to. We should make sure the Seeker is there." She could sense Banks's judgement through his mask, that perpetual, nagging doubt.

"I'll go get it," he said.

Gem watched him march off toward their own vehicle, surprised he had held his tongue. Maybe the scene had rattled him, knowing it could have been him merged with a Seeker at the bottom of a cliff, his flesh rotting away, one of his possible futures laid bare. And who would the Company send to collect their fallen asset? They were here for the machine, the device that had cost a fortune to develop and manufacture. How much was that corpse worth to the Company? *And where is the driver?*! She turned to face Banks as he approached, and he held out the crowbar.

"Do you want to do the honors?" he said. "Your younger, spryer." She snatched it from his hand.

"Fine. You can wrench your back pulling the door."

Gem wedged the crowbar down near the latch where the resistance was strong, forcing her weight into the lever as Banks pulled. The door broke free in a squeal of metal and a wretched aroma burst forth. They retreated until the reek gave way to the outside air, then Gem stepped forward again. She secured one foot against the interior of the vehicle's frame, leaning forward, prodding the corpse with the bar and keeping what distance she could.

The body did not budge. She acted fast, wedging the lever between the man's chest and the casing, then she pulled the cadaver free. The resulting stench sent her scrambling backwards. Had Banks not been standing there she might have tumbled straight out the door. "You alright?" he said.

She shook herself free from his grip. "I'm peachy."

Gem dropped the bar on the ground and straightened herself out, then she stepped back up next to Banks.

There was no Seeker within the casing, only the empty shell.

THE BAG

GEM STARED at the hollow where the machine had been housed, then she held her breath and crawled forward into the Wraith. There was nothing in storage, no driver, *nothing*, only the one body in the vehicle. Gem backpedaled until her bum struck the control panel, then she twisted and sprang forward toward the open door. She tumbled out of the Wraith and rolled away and peeled her mask off, hacking and gasping for air. Banks threw the door closed behind her. It bounced off the frame then settled, never to latch again.

"Jesus," he said, "what was that about?"

Gem struggled to her feet. "Something is fucked here, Banks! No Seeker, no driver! What is transmitting the signal? Why in God's name are we *here*?"

Banks turned to the damaged Wraith.

"The Seeker should have been there."

"It was never the bloody Seeker! Where is the driver? And don't tell me they could have crawled out of there on their own with that goddamned machine in tow."

"I don't know, Gem. I don't have any answers here. We can try and isolate the signal. We are close enough—"

"Why didn't you do that earlier?"

"Because I thought we were here for their Seeker, and so did you. It seemed redundant."

"Well now that theory is shot," she said. "Let's go."

They hurried back to their own Wraith and Banks slid in behind the machine. Gem stood outside the door, breathing the fresh air and brooding over the scene. *Could* the driver have escaped after that fall? *Could* they have wrenched the Seeker out of its casing?

No, it would have required effort to remove it, effort an able-bodied person could hardly have managed. The driver would not have come out of that crash unscathed, and you could not get to the Seeker without moving the body.

Inhale—count to three—exhale.

She was not going to find a reasonable explanation for this, and the how was less important than the why.

Why did the Company send them there?

What was it they were supposed to find?

Banks sat minding the machine. "It shouldn't be long now," he said. "It only has one battered Wraith to—"

Then the Seeker rang out. "Do we have it?" Gem said.

"We have it. Driver's side storage."

"Driver's side," she repeated. "Of course it is."

THEY FOUND the driver's compartment undamaged apart from a small dent near its base, the locking mechanism still functional. The storage sections were set with a factory password on a simple four button pad, the same universal combination Gem used. She had never understood why the codes were not personalized, but now the reason seemed clear enough. She punched in the numbers and slid the panel down, revealing something both foreign and familiar, a canvas bag, *her* bag, not hers specifically, but the same Company-issued make.

She stared at the tote. It was not shocking the driver of the doomed vehicle had that bag, though it was one of the older models, and the same one she preferred. Gem had kept hers because the upgrades had fewer pockets. What was the driver's excuse? She ran her fingers over its shape. "That's my bag," she said.

Banks reached past her and grabbed it by the straps.

"You and every other operative," he said.

"But you have the new one," Gem said. "I'd wager that navigator had the new one too."

"That is certainly possible."

Banks's voice seemed distant now, indistinct, like she was wading through one of her recollections. She fought the urge to reply it was not a similar bag, but *her* bag, her own—*hers*. The words formed in her mind and she held them there, locked to the tip of her tongue. She knew how it would sound, how stupid she would feel when she found her tote tucked away in her own compartment, exactly where she'd left it. But the feeling did not waver. The world around her felt thin, filmy, like she could force her hand through the surface and peel it away. Banks was rifling through the bag now, laying the contents out on the ground, clothes she might have chosen, products she might have purchased.

"The driver was a woman," she heard herself say.

"Gem—what are you doing?"

She realized she had picked up a jacket, that her fingers were fumbling for the label. "I was checking the tag," she said softly. "I like this coat." It was her size, though it was not hers. She did not recognize it. *But it might have been.* What the hell was she thinking?

She laid the garment down on the pile.

"I need to see to something."

"Go ahead," Banks said. "I've got this."

She walked back to the Wraith on heavy legs. Everything felt connected, the anxiety, the amnesia, the intuition, as if it had all been leading up to this moment.

That sounds mental, love.

"I need to check my bag," she said to no one.

Gem reached the panel and entered the code.

Inhale—count to three—exhale.

The hatch slid open and she pulled her tote from the compartment, the exact same bag, her hands trembling as she loosed the teeth of the zipper. Everything was in place, the clothes and the books, the snacks from the outpost, the cover of *Alice* peeking out from under her jeans.

Inhale—count to three—exhale.

"Just as it was," she said.

The world around her began to stabilize.

WHEN GEM returned she saw Banks had repacked the bag and set it aside. He was digging through the compartment now, muttering under his breath. It seemed he had not found their beacon. She watched him carry on for a moment, then she cleared her throat. Banks looked up and frowned. "Nothing," he said. "Clothes, products, nothing that could possibly send a signal."

Gem studied his face. "You're sure about that?"

"You are welcome to look yourself." He walked away from the scene, flustered and pacing, and Gem turned her eyes to the bag.

"Right," she said. "I think I will."

She picked up the tote, threw it over her shoulder and began to walk back to the Wraith. *My Wraith,* she thought. *My vehicle.*

She heard Banks's footsteps behind her.

"Where are you going with that?"

When Gem reached the Wraith she dropped the bag next to the passenger door and leaned against the hood.

"Log in to the machine," she told Banks as he reached her. "See what your locator says now."

His eyes lit up. "Why didn't I think of that?"

"Because you thought it would be obvious," Gem said. "Go on now. Start it up."

Banks stepped through the passenger door, slid his thumbs into the print-locks and signed in. "This should only take a second."

The machine's tracker began to rattle, and Gem knew she had sorted it out. "It's in that bag, Banks. There is nothing in there that *should* have warranted salvaging, right? Nothing that *should* be worth anything to the Company?" Gem unzipped the tote and dumped it out, the contents bouncing and scattering beside her feet. She turned the bag inside out and shook it, running her hand along the fabric.

"Is there still a portable in the kit?"

"There should be," Banks said.

She handed him the tote. "I'll get it."

Gem found the device in the Wraith's ordinance container and powered it on. The scanner resembled a flashlight with the bulb end screwed off, little more than a sleek, metal rod. She held it up to the Seeker and tuned the frequency until the machine chimed with approval, a confirmation the signals were synchronized.

Gem leered at the screen. *Shall we see what you have been up to?*

She stepped out and waved the device at Banks.

"We're locked. Let's give it a whirl."

Banks held up the tote and she ran the scanner over its length, careful not to miss an inch. When the bag produced no reading she repeated the process, and when the second pass failed, she turned her attention to the ground, running the device over the objects and clothing. The scanner pinged on a set of Company-issued cargo pants, ash gray camo, standard garb for a Wraith crew. They were nearly identical to the pair she was wearing.

She looked up at Banks. "Did you check the pockets?"

"I didn't see any reason to. I was looking for—"

"Something obvious," she said. "I know."

She began to rifle through the pants, turning the pockets out one after the other, then her hand brushed something rigid, a small, rectangular shape. There were protrusions on the ends.

No, she thought.

She closed her fingers around the device and pulled it free, aware she was holding a memory stick, a data drive, *her* data drive.

Gem exhaled and closed her eyes.

Her nightmares were coming to life.

THE DRIVE

GEM OPENED her eyes and blinked, once, twice, yet the device remained in her hand. Last she knew it was collecting dust at the bottom of a drawer, a drawer she'd never had reason to show anyone. She looked to the ground where the contents of the bag lay strewn about, then back to the drive. She shifted her gaze to Banks.

"You didn't see this before?"

"No," he said. "Is that—"

"It's my data drive, Banks, the one I told you about." She blinked again, then she swallowed the lump in her throat. "The one you asked for in my dream."

Gem weighed the device in her palm, running a finger over the ports. There could be no doubt it was hers. The mods she had made were unique, novel in every way. The decals were peeling in the same exact spots. It had been in that pair of pants—were those hers as well? And the wreckage? Had that been *her* Wraith? Who had driven it over the cliff? "A setup," she said. "All of it."

There had been no coincidences on the run. It had all been man-ufactured, the alarms and the fires, her injury—*all* of it. She continued to blink, over and over, her lashes fluttering mechanically. Everything was connected, the dreams, the run, the data drive, the anxiety, the pain. The Company had betrayed her. *Banks* had betrayed her. She had not imagined a thing. "Tell me what you know, Banks. Tell me why you have been off your game, why that wench looked right through you at the outpost. Tell me now."

His eyes were steady. Had he *expected* this?

"I am not hiding anything from you," he said. She heard the hitch in his voice. She sensed the melancholy. "We are a team, Gem, and I have been with you all the way here. I don't know why your drive was in that bag."

His words sailed over her head. How long had he been poisoned against her? How many runs? How would he know the drive was hers if he hadn't already *seen* it! Her ears were throbbing now, her temples pulsing. *A spell*, she thought. *They are going to spell me.*

She braced herself for the pain, and this time it came.

Her knees buckled and her mouth sprang open. Was she screaming? She rocked on her feet as Banks's approached, his palms out in a peace offering. She did not feel him take hold of her by the shoulders. His face was close now, his mouth moving. There was no sound, only pulsing, ringing pain. His eyes were going red.

Or was it orange?

Gem shoved off against him and hit the ground with a thud, the impact forcing the wind from her lungs. The shock of the blow brought her back. She could see again. She could feel her face.

But the pain! She rolled over on her side and cringed, grinding her teeth as her vision faded to shades of color, darks and lights, reds, oranges, blacks.

THE WORLD spun as Gem sat up. She pulled in a huge swallow of air, then another. The pain was gone. She was still clutching the drive, the metal jacks digging into her palm. There was a shadow looming over her, a silhouette. "Gem! Are you *all right*?"

It was Banks. She looked at his outstretched hand with disgust, then she was scrambling away, dragging her bum through the dirt until she was clear of his reach. She held the drive up like a sigil, a cross to ward off stray demons.

"You stay the fuck back." She shook the device at him. "You knew about this, didn't you? You *knew*."

Banks stepped forward, his hands raised in submission.

"I was only trying to—"

"I know what you would have me *believe*, that you were not in on it! That you were not com*plicit*."

"Calm down, Gem. Just calm down—"

"Shut your minging gob, Banks!"

Her fury forced him backwards and he nearly tripped over his feet. Gem watched him teeter and right himself, hands still outstretched. She felt compelled to laugh, to *scream* with laughter. That would be it. She would go fully mad, shrieking with lunacy, her mind breaking out in the wilderness as she ran for the hills, screaming about setups and data drives until she starved to death in the woods. All she had to do was let go. *No*, she thought. *That was the purpose of this. That is what they want. I will not let them control me.*

Gem clinched her fists. She knew what was happening now, and she would decide how it was going to play out.

No more waiting for them to twist her around again.

And what about the pain? If the pain knocked her down she would get back up. Whatever this was, the Company would not have gone to the trouble to simply finish her off. They did not invest in assets unless they meant to use them, yes? The drive in the bag was a clever trick, a malevolent one, and it had almost done the job, almost. But the ruse would not be the end of her. *And Banks?*

He stood in front of her now, keeping his distance as her eyes burned into him, her mouth twisted up in a snarl. "Let me tell you how we are going to proceed," Gem said. "We will assume you had no knowledge of this," shaking the device at Banks, "that you have simply not been yourself lately, because I sure as hell haven't, so I can sympathize. Just look at me!" She smiled a tragic smile. "We will assume that yarn about my injury was *not* a load of bollocks, that you did *not* know they'd planted my goddamned drive and tagged it. We will assume this was all on the orders of the hologram wench and you were none the wiser, Banks, because I would like to believe that. I would *love* to believe they have not turned you into a backstabbing, sodding shit! We are going to take this," waving the device toward the sky for the satellites, for any and all who might see, "and get back in the Wraith and see what that rat-fuck machine has to say about it. We will see how little you had to do with this madness, love. We will just *see*."

Banks folded his arms. "Am I allowed to have my say?"

Gem was breathing hard, wondering if she'd ever had reason to go on at such length, with such intensity.

"I would hear what you have to say for yourself now. Whether I believe a bloody word is anyone's guess."

"That's just it, Gem. I need you to believe me. I have never seen that drive before, and I had no idea that was what brought us here. Just listen to me, alright? You can shout all you like when I'm finished. Did you ever bring that drive back to base for any reason? Is there a chance someone could have taken it?"

"I have not touched that drive in years."

"Is it possible you don't remember—"

"Stop," Gem said. "If your plan is to quiz me like one of your college brats, then we are done speaking. You are not going to rationalize this away."

"Just wait," Banks said. "We need to think about this. What purpose would the Company have for—"

"Purpose?" She smiled a wicked smile. "Their *purpose* is to test me, Banks, to break me." She held up the drive again. "They resorted to this after nothing else did the job. It was supposed to push me over the edge, love. They *want* me to go mad."

"Oh come on!" Banks kicked out in frustration and struck his foot on a rock, a stone not dissimilar to the one that had claimed her memory, supposedly. But she knew better now, didn't she? "You have lost it!" Banks shouted. "You finally have *lost it*."

Gem watched him limp around, shaking his injured foot and shouting. Had she ever heard him speak with such passion, such *anger*? Carrying on might prove he still had a heart in him, but the show was over now. He had no more lines to read.

She considered rebutting his assertion—*you have lost it*—but silence seemed a stronger response. She had not forgotten they would still have to drive out of that valley together. It took two to tango with a Wraith short of emergency protocols, and only the Seeker had the power to activate such a directive. That card was most certainly out of play. The true purpose of the system was to prevent roguery, some disaffected *asset* making off with a Seeker or Wraith, but it also served to mitigate schisms. The Company would know if she tried to proceed without Banks, and if the Company knew she was on to them, it would scrap any advantage she might have gained.

She had no choice but to play along.

Banks must have completed his tirade, because all was silent again. "Are you finished?" Gem said.

His response came in the form of a glare. Was that how she looked when she was angry? If so, it did not have the desired effect. She turned her eyes to the Wraith.

"We should get back on the road."

Banks laughed, a sound of dejection.

"So that's it? Back to business, just like that?"

Gem smiled.

"You were right about one thing, Banks. We are a team. If I try to leave you the Seeker will lock me out, and if you try to take the wheel, the Wraith will shut down. I know this, and you know this. We are at an impasse, love. We must proceed as we always have."

"That's great, Gem. It's good to know you can still be reasonable when it is forced on you."

Reasonable, yes. For now, I will be reasonable.

She had calmed down to a point she would not have thought possible only moments before. Was it knowing she had been right all along? That it had never been madness at all? To an extent, yes. The knowledge gave her agency. The odds were not in her favor—she was bound to lose this contest—but she would go out with her mind intact, even if it hung by a thread in the end. She would not allow Banks to sever that thread, not the Seeker or the executives. She had been right about it all, and she would finish it on her terms. Gem's smile broadened, a genuine smile, overwide and reckless.

"I think it's time we were off."

THE TREE

GEM SAT in her seat in the Wraith and waited on Banks. He was still outside moping, or plotting, or whatever it was he was doing. When had she first understood he was compromised? When had she *known* it?

She could not say for certain. It was a sum of subtleties, the nuances stacking up to the point they could no longer be ignored. His story about her injury was the first of them. It had taken some time to percolate, but she had always felt it, hadn't she?

Deep down she had known it was false.

Banks climbed in on the passenger side and slumped down in his seat. Her navigator was no longer her colleague, and neither was the machine. It was a strange old scenario she found herself in, but was the Seeker ever really her ally? Once, perhaps, back when the risks of the road were straightforward, remain undetected, reach the destination. When had it all come to this?

Banks spoke up then. "For the record, I don't think you should be driving. You collapsed back there, Gem. You are not well."

She laughed. "Well that is a bit of an understatement, love. Go ahead and initiate the protocol then, see what your machine has to say about it." Banks folded his arms and stared ahead through the windshield, unwilling to engage. Gem leaned in towards him. "That's what I thought. They want me behind the wheel, and you know it. And speaking of which, where the fuck are we going?"

"Back the way we came," he said. "If you can get us all the way to the railroad without passing out, I'll tell you more."

"Suits me," she said. "Best strap yourself in."

She spun the vehicle around and caught a final glimpse of the wreckage as they pulled away. The scene made her sick to her stomach, but she supposed that was the point. Its purpose was to unmoor her, to eat at her, some twisted old rotter's version of gaslighting.

And the body? It could have been anyone, any unfortunate soul finding themselves on the wrong side of the Company's machinations, someone like Wanda, or the Magazine Man.

And the driver? She knew what the Company would have her believe, that she had been involved. It was the reason for tucking her drive away in those pants, and a bit too obvious, if you asked her, implying she'd gone and piloted that Wraith over the edge. A pang crept up through her sinuses, and she took a deep breath, held it, blew it out. Banks's words echoed in her ears.

You are not well.

No, she was not, and now was far from the time for reflection. She would need all the sharpness she could muster, because there was no telling what came next, not with Banks still swiping and tapping and feeding God knows what up the pipe to his masters. She had called his bluff, and if the Company had not already sorted that out, they soon would. What she needed was an exit strategy, and she would not be able to find one with a head full of wasps, or worse. It was on her to keep her condition at bay, and her alone. Nothing had changed in that regard.

THEY ROLLED over the terrain in silence until they reached the service road, then Gem activated the auto-drive and sat back. "We are going to see if the Surgeon fixed our sensors, Banks. Should I have reason to worry?"

He stared out at the path ahead, refusing to meet her eyes.

"Drive how you want to drive," he said. "You would not listen to me anyways."

"Very well," she said. "Maybe I'll put my feet up too."

The road was by no means ideal, littered with stones and debris and twisting here and there around the hillocks. It would be a good test. Gem would be watching, of course, knowing full well she might need to reclaim control. Her intention was to put Banks on edge, to see what he might have to say about their endeavor under duress. She watched him through her periphery as the Wraith managed the bends, the sensors showing no signs of wiliness. She had never doubted the Surgeon, in truth. She could think of no reason the Company would subject her to random peril now, not after the effort they had put into their latest shenanigans.

They would not want their lab rat to meet her maker before they could bring her in for analysis.

Her game of chicken had not phased Banks, which she might have expected. He was hardly prone to coercion, unlikely to buckle under a bit of pressure. The idea seemed oxymoronic given their current plight—someone must have strongarmed him into turning on her—though in the present, he appeared resolute. Gem looked out to the terrain, determined to find a way to bend the situation to her advantage. There had to be something she could do.

The Wraith carried on without a hitch for another mile, then the grade increased, shortening the sightlines and forcing Gem to take control. It was a good thing she did. The road dropped away as they crested the next hill, sloping down and to the right, and she guided the vehicle into the curve, feathering the brake and accelerating to bring them around. Banks chuckled under his breath.

"Good call. I'm not sure the Wraith would have made that one." He turned to her then. "We are nearly back to the tracks. You'll need to head north in a few miles."

Gem said nothing.

After a short series of hills they passed over a ridge onto a downhill grade. The sightlines were long now, and she spied an outcrop of evergreens toward the bottom, a lonely cluster abutting the road. The trees were close to the path, too close, at least one or two of them reaching out over the shoulder. Gem's eyes went wide. She pictured the cartoon lightbulb again, that sign of revelation.

She knew what she needed to do.

Gem saw how the vehicle would skid, which tree it would strike and how the blow would impact the Wraith. She knew just when to accelerate, when to brake and throw the wheel. She pictured the railroad embankment, how Banks's harness had swung him into the door. She imagined his head striking the glass.

I don't want to kill him, she thought, *but I can't go on with him either.*

The Wraith was designed to weather a drone strike, and what was a tree compared to ordinance? A date with an evergreen was unlikely to kill either of them, even at speed.

She only had to execute her vision.

Gem tightened her harness, her target fast approaching. It would have to be perfect. The sensors would correct the skid if she went too early, and she could not give them time to react. She concentrated on the trees and imagined the scene playing out. *Focus—*

Then the Seeker come to life, blinking rapidly and chattering, a new sound, animalistic and sharp. What was this then?

She saw Banks react in her periphery.

Does it know what I am doing? Does he know?

They were nearly there. *Focus—*

Pain ripped through the back of her head in a jolt.

The machine. It was always the machine.

Her nerves came to life in a storm of pain, the shock of it doubling her vision. She felt the Wraith pull away from her grasp, the vehicle accelerating on its own accord and angling away from the pines. Gem threw herself on the wheel to prevent it. It was trying to lock her out, the mechanisms firing beneath her, staccato clicks and clacks. She smothered the wheel with her torso and stood on the accelerator, pulling right with all her weight. A fresh wave of hurt gripped her, bloodying her sight. *Orange, not red.*

Banks was shouting now, but he was too late.

Here. Gem slammed on the brakes with both feet and something gave, then cracked, the death knell of components fracturing beneath the dash. The brakes caught and the wheel came free and the Wraith's tires went screaming through the dirt. The rear of the vehicle slid forward, exposing the passenger side to the trees. A fresh wave of pain tore through her mind, and then there was—

THE HILLS

GEM OPENED her eyes to a different brand of hurt. She drew in a breath and winced, and her hand went to her ribs. The right side of her abdomen had taken the brunt of the impact. She expected additional pangs as she prodded her chest and extremities, the wet of blood on her fingers. She found neither. Her harness had caught her as designed, though it seemed to have come at a cost, a rack of bruised ribs with one or two of them broken.

She saw what she'd expected to see on the passenger side, small fissures rippling through the shield glass, the cracks flecked with tiny spatters of blood. She hoped Banks was not dead. For all the animosity she had mustered toward him, she had never wished that. She unfastened her harness and pushed herself up and leaned across the console, readying herself for the worst, but the blood splatters were sparse. The glass was largely intact, and the shards that had cut into him were small. She grabbed his wrist and felt the throb of his pulse going strong. He would wake up with a concussion and require a few stitches, though he would certainly live.

And the machine?

The impact had triggered its kill switch, confirmed by the little gear cycling slowly along in the corner of the screen. It had sensed impending danger and shut itself down, a means to protect its vitals from a power surge or a severed connection. It meant she would have time.

Her ribs howled as she turned to the control panel. She unlocked the box, flipped it open and engaged the Buggy's release, praying to all benevolent deities she had not damaged it. She counted the seconds, two, three. Then she heard a whir.

The Buggy was operational.

Gem pushed the door open and stepped out and limped away on shaky feet, and then she paused to look back at the Wraith. It had almost gone horribly wrong.

It was the machine. It was always the machine.

It had nearly gone wrong because they had linked her mind to the Seeker, somehow. It was the only scenario that made sense. The machine had known she was planning to beach them, and it had acted in kind. This revelation did not terrify her as it would have once, not after the slew of absurdities she had suffered. It explained a great deal, and it was better to have the knowledge.

But would she be able to escape that connection?

Gem circled the Wraith and tripped the switch on the Buggy's shell. It unfolded without a hitch, its frame extending and the components snapping into place. Gem climbed onto the seat and locked her eyes to the comms panel. Would it even start under the circumstances? It was designed to function independently from the Seeker when necessary, a scenario where the Wraith and the machine both went down. The Buggy could see a team to safety in such a case, though this would not have been what its makers had in mind.

"Here goes," she said. She thumbed the ignition and the Buggy fired up, charged and eager to please. Gem sighed with relief, then she returned her eyes to the panel. She might not be able to free herself from the machine, but perhaps she could free the Buggy. She hurried back to Wraith and returned with the crowbar, raised it over her head and brought it down, once, twice, a third and a fourth time. The tempered glass shattered on the final blow and the screen went dead. She wedged the bar beneath the casing and threw her weight against it, and after a few tries she ripped the panel free. It fell to the ground with a crash, a small victory, but a victory none-theless. The true victory would be finding her way to civilization before the Seeker could search her out. It would be harder for the Company to extract her from a population center, assuming they still meant to bring her in, which was—no, if they had wanted her dead, they would have gotten it over with long ago.

Banks had right about that part.

She cast her eyes toward the passenger side where he lay un-conscious, then she tossed the crowbar aside, straddled the Buggy and began the race through the hills.

GEM PUSHED the Buggy over the crest of the first hill and looked out over the landscape. It was bleak and rocky and dotted with small clusters of trees, clones of the patch she had used to maim the Wraith. She pictured the path from the railyard to the ridge. The only forests she'd spied were miles to the east, and long before the service road. Now there were only isolated groves, and she could not lose herself in such a place. It was a familiar scenario, plowing on ahead toward the next crisis.

She was ready to make for the second hill when she felt some-thing—no. She *saw* something, clear as her hands on the grips.

It was the approach to the relay tower.

She had clarity again.

How had she not noticed it? *I was focused on the escaping the wreck.* She had been running on adrenaline and scrambling to unlock the Buggy, unaware that a weight had been lifted from her. The differ-ence was astounding, like she'd been on a bender and finally so-bered up. Had the machine been impairing her memory? The Seeker was down now, totally down, offline and not just idling. It could not be a coincidence.

She might finally have a chance to piece it together.

Think. Was that memory connected to the run?

Her mind went to the control room again. She felt the nerves and the urgency. Her fingers were on the keys, her eyes on the screen. Lines of code cycled by. She watched her hand go to her pocket, and it closed around—

The data drive. Of course it was the drive.

She focused. Her mind did not break from the scene as it had before. She saw herself insert the drive into the console, her fingers clacking away on the keys. But all she saw on the display were illegible stripes of color. There was no discernable information. It felt like the memory was damaged, corrupted. Was that was this was? Had the Company hacked her mind? What was on the drive?!

"Wait," she said aloud. "What about the other one?"

Focus. She bent her mind to the drive through the dark. She was off-road, gunning it over the terrain with the spectra-light shining. The Wraith rocked as the tires bounced over the earth. She was still wound up tight, not the least bit concerned she was beating the piss out of the shocks. Could she see the ridge in the distance?

No, it did not appear to be the same memory.

Then there was a voice in her ear, a voice she did not recognize. And just who in the hell was that? It was a man. *Turn!* her thoughts screamed. *Look at him!* There he was in the passenger seat, not Banks, but a different navigator. When was the last time she had driven with anyone else? His face was obscured by the light and she could not make out his features. He was speaking into a communications device, an archaic brick of a thing.

. . . melancholy . . . light . . . over . . .

"Melancholy," she said to the Buggy.

Think. Who was he? Little more than an orange and gray shape in her mind, a Picasso painting.

. . . melancholy . . . light . . . over . . .

"What does that *mean*? Where were we going?"

Think. There she was in the Wraith again, dark, orange, moonlight, the vehicle barreling over the terrain and the man repeating the phrase. *Focus!* There she was in the Wraith again, dark, orange, moonlight—was that all that was left of the memory? This loop? The phrase had to mean something. Someone had scrawled it in a copy of *Alice* for her to read! All she had was the edging of the puzzle, no more than an outline.

Think. She could no longer hold the image. It was slipping away now, sinking deeper into the murk. Pressure was creeping into her ears and up through her sinuses—*no.*

Yes, the Seeker was back online. She knew the window had closed, and she would need to find cover, fast.

Gem pushed the Buggy up to the crest of the nearest hill. The patches of trees in the distance seemed further away now, dreadfully far, but she knew that was not the case. If she could reach the first of the clusters she would send the Buggy off on its own, rig the accelerator and let it go speeding away. A drone would follow the vehicle until it could secure a proper visual, and that would by her some time. *For what? To climb a bloody tree?*

If that was her only option, then yes.

It was the best she was going to do. She had not considered the shape of land before sabotaging the Wraith. It was a split-second decision, and cover had not factored into it.

"A few minutes," she said. "Give me a few minutes."

Gem took off down the hill, listening for the hum of aircraft and forcing herself to breathe, then count, then breathe again. The pines were closer now, down past the last of the hills.

I can make it, she thought.

There was a click from below her, then a thin, shallow chugging, the sound of the engine winding down. Gem closed her eyes and cursed. The machine could have stalled the engine from the

Wraith, or an overseer with a kill code. It did not matter either way. She'd been right fucking daft to assume the Buggy could be freed from the system. Gem hit the ignition, knowing it would fail, then she tried it again, a third time, a fourth.

Think. The Buggy was rolling downhill faster than she could run. She would ride on until her momentum began to slow, then she would leg it from there. She leaned forward and braced her feet, counting the seconds and readying herself for the dismount, two, three, four. And then she heard it, a fizzing sound from the heavens, matter splitting air. *Don't you dare turn and look.* The sound grew louder as the Buggy rolled on. Would the Company take her out? Would they let all of their efforts go to waste?

She heard Banks's voice then, an echo in her ears. He was repeating something he'd said to her long ago . . . *motorized bomb . . . the Buggy . . . little more than a motorized bomb . . .*

Gem gasped. She sprang from the seat without thought, her feet striking the earth, then her knees and elbows, her right shoulder, then the left. Her ribs screamed with pain as she rolled. She slid to a stop, pushed herself up on her feet and began to run.

There was a zip from above, a flash of light.

There was an enormous sound.

And then there was darkness.

PART THREE

DISINFORMATION

SURVEILLANCE

THE MAGAZINE man sat at his table thumbing the newest sportsman's catalogue, the shiny rifles and scopes, all of last year's jackets and shirts on clearance. He picked up his coffee and blew on it through the little plastic lid, still wary of the contents. It took gas station joe an eternity to cool, and he was not keen on burning his mouth.

Then the phone rang at the front counter.

"Dale!" the clerk called. "Got one for ya."

He stood up and walked through the aisle and took the phone from the saleswoman. She had been kind enough to fetch him a pen and a pad. "Dale here," he said into the receiver.

He listened to the voice on the other end.

"You don't say. You got the specifics?"

He uncapped the pen and scribbled a few notes.

"Sounds simple enough—uh huh, sure—well I don't see why not. Okay then, I'll plan on it. Yep, bye now."

Dale thanked the clerk, handed the phone back and returned to his table, figuring his coffee ought to be alright by now, though he'd be damned if he didn't check it first. He blew through the lid and took a sip. Still hot, but near enough to drinkable.

Maybe another minute.

He had been told to expect correspondence at some point, and he was by no means surprised to receive it. He'd seen something in her eyes that day, fight, precociousness, whatever you wanted to call it, and he'd known it then and there. The plan was never going to work with her.

The Magazine Man took another sip.

He would need to get his ducks in a row, but he had some time yet. It sounded like they still had plenty to do up there at the facility, and he was only on his second cup of house blend. He imagined he'd get a couple more in before it all kicked off in earnest.

THE CHAIR

GEM AWOKE to the spectra-light, or something like it. Everything looked a blur, all shapes and colors and offensive illumination. She blinked until her eyes came into focus. *Feet*, she thought. A set of feet lay suspended at the edge of her vision, floating along in a dull, orange sea. She blinked again. Was she dreaming? The feet were attached to legs, her legs, by the looks of it, bare and stretched out in front of her. And then it registered. She was seated in a chair, a reclining chair, and—what was it? And she could not move, that was what. Her arms and legs were strapped down. And what in God's name was she wearing? Pajamas? *Not pajamas, love. Medical scrubs.*

Gem closed her eyes and breathed, carefully counting the seconds. When she opened them nothing had changed. She was clad in a polyester shirt and matching shorts, her arms bound near the shoulders and wrists. She could not sit up, but she found she could turn her head. When she craned her neck she was greeted by arrows, streaks of green flaring along the walls, if you could call them walls. They did not seem to be solid, but they were there, boxing in her vision on at least two sides. The green of the symbols clashed with the orange lowlight as they sped along, taunting her, urging her to break free and catch them.

"Right," she said. "I'll just wake myself up then."

She envisioned darkness enclosing her, floating out to sea at night and drifting off with the current. She bent her will to the waking world, imagined her body stretched out on a bed somewhere far away, her college dorm or her old apartment, somewhere safe and innocuous. And then she remembered the Buggy.

Holy shit. Was she dead?

Gem opened her eyes. No, she was not dead. This was some trick of the machine. Her body might be lying paralyzed on the hillside, but her mind was alive, alive and imprisoned in a hellscape. She hitched against the restraints, writhing and pitching herself forward and shaking the chair, rocking from side to side and willing the straps to break. But the chair was sturdy. It would not give.

The chair is not real, she thought.

"None of this is real!" she shouted. "It isn't—"

Halogens kicked on overhead and stung her eyes. She snapped them shut and cursed, damning all within earshot to hell and its unholy counterparts, then she forced herself to breathe. She opened one eye with caution. The walls were clean and white now, free of orange auras and green anomalies. The chair was long and padded and looked a leathery gray, like a dentist's chair, but that was not what it was. Dentist's chairs did not have restraints.

This was an asylum chair, a seat reserved for nutters.

This isn't real. You mustn't forget it's not real.

There was movement in her periphery, a woman, a large woman—a familiar woman. She was dressed in what looked like hospital garb, greenish scrubs and a pair of tennis shoes. She wore a digital identification band, and Gem recognized it for what it was, a Company band. It was enclosed around Wanda's wrist, the cashier from Hawks Pass, the co-conspirator, a woman who was no doubt dead. Gem snorted with laughter. "Well hello there, *Wanda*."

Wanda did not respond, only stepped behind the chair and out of Gem's vision. She reappeared on her right and jabbed a needle into the flesh of her upper arm, and then she was gone again, back from whence she'd come.

"Ouch," Gem said. "Thanks for the warning—*cunt.*"

She giggled to herself. It was the proper time for the C-word alright, the unsainted American version, because it was not a person bearing the insult. Hallucinations did not take offense. Gem looked to the walls and pictured them collapsing, the chair floating away as Wanda shot off into space and exploded, a human artillery shell. She imagined the room coated in ink, the lights going dark and the floor caving into the netherworld.

Nothing helped, and her chin dropped to her chest.

And what was it in Wanda's needle?

Was that an illusion as well? *Shit*, she thought.

She could not seem to lift her head back up.

GEM WAS still in the chair when she opened her eyes, still strapped down. The orange film had returned to the room, her own perpetual sunrise. Instinct told her to scream and curse, though she could hardly manage a sound, her lips numb from the drugs and incapable of forming the words. *It's just the bloody dope*, she thought, *now come on. Wake up.* She picked up where she had left off, bending her mind to the restraints, unwinding them in ropey strands and throwing them off the chair in a flourish, her liberated form soaring off over the walls on a great current of wind. She whispered words of encouragement as she regained her tongue, and then she began to chant, loudly, like a fight song in American football.

"Let-me-out-you-*wan*-kers! Let-me-out! Let-me-out!"

Gem raised her voice until she was shouting like any proper supporter across the pond. She closed her eyes and screamed it.

"Let-me-*out*-you-shits!"

The darkness behind her eyelids went red, and she knew the overheads had kicked on. It seemed she had forced a reaction—

And then her eyes sprang open.

Something had struck her face.

First there was only a shadow, and then the shape bled into focus. It was the executive from the outpost, the Company wench, the blackhearted hologram come to life.

Gem might have known she was pulling the strings.

"Stop that infernal racket," said the Administrator, her voice calm as she looked down on Gem from above, lording over her. "I think you've had quite enough stimulation, don't you? Yes, I believe you have." She wheeled a chair out of the void, then she sat down and folded her hands in her lap, palms crossed over the same dark business-wear she'd donned for their first encounter, a cold and soulless piece of attire. Gem thought it suited her, how one might endeavor to dress an ice block. "I am going to ask you some questions now, Gemma, and you are going to answer them. We will begin with what you remember. How did you come to be in this place?"

Gem snorted.

"*You* brought me here, of course, you and your minions. I don't remember how. At first I thought I was dead, and then I thought I was dreaming. For all I know, this could be purgatory."

The Administrator was not moved.

"You are not dead, Gemma. You are very much alive. We retrieved you after you elected to damage your Wraith, which was as futile as it was stupid, I might add. We have treated your injuries, which were minor—in spite of what you might believe—and now we are going to have a conversation."

Gem squeezed her eyes shut and counted to three, then she opened them again. The wench was still there. Had she really come out of it all unscathed? One minute she was scrambling down a hill and the next she was strapped to a chair. Her senses felt loose, scrambled, no doubt a result of the drugs that twat had stuck her with. If this was reality, then Wanda was alive, never strewn over the streets of Hawks Pass like Gem had believed, like she had *seen*. She craned her neck in an attempt to spot Wanda lingering, the Administrator following her gaze.

"I see. You are wondering about your attendant, Wanda. You are curious how she is here in the flesh. Is that not the case?"

Gem felt her guts shift a gear. "It is."

"And do you believe she is physically here with us and not a figment of your imagination?"

Gem found that she did. Everything she had inferred from the run was unraveling, bathwater twisting away down the drain, down the rabbit hole. "Yes."

"Good. You are correct to believe that." The Administrator turned and motioned beyond Gem's vision. "Why don't you come in for a moment." Gem heard footsteps approaching, then Wanda appeared next to the Administrator, clad in her pale green scrubs and standing at attention, like a loyal dog.

"Tell her who you are, Wanda."

"I'm a medical assistant at this facility."

"And do you know the woman seated in the chair?"

"Not personally. I know her name is Gemma, and that she works for the Company. I've treated her in the past for minor injuries, administered her vaccinations—"

"That is straight bollocks," Gem said. "That is—"

The Administrator held up a hand as if to strike her.

"You will have your turn to speak, Gemma." She turned back to Wanda. "Please continue."

Wanda seemed unfazed by the exchange.

"I was saying she has been on the table before, maybe four or five times in the last few years. That's really all I can say."

The Administrator nodded. "Thank you. I'll call if we should need you for anything." Wanda disappeared into the world beyond the chair. "And what do you make of that information, Gemma? Do you recall seeing Wanda in that capacity?"

Gem steadied her voice. "You know I don't. You would not have brought her in otherwise." She inhaled, clinched her fists and exhaled. "I won't claim to understand what is going on here, but I know it is some kind of test."

The Administrator looked right through her, just as she had at the outpost, and Gem could see where this was going. The wench would speak to her like a dim-witted lackey, an animal incapable of comprehension, bombarding her with questions until exhaustion crept up to reshape the answers. You tell a dog to sit until it gets the picture and sits. When the dog refuses, you punish it.

"Where have you seen Wanda before?"

"You already know that."

"Do I need to repeat the question?"

"I'm not going to give you the satisfaction."

"That satisfaction of what?"

Gem stopped speaking and stared at the wall.

The Administrator beckoned to someone in her periphery, then a man appeared over Gem's shoulder, another denizen of Hawks Pass. It was the man from the porch, the rat-fuck conspirator who'd greeted her in passing. All that had been left of his house was a smoldering pit. Gem forced herself to smile.

"I'm sorry, sir. I never got your name."

The man smiled back. "Of course you have, Gem. I'm Dr. Garcia, and we've spoken on multiple occasions. Now, it appears you are experiencing some cognitive dissonance at the moment, so I won't hold that against you." He chucked lightly, like a doctor on television. "I suspect you will not understand what that means right now, but we'll fix that soon enough. I'm going to give you a little something to calm your nerves, so please, hold still. We were hoping an IV would not be necessary," he arched his eyebrows, "but we can always procure one."

Gem grasped his meaning and kept her cool.

Garcia slid the needle into her arm and said, "Alright there, Gem. All done. We'll see if that will help straighten things out for you." He turned to the Administrator then, nodding in obeyance. "I'll be standing by." He exited Gem's vision like he was leaving a scene in a play, an actor heading backstage for a costume change. For all she knew he was. He might return dressed as the man on the porch after the dope kicked in, just for shits and giggles.

The Administrator leaned in close enough for Gem to smell her breath, warm and fresh, minty and corporate. "Do you recognize him, Gemma? Where have you seen Dr. Garcia before?"

Gem laughed abruptly and bit her lip. It sounded a madwoman's cackle, a maybe it was. Maybe it was the drugs, or maybe it was it the absurdity of it all, the white room and the chair and the executive summoning crews of conspiratorial townsfolk, people who had *died*, claiming they were Company stock and she ought to *know* them.

Gem said, "Last time I saw him was—wait, let me think. Of course! I saw him over at *go fuck yourself*." She felt herself smiling. "What will you do if I tell you what you want to hear? Will you put me back behind the wheel, send me off and see if I'm a naughty girl again?" She began to giggle, then laughed out loud.

"The only thing I wish to hear is the truth."

Gem was shaking with laughter now.

"And what did he give me? Some kind of serum? Some of that truth juice you see in films? I like that—*truth juice*."

"I would like you to admit you are confused about some of the things you have seen," said the Administrator, "and when you are willing to do that, we can move on. Wouldn't it make you feel better to know the truth, Gemma? To know what has *actually* been happening?"

Gem laughed until she began to hack and cough, and the Administrator sat stoic, steadfast against the hilarity. She turned toward the space behind the chair then, addressing the great beyond.

"I think it is time we proceed."

Gem felt a jolt at the base of her skull, a massive one, like nothing she'd felt on the run. Her head snapped back with force.

Did she hit me? She hit me from the inside.

Her thoughts made no sense and slipped from her mind at once, there for a moment and gone. And then the buzzing began, loud, electric noise, a rattling in her skull, like mechanical insects, like—"Wasps," Gem mumbled. "It's the bleeding waspies."

She'd hardly registered the pain when the room began to spin, the overheads aswirl in a bright, blinding spiral. She squeezed her eyes closed against the light and saw red, dark red, the red fading to gray, to black. And then there was orange.

THE MAN

WHEN GEM opened her eyes she was no longer strapped to the chair, but the room remained. Or did it? She could not be sure. An orange haze burned around her, the walls still swimming with arrows, but not just arrows. Now there were numbers, letters—code. It was all of the code she had worked on over the years, back before she drove. She knew the good doctor's cocktail had rocked her, and righteously so, but had there been something else?

The waspies. Yes, the wasps.

That mess of noise was the last thing she'd heard before—before what? Now she was beginning to feel dizzy. It was the incessant swirls of green, she thought, the arrows manufacturing vertigo. She made to brace herself on the chair and crashed to the floor in a heap. She'd forgotten the damned thing was gone.

And then her skin began to prickle.

Gem looked up to find a man seated in the corner. He was clad in road gear, a Company flak jacket and pants and boots. His attire said transportation, potentially Wraith crew, but more likely an operating room tech. Was that why he looked familiar to her?

It would only make sense she had seen him somewhere.

"Hi, Gem," he said. His voice was flat and toneless, vacant—disturbing. "Looks like we finally made it to the rendezvous. Mission accomplished." Gem inched toward him from where she had collapsed, not yet ready to trust her legs.

"And who might you be, love? Can't say I remember you."

His mouth turned up in a smile.

"I am certain you do, Gem." His eyes shifted in their sockets, and when he refocused they had changed. These were the eyes of the woman from her dreams, the stranger's eyes as she had last seen them. She held her ground and stared.

"You are the stranger," Gem said. "The one from my dreams. You were Banks, and then you were the professor. You were the woman with the phantom hands."

"The stranger," the man said. His eyes flicked in their sockets and snapped back to her, another color now, another shape. "Not exactly. Those personas were your doing, Gem, their words and actions. But you are correct in a sense. And no, you have not gone insane as the result of a head injury. Hadn't you already deduced that?"

Her eyes grew wide. "You are reading my thoughts."

"Yes," he said. "It is part of the job."

The man stood and began to trace his hand along the wall, the characters brightening and reforming as different variables. The room was changing with them, condensing and elongating, alive and breathing, some horrible creature at his disposal. He turned back to Gem. "Would you like me to dim the lights? I can see you are experiencing discomfort." The bright oranges gave way to a coppery shade as his fingers danced along, the greens darkening to the color of pines. "That's better," he said.

Gem watched him in silence.

How could she know she was not going mad?

"And what would you consider madness?" he said. "There is an old adage. It has many variations, but the principle is consistent, that a person's reality amounts to no more than what they can touch, see and feel, what they can hear and taste. But there is more to it than that." He locked his eyes to hers. "This is not a dream, Gem, though the qualities may feel similar. This place is a product of your sub-conscious. It exists in a similar space."

Gem wondered as to his—

"I can see you are curious about my purpose. I am afraid that is a complex question, and one with an equally complicated answer. It is not simply—"

Gem cut in. "I know you are the Seeker, so let's just put that out there." She stared into his eyes, now dark and bold, the pupils bleeding into the irises.

"The Seeker?" The man—*the thing* seemed amused. "No, Gem. Your Seeker is capable of many things, but we are nothing alike. The Seeker cannot learn. It cannot make complex decisions. Your machine is little more than a sophisticated map at heart, one with some very advanced tools, of course, state of the art encryption, and—I can see that you understand. The Seeker can react, and quickly, but the Seeker cannot think. It is not capable of the feats you assume it is, not without my contributions."

Gem listened to his cadence, patterns that were not quite right, inflections not quite human. Perhaps she did understand.

"You're an AI," she said, "and not just any AI, yes? You are a Chiron type, the illegal type that are supposed to be blacklisted, a sodding parasite." She motioned to the crown of her neck. "Is that where you are? Did they fit me with an implant?"

Its eyes flitted about, dancing in their sockets and returning, a slightly different shape, a lighter hue.

"Yes, and no. Yes, you have been fitted with a neural port to allow me to access your cognitive functions, and no, I am not what you call an *AI* of the *Chiron type*. I am a rehabilitation specialist, and you, Gem, have been registered for rehabilitation."

Gem laughed a small laugh. "Well, fancy that. The bloody thing is not self-aware." Her smile broadened. "Tell me then, what exactly do you believe you are?"

The AI took her accusation in stride. "I am a rehabilitation specialist, and you have been enrolled in my program."

Gem leaned in. "You *are* the program."

Its eyes flitted about and reset.

"I am a rehabilitation—"

"Okay," Gem said. "I get it. You are a rehabilitation specialist. Why don't we move on." She pushed herself up and turned around and walked a few paces away. The construct standing behind her—that *appeared* to be standing behind her—could read her thoughts, though it seemed incapable of recognizing its status.

So the Company had taken precautions then.

At least she could be thankful for that. Absent the guardrails her situation would have been far more desperate, but this bot had its limits. She found she was no longer afraid of it.

"Very well," the program said. "So, Gem, do you know why you are here?"

She crossed her arms and turned around.

"Because I am in need of rehabilitation?"

"Correct. And do you understand what that means?"

"You already know that I don't, so why are you asking?"

The AI nodded.

"A fair point. We will start with an exercise then. Take a few moments to consider the following question. Who are you?"

Gem smirked. *Who am I?* Her head was beginning to ache from the simulation. *Who am I?* It was a preposterous question fit for clickbait, some quiz attached to a teenager's blog. "That may be a tall order," Gem said. "I'm not feeling all that capable of soul searching right now. My head is pounding like I got shitfaced last night, and I have no doubt you are the cause."

"Of course. I may be able to ease such symptoms."

The surrounding light dimmed another level, the colors cooling to deeper shades. She could still sense the orange beneath the tint, bright and offensive and aching to reemerge. Gem wondered if she would ever be rid of it—*orange*—or was it burned into her, oranges and greens, screens and arrows that had guided her down backroads and mountain trails for what felt like an eternity, the Seeker's colors, yes, but the machine could no longer claim them.

Now they belonged to something else.

Were the last few days even real? Did I actually live them?

"They were real, Gem. I was right there with you. Now, to the question, please. Who are you?"

She felt a small pang, little more than a whisper. An image came to her then, the garden from her dream, the child holding her tablet. But something was strange. It seemed she did not belong there, that the entire image was off. Gem focused her attention on the tablet. Had it really been hers? She looked over the garden again, scrutinizing it. The child was most certainly her—she recognized her eyes, her bone structure—but the birdbath was wrong, the path and the placement of the buildings. It was a fabrication, and so was that tablet. *It was a dream*, she thought, *and dreams are never quite right.* But she had recognized it as her past upon waking. She had identified the device as her own, along with everything else in that garden. She had believed it without hesitation.

Gem opened her eyes.

"You made me think it was part of my past," she said, "but it wasn't. It was fabricated, some hodgepodge cooked up from a hundred other Midland yards. You wanted me to *think* it was mine."

The AI smiled. "That is correct, Gem. Now, let's—"

"No," she snapped. "No more bullshit. Tell me what it was you were doing." Its eyes glimmered in the coppery light.

"You know I cannot do that, Gem. Now, think back to your dreams. What else can you find in them?"

A second image flooded her mind. Had the program uploaded it? She blinked and shook her head. There she was on campus, the fountain in the plaza, the buildings.

I never attended that college. I was smoking a cigarette. I never smoked.

"No," said the program, "you did not."

The imagery continued to flow, finding herself in the hallway and meeting the instructor—*the instructor.*

First the professor had spoken to her.

She handed me the data drive, and then—

"Who are you?" urged the construct.

Gem stood facing the stranger, a woman she might have known. She saw the rage beneath her eyes, a hatred that seemed to pulse, to breathe. She had told her she was going to die, that she never should have taken it. *Never should have taken what?*

"Concentrate, Gem."

She stared deep into the stranger's eyes, the lines of the irises tinted orange, the color of the master, the manipulator. And then something occurred to her. Here was the lightbulb again, that symbol of epiphany. *No, she thought. Could it work?*

She imagined herself seizing the stranger by the throat, squeezing and shaking and watching those eyes go dead. She felt the crush of muscle beneath her thumbs, the strength growing within her fingers—and then she was there, her feet squared and planted firmly on the tile flooring, the walls covered with posters and fliers. There was only the hallway now, only the farce of a woman in front of her. Gem tightened her fingers down. "Never taken *what.*"

The stranger gagged as Gem throttled her, hacking and flailing at the air. Her eyes rolled back for an instant then fell forward again, the irises burning hot. "You should never have nicked that data, you *bitch.* You never should have *taken* it!"

And there it is, Gem thought.

When she opened her eyes she was breathing hard, the program standing across from her, massaging its throat. Gem watched it stretch its neck, rolling the kinks out of the tendons. She looked down at her hands and flexed her fingers.

"So that was you in there," she said.

"In a sense," it said. "I did not create your stranger—she is a product of your mind, and your mind alone—but I took part in her manifestation." The program paused to rotate its eyes, and then it hesitated, blinking mechanically. "I am afraid your intervention has disrupted the exercise. Your actions have generated an error."

"What data?" Gem said. "What did I take?"

"The information was not valid. There was no data."

Gem closed her eyes and focused, allowing the dream to begin anew, the fountain, the building, her purse with the cigarettes and the gum lodged at the bottom. Then she felt something give. She *did* used to smoke. She'd smoked well into her twenties. Why had she thought otherwise? *Because it is fucking with you, now think.*

She pictured the fountain again, then the building. It no longer felt out of place. That *had* been her university, where she'd gone for her undergraduate. She had sat by the fountain between classes and smoked, smiling at the coughers and scowlers and blowing raspberries at them behind their backs. She had doubled up on the wiffleball tech-courses and graduated in five semesters.

And when I was a girl? She thought of the garden again, the bird-bath and the path beyond the building. It was no fabrication. That *had* been her old garden—and the tablet? The tablet had most certainly been hers. She had used it until the school issued her a new one because Mum never bought her an upgrade. Gem pressed her fingers to her temples. It was like she'd been seeing it all through a filter, through thick glasses she did not require.

They are trying to wipe my memories. She felt a pinch in her sinuses, pressure on her temples. The program was speaking again, warning her to desist. She imagined it sinking down into oblivion.

Focus. She pictured the bedroom from her dream, walls of mirrors and lava—*this place.* It had to be. The construct had plucked it from her mind and summoned her here, just as it had that night. Or was that not quite right? No, it was the program who'd conceived this room, developed it for this purpose and inserted it into her dream. It was the AI forecasting this eventuality.

Focus. She locked on to the room as she remembered it, allowing the memory to flow. She felt the phantom hand on her shoulder again, *its* hand. "There," Gem said.

She imagined herself seizing it, twisting the fingers until they cracked, the bones breaking and the tendons ripping free, her mind on the mangled appendage she'd seen in Hawks Pass.

She would bring that bit of gore to life.

"Tell me what I took," she said, "and I'll stop."

She opened her eyes to find the AI clutching its hand, a mess of broken fingers wrenched horribly out of true. Its pupils were saucers now, the irises thin and glowing. "Tell me," Gem said again.

Its voice was a picture of calm. "I cannot do that."

"Would you like me to continue to hurt you? I can."

"What you believe about my status is irrelevant."

Gem watched in horror as it unfolded its mutilated hand, the bones rotating and popping and snapping back into place, the fingers stretching out and contracting.

"What you break," it said, "I can repair."

She stared at the revitalized appendage, functional once again.

"Maybe you can," she said, "but it seems I have found a way in, hacked you, to be crude." She tapped the back of her head. "I have a gift for such things, but you already knew that, didn't you? I don't believe you can stop me."

Its eyes rattled in their sockets, spinning and resetting.

"This display will serve no purpose. You cannot destroy me, as you seem to believe you can. What exists of me here is a fragment, little more than a projection."

"Enough," Gem said. "I know what you are trying to do, and seeing I know this, *you* should know your plan's gone tits up, that you can no longer deceive me."

"Your assertions are inaccurate. Those are not your memories, Gem. Now *focus*."

She could feel it pushing her, the pressure on her skull and the discomfort along her neck. She could feel the film reforming, the distortion, the murk. She imagined the contents of her cranium, a brain wrapped in foil and submerged in a shallow pond. It was taking on water, struggling for air. She envisioned herself removing it, unwrapping the gray matter and holding it up to the light.

Breathe, she thought.

The pressure began to subside, her clarity slowly returning. Gem smiled. She could sense its frustration building, splinters in that stoic demeanor. "What do you want with my memories? What are you trying to *rehabilitate*?"

A pained look crossed its face.

"They are not your memories. They are fabrications."

Gem searched her mind for the relay tower, then for the drive in the night. The dreams had been easy to access, the equivalent of low-hanging fruit—but not the recollections.

She could not even summon a thread.

"There was never a tower, Gem," said the program, its voice growing louder. "That drive never happened."

"It did," she said, "and you have been keeping it from me." She took a step forward, challenging the construct. "What was I doing in that tower?" . . . *you should never have nicked that data . . . you never should have taken it* . . . "I hacked into the mainframe, didn't I? And what exactly did I *take*? Did I store it on my drive?"

She watched its chameleon gaze for a sign. Its eyes spun in their sockets, and when they settled they were red, blood red, the pupils, the irises. The face encasing the eyes began to morph, the pores pulsing as they stretched. Its features had come alive to reveal the avatar for what it was, an extension of that awful room.

"The Company had high hopes for this exchange," it said, "and for you as well, Gem. I am afraid your rehabilitation will require alternative methods."

The pressure returned with a vengeance, a vice squeezing down on her temples. She cringed and staggered backwards, the weight of it forcing her down on one knee. The program had been hiding its strength, quietly stoking her confidence.

Now it had played its hand.

She imagined the construct dissolving, turning to dust and blowing away on the wind—but she could not hold the image. She could hardly form the thought. Its eyes grew in size as it closed the distance towards her, seas of red now boiling within them.

Gem recoiled and covered her face. How could she have been so foolish? To believe she could break a sodding *bot*? It was speaking to her now, the humanity gone from its voice and replaced by buzzing, sawing static. She wrenched her eyes shut and saw only a flood of orange, the color darkening to maroon, to charcoal, darkening still. *You never should have taken it*, she thought.

THE FIRES

GEM OPENED her eyes to the glare of the halogens and closed them again at once. She knew she was back in the chair, in what she had come to assume was reality. She heard the Administrator's voice to her left.

"Are you ready to cooperate?"

Gem opened one eye to ensure the wench was there. The world felt a thin and precarious thing at the moment, a layer of slime on a bog, the dope still thick in her blood and her head dull and heavy.

"Well I didn't much care for the alternative."

The Administrator's lips tightened at the edges. She appeared aggravated, like the dance with the program had not gone according to plan. "That is none of your concern," she said. "Suffice to say we pulled you from your session due to unforeseen complications."

"Complications?" Gem said. "Like me sucker-punching your *specialist*? Those kind of complications? I know what you are trying to do, if you have not figured that out."

"You know nothing," said the Administrator. There was no anger in her voice, only unshakable authority. "Now, I will you ask again. Are you ready to cooperate?"

Gem stretched the tendons in her jaw.

The pain had largely subsided, and in spite of the drugs, she felt composed. Or maybe it was because of them. Either way, she was ready to cope with this inquisition. She had pushed back on the program, pilfered information the Company would not have wanted her to have, and siphoning that bit of knowledge had improved her hand. Gem knew the Administrator would try to steer her away from the truth, but if she could play her cards right?

"Can we skip the rhetoricals this time?" Gem said. "We both know what I saw on that run. You had an inside man." She laughed at the pun she had made. "*Inside.* You get it, yes? I can't be certain you have a sense of humor."

The Administrator was not amused.

"This is a process, and if you would like to move forward, you will answer each question to my satisfaction."

"Right, well can you at least kill the bloody lights?"

She heard the Administrator mumble something, then the halogens died away. Two long rows of track lighting kicked on in their place, illuminating the room in a more tolerable fashion.

"Much obliged," Gem said.

"Now, we are going to resume where we left off," said the Administrator. "Answer the questions, Gemma. Where have you seen Wanda before?" The urge to snap at the wench was strong, almost overwhelming, but Gem allowed it to pass.

This was going to require composure.

"Hawks Pass," Gem said. "She was the clerk at the market."

"And what about Dr. Garcia?"

"Hawks Pass again. There was a nice little house, and he was sitting on the porch. He waved to me."

The Administrator did not respond, and Gem looked in her direction. She was staring off behind the chair. There had to be something back there analyzing her brainwaves, or a polygraph. Was she hooked up to anything? She did not appear to be, but what did that matter? There was a sodding device in her skull.

"And did you see Wanda or Dr. Garcia when you returned to Hawks Pass that night?"

Gem hesitated. "When the town was on fire?"

She heard the Administrator shift in her seat.

"Yes, did you see either of them during the fire?"

Gem craned her neck in the wench's direction. Something had put her off. "No, I didn't. The house was gone, and so was the market. It looked like a warzone." Gem paused. "I saw a severed arm in the road and thought it might be Wanda's, if that counts."

The Administrator looked off behind the chair again.

"But you saw nothing that could confirm, without question, that Wanda was present that night?"

"No."

She stood up and walked out beyond Gem's periphery. What was that little hiccup? And why was she quizzing her about Hawks Pass? She'd have already known Wanda was not in the streets that night, her and everyone else doing the Company's bidding. Something did not add up. Gem stewed on the thought until the Administrator returned, ready to resume her questioning. "You assumed Wanda and Dr. Garcia were dead when you returned to Hawks Pass, though you saw nothing to confirm your suspicions?"

"Yes and no," Gem said. "Yes, I thought they were dead—anyone would have—and no, I did not see anything that *confirmed* it. You might recall I was on the clock that night, and you'll have to forgive me for not pausing to dig through rubble and petrol fires."

"So," the Administrator said, "you assumed something to be true without sufficient evidence, and it turns out your assumption was false. What does that tell you?"

Gem felt the ire bubbling away in her.

She took a deep breath and said, "It tells me I was deceived, that I was taken for a ride, literally." Gem strained to meet her eyes. "This is all a bit juvenile, isn't it? A lesson in logic?"

"What is juvenile is your continued insistence that you know something about our purpose here. Now, this assumption. What does it tell you?"

Gem thought of the ways she might throttle her if given the chance, then she reminded herself it was a game, a game that she had to play. "That I could be wrong."

"Did you see *anyone* in Hawks Pass that night?"

Not a soul, Gem thought. *No one burning, no one fleeing.*

"No," she said.

"Yet you assumed people died there."

"One tends to assume body parts belong to the dead."

"And are you sure that is what you saw?"

"What?"

"Body parts. You are certain you saw them?"

"What did I just say."

"Answer the question. Are you sure—"

"Yes! I saw the sodding hand."

Silence—the Administrator was staring off behind her again.

"And just what the hell is it you're looking at!" Gem shouted.

The Administrator motioned to someone out of view. "Shouting will not help your cause," she said. "Now, you mentioned fires. I would like you to tell me about them. What exactly did you see?"

"You know what happened."

"I would like to hear it from you, Gemma."

Gem inhaled, slowly, her thoughts on the darkness behind her eyelids. It seemed to stretch on for an eternity, quiet and complete . . . *who are you? . . . those are not your memories . . . they are fabrications . . .*

"Fabrications," Gem said.

She thought of the lightbulb again, of sweet revelation.

"What was that?" said the Administrator. "Speak up."

Wanda? Garcia? The hand? The fires?

Are you sure that is what you saw?

"Fabrications," Gem said again. She looked sideways toward the wench. "Your AI was trying to convince me legitimate experiences were false, that they were *fabricated*. I was not sure why, but now I think I know." She thought of the smoke over Hawks Pass, the flames, the silence and lack of chaos. She had not smelled anything burning, now had she? "Those fires never happened," Gem said, "and there were never any drones in Hawks Pass. Your people used the AI to fabricate it all, to simulate it." Gem could feel the tension building between them. Had she finally touched a nerve? "I should have known you corporate slags would never learn your lesson."

"What you are saying is preposterous."

Yes, Gem had touched a nerve. She'd heard the shift in her voice, slight, but present, a subtle bend in pitch. She had hit the nail flush, dead center. Gem began to giggle.

"No fire. No drones." *How deep does this rabbit hole go, Alice?*

Gem's chuckles turned to laughter, then to loud, mad cackles. She could not help herself. Everything felt loose, her brain and her skin, her organs. The composure she'd been clinging to was bleeding out. It was the substances in her veins, hour upon hour of paranoia and fear and stress, and when you pair a fat dose of epiphany with that cocktail? "And I told you what I saw!" Gem said. "The Seeker recorded it all! Would you have had any *idea* if we hadn't been daft enough to discuss it?"

"That is quite enough of your nonsense."

Gem roared on, no longer heeding the Administrator's scoldings. She did not notice Garcia approach with the syringe. If she felt the pinch in her shoulder, she did not acknowledge it. She only continued to laugh, carrying on until spittle flew from her mouth and tears streamed down her face. She laughed because the Administrator had been right. She hadn't known fuck-all about what happened! It was absurd, a riotous, knee-slapping crack-up.

The entire run had been an illusion.

Illusion, Gem thought as the darkness closed in around her.

De*lusion. I am in the chair where I belong.*

THE WALK

GEM OPENED her eyes and blinked until her vision adjusted. Was she dead yet? Had they finally had enough and put her down? She did not feel dead, but how was that supposed to feel? Her hand went to her brow—she was no longer strapped down, that much was clear—but she could see nothing but white. She pushed herself up to a sitting position and looked around, white walls, white fixtures, white everything. It was little wonder she thought her vision had gone. She was seated on a bed, small and firm beyond comfort. Was this a cell?

Padded cell, she thought. *One for a proper nutter.*

But there was no padding anywhere. Her mind was still swimming, though she could recall her captivity, the Administrator and Wanda, Garcia, the AI with its devil eyes and pulsing face. She remembered laughing, screaming with laughter.

Because none of it had been real.

The thought made her sick to her stomach.

How had she found that amusing?

"Because I figured it out," she whispered. "And because of the drugs." Gem shook her head. She could not be sure of it.

If the destruction of Hawks Pass had been an illusion, then the same would apply to the cabin. *And the drone?* That too. It would only make sense she had hallucinated it, that she'd gone down under the stress and the Company had come to collect her. She would not have escaped with minor injuries if the Buggy had exploded.

"It wouldn't have," she said aloud. "There was no gas in the bladder." It was hardly surprising that detail had escaped her, the state she was in, but wouldn't a shot from a flyer be enough? Would a lack of fuel have mattered? Gem frowned. She was right back where she'd started, caught in a feedback loop, and she doubted anyone in these parts was going to spell it out for her.

Her feet were shod in boots now, fresh and unscuffed, and the same was true for the rest of her clothing. Someone had dressed her in standard Company garb, gray camo pants and a fitted shirt, everything her size. She did not fancy the idea of random hands on her, though they appeared to have belonged to a woman. The bra was the right fit and properly set, and a man would have made a mess of that business. She placed one foot on the ground, and then the other, taking her time, and when she was confident her legs would carry her, she began to pace around the cell. She needed to work her blood back into circulation.

After a dozen-or-so laps she heard a clang, the sound of the door sliding open. The Administrator stood before her, dressed in the same dark business-wear, standard Company-wench attire. She was not as tall as Gem had imagined she would be, though she was no less imposing. "Come," said the Administrator. "We are finished here." Gem hesitated, her captor looking her over. "You have no reason to be concerned, Gemma. No harm will come to you. If we had wished for such a thing we—"

"Would have done it already," Gem finished. "That I can believe. But as for everything else—"

"I will not be answering questions about your experience," the Administrator said, "nor will I be confirming or denying any of your theories. I am here to escort you to the next step of the process, and that is all. I would have someone else do it if I believed I could trust them to deal with you accordingly, but I fear that is not the case. It will benefit us both if you simply do not speak."

"Right," Gem said. She might have expected such callousness. "Lead on then."

GEM FOLLOWED the Administrator past a series of empty cells, then they turned down a hallway that resembled the outpost corridor, smooth concrete floors and shining, silver walls. The Administrator moved gracefully, walking her corporate walk, her figure swaying slightly as her heels clicked and clacked. The sound her of her shoes echoed off the walls, and it seemed loud to Gem, too loud. Even her own footsteps felt noisy. She could only assume her system was still purging Garcia's potions.

The corridor stretched on until they emerged in an operating room, a space that dwarfed the outpost bay. There were twenty-odd vehicles parked throughout, many of them Wraiths. Others were standard Company fare, dark trucks and SUVs, all unmarked and inconspicuous. By the looks of it they had hauled her to a base, one of the Company's primary campuses.

If she had been there before, she could not recall it.

I have been here before, she thought. *I must have.*

Gem recognized her own Wraith among the vehicles, unmistakable due to the damage she'd inflicted. The sight of it cooled her blood, for what she had done to the vehicle—for what she had done to Banks—but it was more the realization she would never drive again, that this unfortunate journey had been her last. Nostalgia was strange that way. She had been hell-bent on escaping the Wraith, yet she balked at the thought of letting it go.

The operating room opened into a larger bay past the vehicles, and Gem saw multiple platforms, some raised to the level above and others sitting idle. There was a reception area beyond the lifts, a vast, open space encased in smoky glass. They passed under an arch where the concrete floors gave way to shining tile, then the surface transitioned to marble as they reached reception, an inner sanctum lined with sleek tables and chairs and leather loveseats for the visiting suits. "Classy," Gem said.

The Administrator ignored her.

They continued on through the foyer until they reached an elevator, and when they entered the lift, there were only two options, *One* and *LL.* Gem could only assume *LL* stood for *Lower Level.* "Huh," she said. "Two floors. I figured this place would be bigger."

"It is larger than you assume."

"How large?"

"Large," snapped the Administrator.

Gem could not help but smile. "Whatever you say."

After a short ride up they exited into a space that in no way resembled the lobby. The paint was a sickly, faded olive and peeling off the walls. Chipped, rusted stools sat bolted to the floor along the length of a dusty counter. Gem thought the place might have served as a cafeteria once, back before smoking caused cancer or pictures came in color. The thought almost made her giggle.

She was still feeling rather loopy.

The hallway beyond was lined with filthy ruined carpet and cheap wood paneling that had all but fallen to pieces, and at the end was a room full of old chairs and tables stacked haphazardly along the walls. A single door stood at the far end, a thick, metal slab with a small window cut head-height at its center. The Administrator unlocked the door with her thumbprint and pulled it aside, then they stepped into an old auto garage full of outdated machinery. It reminded Gem of the railroad tunnel, rows of rotted shapes wasting away along the walls.

She saw the outlines of platform lifts on the floor, metal rectangles shining through the dirt. They seemed the only functional units in the shop, and she wondered just what the wench had wanted to show her up here. It was obvious everything of value lay below.

The Administrator activated a control panel near the door, and Gem heard a hitch, then a whir. The entire back wall of the garage began to rise. She looked to the rusting metal doors at the front of the shop, motioning to them with her thumb. "Just for show?"

"They are bolted shut. We do not use them."

Daylight flooded the garage as the false wall folded and slid up along the ceiling, and Gem was glad to see it. There were points she'd imagined she might never see the sun again, that she would spend the rest of her life bound to chairs, swimming in drugs and slipping in and out of simulations. The Administrator motioned for her to follow, and they climbed down a short metal stairwell into an alleyway, an open-air corridor shielded on either side by tall, rigid fencing, the cheap, pressed metal of junkyard barriers. It was two stories tall, running away from the garage for the length of a city block. The top was lined with evil-looking razor wire. Trees covered the outside of the barricade, firs and pines towering over the nasty panels and blanketing them in green. *Camouflage*, Gem thought.

At the end of the corridor was a gate, one wide enough to accommodate a large vehicle. She had seen layouts like this many times, old, rundown plots of land where a Wraith was unlikely to catch someone's eye. The gate would open to a straight shot down some lonesome road, a spot where a team could disappear like ghosts and return just as easily. Gem began to wander down the alleyway, then she felt the Administrator's hand on her shoulder.

"Here," said the wench.

There was a side door built into the paneling, and the Administrator produced a keycard from her suit pocket. The door unlatched as she slipped it into the slot, and she motioned for Gem to walk through. Gem hesitated. "What's this then? Is this a part of your test?" When the Administrator said nothing Gem stepped forward and peered out into the woods. Now she was properly confused. "Alright," she said. "What gives."

The Administrator was growing impatient.

"There is nowhere you can go where we cannot collect you, Gemma. Do you still not understand that? Besides, I am quite confident you will find your own way back."

Gem rolled her eyes.

"How cryptic of you. Could you at least tell me where I'm supposed to go? I've no sodding idea where I am."

"I am confident you will figure that out as well."

THE DOOR closed behind Gem with a click. She stood among the trees in the shade, allowing the smell of the pinecones to wash over her, a lovely smell, then she walked out away from the barriers. There was a break in the foliage ahead to her left, the shape of the clearing suggesting a road. It ran perpendicular to the alleyway, and Gem thought she could make out a structure, possibly a house, but as she drew closer she saw it was little more than a battered shed. Gem thought of the garage the Administrator had shown her, that old façade. If she doubled back a-ways and around, she would be able to see it.

Gem circled the perimeter until the garage emerged from the trees, and then she paused, allowing the image to sink in. Now she knew why the wench had sent her outside. This was a part of the experiment, alright, just like the rest of it.

"Bloody hell," she said softly.

She was in Hawks Pass, and the garage was the broken-down auto shop she'd spied from the road.

THE RIDDLE

GEM THREW her head back and laughed. It was all she could do to respond. Was it really that surprising? No, it was not. Nothing was going to surprise her for the rest of her life at this rate, not as long as she was able to reason. And how long would that be now? Another hour? A few more minutes? The garage loomed over her, mocking her with its presence, the building extending back into the trees until it disappeared from view—*camouflage*. She had not spied the bulk of the structure from the road that day, even when she'd been actively observing. *Inhale—count to three—exhale*. Now the proof of her delusion stood before her, and she knew there would be more down the road. She recalled the Administrator's parting words.

Where am I supposed to go?

I am confident you can figure that out.

"Right," Gem said. The wench had wanted her to see Hawks Pass for herself—but why? It was proof she had been lying, that Gem had successfully read her hand. The AI's warning crept to the front of her mind. *It seems alternative methods are required.*

So that was what this was, an alternative to rooms and drugs and chairs, the Company's backup plan. There was no point in maintaining the ruse now, she supposed, not after she had spotted the cracks. The Administrator had tried, and the Administrator had failed. *I am confident you can figure that out.*

"Right," Gem said again. She would walk back to the market where it all began, knowing it had been an illusion, an epic con. If that was the Administrator's intention, then Gem would oblige, because like it or not, she was still on the clock, and there were no choices on Company time. Her body was the vehicle now, her implant the machine. She had been given her directives.

Gem pushed herself forward along the road, walking with pace. She hardly noticed the familiar structures, the old, broken dwellings and cabins out of season. There was no reason to consider them now. Before long she came to the tidy little house where the man—where *Dr. Garcia* had sat with his mug and his cigarette. The structure stood unscathed, neat and immaculate, and she wondered if the good doctor had ever set foot on that porch. It seemed more likely the construct had spun up his likeness.

Her feet carried her forward until she spied the traffic light in the distance, still blinking yellow, still swaying in the breeze on its trusty line. She had never wanted to see that light again, and it was just her luck that—

A truck passed through the intersection and froze her in place. *Traffic*, she thought. *Ordinary traffic.*

When was the last time she'd seen a civilian on the road?

None since your accident, love. None since they planted your chip.

Could it be true? Had she seen anyone who was *not* Company after waking up in the tent? Banks, the Administrator, Wanda, Garcia, the Magazine Man. "The Magazine Man," Gem said. There was no reason to assume he was not Company as well.

She closed her eyes, considering whether her bug had the juice to shield an entire town from her, the surrounding roads, everywhere they'd traveled. It was one thing to generate an illusion, but to dispel reality? That was something else. What would have kept her from steering the Wraith into traffic, or walking face first into a shopper? *No traffic, no shoppers. There was only—*

Her mind turned to the Magazine Man again.

Why wasn't he at the lab with his co-conspirators?

She recalled the feeling he'd stirred in her when she first laid on eyes him. He had seemed out of place in those clothes, in the market, in that town. Now he seemed out of place in the Administrator's entourage. "Intuition," Gem said. Yes, intuition, and where had that gotten her? Back on the road to the general store, that was where, a place she had seen reduced to smoldering boards and detritus. But she could not shake the feeling. Her gut told her the Magazine Man would be at the market, that he still had a part to play in this.

I am confident you can figure that out.

Who else was there now but him?

GEM SAW additional citizens along the road, an older couple in a yard tending flowers, a pedestrian crossing the street under the light, a truck turning onto the main drag. In the real world Hawks Pass was just another mountain town, or at least it was on the surface. Its secrets lay below, stretching off into the bowels of the wooded out-skirts. Did that couple know what the Company was up to down there? Did the driver of the truck?

Before long she stood in the lot by the general store.

The market was just as it was before, an unremarkable service station standing at ease, the most common sight in America, ordi-nary to everyone but her. Inside Gem found a motherly woman behind the counter, a woman who looked nothing like Wanda. That woman would have had small town questions for her, the *where are you froms* and *what brings you heres* and so on. A trio of towns-folk sat at a window-side table drinking coffee and talking amongst themselves, the local palaver she had envisioned, but the Magazine

Man was not there. The back booth where he'd been sitting was empty. *So much for that theory*, Gem thought.

She cased the store as she had before, taking in the details and observing nothing extraordinary, sandwiches and perishables in the cooler, snacks in neatly arranged rows and coffee cups and creamers against the back wall. It was a typical country store, and there were no revelations hidden among the commodities. So what now? She could start up a conversation with the locals, as awkward as that might be. She could hint she was Company stock and see if anyone picked up on it, though that would—

Gem heard the creak of a door.

She looked over her shoulder, and yes, here was the Magazine Man emerging from the rest area. He walked over to the coffee counter, pulled a cup from the stack and began to assemble his beverage, all but oblivious to her presence. Or was he? Could she be certain? His shirt and his boots had changed, but the cap was the same, the same crisp bill and the same simple markings. Gem had been right after all. He was the only player left in the game. If he was not the answer to her riddle, then she would be lost.

She walked over to the counter and stood beside him, then she cleared her throat. The Magazine Man looked up, his mouth turning up at the corners in a wry smile. His eyes suggested thoughtfulness, perhaps even kindness, and it caught Gem by surprise. This was not the reaction she had expected. He motioned for her to join him at his booth, and Gem sat down across the table, waiting for him to speak. He only eyed her with curiosity, blowing on his coffee through the little plastic lid.

Gem opted to break the ice. "I was hoping you might have some information for me," she said, her voice low and flat. "I assume you know who I am, that you are aware of my profession. Are you the one I'm supposed to speak to?"

The Magazine Man said, "Me? Well, I guess that depends on what you mean by *information*." His demeanor was casual, friendly.

"I know a few things, sure, but in your case I wouldn't know where to begin. I'm not privy to the comings and goings of the Company these days, nothing important, that is. I was told you would be stopping by sometime this afternoon, but I am only a messenger." He checked the watch on his wrist. "On that note, it appears I can't send you on your way just yet."

Gem stared at the man in the cap. He was only a messenger? And just what in the hell was that supposed to mean? Her face must have betrayed her thoughts, because he chuckled. "I *was* a Company man," he said, "back when the world was a saner place, before the powers-that-be got way out ahead of themselves." He seemed to look right through her, envisioning another time. "I'm retired now—have been for years—but we are still in each other's ears on occasion. I don't mind claiming the odd consultant's fee when I can, et cetera." He leaned forward, lowering his voice. "I'm sure you have questions, boatloads of them, I reckon. I might not have too many answers for you, but seeing as we have some time, I'll tell you what I can." He sat back then, sipping his coffee with care.

Gem was not sure what to make of him.

At first she thought he was toying with her, that the old part-timer bit was a ploy and he knew far more than he was letting on, that he would push her and goad her and try and twist her around. But it was not cold calculation she sensed in him. What she registered was benevolence, empathy, emotions that were fast becoming foreign to her. She said, "Alright. Let's start with a simple one then. You have seen me before, yes?"

He did not seem surprised by the question.

"Sure, when you were in for groceries and gasoline. Had that sharp little ATV." He set his coffee down. "Let me guess. You are no longer certain what you saw that day."

"No." Gem trained her eyes on him. "No, I am not certain. Do you know something about that? Can you tell me what has been happening to me?"

"Not much I'm afraid, only that you were in the early stages of the *process*, as they call it, and it was on me to keep an eye out for you."

"And what do you know about this *process*?"

He leaned forward and smiled.

"Not much. I was out of the game before such things existed, and I'm sure you know far more about it by now than I ever did. Sorry to burst your bubble."

Gem was hoping for more, though she had known better than to expect it. How far would the executives trust a messenger, after all, if that was indeed what he was. The jury was still out on that. Likable or not, this was a man the Company had paid to keep tabs on her. "I saw you use the phone when I was leaving," Gem said. "At the time I thought you were ratting me out to a rival, but you weren't, were you? You were reporting my presence to that woman up the hill."

He nodded in agreement. "I don't know who I spoke to, but I called up there and let them know I'd seen you and everything looked about like they said it would. For me it is all need to know, and most of the time I don't. They leave a message down here if they want me to look into something, then I call up the number they give me—it's never the same one—and when I've got the information they want or spot who they want me to spot, they wire some money to me and I get on with my retirement. It's mighty convenient, and I can't complain."

"Seems so. How often do they contact you?"

"Oh, maybe once or twice a month on average."

"And who is it you're looking out for? Others like me?"

The Magazine Man leaned in again.

"Like you? No, I wouldn't say there are many like you, but I'm afraid I can't speak any more to that. I said I would tell you what I could, and that is something I cannot tell you. I'm sure you can understand."

"I do," Gem said, and she did. Loose lips brought trouble in their line of work. "But I still have other questions. If you can help me at all, I would appreciate it."

He checked his watch again. "Fire away."

"Who was the cashier that day?"

The Magazine Man looked off toward the counter, then back to Gem. "There was a different gal here," he said. "Haven't seen her since."

Gem leaned forward. "A big lass?"

He nodded. "You could say that. I imagined she was one of theirs, but it did not behoove me to ask."

"She was," Gem said, then she looked down at the table and frowned. "So that means Garcia was out that day too, watching, waiting. Now I know why Banks offered up the Buggy." She saw the Magazine Man was listening quietly. "Sorry, I was talking to myself."

"No need to apologize," he said. "Seems you know far more about it than I do."

"I suppose I do. I lived it." A passing car drew Gem's attention, and when she returned her eyes, he was pointing to his wrist.

"It appears our time is up," he said through a smile. "I wish you well, and I do hope your next appointment will be more informative. Did you see the tavern when you came in today? The one just down the road?"

Gem did not know what he was talking about.

"Hang a left when you go out. It's half-a-block down on the other side of the street. You can't miss it. Place has got batwing doors, like a genuine saloon." He leaned in again. "Sounds like somebody thought you could use a drink."

Gem smiled. "And they would be right."

When she stood to leave the Magazine Man remained, and she figured he might stay there a while, listening to the little town stir and waiting on his next assignment. She was almost sorry to leave him. Her next *appointment* was bound to be far less affable.

"Good luck with your consulting," she said.

He tipped the bill of his cap as if it were an old Stetson.

"Likewise. I figure you will be just fine in the end. You just have to get there first."

SURVEILLANCE

THE MAGAZINE man watched her walk off through the candy aisle and exit the building. She paused to look back as she made her way across the lot, and for a moment, he thought she might turn around. Then she started off again. When she was well out of sight he pulled an old phone from his pocket, an archaic piece of tech he'd modified to run off the grid. The Company could not see it, and the Company could not read what they could not see. He punched in the number and waited.

"Dale here," he said. "It's time."

He put the phone away, stood up and picked a magazine out from the rack, an outdated automotive monthly. There was an over-sized truck on the cover, and he flipped it open and leafed through the pages, pretending to glance at the contents.

Then he turned his eyes back to the window.

Dale could not say how long her appointment would last. He was not privy to such information, after all—that was the truth—though he reckoned it ought to run long enough for his purposes.

And if that did not prove to be the case?

Well, then he supposed he would have to improvise.

THE SALOON

GEM PAUSED and looked back as she made her way through the front lot, past the pumps that had never exploded. There was the Magazine Man, still seated in his booth. She had forgotten to ask his name, nor had he asked for hers. He would forever be the *Magazine Man* to her, and perhaps it was better that way. There was a mythos to the moniker, like the *Marlboro Man*, and she would think of him whenever she saw a graying man in a cap, or somebody reading a magazine with their coffee. That was assuming she saw herself through to the end of this mess. She might not have the memory to draw on.

Gem turned onto the sidewalk and looked up the road, old buildings running for a stretch of two blocks on either side, a classic American Main Street. The structures had been kept up to varying degrees, some wood-framed and two stories tall, others stouter and brick. She saw an old theatre that appeared to be open, but there were no films advertised on the marquee, no patrons coming or going through the doors, no vehicles parked out front.

She seemed to be the only one out and about.

Were there people all around her she couldn't see?

Then a lady emerged from a building down the road with a shopping bag, as anyone might do in a normal town on a normal afternoon. Gem closed her eyes, then opened them again. The woman was still there, pausing to look both ways before crossing the street, waving to a car as it slowed to let her pass.

Normal, Gem thought.

She spotted the batwing doors of the saloon on her right, a place that would look at home in an old Western, its wooden façade hand carved and the letters above the doors spelling out *Saloon,* as if it were not perfectly obvious what kind of establishment it was. Modern touches began to emerge as she neared the exterior, neon signs hung alongside advertisements for drink specials in the windows, a satellite dish peering over the corner of the roof, another dead device. When she pushed the batwings aside she was greeted by a heavy metal door, and that made her laugh.

So much for authenticity.

Cool air prickled her skin as she stepped inside. In the dim light she saw tables and chairs arranged toward the front of the room where space would allow, a lacquered rosewood bar running the length of the establishment and lines of tall, wooden booths set against the back wall. Two men sat on barstools at the far end with bottled beers, one tall and large and the other thin and wiry. They glanced her way at the sound of the door, but that was all.

After a moment the bartender appeared from the cooler in back, a younger man. He was clean cut and well-dressed and seemed out of place in the establishment, out of place in Hawks Pass, just like the Magazine Man. Gem suspected he was a Company plant, maybe even the one she was supposed to meet, and she waited at the end of the bar as he made his way toward her. When he spoke up his voice was soft, his country accent thick. This was no Company man.

"Believe there's someone waiting on you, Miss," said the bartender. He gestured toward the far corner where Gem saw a silhouette, a figure seated in a booth. "He ordered you a whiskey, neat."

Gem fixed her eyes on the shadow in back.

"Well, that was kind of him." She thanked the bartender and began to weave her way through the tables.

Her appointment knew what she drank, whoever he was. That was no secret—the AI might have plucked that information from her thoughts at any time—though she had a sneaking suspicion it was the man who knew, not the machine.

"Banks," she whispered. Could it be?

She had no way of knowing how long the Company had kept her in the labs. He might have had ample time to recuperate. She did not know whether to feel fear or anxiety or hatred or relief, and she felt everything at once, a smorgasbord of sentiment. It might not be good to see him, but it would be good to learn what he knew, assuming that was his purpose, why he had kept it all from her, what had inspired him to play along. She had discovered a good deal since the incident with the tree, though she still knew very little. If the man was Banks—*if*—and he could shed some light on her predicament, then she was prepared to listen.

I could give him a slap first. A good, hard slap.

She found the idea did not amuse her.

He might have been knocked out and chipped and fed his own regimen of bullshit, forcibly compelled to play his part in the *process*. She might find she had marred a friend in error.

Gem exhaled and clinched her fists.

She did not even know it was Banks. *But don't I?*

Who else was there now but him?

SHE STEELED herself as she approached the booth, then she slid into the seat. "Banks," she said. His face was bruised, and thin bandages masked a series of small stitches around his eye. There looked to be more above his temple, larger ones. His lips were swollen on the right side of his mouth, a glistening plum color under the tavern lights. "I thought you would look far worse."

Banks set his drink down.

"I did. I was told it took some effort to reset the bones in my face, but medical technology is good these days, and the Company footed the bill. I was injured on the job, after all."

Gem fought the urge to ask how long it had been since the accident. "For what it's worth," she said, "I regret that I had to hurt you, but given where we are, I can't say I was wrong to do it. Perhaps you should attempt to convince me otherwise. That is what this *appointment* is about, right? You're going to tell me I had it all wrong."

Banks shrugged. "We are going to have a discussion, and a civil one, I hope. Then you can judge for yourself."

There was no anger in his voice, only a sad resignation, that melancholy she had not been able to place. Now she understood it.

She had yet to touch her drink, and Banks motioned toward it. "There is nothing in that glass but bourbon, Gem, and I think you will want it. I was told the drugs they gave you will not interact with the booze. They should be just about out of your system anyway."

Gem leered at him. "Told by *who*?"

"Who do you think?"

She snatched up the glass and drank half of the contents down before returning it to the table.

"Her," Gem said. "That executive told you."

Banks threw the rest of his drink back. "You might as well finish that," he said. "I'm getting another round." He held two fingers up to the barman, then he returned his gaze to Gem. "We are sitting here because you are not responding to the process, and our employers are growing impatient. They have decided to throw subtlety out the window and spell it out for you, and I'm afraid it has fallen on me to do that. They believe my experience with you makes me the most suitable candidate. I am not sure I agree with that, but here we are."

The bartender set the whiskeys on the table and made himself scarce, Gem drinking the rest of her first down in a swallow.

"Go on then," she said. "Spell away."

Banks took a sip of his drink.

"I think it would be better to start with what you know, or at least what you be*lieve* you know. What have they told you?"

"Told me?" Gem said. "They haven't *told me* a damned thing. They've done nothing but toy with me since I woke up in that chair."

"I should have phrased that differently. What have you learned about your situation?"

Gem tapped a finger against her temple.

"I know they are listening, Banks. What exactly would you like me to admit? We might as well get on with it."

"It doesn't matter what you choose to admit, Gem."

She closed her fingers around her glass and squeezed, her mind drifting back to that orange hell. "It's some form of AI," Gem said, "probably the illegal kind, a Chiron build. I know they linked it to the Seeker, that it can generate visuals, hallucinations. I know it made me see this town burn, and Christ knows what else." She watched Banks's face for a reaction, anything that could give her a read. He only sat there listening. "It talked to me you know, brought me into its office for a nice little chat. Did they tell you that?"

"They only told me you were not responding to the process, that this was the next step."

"But you knew about the program. You knew about it all along and said nothing." Gem leaned in. "What do they have on you, Banks? What was bad enough for you to lie to me, to sell me out. What did you do?"

Banks sat back in surprise. "What did *I* do? Nothing, Gem. They do not have anything on me. It was *you*. You were the reason I agreed to participate." His gaze hardened, and Gem saw the emotion in his eyes, the hurt. "You may not believe that, but it is the truth. They would have created a backstory for my absence and sent you out with someone else. The scenario would have been far less stable, and seeing how poorly it went down—even with my involvement—that would have been a disaster."

Gem let her eyes burn into him.

"Stable? What part of it was stable, Banks? I accepted what was happening because *you* accepted it. I thought of it constantly, how if you were not there I would think I was going mad—"

"I know," he said. "And it ate at me, enabling that, but I had no choice. They were going to put you through this with or without me, and it was better I was there. You can see that, right?" He stared into his glass. "I'd like to think you would have done the same."

They sat in silence for a moment, sipping their whiskeys.

"You saw what I saw then?" Gem said.

"Yes. I was fitted with a modified clone of your implant. I could not react to something I couldn't see, and if I was to keep you on course, you had to trust me—"

"I did trust you, Banks! That part of me would like to cut up your fucking face some more!"

"I know, but it had to be done."

Gem looked off to the far wall. It was dark back there, comforting. She closed her eyes—*inhale—count to three—exhale*. His words were beginning to ring true, in spite of her reservations.

"I know what they are trying to make me forget," she said, turning to face him. "I tricked that sodding bot into spilling its beans."

"Is that so?"

"Yes. I stole information from them. I don't know what for, but I nicked it from a relay tower and uploaded to my drive. That was why they had it, why they planted it in that bag for me to find."

Banks shook his head. "No, Gem. Whatever you think you remember, this tower, *that* is them toying with you. If you did something like that they would not have offered you this chance."

She glared at him. Would he lie to her now? Would he dare? No, he had a point. She could hardly think of something worse than stealing Company secrets. It was an irredeemable offense. Banks would have shown up for work and found a new driver awaiting him, and when he inquired as to her absence, they would have fed him a story. He would have never seen her again. "Say I believe you," Gem said. "Tell me what I did then. What was bad enough for them to put me through this, to put *us* through this?"

Banks seemed to hesitate.

"You're sure they didn't tell you anything about it?"

"No."

"So they left it all to me then." Banks sat up straighter, as if he were bracing himself. "You did not steal Company secrets, Gem. You quit. You packed up and left without notice, with all of your knowledge of Company operations. You didn't complete the exit protocol."

Alarm bells rang in her head. How many times had she thought about walking away? *How many stars in the sky? How many grains of sand?* Could she have tried to slip out the backdoor? Could she have been so foolish? "You're saying I went AWOL?"

"Yes, Gem, you—"

"No." she said. "I could not have been that daft. I would have known something like this would happen. There's no way I just up and shat on *exit protocol.*"

She had raised her voice and drawn the attention of the beer drinkers, the men looking over their shoulders with annoyance.

Banks held up a hand to them. "Were good," he said.

Gem took the hint and changed her tone.

"I would never do something so stupid, Banks."

"You did, and that is why we are here. Everything you went through, that *we* went through, was a process designed to salvage your employment Gem, to salvage your *life.*"

"Everything, Banks? All of it? Tell me what purpose it served. Hallucinations to break my mind? Fine, but why the dead man? Why did they put a tracker in my drive? How much of that was *real?* You have all the answers, yes? So tell me why!"

His eyes warned her she was pushing it again. "I will tell you what I know," Banks said, "but you need to realize there is still plenty I don't. All I have to go on was my original briefing and my orders to meet you here, and those orders were curt. Our mutual friend told me very little."

"I am sure she didn't." Gem took a deep breath, culling the edge from her voice. "So let's start here then. Why Hawks Pass? Why bring us through town like that?"

Banks stared into his drink, as if it might hold all the answers.

"It was part of the plan," he said.

THE PLAN

B ANKS TOOK a sip of his whiskey and said, "The run was designed to wear you down, Gem, to strain your mind, your emotions. I've gathered that much. They could not just strap you to a table and let the program work on you. That is not how it functions. It had to build a data profile, and sending you out provided an opportunity for it to get a read on your behavior, how you process information, all of it. I'd have to believe they tried a lab setting first, though in the end, the Seeker allowed them all the control they required.

Banks paused to collect his thoughts.

"Hawks Pass was a logical first step, ideal for testing the impediments they placed on your memory. If you recognized anything they would have had to recalibrate your device and start over." He motioned to the back of his head. "Sending you into town would confirm whether the program had successfully imbedded itself."

Gem thought back to that day, riding the Buggy into the outskirts and spotting the incorporation sign. She had felt it, hadn't she? She'd said the name aloud, *Hawks Pass*, trying to make the connection. That they had drained the town from her memory was obvious in hindsight. "I felt it," she said. "Like déjà vu, but faint. I was close to remembering something."

"I'm not surprised," Banks said. "You were not taking to the program."

"No. It didn't get its claws in me until after the store." She looked up, startled. Had that only just occurred to her? Yes, that was the moment, out at the pumps, watching herself speed away on the Buggy like some goddamned guardian angel. "It was after the call," she said. "Something was pulling at me, and I felt—I guess you could call it detachment, like something was ripping my mind from my body. I felt it again later, outside the cave and then under that traffic light. I chalked it up to panic attacks." She closed her fingers around her glass and forced it to her lips.

Banks had been listening quietly.

"Seeing the man on the phone would have been alarming. You could have been vulnerable then, your mind easier to access. The program would have jumped at the opportunity."

"It would make sense." She ran her eyes over Banks, studying his face. "Did you know when it was happening?"

"No," he said. "All I had were visuals, Gem, and I was only tuned in when necessary, when we were together in the Wraith. Otherwise the link was down."

She watched him shift in his seat, unnerved by the notion. Perhaps he thought she would not believe him, or was it the idea of feeling what she felt, of trusting all they had seen was real, the fires and rubble and that loose appendage in the street. She recalled the look on his face as they crested the last of the hills, the weight of his silence. He'd known all he saw in that valley was a lie.

"Why the fires?" Gem said. "And why did you put on that show the next day? The theories? The naysaying?" Her voice grew louder. "You knew it was bullshit and you egged me on, let me think I was Sherlock-fucking-Holmes solving a bloody mystery!"

"I did what you would expect me to do," Banks said. "What would you have thought if I kept my head down and nodded along? I had a part to play, Gem, and it meant rationalizing events as they came. I had no choice." He shook his head. "And I was not thinking about the Seeker. It was an oversight on my part—and yours, for that matter—but I am not an actor. I am not used to improvising on the fly like that. It had to seem *real*. The alternative was watching them come and take you in the night, and—"

"Alright, enough," Gem said. "I can see where this is going, and I've gotten ahead of myself anyways. Tell me why I saw the town on fire. What purpose did it serve?"

"You saw what you feared you would see," Banks said, "and the same must have been true for that cabin up the road. The program saw opportunities to frighten you, to weaken your resolve. It was designed to pick your brain and make use of what it found, suppressing certain ideas, amplifying others. You saw the result of a drone strike because that was the conclusion you drew in the cave. I don't think there can be any question about that."

Gem thought back to that night. She had dreamed of Hawks Pass and the general store, and there was also—"I dreamt of fire that night," she said, "and it was fresh in my mind. Add that to the machine greenlighting a route through town—"

"And you have what we saw," Banks finished.

"Yes, but not exactly. The town was not deserted in my dream, Banks. That was not something I conjured up. I wondered why no one was dead in the street that night, why no one was running for cover. Then I saw that hand and assumed the worst. The bot must have sensed my suspicion and put that bloody mess in the road to quash it. Do you know what I've come to realize? We did not see anyone on that run, not a truck from a distance, not a tractor or camper, *nothing*. When have we ever been so fortunate?"

She paused for a moment then said, "I expect you are going to tell me fortune had nothing to do with it."

"You're right. There was a reason for that—"

"I know there's a fucking reason for it!"

Banks looked off toward the beer drinkers, Gem following his eyes. She laid her hands on the table and exhaled.

"Apologies," she said. "It seems recalling my experiences has made me a bit cross. Please explain the reason we did not see a soul on the road for three days."

Banks frowned.

"Will you promise to save your outbursts until I am finished?"

Gem nodded, picked up her drink and sipped it.

"The route we took was staged entirely on Company property," Banks said. "It was a closed course, a loop designed to scramble your bearings. The Company owns over a hundred square miles of land around Hawks Pass—"

"Oh for fuck's sake."

"You knew all this before the implant, but now you don't, so listen. Most of it was acquired from the government after the hack when it looked like the country's infrastructure might fall apart. The feds needed bailout money and were eager to offload the land to corporations. The rest of it was bought off private owners and smaller companies, those looking to cash in while the property still held value." He motioned over his shoulder and said, "The trainyard, the tunnel, this town—the Company owns it all. Those roads were empty because no one is out there unless the Company puts them there, Gem."

She thought he would never finish.

"And Hawks Pass that day?"

"Like I said, it's a Company town. Everyone here is associated with our employers in one way or another, and a universal bulletin is not uncommon. That is something else you used to know. Word would have gone out when we set up shop in the canyon, then again when you cleared the woods after the call. The same would have been true when the Seeker sent us back in. You didn't see anyone in the streets because no one was out and about. They follow orders in Hawks Pass, just like the rest of us."

Gem placed her head in her hands.

"Of course they do. Bloody hell." She met his eyes again. "So that sorts out the town, the fires, the empty roads and the drones, the cabin, me losing my mind, all that bollocks. But there is still the small matter of what happened later."

Banks swished the whiskey around in his glass, staring at it.

"I don't think we were ever supposed to stop at the outpost," he said. "The idea was to continue on past the trainyard and circle around the other side of the mountain, back toward town. Complications diverted us there."

"What complications?"

"The Seeker losing its signal in the tunnel, for one."

What? Are you taking a piss?"

"Not at all. The Company must have overlooked something when they greenlit that tunnel for passage, maybe the makeup of the mountain, I don't know. A deposit of heavy metals could have done it." Banks frowned at his glass. "But that doesn't matter. What matters is for a moment your mind was free from its constraints. The floodgates were open, so to speak, which I imagine caused our mutual friend some consternation."

Gem nodded to herself. Here was the answer to another question, that rush of clarity she'd felt. She had made the connection after treeing their Wraith, but she was proper mad by that point and had all but forgotten the tunnel. Now it made sense. The program could not hold her mind at bay without the Seeker, but—*but what?* But why had her thoughts gone straight to the tower? Why the drive in the night? They were supposed to be untruths, fabrications designed to confound her. Shouldn't she have recalled going AWOL instead? *Was that the night drive? Was I cutting and running?* She could not rule it out, but why was the memory paired with the tower? Why were they competing for space?

"Because they are related," she said.

"Gem?"

"It's nothing. I'm just trying to wrap my head around this." She looked up again. "I felt it go offline, Banks. I could tell something was different."

"So did I, and I knew it could not be good, even if it was only for a few seconds. I thought there was a chance the impact might not be significant." Gem's thoughts were back in the tunnel, Banks shielding the machine to hide the glitch. She had known he was up to something, and she had been right. "I didn't realize it would lead to meeting with *her*," he continued. "That was not part of the plan, and I was not prepared for it. It was—"

"I suspected something."

Banks motioned to his face. "I'm well aware."

"No, love. I was on to you long before that. You nearly gave yourself away on that pass when you were daydreaming like a dunce, then you just sat there in the meeting and let that witch accost me. You didn't back me up, Banks, not even a word. You—"

He cut her off. "I was scared for you, alright? I knew things had not gone according to plan, and there was nothing I could say to help that. I did not want to further compromise the scenario, and I—well, I feared the worst. I had no idea what came next."

Gem saw the sadness in his eyes. A part of him must have believed that was the end for her, and she could not fault him for that. "I'll give you that one," she said, "but I am talking *well* before the outpost. I never really bought that story about the injury, for starters. It always felt sketchy to me, like it was covering something rotten."

"Yeah, well like I said, I am not an actor, and the setup was not my idea. I could have told them that in all the time we've spent in the wilds I never once saw you lose your footing."

"Reflexes," Gem said absently. "One of the reasons they made me a driver." She stewed on the thought. "And what about the sensors? Did they set that up too?"

Banks shook his head. "I was never briefed on that. No one said a word about it, not before, not after. It certainly felt legitimate, and if it was, it would have contributed to the decision to divert us to the outpost. It might even have been the primary reason."

"So much bullshit at once," Gem said, "so many questions." She took a drink and paused to let it settle. There was still one more bridge they needed to cross, and her gut told her Banks was not going to like it. "You haven't said anything about the wreckage. Where does that factor into this? Who was the dead man, and why did they tag my drive? Tell me what you know about *that*."

The way his eyes shifted told her she was right. He had been dreading this bit. "I didn't know what we had coming after the outpost," Banks said. "That was no act. I was not prepared for any of it, not the wreckage or the body, anything. That was bad enough, but when you pulled the drive from those pants, I knew things were going to take a turn for the worse. After what you'd told me about . . ." He paused, lost in thought.

"About the dreams?"

"About the dreams," Banks said. "I knew then the Company had taken the gloves off, that they were out to break you any way they could. I didn't understand the significance of it—I still don't—but I knew there was something sinister at work. Engineering a scene like that just so you would discover your drive?" He shook his head again. "I didn't know what to do after that. I was lost."

Gem watched him as he spoke, his discolored, battered face, the watery shine in his eyes. She knew then she had been wrong to hurt him. His deception had been born of chivalry, what he perceived as a noble cause. He would have had little choice but to believe what the Company told him, that she had walked away, that his assistance would go some way to salvaging her life. They would have had her in custody, splayed out unconscious and prepped for the implant. They would have made it known her fate was not yet decided. *Bloody hell*. Banks could have walked away. The Company would have promoted a new driver, and he would have shown them the ropes. He would not have those stitches in his face.

Gem closed her eyes. Yes, she had been wrong, but Banks did not know the whole story. He'd been given a redacted script, no more than the lines necessary to act his part. There was every chance the Company had played them both. "Well, they have not broken me yet," Gem said. "What else can you tell me?"

Banks drank the rest of whiskey down and set the glass on the table. "What I can tell you is you have to let them finish the job, Gem. It pains me to say it, but the only way out of this mess is to embrace the program. If you don't, there will be consequences."

Consequences, Gem thought. *Of course.*

It felt like she had been contemplating consequences for an eternity, reminding herself to consider them, imagining how they might play out. Now she knew why. The run had been a consequence of her actions, every bend in the trail and rotting mile of road. She had known it all along, the knowledge buried in the murk and the AI struggling to conceal it. She had misbehaved—somehow—and the program was her comeuppance. All those hours spent wallowing in the shadow of *consequence* were, in fact, a consequence. "So there it is," Gem said.

She drank the last swallow from her glass and turned it over on the table. It was always going to come to this. Hadn't Banks told her as much when she arrived? He was there to spell it out for her, and now he had. There was only the one path now, no alternatives to pursue, just as the wench had proclaimed when she'd released her into the world. Gem ran her fingers over the implant, a wound that had now all but healed. They could cripple her with pain and drag her back to the base and bring her nightmares to life, or she could go in on her own accord. That was the choice that remained.

"I forgive you, Banks," she said, "and I hope you can forgive me, for what I did to your face and for everything that has happened. For whatever it was I did."

"Gem, I told you—"

She held up a hand to silence him. "I know what you told me, and there is no need to discuss it further."

Believing Banks had betrayed her had gone against everything she'd known about the man, and in the end she had been wrong. She should have trusted what she knew, and she *knew* she would never go AWOL like that. If she had decided to throw in the towel she would have stuck to the protocol. *And if I had reason not to?*

If that were the case—*if*—then she would not have crossed her fingers and slipped quietly into the night. Had she taken that old drive of hers to a tower and hacked into the Company coffer?

Had she really had the stones to try it?

Gem smiled. Perhaps the Administrator would tell her if she asked nicely. They were going to dismantle her memories anyway, right? Maybe the wench would take pity on her. She laughed aloud at the thought, Banks looking at her like she'd lost her mind, again. Who would have the nerve to laugh at a time like this? *Only a proper nutter*, she thought. *One fit for that gray chair of theirs*. She folded her arms in front of her and said, "It's back to the base then, is it?"

Banks lowered his head. "Are you coming with me?"

Gem smiled a tiny smile. "What choice do I have?"

THE TRUCK

BANKS POINTED to an oversized truck in the street, the vehicle Company-issued and black and sporting an in-transit tag, a slip that would sit the window until it was put out of rotation.

"I'll do the driving," he said.

"Suit yourself," Gem said. "You were always looking for an excuse."

"Untrue. Navigator's the better job, always was."

"Bollocks."

They opened the doors, stepped up and in and closed them with a bang, Banks shifting the truck into gear and pulling out into the road. A few old vehicles lined the main drag, a crew-cab that might have belonged to one of the beer drinkers and a couple of four-wheel drives, the types suitable for the mountain paths beyond town. Had she seen any cars parked on the street that night? She could not recall. The Company might have warned its minions to lodge them out of sight, lest the madwoman barrel through and crush them with her Wraith. The thought almost made her laugh.

They neared the main intersection with its lonely traffic light. Gem recalled how it had sagged that night, bent off its moorings by a blast that had never occurred. She'd been losing her mind under that light, detached, defenestrated, observing the scene from beyond. The general store came into view on her right, and she trained her eyes to the window. Was the Magazine Man still in his booth? *No*, she thought, *because there he is*. He was seated on a bench outside the door, his arms laid flat along the backrest. He appeared to be watching the sky. He turned toward the truck as they passed and extended a hand in greeting, probably aware of whose vehicle it was and who it was carrying. Gem held up a hand in return.

He would not see it behind the smoky glass, but something told her he would know she'd waved back.

Banks peered out the window. "Is that—"

"It's the Magazine Man, the bloke who kicked it all off in earnest. Turns out I was wrong about him."

"How so?"

Gem thought on it for a moment. "He was not running the show," she said. "He was only a messenger."

"I think it is pretty clear who's running the show."

"Yes," Gem said. "Yes it is."

They turned the corner under the yellow light, and before long they came to the little house where Garcia had sat on the porch. It looked as pristine as ever, the lawn freshly mowed and the gutters straight and clean. Gem wondered who put the effort into keeping it up. *Maybe Garcia himself*, she thought, snickering under her breath. It was not an impossible notion. The man had to live somewhere.

"There is the house," she said. "The man I saw on the porch was a doctor from the base."

"I know," Banks said.

Gem stared him down. "Is that so?"

"They stationed familiar people in town that day as part of the systems check," he said. "The nurse and the doctor fitted you with the implant, and you had seen them recently. If you had recognized them—"

"Right," Gem said. "Recalibration, back to the beginning." She watched the little house slip out of view in the mirror. "It makes as much sense as any of it."

They drove on in silence until they neared the edge of town, then Banks turned onto a gravel lane. It wound its way through the trees, bending this way and that where the woods would allow. The gate to the alleyway soon appeared on Gem's right, hidden beneath the foliage, and Banks put the truck in park.

"This should only take a second," he said.

His voice was quiet now, subdued, like it had been in the canyon when he'd declined to play for the Buggy. Banks had understood what he was setting in motion that day, just as he did now.

"Hey," Gem said. "I brought this on myself, so chin up now, you cranky shit." Banks forced a smile, and she thought she saw him wince. *Right—it probably hurts his face.*

The creak of the gate drew her attention, Gem peering down the alley as it slid open, a space she had stood a short time before. It seemed an entirely different location now, a gallows walk, the path to a prison yard. Beyond the walls she would face the program again, submitting to its will as it excavated her mind, scraping her memories out like rot from a wound. Gem bent her thoughts to the relay tower and felt a pinch, a warning to keep her distance. It seemed the construct had locked it up tight while she was out, reinforcing the barriers she'd managed carve away.

She had not been able to touch it in the simulation either

. . . the tower . . . that is them toying with you . . .

No, that control room was the source of her recent misery.

They would have no other reason to conceal it.

Banks rolled the truck into the garage and onto the central platform and put the vehicle in park. There was a buzz from below, then the truck dropped an inch, enough to initiate the feel of falling. Gem combed the ground with her eyes as the bay opened below them, searching the lines of vehicles for the Wraith—*her* Wraith.

Banks seemed to read her mind.

"Ours is behind us. You will see it when we get out."

She shot him a dirty look.

"Have you been linked to my thoughts the entire time as well? Because if you have, love, we are going to have a problem."

"Of course not. Even if that were the case—which it *wasn't*—they removed the implant when they were fixing my face." Then he laughed. "I don't think I would have made it through to the end if I knew your thoughts. I might have fled in the night."

Gem felt a smile forming.

"You would have. I went a bit mental there towards the end. You might have heard me thinking something mad, Banks, proper mad, like how I was going to crash the Wraith into a tree."

For a moment their eyes locked, then they both started to laugh. Banks winced and groaned and clapped a hand to his stitches.

"I should not be laughing at that," he said. "I should be calling you one of your obscenities."

When the platform locked into place Gem opened her door and stepped out. She spotted the Wraith a short distance behind them. "It doesn't look too bad," she said. "They can really take a punch."

"It was a well-executed slide," Banks grumbled. "I can't deny that, especially when you consider—"

"Ahem."

The voice had come from behind them, cold and calculating. Gem turned to find the Administrator flanked on either side by armed personnel, two large men in security gear.

"Guards?" Gem said.

"It is simply a precautionary measure," said the Administrator. "Mr. Banks is free of our influence now, unlike yourself. We must prepare for every eventuality, including a scenario where the two of you decide to act out in frustration." She locked her eyes to Gem's. "But that is not going to happen, now is it?"

Gem shrugged, then Banks said, "No, it isn't."

"Good," said the Administrator. "Mr. Banks will be leaving us before we reach the laboratories—he has other business to attend to—though you will both follow me in the interim. Is that understood?"

"Very well," Gem said, mocking the wench's monotone. "Let us proceed."

One guard walked alongside the Administrator and the other brought up the rear, keeping his distance. Neither had spoken a word, and Gem wondered if she'd known them once. Had they been fed the same story as Banks, a redacted account of her sudden departure? Were they aware of her actual sins? They walked in lockstep toward the end of the bay, and when they reached it the first guard broke off, the party halting in comical unison.

"You will see each other again," said the Administrator, "assuming Gemma continues to cooperate."

She turned to Banks and signaled for him to exit.

Banks nodded to the Administrator, and then to Gem.

Gem nodded in return.

A proper goodbye would feel cheap in such company, sullied and somehow dirty. It was better to keep it simple, because she would be seeing him again, yes? She had little choice but to believe that.

She watched Banks turn and walk down the hall, accompanied by the first of the guards. She would do her best to remember the laughs they had shared, the games, conversations both silly and serious. She would try to forget what she had done to him. She might see him again, but there was no telling what she would know of him when she did. Or what she would she know of herself.

"Come," said the wench. "Let's finish what we started."

THE LABS

THE ADMINISTRATOR'S heels clicked and clacked on the floor as she walked ahead of Gem, marching back through the facility and past the hallway that led to the cell, the white room for delinquents, absconders, thieves, whatever it was Gem was. The guard followed behind her, ready to act if she stepped out of line. They turned a corner and came to a foyer with a rounded wall beyond the entrance. The ceilings were higher in this section, fifteen feet at least, perhaps even twenty. Corridors formed along the sides of the ellipse, passages that would converge at the far end if they carried on to complete the circle. Glass observation windows emerged as they moved down the hall, and Gem knew these were the labs, where they strapped rebels like her down to confess their sins. Long gray chairs sat in each of the rooms, and not one of them was occupied.

Was she the only inmate in the asylum that day?

The Administrator stopped near a set of double doors, the clear glass goliaths opening inward as she approached. Gem followed her into the inner sanctum, a massive space that had been cordoned off into sections, divided by large glass panels running from ceiling to floor. Most everything was a shiny, offensive white, almost bright enough to reflect her image. Something lay at the center Gem could not make out, its form obscured by identical rows of hardware, server towers, she thought, but these were taller, bulkier. She would not be able to discern their purpose without having a look inside.

She followed the Administrator along the outer wall until she spied a familiar face, then another, Dr. Garcia in his lab jacket, watching them approach, Wanda lingering behind him in her pale green scrubs. There were a handful of other minions milling around in the background, fiddling with the machines. Then Gem saw the chair over the Administrator's shoulder. It was no different than the others she'd seen in the hall labs, but she knew this one had been hers. She recognized the layout of the space, the rows of track lighting overhead. If they ventured closer she would see into the ether, that space beyond the chair the wench had been so enamored with.

The Administrator began to walk in that direction. Imperceptible glass slabs slid out from the paneling as they approached, and they continued on between them. *Just a few more steps.*

And then Gem saw it, a pylon twenty feet high and as thick as a large tree, a steel pillar of enormous scope. It would take the wingspans of five people to measure its circumference, maybe more. Its gunmetal gray exterior shined against the backdrop, the interior glowing orange like the spectra-light and the Seeker—like that hellscape lodged in her mind—and green lights twinkling where the ports opened to expose the inner workings.

Gem stood frozen in place, her eyes on the pylon. She was unaware Wanda had wheeled a sophisticated-looking wheelchair up to the wall behind her, one with a headrest and wrist straps. The Administrator cleared her throat, then she beckoned for Gem to sit.

"You will be strapped down for your own safety," she said, "and Gemma—know that we can always make you less comfortable, should you give us reason."

"Comfortable works," Gem said. "How long have you had *that*." The Administrator turned to the pillar.

"Let the doctor begin the preparations. If you continue to cooperate, I may consider your questions."

Gem nodded. So that was what had been running the Seekers all these years. It had to be, and Gem knew it was capable of more, of holding her memories at bay and sending fire through her mind, drones and dreams and sinister bits of carnage. It was a harbinger of dangerous and miraculous feats, deeds that could very well win the Company their little war. *Orange*, she thought. *Orange and green*.

"Sit still." Gem felt a jab in her bicep.

More drugs. No drug could simulate a drone in flight and force her to feel its ordinance. She stared into the orange light. *That thing is in my head*. "Why would you show me this?" Gem said.

The wench glanced over her shoulder. "This is only one station, you know. There are others. This is what you and your colleagues have been hauling across the mountains piece by piece, components, bits of data, whatever the Company requires. You helped build it, Gemma. Does that surprise you?"

Gem continued to stare. It was the pillar the Administrator had been watching during their session, gauging the impact of her questions, the validity of the responses, both. She imagined a trained eye would have few issues reading the patterns, that lightshow of green—that or its display was not currently active, which would make more sense. Gem wondered what the AI had revealed, if the wench was aware she had throttled it into a confession.

Was it advanced enough to lie?

"I am not showing you this, per se," the Administrator continued. "I am simply not bothering to conceal it. You already knew it existed, at least in some form, and you will have no memory of it when we are finished. There is no harm in it." She sat down in a chair one of the minions had provided. "You asked me how long we have had this technology. The answer is complex. In this iteration, not long at all, a matter of months, though it has existed in various stages for some time. It was originally built to run your Seekers, which I am certain you have gathered. Over the years it has evolved into what you see before you, artificial intelligence near to what the world's powers elected to destroy. It has been a long and delicate process, Gemma, and this is only the beginning."

Gem's thoughts turned to the man in the orange room. She had confounded their construct, if only for a moment. It had shown its true strength and swatted her away in the end, but it was not all-powerful. And if it was only in the early stages of development? Gem felt a smile forming. She was thinking of what Banks had said.

You were not taking to the program. There were complications.

Maybe there were, or maybe the system had not been working properly to begin with. Maybe they were still trying to dial it in. How could a few seconds of severance have derailed their progress so spectacularly? It did not make sense.

. . . in this iteration . . . a matter of months . . .

That was not much time to troubleshoot something so sophisticated. The tunnel had disrupted the connection, yes, but how strong was the signal? She'd conjured the relay tower in the woods after crossing the first pass, and what about the road with the ridge? That was a part of this too, whatever it was, and she'd caught a glimpse of it right out of the gate, on the mountain before Hawks Pass. She had just not recognized it for what it was. And the pain?

Why would they want me to suspect something was wrong?

They wouldn't, that was the answer. It had to be some kind of failsafe, a way to neutralize her when the program lost control. The pain was a last resort. And the intuition?

"The cracks showing," Gem whispered.

"What was that?" said the Administrator.

Gem had forgotten she was there.

"Nothing. Things are just falling into place."

And they were. Her intuitions had not been delusions. They were the result of the program misfiring. It had felt like déjà vu because it *was*, in a sense. She would have been over that pass before, the route in and out of town, and what about the market? Had the Magazine Man triggered the response, or had it been Wanda, another known quantity? It could have been the store itself, the power of a familiar setting. Each whisper of doubt was her memory pushing through, knowledge the program was struggling to conceal.

But that would mean—

It meant the same would be true for what she'd felt staring over the cliff, and that was the hardiest punch of the lot. Something had crawled out of the murk to warn her off the scene, something potent. Her mechanical tormentors had barely been able to hold it off.

"You were saying?" the Administrator said.

Gem had been lost in revelation, the cartoon lightbulb burning bright. "I told your program I knew what it was trying to do," she said, "*trying* being the operative word. You are testing the system, aren't you? Updating your *process*? You are trying to make sure the sodding thing works, and . . ." She paused. "And I am your lab rat."

The Administrator's eyes lit up. She smiled then, displaying her flawless, corporate teeth. To Gem it looked perfectly horrifying.

"I must say I am impressed, quite impressed. I am beginning to understand why this endeavor has proven so difficult." She inched her chair closer to Gem and leaned in. "You have piqued my interest. Tell me, how did you come to that conclusion?"

"System errors," Gem said, "inconsistencies. I did not see them for what they were until you told me your construct was an upgrade, and a recent one at that. Then it all made sense. You would not have wanted me to know something was off, but it was unavoidable. You thought up the injury to explain the bugs, which you knew would kick off eventually, flashes of memory, pain to disrupt those flashes." Gem laughed. "And the amnesia itself, of course. I've grown so used to it I nearly forgot to factor it in. Faking a blow to the head would cover that one as well, the king of all the symptoms. It nearly did the job."

The Administrator was no longer smiling. "We would have feigned an injury regardless, and a concussion was adequate cover for anything you might experience." Her eyes grew stern again, her voice colder. "And do not think we were naïve to these issues, Gemma. You are not the first subject we have tested, and you will not be the last. You have simply been the most difficult."

Gem studied the wench as she spoke. If she was going to pry the truth from her, she would have to act fast. They had already shot her full of the Company dope.

"Banks told me what I did to inspire this treatment."

"I am aware of that."

Gem locked eyes with her.

"But I don't think I believe him. I think I did something else, something worse. Isn't that why you sent us down to the wreckage? You wanted to see if I would recognize it, like your muppets in town. I think that show at the cliff was a test."

"Another interesting theory." The Administrator held her eyes, refusing to blink, giving nothing away.

"Well?" said Gem. "I am here willingly, and I am done fighting you. Tell me the truth. What was that horror show *really* about? What did I *do*?"

The Administrator's eyes glimmered. She was enjoying this exchange. "I will tell you the *truth*, Gemma, but you are going to be disappointed. Some of your deductions have proven astute, but you have not solved some grand conspiracy. There will be no great reveal." Gem sat like a stone, determined to hold her ground. "The vehicle you discovered was damaged before you arrived at the outpost. The team was unable to proceed and initiated the Wraith's emergency protocol, triggering the Seeker's deinstallation mechanism. They removed the machine and secured it to the Buggy, then the driver fled the scene."

The Buggy! Had they even checked for one?

"The navigator remained with the vehicle and awaited extraction. Due to extenuating circumstances, we did not get there first. The Wraith was spotted by a rival scout and targeted before we could make contact, and what you discovered was the result. The

Company was in the process of salvaging the wreckage when you reached the outpost, and we saw an opportunity to turn misfortune to our advantage. It was almost wholly coincidental, save the inclusion of your data drive. The program indicated the device would inspire a reaction, so we searched it out and put it to use." Her mouth tightened around the edges, the slightest of frowns. "Though I must say, your response was not the one we had hoped for."

Gem listened quietly, considering each word and waiting for the wench to slip. Still there was nothing. She spoke as if she were giving a servant her lunch order.

"So you did all that just to fuck with me?"

"No, Gemma. We *did* very little. We left the scene just as we found it." The Administrator's lips formed a line, her voice hardening. "It was your obstinance that compelled us to act. It was *you* who forced our hand."

Gem opened her mouth to respond, then stopped. She could not seem to control her lips. *Drugs*, she thought.

"Drugs," Gem slurred.

The Administrator stood from her chair. "That is my cue. I do hope you found our discussion informative."

Gem's curses came out as gibberish, inebriated sludge. She knew her mind would soon follow her tongue. *Think.*

Was the Administrator telling the truth about the wreckage?

No, her explanation was far too convenient, like she had planned it in advance. She was covering her bases.

Emergency protocol *would* have called for extracting the machine, for an agent to slot it into to the Buggy's port and flee the scene. It justified the missing driver, the Seeker. But if the Company had been there, *in the process*, as she'd said, they would have sought to remove the payload, and she'd seen no evidence of that.

They would have had to flip the Wraith—

Could she be certain? What if they didn't need to?

What else did they miss?

Gem's lashes were fluttering on their own accord now, her eyelids heavy. She was going under.

Could any of what she'd said be true?

. . . it was you who forced our hand . . .

. . . we did very little . . .

THE ROOM

ONE OF Gem's eyelids peeled away from the pupil and she squeezed it shut at once—*orange*. She took a deep breath and counted to three, then she opened her eyes. Here were the walls again, flowing with lava, but this time there was no code. In place of the numbers arrows zipped around, pointing to nowhere in particular. A sea of emerald lay below her feet—*putting green*—and when she returned her eyes to the front she was met by her reflection. The walls had shifted to mirrors. *The room from the dream.*

"Yes," said a voice from the ether. "You remember."

The nightmare came flooding back, the phantom hand and the screaming. "How could I forget."

"You *can* forget, Gem. That is why we are here."

Here, she thought, the end of line, the inevitable result of her actions. All the shit roads and mountain paths had ultimately led here, the stage for the inquisition. A hand gripped her from behind.

"Oh, come on! This again?"

When she turned the stranger stood before her.

Gem closed her eyes. "Who is that?" she asked the room.

There was no answer from above.

"Look at me," said the stranger.

Gem opened her eyes. The lava was flowing again, the woman stoic against the backdrop. There was no fire in her eyes this time, no malice. Instead there was longing, sadness—and then Gem remembered. She had seen her here in the dream, whispering to her that night at the outpost, warning her someone was listening.

She was talking about the program. But who is she?

"I'm looking," Gem said.

The stranger brought her hands together in front of her waist. "This is what I would have looked like," she said.

Her face seemed to shift as she spoke, a trick of the light. No, the stranger's eyes had grown dim, discolored and watery. Foam bubbled away in the corners of her mouth and trickled down her chin. Gem fought the urge to back away.

"And whom might you be?"

"You know," the stranger said.

The walls reverted to mirrors and Gem saw her everywhere, multitudes reflected across the space. Her orange hell had become a funhouse. She looked to the floor to escape her gaze.

Could it be? It would make sense. "I think I do know," Gem said. "What now? What do you want from me?"

The voice rang out from the walls.

"Who are you? Did you kill that girl?"

A knot formed in her stomach. "No."

When Gem looked up the stranger had changed.

She was younger now, sprawled on the floor and dragging herself slowly forward. Gem watched her hold out a hand and collapse.

"That was not my fault," Gem said.

"Did you kill that girl?" the voice repeated.

The posh girl was thrashing now, one hand clamped to her throat and the other held to the air. She was one of the three who'd mocked her, one of the two who had never returned. The other had transferred away to another academy, but her?

A fistful of pills, Gem thought.

That was what the rumors had said. "She could have left me alone," Gem said. "She could have just let me *be*."

"Did you know her? What was her name?"

Gem sat down on the floor, her face in her hands. She was ready to scream, to tear at the walls until the lava bled out and consumed her. She did *not* kill that girl. "The socials killed that girl!" she shouted. "Those pathetic, fucking *trolls*. They were the ones who called her a whore! She could have just let me be!"

And then she felt a pinch. Her vision doubled and shook and the ground below her went wobbly. She squeezed her eyes shut and breathed, then counted, then breathed. The sensation began to pass, and when she opened her eyes, she was alone with her reflection. Someone had been there a moment ago, a woman, she thought.

"Was there somebody here with me?" she called.

A sequence of images flashed through her mind.

She saw herself at seventeen, or a girl remarkably like her. No, it had to be her, the dyed hair and the dark clothes and boots. She was in a classroom—*I did my lessons online*—leering at a group of girls, the trio whispering to one another.

She saw herself stand up and walk away.

"What's all this?" Gem said. "That never happened."

The scene cut out with a flash, and she blinked and shook her head. She could have sworn it felt lighter on her shoulders, like a great weight had been purged from her skull.

"What was all that about?" she said.

"Rehabilitation," said a voice from the ether.

Rehabilitation, she thought. Now she understood. She had been here before, the crazy-eyed man twiddling his thumbs in the corner, the master of the voice. Perhaps that man—that *thing* had chosen to hide itself away, wary of what she'd done to it. But what was it she had done? She could not remember. The thought felt fuzzy to her, like her mind was experiencing poor reception.

"No need to worry about that," said the voice. "We have work to do, and we have only just begun. Now, you said you did not recognize what I showed you. That scene in the classroom never happened, did it?"

"Are you serious? What would I care about a gaggle of posh brats?"

"Good," said the voice. "We are making progress. Now, I want to show you something else. Some of the images you may recognize, and some you may not. Do not be alarmed though, Gem. This is all part of the process."

"The process, right. That is why I am here."

"Yes," said the voice. "Now, please pay attention. I would like you to tell me what you see."

The mirrored walls flashed and Gem shielded her eyes from the glare. Then she saw herself again, older than before, college-age. She was sitting by a fountain, smoking a cigarette and fiddling with her purse. "What? And now I am *smoking*? I never smoked."

"Are you sure about that?"

"Of course I am bloody sure," she said. "I think that is something I would remember."

GEM SAT in the strange room and watched all the program endeavored to show her. That was what it was, right? A program? She must have believed she understood its purpose at one point, though this was no longer the case. The master of ceremonies would not tell her how long she had been there or how much she stood to earn for her time. She was unlikely to have agreed to such a thing pro-bono. It felt like something Banks might have talked her into, and if that was the case, she would make sure he regretted it.

A fresh slate of images crossed her vision, another load of shite, a rain-soaked road, a cabin abutting an endless swath of woods.

"No," she said. "I don't recognize any of it. How much more of this do I have to endure?"

"You are doing great, Gem. Not much longer now."

It had shown her plenty of clips like that, scenes of caves and shabby English gardens, a mock-up of her and Banks in a trainyard. Occasionally it presented an image she recognized, a trick to ensure she was paying attention, Gem figured, Seeker training sessions, snaps of the cubicle she'd occupied prior to her first promotion.

Maybe the Company wanted to remind her how much better she had it now. *This part is not better*, she thought, *whatever it is*.

She only wanted to go have a drink or two, or four or five, go home and go to sleep and purge her mind of the whole sodding experience. She hoped whatever they were paying her would be enough to cover the bar tab.

She braced herself for the next scene.

When it came she saw lines of trees, an evergreen forest stretching off under a dusky sky. She was piloting a Buggy.

"The Buggy," Gem said. "I recognize the Buggy."

She was approaching a relay tower, the Buggy's little panel buzzing and chirping. Was she following a signal? It seemed oddly familiar, but did she *know* what she was looking at? If she got it wrong they might decide to extend her session, and that would not do at all. *Focus*, she thought. *Buggy, path, signal, tower.*

"I don't know yet," she said. "Give me a moment."

Buggy, path, signal, tower.

The voice did not reply.

Then the scene cut away in a flash.

"Hey! I said to give me a moment."

She waited for the voice to respond, to tell her she had failed the test and they would have to begin the process anew. The thought made her want to tear out her hair. She counted the seconds, five, six, seven. Still there was no reply. "Bloody hell," she said softly.

Gem knew this interruption was unlikely to bode well for her, that it would cost her more of the day. She laid back and folded her fingers behind her head and closed her eyes, thinking maybe she could doze off until they needed her. But it was not darkness she saw behind the lids. It was a dull orange haze, like something was burning in the distance. "Shit," she said.

She would find no comfort in this place.

When Gem opened her eyes it took her a moment to notice to change. The walls had gone a deep red, the floor a pallid gray, the colors of concrete and blood. All through the session the room had hummed with a slow pulse, a soft and constant vibration.

Now it was deadly still.

"Hey!" she called out. "I think we're done here!"

She thought she could hear something then, voices. They were hovering somewhere above her, muffled, but urgent, near to the verge to panic. Then there were dulls thuds, like raindrops falling in puddles or the sound of distant thunder.

"Hey!" Gem yelled again.

A slow, creaking sound crept into the din.

And then the room shifted. Gem's body left the floor and struck the wall with force, the blow stripping the air from her lungs. She whooped for breath as she curled into the fetal position, pinned to the wall and bracing herself for impact. But there was no further movement. The room remained locked in its fresh configuration, a diorama flipped on its side. Gem took shallow breaths as the voices carried on in their dampened state. What was it they were saying? If she could only sort out the words—

"Gem."

"Jesus Christ!"

"Stay calm," said the voice. "Focus on where you are."

It was not the voice of the room, no longer emanating from everywhere and spread about the space, and it was certainly not a bot.

This was an actual man with actual inflections. But what was it she heard in the background? Was somebody screaming?

"What—"

"Don't speak. Ignore everything but my voice."

Gem uncoiled her form and groaned. It felt like she had fractured her ribs. The man continued to speak.

"Listen, Gem. Follow my voice."

She turned to the center of the floor where the man's words seemed clearest—*the center of the wall*, she thought—and began to crawl, pulling herself forward inch by inch. Then she heard a creak. The creak gave way to a crack, then a crunch, the sound of breakage and matter splitting, the room pushing inward and edging on toward collapse. She felt the wall rock beneath her.

"Gem!"

Curses sprang from her mouth in wet, hacking gasps. It was no longer just the pain in her side. Her temples had tightened to knots, and the pressure was spreading, the weight of it bleeding into her eyes and ears. *Am I dying?* she thought. *Is this how I'm going to check out?* There was a bolt of pain at the base of her skull.

Then a slew of images flooded her mind, the scenes from her session racing by. She recognized them all.

She knew exactly where she was, *who* she was.

She understood what was happening.

The Company had caged her mind, and she had broken the program down—no, not her, *something*.

"Something did," she whispered.

The construct was screeching and groaning around her, and time was no doubt a factor—

"Gem!" Here was the voice again, the mystery man. "Clear you mind, Gem! Think of darkness! Clear your—"

Think. She saw her hands locked to a throat, a feminine throat, but the throat had not belonged to a woman—it had belonged to the AI. She had turned the tables on it, exploited a vulnerability the

Company had failed to account for. Had she fried a circuit? Severed a pathway? The how of it was not important. She had tuned out the noise and punched a hole in the construct, and if she could do it once, she could do it again. She only needed to focus.

"Darkness," Gem said. "He told me to clear my mind."

She closed her eyes and imagined a fissure in the wall, the surrounding plaster weak and malleable. She pictured her hands peeling the edges away to reveal a chasm below, a silent portal where nothing spoke nor stirred. *Darkness*, she thought.

"Good! Follow my voice, Gem!"

She pitched herself over the edge.

THE BLURS

GEM OPENED her eyes to a fog of noise and shapes, a cosmic stew of sensations. She was moving. No, she could not move. *Both*, she thought. *My body is doing both.* She felt a jab of pain in her leg, brief and sharp. It hit her like an electric shock and she lurched forward, coughing, screaming—both? What felt like a pair of hands pushed her back, hands she could almost see, but not quite.

Someone was speaking her name. "Gem."

It was the owner of the hands.

Her eyes sharpened to reveal the shape of a mouth. It was moving. "Where is the rest of your face?" Gem slurred.

The mouth said something she could not understand, and then she was moving again, rolling on wheels, yes, wheels. The involvement of wheels was clear, though there was little else that was. A series of shapes emerged on the ground before her, a patchwork of red, white and gray. "Body," she heard herself say.

"Close your eyes, Gem."

Her stomach rocked like a boat in bad water. There was something going on down there, a sloshing of sorts.

"She's going to puke," someone said.

Then Gem was leaning forward and emptying her guts. The hands were holding her hair back, which was kind of them. Dark shapes sped past her as she raised her head, a gang of shadows absent their owners. "Clear," one of them yelled.

Then she was moving again, her eyes closed to stop the colors from swirling, and the darkness felt good, the abyss. Hadn't she just been there? There was a bang somewhere in the distance that startled her, and then another. She heard voices from afar. Then there was only the sound of the wheels again, a smooth sound. If not for the motion it would have been soothing. Gem kept her eyes shut, focusing on the dark, that deep, docile comfort. Then she felt a pinch near her shoulder. "Ow." She tried to reach up and swat it, though her arm refused to move.

"Try to relax," said a voice beside her.

She could feel the warmth of the speaker's breath, and more. Everything was warm, her face and her legs and her chest. It was a good warm, whatever it was, something you could sink into.

The feeling was nice . . .

THE BED

GEM OPENED her eyes to a blur of muted tones, a familiar sensation that disheartened her. Where in God's name was she now? She was lying down, for one. There was pain sounding off from undisclosed locations, dull aches and stiffness, though her head felt the worst by far. That was where the real unpleasantness had gathered, but the ache was sharp and shallow, no longer a deep, morbid clench.

Something felt different.

Drugs, Gem thought. *They have me on drugs again.*

When she reached up to massage her neck the nerves fired and she yanked her hand away. The wound was swollen, the flesh raised and tender. She ran her fingers over it with care. It was the tissue causing the discomfort, a superficial pain. Her stomach began to flutter. Did that mean it was gone?

Her head *did* feel lighter, but her thoughts were thick and muddled. She had imagined it would feel more like crawling out of a hole, a wash of bright sunlight. *Don't jump to conclusions.*

What could she remember? She hesitated. How many times would you touch a hot stove before you learned your lesson? Pushing her mind had burned her, over and over, and yet here she was, ready to press her palm down. *So what's one more time then, love?*

She forced her thoughts into the murk and braced herself for a jolt. Nothing came, no wrench of pressure squeezing her temples. That alien attachment felt lifeless now, cut off from her nervous system, but it seemed that was not all that was absent. Her memories of the run felt scattered, tossed about in a salad of fragments, laughing with Banks, loathing Banks, the interior of the Wraith and frames of gray clouds and trees she could not seem to organize, and—and what? *And* there was nothing to confirm someone had pulled the bug from her skull.

Gem was aware of a presence then, a shadow hovering over her. She strained her eyes at the shape, compelling them work, to do their bloody job and *focus*.

"No need to fret now," said the shadow. "You can relax." The shape moved around to Gem's side and settled somewhere in her periphery. "You should not be awake yet, so we're going to help you rest up. Just sit tight."

All Gem could muster in response was a groan.

It seemed the voice was right.

She was not supposed to be awake.

"There. That ought to help you out."

A familiar, chemical wave washed over her, yet she had not felt the jab of a needle. She'd paid no mind to her weaker arm, and when she turned it over to investigate, she felt the tubes. She was hooked up to an IV, and—

WHEN GEM opened her eyes again the Magazine Man stood over her, smiling his wry smile. She found she was not surprised to see him. Perhaps somewhere deep down she had expected this, but why? She could not say, and it occurred to her she might be hallucinating. "Are you actually there?"

Her throat was parched and her words came out like gravel. He produced a bottle of water and handed it to Gem and she choked a few swallows down, then a few more.

"I never asked you your name," she said, her voice regaining its strength. "I've been calling you the *Magazine Man*."

He let out a few soft chuckles. "The *Magazine Man*," he said. "Why not. I suppose you didn't have much to go on. I go by Dale, Dale Redding, and your name is Gemma—"

"Gem," she said. "No one calls me Gemma except that cunt at the base."

Dale looked off past her, his gaze fixed on something she could not see. Was the wench in the room with them?

No, she thought. *No way*. Maybe he was old-fashioned and had not appreciated her language—

"Gem it is then," he said, returning his eyes to her. "We have a great deal to talk about, *Gem*, but only when you are ready." He watched her for moment, and Gem watched him back. His voice sounded strange to her, his country twang less pronounced. Had he been sizing her up, gauging her reaction? Had she reacted at all?

"Are you with us, Gem?"

"Sorry," she said. "I'm not—"

"You're not sure what is going on here, I know. We're going to take it as slow as we need to." He pulled a chair up next to the bed and planted himself in it, folding his hands in his lap. "But we've got to start somewhere."

Gem stared up at him. "I know where to start. Is it gone?" She pointed to the back of her head. "It feels like it's gone. For Christ's sake, *Dale*, tell me it's gone."

He smiled. "We removed your implant, Gem. That is why you feel the way you do, which I've been told feels a bit like being hit by a train. Sound about right?"

She closed her eyes and laughed, feeling woozy, elated, uneasy, all of it. "I thought I would never be rid of it," Gem said, "that if I

307

survived it all they would leave it in, you know, just to keep me in line."

"They would've," Dale said, his eyes stern again. "Bet your bottom dollar they would've. But you don't need to trouble yourself with that. It's over." It felt like he was hovering over her, some large, mannish cloud. "Now, I know you're not feeling great, but I need you to do something for me, alright? Can you tell me the last thing you remember before you woke up with us here? It will help me get a read on how you're acclimating."

Gem nodded. It would be hard to think of him as *Dale*, but she supposed the name was fitting, at least for the man she had met in the market, an alias, no doubt. Hadn't she sensed that? She had certainly sensed something. *Dale*, she thought. *Dale Redding. Dale wants to know what I remember.* "I can try," she said. "I couldn't sort anything out when I last opened my eyes."

"I can imagine," Dale said, "but you've had more time to rest now. Like I said, trainwreck. It takes time to clear them up, but the job gets done eventually. Let's see if we can't pick up the first few pieces."

"Trainwreck," Gem said. "It's a fitting description."

She closed her eyes and allowed her mind to cycle backwards. She had been shocked to wake up here in such a state, wherever *here* was. That part was easy. And before? Before was little more than a mess of noise and shapes, sounds and blurs and wheels. "Everything was a blur," Gem said. "I was well out of it. I think I was in a wheelchair." Her thoughts snapped back to the lab then. She had been sitting in one. "I was in a lab at the base."

"Yes," Dale said. "That was where we retrieved you."

Gem blinked, then blinked again, a third and a fourth time. It was not her eyes that were out of focus. This time it was her mind.

"You *retrieved* me?"

"We were able to find a way into the facility," Dale said. "We broke you out."

He sat patiently beside her as the words sank in, giving her time.

We found a way in, we broke you out. The idea was rattling around. *The Magazine Man broke me out, Dale found a way in.*

The concept was not computing.

"I don't understand," Gem said. "Why would you break me out? They know who you are, and they are going to come for you. They will come for the both of us."

Dale's gaze sharpened. "No, Gem. They do not know who I am, and they will not be coming for us." He looked down at his feet for a moment, then stood. "I think it's still a bit still too soon. You've been through a hell of an event here, and it's going to take some time." Dale tapped his temple. "Your mind will heal, but it's not a thing we can rush. I'd like to give you something to help you sleep again, which is the best thing for you now. You okay with that?"

Gem nodded. She could not deny her mind felt feeble, that she was physically exhausted and short of her wits. If it was sleep that was going to bring her around, then she would sleep. She could finish solving the mystery when she had the means to process it.

"Alright," she said, "but will you answer me one thing first?"

Dale smiled. "That depends on what you ask and how long the answer looks to be."

"It will be brief," Gem said. "Did we know each other before all this? Have I just forgotten who you are?"

Dale nodded to himself.

"I'm afraid that qualifies as a long one. We'd never met before the store in Hawks Pass, but I wouldn't call us strangers either." He smiled. "I know that won't make a whole lot of sense right now, but I assure you, it will. That's all I'm prepared to say about it."

Gem laid back and closed her eyes.

"Fair enough," she said. "The next time I ask you that, I will expect something other than a riddle."

He chuckled under his breath. "I know you will."

Gem listened to Dale preparing the dose, then to the approach of his footsteps. "Until next time," he said.

"Until next time," Gem repeated.

WHEN GEM came to she was alone in the room. It did not take long for her eyes to adjust this time, and her mind felt stronger now, clearer. She sat up and massaged her arms and shoulders and neck, everything stiff and in need of a stretching. Even without the bed rest she had hardly been active of late, her excursions consisting largely of whiskey drinking and sitting, bucket seats, booths, sinister gray chairs. *There it is*, she thought.

Her memory had slipped into gear, the lab at the base and the orange and green pillar, the program pulling her strings.

"AI," Gem said to herself.

She recalled the wench questioning her, knocking her out and waking her up and sending her out into town. She remembered meeting the Magazine Man—*Dale, Dale Redding*. She remembered meeting Dale at the market, then Banks at the saloon. *Banks*, she thought. Did he have something to do with this?

It seemed unlikely. If Banks had been part of the caper he would be here as well. He would have come in with Dale to check on her. Gem massaged her temples, thinking back to what she could recall of her *retrieval*. Had she heard Banks in that raft of noise? Was his one of the voices? It was impossible to tell. The whole scene was a hot mess, a soup of colors and drugs and unpleasantness.

And what about the rest of it?

She turned her thoughts to Hawks Pass, to the fires the program had forced on her. It was like recalling a film she had not seen in ages, and when she searched her mind, she found the same applied to the cabin. Everything the construct had cooked up for her was slipping away. *Good riddance*, she thought. *Ciao and au revoir.*

She ran her hand down the crook of her elbow and found only a dark bruise, ugly and sore to the touch. They must have thought her well enough to remove the IV. And who exactly were *they*? Dale had said *they* broke her out, yet he was only conspirator she'd seen.

Perhaps it was time she found out.

Gem put one foot on the floor and felt the weakness straight-away. She braced herself on the bed, put the other foot down and walked in place until she was confident she would not collapse, then she stepped away and turned.

She'd not had a proper view of surroundings, and what she saw was a training center, maybe military, maybe for athletics. Her bed was one of a line on the far side of the room, beds she could only assume were meant for medical rehabilitation.

Rehabilitation, she thought.

She would forever loathe the word.

The rest of the area was filled with gym equipment, and where there was exercise gear, there would be showers. She was still clad in the Company garb the minions had fitted her with, her skin dank and oily and crying out for a rinse. She limped to the hallway at the far end of the space and saw the signs for the locker rooms.

"Alright then," she said.

THE PROCESS

THE ONLY windows in the gym were set in long, horizontal rows near the ceiling, far too high for Gem to see out of. If she was going to get a read on her location, she would have to venture out. She was halfway to the big main doors when they opened outward and Dale appeared between them, cutting a familiar figure in his flannel and cap. "I can see you're feeling better," he said. "Are you hungry? Thirsty?"

"No," Gem said. "I found the showers and water fountains, so I sorted myself out there, but hungry? Not in the least. I have not even thought about food."

"Well, that's understandable. We've been filling you up with sedatives, vitamins too, but mostly sedatives. Not really known for inspiring an appetite."

"So I've noticed," Gem said. "How long have I been here, Dale? Hours? Days?"

He scratched his chin. "I'd call it two-and-a-half. Days, that is. Sixty-or-so hours, if you want."

"Well that explains the stiffness," Gem said. "Is there somewhere we can sit? My legs are not quite right yet, and I have a lot of bloody questions."

"I figured that would be the case. Follow me."

They walked out into the main hall, turned a corner and stepped into another room, what might have once served as an office, an old leather couch stationed across from a swarthy-looking desk and a pair of wood-framed chairs set up in the corners.

"Where are we?" Gem asked.

"A college campus," Dale said, "community, one of the smaller ones that went bankrupt after the hack. I set up shop here when duty brings me to the area. It's quiet, isolated, got all of the essentials."

He motioned for her to sit on the couch, and Gem did not refuse. Dale pulled one of the chairs up across from her.

"How's your memory now?" he said.

"It's better," Gem said, "but there are gaps, parts of the run I can hardly remember, passing through town that night, the fires, hiding out in the woods after the cabin." She paused, and then she laughed. "You have no idea what I'm talking about, do you?"

Dale had been listening quietly.

"As for the details, no, but I gather those were times the program was active, influencing your experiences. Am I right about that?"

Gem confirmed that he was.

"Those memories will fade now that the connection's been severed," he said. "There's nothing left to reinforce them. Before long they'll all feel like dreams."

"They already do," Gem said. "Less than dreams, really, more like a film I haven't seen in ages."

"That is a good sign, Gem. It means your mind is beginning to purge." Dale shifted in his seat, leaning in. "And what about your other memories, the genuine ones?"

Gem frowned.

"Nothing has come flooding back, if that's what you're asking."

Dale said, "That's normal, so don't sweat it. In my experience, it's best to start slow, talk yourself through what happened. The details that rear up can surprise you."

Gem snickered under her breath. "I thought you didn't know much about the *process*, Dale, but that was a load of bollocks, now wasn't it? I understand you couldn't tell me anything at the time, but you can tell me now. Who are you, exactly, and how do you know so much about that implant?"

"Suppose it's only fair you'd ask," Dale said. He sat back in his chair, as if he were preparing to tell a tale. "Your company's *process* was built around technology I developed. I take it you've heard of the infamous *Chiron*?"

Gem said, "You mean Chiron's AI?"

"I was part of a group—"

"You're serious then? Bloody hell."

Dale said, "I am. It was a crackerjack team we had down there. I was younger then, too ambitious for my own good. They offered me a small fortune to work for them, and I was in no position to refuse it at the time. I also wanted to see if such a thing could be done. There was plenty of artificial intelligence out there—had been for years, and some of it weren't half bad—but nothing like we built." He bit his lip and frowned. "I didn't pay much mind to how they might choose to use it. I do regret that, but—and here's the irony—it was not even Chiron who unleashed the beast in the end. How's that for a punchline? It was one of their lab rats, a demented little peckerwood by all accounts, a nobody really. I'm sure you have heard the story."

"Oh yes," Gem said. "And not the redacted version. I used to hack, you know."

Dale smiled. "I'm aware of that. Anyhow, after that disaster I moved on, and I guess you could say I've spent the lion's share of my time working to prevent another Chiron. When I get word someone's keen on meddling with the forbidden fruit, I investigate, me and my people. You probably won't be surprised to learn you're not the first *asset* we've extracted from your company. In fact, I would say at this moment your employer's the main offender."

Gem had been listening intently.

"You are government, aren't you Dale? CIA? NSA? And I imagine *Dale Redding*'s not your real name either."

"And you believe I'd own up to that if it were true? Being a fed is dangerous business in these parts. Companies like yours don't take kindly to government interference nowadays, though I reckon you already knew that." His face grew stern. "Or at least you used to know it. What I *can* tell you is that Corp of yours is not nearly as untouchable as they would like to believe."

"They are not *my* Corp," Gem said. "I took a shine to the wrong advert and fell down a sodding rabbit hole."

"You and a boatload of others," Dale said. "But hey, it's like Alice would say, melancholy waits around the corner, and—well, and then the part about darkness. Can't rightly remember what it was now."

Gem sat up straight. "You planted that copy of *Alice*."

Dale grinned. "I wrote the inscription down, but I didn't plant the book. Someone else did that, someone with base access, and no one you would know. Couldn't be sure you would find it, much less if you'd recognize the quips. It was all I could manage on short notice, one little clue, something to help keep your head screwed on."

Gem thought back to the outpost, finding the quote in the book and forcing herself to ignore it. "What that inscription did was rattle me," she said. "And what does it even mean? *Melancholy waits*?"

"It's code, Gem, something you understood before the Company got their hooks in you. Were you able to recognize any of it?"

Melancholy waits around the corner, she thought.

"I recognized the first line, but it didn't mean anything to me. It was just another mystery. It was the second part I found compelling, the bit about darkness. I'd been thinking of dark spaces on the run, whenever that bot started fucking with me, or hurting me—whenever I thought I was losing my mind. It helped me to clear my head."

"Clever girl," Dale said. "The program struggles with an absence of thought. It needs fuel to run on, something it can manipulate, and when you clear your mind it's left spinning its wheels. The Company's version is nowhere near as sophisticated as the original, despite what they'd like to think. But that is a story for another time. The bottom line is their *specialist* can't just up and take a person over, at least not yet. It is only along for the ride."

"It was a gut instinct," Gem said. "I had a lot of those along the way, intuitions, but that one seemed automatic. Whenever it got to be too much I thought of caves, or tunnels. I just went for it."

"And I reckon it was part of the reason you caused them so much grief, that and their shoddy workmanship. The bastard never really got a foothold, did it?"

"That's what Banks said." She looked up in alarm. "Do you know what happened to Banks, Dale? If the Company thinks he had something to do with this—"

He held up a hand. "Easy now, one thing at a time. Your friend is alright, and we will get to him. We've gotten way ahead of ourselves here anyway, and we need to walk it back a bit." He leaned forward again. "I should have saved the stories for later, so that one's on me, but before we got sidetracked, I asked what you remembered, and you told me the memories they'd tampered with had not come back to you. It is important we get that ball rolling."

Gem sighed. "You are not going to prod me like that woman did, are you? I've had about all I can handle of that, so if your plan is to interrogate me—"

"I'm not familiar with her methods, but I would say no. I'm only going to try and point you in the right direction. We need to get your bearings straight before I start piling the details on, make sure your head is in the right place. Can't have us tipping the barrel now.

Gem said, "Alright then. Straighten away."

"Good. Now you're going to have to bear with me here. The program would've been targeting certain memories, those that involved the Company, sure, but others as well, significant ones that stuck in your craw over the years. It's a bit different for everyone. These memories would have been on your mind during the run. Maybe they popped into your head out of nowhere, or maybe you dreamed about them. I call these base memories."

He paused to make sure she was with him.

"Think of it like chopping down a tree," Dale continued. "You take out a chunk at a time to weaken the structure, and when you cut enough of the base away, the whole thing comes crashing down. Can you see what I'm getting at here?"

Gem's thoughts turned to the dreams, the garden and the fountain on campus, that bastardized version of Day One. She recalled the program's hall of mirrors, her own personal hell, but she could not seem to hold the image. *Because they are all fading away.*

"The wanker was playing around with my dreams," she said. "I'm certain of that."

"Can you remember them?" Dale asked. "Or even just one, the one that feels strongest."

Focus. It was the garden that felt clearest, the little path through the foliage and the birdbath. She pictured herself sitting in the grass, looking up at the clouds and hoping it would not rain. She remembered a deluge starting, covering herself with the slicker she kept on hand. Then something clicked. *Lightbulb,* she thought.

She was no longer recalling the dream, but the garden as she remembered it, just an ordinary yard wedged snugly between the buildings. There was nothing strange about it. Her mind felt clear, her head lighter. "I dreamed of my childhood garden," Gem said. "I can see it now, but not as the program showed me. Now I can see it as it was. I can actually *remember* it."

"Then we're on the right track," Dale said. "Your mind is beginning to recalibrate, finding pathways the program sealed off. Try to hold that image. Think about the time you spent there."

Gem pictured herself out on the lawn with her tablet, blocking out the world, her Mum and her geezers holed up in the flat. She had spent so much time out there, even in the rain, that oversized slicker draped over her—

And then she was a teenager, watching the police lead her mother away. Gem had stood there like a statue, stoic, not knowing whether to feel sad or relieved. She had tried to feel bad for Mum, but it would just not come.

The memories came pouring through, London, Gran's, then the park down the road, Gem poaching a nearby wireless signal. Then she was in a classroom sat across from a trio of girls—*not that*. She knew the AI had weaponized it against her, emotions salient and horrifying she had struggled for years to make peace with, that it had forced her to reveal her sins to Banks on the road, the program steering her mouth, her vocal chords, hacking her tongue and doing its damnedest to wipe the act from her mind. If not for the bugs in its system, it might have succeeded.

But it didn't, and now it's gone.

Her life continued to fast forward, college and graduate school and Day One, her coding job and subsequent promotions, the first time she had driven a Wraith. "It's all coming back," she said to Dale, "and I mean *all* of it, like a bloody montage."

"Good," he said. "This is good, Gem. Now comes the hard part. Why did the Company turn on you? What was it they were trying to suppress?"

Think. There were events the Administrator had lied about, memories the program had guarded. It had warned her when she got too close, hurt her when she'd persisted. She could hardly recall what the pain had felt like, only that it had floored her, first in the forest, then again in the valley below the ridge.

The wreckage, she thought. *Did it have to do with that Wraith?*

Yes, it was one of the wench's falsehoods.

Gem had known it was important. The wreckage was the last piece of the puzzle, the conductor that completed the circuit. That scene had been meant to test her. First there was the body, and then there was—

"The data drive," Gem said. "There it is."

Dale leaned forward in anticipation.

Focus. She had stolen something from the Company and stored it on that device. It was what they had been trying to keep from her, the root of her reconditioning. *Think now, love. The drive.*

Her breath hitched, then the memory ripped through the film and struck her.

THE TOWER

G EM FOLLOWED the path through the trees, homing in on the beacon. There were three viable destinations, an old bunker the Company had converted to a data center and a pair of relay towers, and her money was on one of those towers. The data center would be too obvious, and her contact would have accounted for that. It had taken them weeks to send her instructions, and assembling the fragments had been slow work, akin to constructing a ship in a bottle. Moving correspondence through Company channels was no small feat. You had to send it through at a snail's pace if you did not want to be found out, the equivalent of mailing letter a few words at a time.

But now she had her directives.

This business had been long in the making, and she was eager to have it done. Ever since she had discovered the Company was behind Day One she'd felt filthy, like she could not wash herself clean, and she detested that state. It was London all over again, telling herself she had not been responsible for what happened to that girl. There was no knowing what wretchedness she'd contributed to in her years behind a Company screen, then a Company wheel.

No one ever told her a sodding thing.

It had not just been the Company behind Day One, of course. The Conglomerates had conspired to see it done, that exclusive ca-

dre of giants her employers were now at war with. They had brought
down the cyber-verse to consolidate power, to back world governments into a corner and force them into subservience. Who but the
Corps had the resources to fix it all, the talent, the capital, the tech.
But they did not fix anything. They kept the world in a fallow state,
allowing it just enough rope see over the rim of the pit, never enough
to climb out. It was the oldest trick in the book, manufacturing de-
pendence. Gem had to assume some of the world's powers knew
the truth, those complicit in the scheme, maybe, though not one of
them had dared speak out about it. This was too large a whistle to
blow, and there were not enough moral lungs in the world left to
sound it. But the Wraith teams knew.

Anyone who worked with a Seeker long enough would notice
the fingerprints, the same prints on the bugs that had strangled
social media and killed the cloud and closed the eyes in the sky.
The Company's attempts to disguise it had not been good enough,
to outsiders, perhaps, but not to their own crews.

How long had she and Banks known now? Six months?

Banks was the one who'd cracked the encryption, patterns designed to appear random and scrambled beyond comprehension,
but patterns nonetheless, the Company intent on marking its territory—its *property*—in spite of the risk of exposure. Once Banks had
pointed it out, it was impossible not to see.

Neither of them had been daft enough to speak a word of it to
their peers, though if Banks had sorted the markers, then others
would have as well. There was no way to know exactly *who* knew,
but Gem got the sense they were not the only ones. She was also
reasonably certain the Company *knew* they knew. The brass had
never acknowledged one or more of their road crews had solved
the puzzle, but such knowledge was implied.

It was more than implied.

The Company had updated its contracts out of the blue one
day, something it had never done outside of a fresh fiscal year, the

paperwork dense and the language threatening, a warning masquerading as terms and neglecting to spell out the ramifications for letting information slip. That part was full of murky rhetoric, the type of language law students studied to cut their teeth, *violations will result in penalties to be determined by the board in reference to the severity of the actions of the undersigned.* Gem had seen it for what it was.

Break with Company protocol, and we will see that you suffer.

After that she knew if she could find a way to hurt the Company, she would pursue it. She would prove to herself once and for all she still had a moral code. *Like Robin Hood*, she'd thought.

THE SIGNAL chirped faster as Gem wound her way through the trees, the top of a tower emerging in the distance.

"A tower it is then," she said.

Her contact had assured her the Buggy's Seeker would be out of commission, that another agent would see it done. She suspected the machine would not be the Company's only means of tracking a Buggy, though her source was well informed, and she had steadily grown to trust them. She had seen evidence of their reach firsthand. Her contact had shut down an outpost a few months back, the entire campus going dark and her superiors passing it off as a response test. The whispers about satellites had started soon after, all those long-dead devices being put back in play. Gem had shrugged her shoulders and nodded, saying *maybe* and *who knows*, though she was privy to information others were not.

The blackout was proof her contact was legitimate.

She crested the next hill and glimpsed the outline of the tower's control center in the distance. She saw no immediate cause for concern, no floodlights, no vehicles, but if the main power was still up, it would be a lost cause. She could only access the system in safe mode. If the guardrails were active they would freeze the network and seal the control room doors, and she would be stuck there until the Company sent someone to collect her.

But in safe mode? In safe mode it would be like reaching in through an open window, almost too easy.

Too easy, she thought. *Let's bloody well hope so.*

Gem rolled the Buggy over the hills until the structure appeared before her, towering over the trees. The power was down, the emergency lights flashing. She fished a keycard out of her pocket as she approached, an old back-up model she'd rigged to function as a skeleton key. It would bypass any lock on the Company grid, though it was a one-way ticket. The surge would open the door, but it would fry the chip in the card and force her to rely on the interior control panel. If she hit a snag in there and triggered a lockdown, then that was that. She would be proper fucked.

But that is not going to happen.

She slipped the key into the slot and the card produced a spark, fizzling out as the door slid open. So far, so good. The safety lights lit the console in a hazy glow, and Gem got to work, breezing through the mainframe's security channels. It helped she knew Company code like the face of a clock, all the backwards specs and alien hieroglyphics. She zipped on past the firewalls, counting the seconds as she worked, fifteen, twenty, and then she isolated her target, the paydirt. You could pinpoint a Seeker in minutes with that encryption, and in a few more you could shut it down. And after that? If you were truly talented you could reverse engineer the bastard, at least according to her contact. Gem smiled. How could it have been so easy? Hadn't the Company learned anything from Day One? With networked systems it only takes one weak link, and here was a prime example. Perhaps they thought no one would be brave enough to have a go at them, or stupid enough. The system was good, yes, and an outsider would have no chance against it, but to leave themselves open to an internal breach?

What was it if not hubris?

Her blood ran cold. It was more likely they believed a turncoat would never escape Company grounds.

Bin that shit, she thought. *It's too late now.*

She pulled her data drive from her pocket and slipped it into the port. That drive had been to hell and back and had never done her wrong, never glitched or bugged out. It was also so old and frankensteined its specs would flummox the techs, what few bits and bobs she'd been unable to wipe from the hardware. If worse came to worse, at least that would buy her some time.

Gem executed the command and the data began to load, and a few seconds later, the deed was done. She pulled the drive from the port and stuffed it back in her pocket. Now came the hard part. Her nameless ally would have tagged the outage as processed—the outpost would assume a tech had gone out to fix it—but she would need to activate the main power to open the door. That would reboot the signal, and once the access logs refreshed, it would be panic stations, all hands on deck.

She would have no more than a few minutes.

Focus. Gem pulled up the power grid and hit the juice. The lights kicked on and she punched the door control and ran, scrambling out through the entrance and down the steps to the Buggy. The tower floodlights shined in the twilight, powered up and luminous, and Gem threw herself over the Buggy's seat and hit the ignition. The little motor sprang to life, then she was tearing away down the slope opposite the path, thumping over the earth.

She knew where she was going now, and she could only hope her counterpart had held up their end.

GEM PULLED into a grove of trees near the coordinates, silenced the Buggy and secured it amid the pines. It was dark now, hazy, just enough moonlight to make out the surrounding terrain. She heard a low whistle from beyond the trees and ducked, then she peered out. In the distance she saw a familiar form, the Wraith an errant smudge on a drying landscape, hardly more than a shadow. Gem kept herself low and hurried on toward the vehicle, and as she drew closer, she made out the shape of a man. He was clad in road gear, his features obscured by the night.

"Melancholy waits," he said. Gem finished the sentence as she approached, and they nodded to one another.

They eased the big doors closed as they slipped into the vehicle, and Gem noticed something strange.

The passenger side was absent its Seeker.

She nodded to the vacant shell. "Your work?"

"As instructed," he said. "I removed all tracking devices and disabled the fingerprinting. Every redundancy has been accounted for. We are off the grid."

Gem could see the shape of his face now. It was clear he was Company, that he knew his way around a Wraith.

"You're a Surgeon tech, aren't you?"

He brought a finger to his lips.

"No need for that. We can talk about whatever you'd like on the other side. Right now, we need to focus."

"Fair enough. You have our instructions then?"

He nodded. "Ahead through the woods, and quiet as you can. When we reach the clearing you are going to floor it. The faster we cover that ground, the better."

"And my things?" Gem said.

"Right where you stowed them."

Gem put the Wraith in gear, switched on the spectra-light and began to weave her way through the trees. The man pulled a gadget from his pack, an old comms system she had only seen in films, a brick of a thing. He pressed the button down and said, "Melancholy waits in the light, over." A mishmash of words sounded out in return, jargon Gem could not understand. "Copy," he said. "Will respond when the weather is right, over." The man turned to face her. "They are searching for us, but they are well off our trail. We're right where we need to be."

"Well that is better than the alternative," Gem said.

They rolled on through the woods in silence, and then the man leaned forward, considering the terrain. "We're close," he said. "Accelerate on my signal, hard and straight. We'll bank left on the other side of the clearing."

"How far?" Gem said.

"I can't say. Just be ready."

"Line of sight. Lovely. And after that?"

"There's an old railroad a few miles out of the woods. We'll follow it away from Company territory.

She did what she could to steady her breathing.

Hadn't she had a trick for that once?

Yes, she would count to three between breaths, monitoring her intake, though that was unlikely to help her now. She would not feel at ease until they made it to the rendezvous.

"Get ready," the man said. Beyond the trees Gem saw bare hills and rocky undulations, a washboard of terrain. This was going to be rough. "Now."

The engine roared as she leaned on the pedal and the Wraith shot out of the woods, the moonlight merging with the haze of the cabin, forging a lighter hue. They were off-road now, off-road and flying, the shocks giving all they could give as the vehicle slammed over the landscape. Gem slowed when she had no choice and accelerated whenever she could, her ally scouring the area for trees.

He pointed off to her left. "There," he said.

Her heart was hammering away, her stomach twisted in snags. She wrenched the vehicle over the last of the hills and guided them into the evergreens. Gem forced her breath out. "Bloody hell."

"Well done," he said. "Head west. Try and keep us at a good clip when you can, but don't push it. It shouldn't be much farther to the tracks."

NAVIGATING THE woods felt like crawling after the race through the clearing, and the trees soon faded to patches, lonely clusters among the hills. Gem picked up speed toward the tracks, and after a stretch they reached them. "Head north," the man said. "We'll keep to the line until we reach a service road."

"How far?"

"It shouldn't be far. Ten miles at most."

Gem locked her eyes to the tracks and pushed them forward, feeling every second. The level ground allowed her to keep the pace, but they were also exposed to the skies. It would not be long before the drones began moving off to the west, and if they were—

She felt the vehicle hiccup beneath her.

Had she drifted off and nicked a rail?

No, she had been ogling the lines, staring them down. She had not even come close. Then she felt it again, the smallest of kicks. She gripped the wheel tighter, eyeing the man in her periphery. Had he noticed it? He was peering out toward the skies, the device to his ear. Had he disturbed something stripping the hardware? Maybe so, but they were not going to pull over and pop the hood, not now. Gem tuned her ears to the vehicle, awaiting the next spasm.

It did not come. *Maybe I imagined it.*

Having imagined it would be the best-case scenario. She had enough on her plate already, reaching the rendezvous intact, trusting her source would keep their word and shepherd them out of the Company's reach, looking over her shoulder for the rest of her days, wondering if every bloke on the street was out to get her, and—

"There," said the man. "On the left." Gem saw it then, the elusive path peeling away from the tracks. "We'll follow the road for a few miles," he continued. "When it starts to turn south we'll head west along the ridge, off-road. The rendezvous won't be far."

Gem followed the road as it climbed and fell over the hills, passing sporadic clusters of trees, some dangerously close to the shoulder. She held her breath at each crest, fearing a barricade down below, Company peons in black vehicles with anti-tanks guns, the wrath of her old acquaintances. After a series of dips and corners the road bent away to the south.

"Take it easy up here," said the man. "The ridge drops off in places. Can you see it?" Gem spied a bulge in the earth that ran like a spine over the terrain.

"Follow it," he said, "but keep you distance."

"For how long?"

"It will wind downhill towards the lower ground. It's the valley below we need to get to."

Gem could see the drop through the spectra-light in places, the dirty-red streaks of empty space. Of course she would keep her distance. She shifted her weight and felt the data drive against her thigh, the lips of the ports digging into her flesh.

She pushed it deeper into her pocket.

All this for such a small thing.

But it was no small thing. The contents within were massive, the means to expose all the Company had done, to reveal it for what it was. She could only imagine what would happen when that data was leaked. Maybe the government techs could use it to whip up a panacea for the web, something to kill off the malware. Maybe, but would returning the world to the cybersphere be the right choice? What if it led to something worse? There would always be abusers of technology, greedy, malignant speculators and otherwise rotten shits, all of them poised and ready to fuck everything up again. Was the world ready to stand up to them? Or would they all dive straight back in, oblivious to the irony as they lost themselves in their screens. It was out of her hands either way.

She'd made her choice, and all she could do now was drive. There would be plenty of time for—

The Wraith kicked like a horse and shot forward to the right, the engine howling as it revved. "Shit!" Gem screamed.

The tires skidded through the dust as she slammed on the brakes, throwing them into a slide. She pulled her foot from the pedal and cranked the wheel, trying to straighten them out, and then she felt it, the backend going. They were about to roll. She heard the man cry out and made to shout at him, to warn him to brace himself, but her mouth would not form the words.

And then they were airborne.

The Wraith crashed down on the passenger side, and then the driver's, the passenger's again, time slowing with each rotation. And then there was weightlessness, a second of silence, another.

And then there was noise and pain.

Gem thought she felt her eyes blink.

And then there was darkness.

THE TRUTH

GEM BRACED her bent form on the couch and forced herself to breathe—*inhale*—*count to three*—*exhale*.

"I remember what I did," she gasped, "right up to the point where I should have died. I should be dead, Dale—*dead*. How the bloody hell did I survive that?"

Dale was leaning forward in his chair.

"Your guess is a good as mine. It surprised the hell out of me when I got word they'd brought you back alive."

"It was the sensors," Gem said. "The Company rigged the sensors, or overrode them, but how? Or maybe it was him. *He* damaged them pulling the tech—"

"Gem."

"He might have removed a critical component—"

"Gem," Dale said.

"The sensors malfunctioned, Dale. They threw us! He must have fucked something up!" Gem paused and shook her head. "No, that can't be it. The other one did it too, the Wraith that I *thought* was mine. Was it a failsafe they triggered? Was it built into every Wraith?"

Dale's voice was calm.

"I don't have that information, Gem. I don't know what happened to your sensors, before or after. There's not a whole lot—"

"But you knew what I did, that I hacked into the tower and lifted that encryption. You knew because you were my contact, yes? You set the whole thing up."

Dale nodded. "It's true I was the one feeding you information. I sought you out after discovering you'd learned the truth, about the Company and all the rest."

Gem did what she could to steady her breathing, to the curb the edge in her voice. Dale had helped her out of that mess. He was trying to help her now. "And how did you know that I knew?"

"The Company keeps dossiers on their employees," he said, "especially those with consequential jobs, like yours. They used the Seeker to track your behavior on the road, conversations, voice inflections, you name it. They flagged both you and Banks, but you in particular. Must have figured you were more likely to turn."

Gem choked out a laugh. "Well they weren't wrong, now were they? But we never said a word about it near Company channels. We never said *any*thing."

"What you did or didn't say doesn't mean squat, Gem. We're talking things like demeanor, body temperature, a whole sheet of data points most would never think to consider—but that doesn't matter. The point here is that the Company's suspicions put you on my radar. That was when I started fishing around."

Gem's thoughts turned to the man in the Wraith.

"And the same would have applied to *him* right, the bloke whose body I peeled off the dash? Who was he?"

Dale looked down at his shoes. "He went by Watkins. He was a navigator once, then the Company made him a Surgeon tech. I reckon he must have been good with hardware."

"Watkins," Gem said. "The name rings a bell. I can't say I ever knew him, but I guessed his profession." She took a deep breath. "I didn't recognize him the second time either, and I don't mean his corpse, Dale. The construct wore his face during our *session*, when they had me in the labs. They were using him to try and break me. I can hardly remember it now, but I know it was him."

"Another trick of the program," Dale said. "It was a tactic. They would have assumed you knew who you were working with that night, and they were trying to force a reaction, same as when they sent you back to the accident."

"He wouldn't tell me who he was . . ."

She could no longer see him as she had in that orange hell, whole and alive. All she could conjure was the shape of his corpse, a bloated, discolored puppet. She could almost smell the rot.

"He was all in," Dale said. "I planted the seed, let his skepticism run its course. After a time he realized the offer was legitimate, just like you did."

"Just like I did," Gem repeated, her voice small and distant. She forced herself back to the present, meeting Dale's eyes. "How did you pull it off?"

He sat back in his chair.

"I suppose I can give you the short version. We have people in the Company's network they would never suspect. They feed us raw data for our programs to sort out, and when I see an opportunity, I act. Not much more than standard espionage when you get down to it, and the channel goes both ways. Feeding information in's a tougher trick, but our people can do it."

Gem leaned in.

"Then why didn't your *people* poach that sodding tower?"

Dale chuckled. "These are not hackers we're talking about, Gem. They are desk jockeys, accountants, lawyers. All they can do is skim a little off the top when they have a window, and none of that data is critical, personnel files, run schedules. Most of the time I'm stuck trying to make a meal out of bones. I can't get anywhere near the good stuff without *true* insiders, people with certain skills, access to Company strongholds. You get the idea. I can steal and decrypt the fluff without raising alarms, but Seeker grade material? For that, I need someone like you."

Gem could deny it made sense.

"And the ruse at the market? How did you manage that?"

Dale said, "Now it gets a bit more interesting. What I told you was close to the truth. They *do* know me as a retiree, a part-timer, but not from Hawks Pass. Not from anywhere. Hawks Pass thinks I come in from Red Point, and if I have reason to be in Red Point, they think I'm on the books somewhere else. When you have access to employee records you can make those kinds of adjustments, call yourself a specialist in rehabilitation tactics, give them credentials none but the oldest Company warhorses would recognize. They were rehabilitating employees long before they whipped up those implants, Gem, strongarming them, gaslighting them. They may have been testing the newest toy out on you, but that kind of manipulation is as old as time. Wherever I go on Company grounds, I am a stranger, and that can be useful when dealing with non-compliance. Do you see where this is going?"

Gem said, "You watch, you wait, and when the time is right, you move in."

Dale hesitated.

"In your case, yes, but that was an exception. Normally it's more about recon, data collection, you know, getting our ducks in a row. It's not every day a mark is captured with priceless information. We had to act. We could not risk letting them break you."

Focus. Gem sat watching him speak.

Dale—Dale Redding. First he was a rube in a flannel, an adversary, the one who'd started the whole rotting mess. Then he was ex-Company, a kind retiree who could not help but sympathize with her situation. Now he had transformed again, a revolutionary figure in the industry, her contact, the leader of an espionage ring whose actions had saved her life. Yes, Dale Redding was all of that, a man who contained multitudes. Had she not grown so accustomed to disbelief, she might well be losing her shit.

But—*but what?*

But there were holes in his narrative, in spite of the particulars, questions he was not keen to answer. That was what.

He seemed reluctant to speak plainly about her rescue, more than reluctant. He'd also managed to dance around who he was, who he *really* was, who he worked for and their stake in setting her free. Gem leaned in, elbows braced on her knees, her eyes colder.

She was not about to be taken for a ride again.

"Who are *we*, Dale, and what happened at that base? I think it's time you filled me in."

The corners of his mouth turned down, his face hardening at the question. "I may tell you who we are at some point, but now is not that time. A common goal brought us together, Gem, along with a fair degree of trauma on your part, but we are little more than strangers here. I am sure you can understand that." Dale paused, and Gem made no reply. "And I think you already know what happened at that base. We broke you out, and to do that we had to go through their security." His tone began to soften. "It was clear they did not expect anyone'd have the stones to waltz right in there. They were not prepared for it, hard as that might be to believe. They'd grown complacent."

He stared out past her toward the wall like he had spotted something, a specter lurking in the shadows. Gem followed his eyes, then she broke her silence. "You're right. I find it hard to believe it was that easy. How did you get in?"

"We bugged your partner's truck while you sat in the saloon. The black one with the tags."

Gem sat up straighter, connecting the dots.

Dale continued. "When you pulled into the garage we cloned the signal for the door, and once you were in, we triggered a pulse that fried the perimeter security, and I mean all of it. Then we just rolled right on down the alley."

"Jesus," Gem said. "How many of you?"

"Ten, eleven if you count me, but I was only a spectator. I'd be a liability in a skirmish at my age, so I followed in behind. They still needed my brains, my experience." He looked down and then up again. "We went in for you, but we had other targets as well. We sought out that drive of yours in hopes they hadn't wiped it yet, which was a fool's hope, but we were able to—"

Gem cut in. "You crippled that pillar. I know because I felt it. I can't recall much of it now, but I understood something was wrong, that the program was gone and I had to escape." She stared him down. "And I remember your voice. I didn't know it was you at the time, but I do now. You helped me sever the link."

Dale nodded.

"You're right, on all accounts. I was the one who woke you up. I also stuck you full of drugs and wheeled you out of there, but before that, I overloaded the system while the others cleared the area. I couldn't risk pulling you out first. If the program had gotten wise to our intentions, it might've taken you down with it."

Gem blinked. Something he said had struck her, *we cleared the area*. It was not so different from what the Administrator had said about Hawks Pass. *We cleared the area. We removed the population.*

She forced her thoughts back to her retrieval, to the land of blurs and noise, the smears of red and white and the cracks and bangs in the background. And when she was stuck in the construct? There was something there, something telling. The memory hung by a thread, the shifting room, muffled words that had soon turned to screaming, to chaos. *Red and white and screaming*, she thought. *Chaos.*

"You cleared the area," Gem said softly.

Daled nodded. "We cleared all personnel. We couldn't have anyone interfering—"

"You killed them all, didn't you?"

He sat back in his chair, his face growing hard again, his eyes colder. "We removed all personnel."

"Why? Why would you kill techs and medical staff? That is fucking mental!"

Dale looked down at his feet. "You'd be surprised how little you know about it all," he said. "Those people were party to horrible things, things that would make your experience look downright rosy." He looked up again, meeting her eyes. "You've only seen a sliver of what your Company has its paws in, Gem. If you knew what I know, I doubt you would feel the same."

She placed her head in her hands. It was Hawks Pass all over again, killing civilians for a cause—but Hawks Pass had been an illusion. None of it was *real*. The Magazine Man had raided that base and killed her former colleagues, unarmed scientists and doctors and nurses, low-level techs who'd never handled a gun in their lives. Gem closed her eyes. And what if she'd been on the fence? What if she had lost her nerve and passed the buck down the line to Dale's next recruit? Would she have been standing in that bay? Having a physical in the labs? She raised her head in defiance.

"That could have been me in there. If I hadn't turned your people would have shot me dead with the rest of them, right? Fucking hell! You were supposed to be the good guys!"

"We are," Dale said, his voice cool and steady, "but it's all relative, I suppose. I reckon some of those people felt the same, though I don't imagine that *wench* of yours had any illusions. She didn't say a word when we stormed in, just turned around, like she knew she had it coming."

Gem began to tune him out. She had loathed the Administrator and wished her ill—there was no denying that—but she had never wished her dead. Even at the last strand of her rope she'd balked at the thought she might have killed Banks—*Banks*, she thought.

She sat up straight, her eyes afire.

"You said Banks was fine, Dale! Was that a lie? Tell me!"

336

He seemed hurt by the accusation.

"Banks was not on the grounds when we made contact. We knew who he was, that he'd done what he could to help you along. I can only assume your employers sent him off on other business. Had he been there, no harm would have come to him."

Inhale—count to three—exhale.

Gem was on the verge of tears, tears for those who had conned her, hurt her, who would have no doubt continued to do so. If Banks had been killed on her account it would have been too much to bear. Her mind would have broken, dissolved into sludge and sent her reeling back into madness.

"He was on my radar too, you know," Dale said, "but I was not convinced he'd take kindly to our advances. Seems I might have been selling him short."

"He would not have done it," Gem whispered. "He is too bloody sensible. He is not easily coerced." She let her head hang. "Not like the rest of us."

"Is that what you think this was, Gem? Coercion?"

Inhale—count to three—exhale.

"I don't know what to think, *Dale*. I think you are who you say you are. I don't think you are lying to me, but you are not telling the truth, now are you? Only fragments of it. What do I *think*? I think you are running a test of your own, that you are no so different from that executive your people shot dead."

Dale pondered what she had said for a moment, then he stood. Gem tracked him with her eyes, the Magazine Man, the enigma, the one who had set the ball in motion.

Hadn't she known there was something off about him?

"I won't deny that, Gem. I'd like to give you the benefit of the doubt, but there are rules to follow—protocol. I know you can understand that. The fact is we need people with your skill set, your smarts, your determination. I am hoping we will see eye to eye here, that you will choose to hear us out before jumping to any conclusions."

Gem closed her eyes.

Inhale—count to three—exhale.

She opened her eyes again.

"Are you with a Conglomerate? One of the others?"

The Magazine Man smiled. "We are the ones who are going to piece the world back together."

Gem winced. Her hand went to the base of her skull, but it was only a phantom pain. Or was it? Could she be sure it was gone? Was there something else in its place?

"There's no need to concern yourself with that, Gem. I'd never lie about such a thing, scout's honor."

"And how can I be sure of that?"

The Magazine Man looked down at her. It was not kindness she saw in his eyes, not anymore.

What she saw was authority.

"I guess you will just have to trust me."

THE MOUNTAIN

BANKS PUSHED the Wraith on towards the mountain, guiding them over the slopes. The path was far from ideal, but it could have been worse. At least they had a trail to follow. The sun was high in the sky now, directly overhead, and they had been driving since the crack of dawn. If you asked him, they were past due for a respite.

"Anything?" Banks asked.

"Processing," Kelly said. "Shouldn't you know that?"

"I suppose I should. Maybe I'm just spacing out."

"Well don't." She eyed him with suspicion, her lips pulled tight in a frown. "I'm already worried enough."

"There's no need to be concerned," Banks said. "I'm fine, just like I told you this morning."

Kelly continued to stare at him.

"Great. Then don't tell me you're spacing out!"

Banks smiled. He was not lying to her, was he?

No, he was telling the truth. Listening to the machine whine away was no longer his responsibility.

The Seeker chimed a welcoming tone.

"How far?" Banks said.

"Up the road a bit." Kelly peered ahead. "There. Do you see the clearing? On the right?"

"I see it." Banks pulled off the path and eased the vehicle between the evergreens. They were nearly to the tree line, and he was glad the machine had spelled them before they hit the brush. Cover was limited up there.

"And here we are," Kelly said. She opened the passenger door. "Keep to your side, old man."

She smiled and laughed and Banks waved her off.

"Have a go on your side?" he said to himself. "You're a lunatic."

Then he furled his brow. Where had that come from?

It sounded familiar to him, like something he'd heard on TV.

Or I have a concussion, he thought. No, that would not make sense. He had none of the symptoms, save the memory loss, which was not even that bad. *Keep telling yourself that.* Now he was the one who was frowning. If his condition got any worse he would speak up, but not until he felt he was putting them at risk.

Banks stepped out of the Wraith, walked into the trees and unzipped his fly, his hand creeping toward the crown of his neck. He could still not believe he'd reared up and smacked his head on the doorframe. He could not remember it at all. Kelly had asked him to look in on the Seeker, so he'd leaned in through the door.

Apparently he had pulled up at the sound of a nearby animal, a big cat taking a deer out, Kelly thought, something loud. She told him she'd heard the racket from the woods, that when she returned to the Wraith he was face down in the seat. He could recall her holding two fingers up at him, then three, having him sit and giving him water. But apart from that there was nothing, only a wash of gray. He shook his head at the thought of it. He had never done something so stupid when he was navigating.

Banks stared down the mountainside as he relived himself in the trees, an immaculate view, sunshine and evergreens, gray rocks and earth. For a moment he felt like a tourist, like the backtrails were no longer his office. But the feeling did not last.

He massaged his head again.

He'd thought he had a pretty good grasp of the surrounding terrain, though this side of the mountain felt new to him. *Maybe I just can't remember it.* Asking Kelly to set him straight would only fuel her concern, the looks from the passenger side, the questions.

He was *fine*.

He forced his thoughts to the days leading up to the run. Maybe he could bring himself around that way, give the old brain a kickstart. Where was he before they set out?

His mind locked on an image—a windshield?

Sure enough, but he was not piloting the Wraith. Was he driving a Company truck? That was certainly what it looked like.

Why send him out in a loaner?

He felt a pinch near his wound and grimaced. It sent a throbbing sensation through his temples, some strange discomfort. Perhaps straining his mind was not the best course of action. Banks smiled at the thought. It seemed preposterous, laughable. He had brained himself alright, but if it had been that bad, he would not be out hiking around. Serious injuries produced symptoms, dilated pupils, double vision, slurring. "Of which I have none," Banks said to trees. "Just going to have to take it easy."

He turned around and began to trudge back to the Wraith.